3995

Child's Play

CHILD'S
PLAY

Alison Taylor

WILLIAM HEINEMANN : LONDON

Published by William Heinemann in 2001

1 3 5 7 9 10 8 6 4 2

First published in the United Kingdom in 2001 by William Heinemann

The Random House Group Limited
20 Vauxhall Bridge Road, London SW1V 2SA

Random House Australia (Pty) Limited
20 Alfred Street, Milsons Point, Sydney,
New South Wales 2061, Australia

Random House New Zealand Limited
18 Poland Road, Glenfield,
Auckland 10, New Zealand

Random House South Africa (Pty) Limited
Endulini, 5A Jubilee Road,
Parktown 2193, South Africa

Random House UK Limited Reg. No. 954009
www.randomhouse.co.uk

A catalogue CIP record for this book is available from the British Library

Papers used by Random House are natural, recyclable products made from
wood grown in sustainable forests. The manufacturing processes conform
to the environmental regulations of the country of origin

Typeset by SX Composing DTP, Rayleigh, Essex
Printed and bound in Great Britain by
Mackays of Chatham Plc, Chatham, Kent

ISBN 0 434 00481 2

For Dorothy Bulled
for the title

The Hermitage school, the characters and the events in this novel are wholly fictitious.

Sukie received the whispered message as the girls were filing out of the refectory after tea.

'Imogen wants you to meet her in the stable yard at half-eleven. Tonight.'

Even as her heart leapt with joy, her mind was flooded with doubts. 'Why?' she asked, searching the messenger's face. 'Why there, and not her room?'

The other girl shrugged. 'How should I know?' She began to walk away. 'I'm simply telling you what she said.'

Sukie went to her own room and stayed there for the rest of the evening, counting minutes, so agitated that she only remembered about supper when Torrance knocked on the door to remind her.

'I'm not hungry,' she said. 'I think I'll have an early night.'

Torrance frowned at her. 'You don't eat enough.'

'I'm OK.'

'You're not "OK",' Torrance snapped. 'You're really beginning to worry me.'

'I *am*,' Sukie insisted, wanting to be left alone. 'Honestly.' She smiled. '*Honestly!*'

Once Torrance had left, albeit with some reluctance, Sukie leaned on the window ledge, watching night fall about the trees and the grounds. A breeze stirred the leaves now and then, and blew in gently on her cheeks. Shortly after ten thirty, she went to the showers.

At eleven fifteen, clad in jeans and T-shirt, she walked quietly along the corridor to the fire exit. She met no one and no one heard her leave the building, for the door alarm had long ago been disabled. The girls could go in and out at will, or smuggle in anyone they wished.

When she reached the bottom of the fire escape, a figure materialised in front of her.

'Hell, you gave me a fright!' Sukie exclaimed. 'What are *you* doing here?'

As she set off down the path, the girl who had earlier delivered Imogen's message fell into step beside her. 'Just keeping an eye on Imogen,' she replied.

Sukie glanced at her. 'And you're very good at that, aren't you?' she remarked sarcastically.

'Matron calls me "a real little Christian".'

'She wouldn't if she knew the facts,' Sukie retorted, raising her voice as a military jet screamed overhead. 'You only clean Imogen's room so you can pinch her things.'

'That's a lie!' The girl stamped her foot and, in so doing, kicked a stone. It clattered down the path for several yards before rolling into the muddy verge.

'Be quiet!' Sukie hissed. 'You'll wake people.' She quickened her pace, hoping her companion would take the hint and return to school.

The girl glanced back at the building, and saw Torrance at her bedroom window, bright pale hair slung about her shoulders. After a moment's thought, she trotted after Sukie. 'It *is* a lie,' she insisted, when she caught up with her. 'I never touched anything except her pendant, and I only borrowed that!'

'You stole it,' Sukie said wearily. 'And you lied to me when I found you with it.' She hurried on towards the stables. 'It wasn't very Christian to tell me she'd given away my Christmas present, was it? That really hurt.'

'Well, she's got it back now.' The girl's voice was low and sullen. 'So you won't have to rat on me, like you threatened.'

Sukie made no response. After all, what right had she to judge others? It was her own, wilful stupidity that had destroyed both Imogen and their friendship, and left Imogen at the mercy of all comers.

The yard was empty. Easing open the stable door, Sukie searched each stall in turn, then looked in the tack room before going back outside. 'Where is she?' she demanded.

The girl shrugged. 'She must have gone for another walk.'

Sukie grabbed her by the shoulders. 'Another walk? She'd be hard pushed to get this far!'

She twisted free. 'That's all you know! She often comes out at night, so she can practise without half the school watching.' Smugly she added, 'And I help her!'

Sukie could barely hold back her tears. I should be beside Imogen, she thought; I should be helping her, caring for her, trying to undo some of the dreadful harm I did.

'She's probably gone to the Strait,' the girl offered. 'She likes the view.'

Without a word, Sukie ran out of the yard and into the woods, along the path that made a short cut to the water's edge, expecting, at every turn, to come across Imogen, lying fallen, hurt and helpless. I couldn't bear that, she realised; I couldn't bear causing her more pain. She skidded down the last few feet of path and stood in the mud, looking in vain for the friend she had loved like a sister for as long as she could remember.

Out in the Strait, where even at night the water was luminous, the currents already ran fast, although the tide would not peak for a few hours yet. Close by, the water was pitch black, lapping stealthily at the edge of the land.

Hearing a movement behind her, Sukie whipped round.

'I can't think where she's got to,' the girl remarked. 'She definitely said half-eleven.' Peering at the ground, she screwed up her face in puzzlement. 'If she'd been here,' she commented, 'her stick would've left marks, wouldn't it?'

Almost frantic with worry, Sukie again grabbed her shoulders, and began to shake her. 'Where is she?' Her voice rose. 'What's going on?'

The girl pulled away, so violently that she stumbled and fell.

As she scrambled to her feet, a glimmer of light caught Sukie's eye. 'Oh, God!' she whispered. 'You *didn't* give it back to her.'

Even in darkness, the diamond found light to absorb and transform into cold and sinister brilliance. The girl fingered the chain round her neck, then dropped her hand as Sukie advanced, to raise it again in a stunning side-on blow as she came within striking distance.

Sukie collapsed, face in the mud. Hesitating only briefly, the girl snatched up a broken branch and brought it down with every ounce of her strength on the back of Sukie's head. Tossing aside the branch, she grabbed her arms and began dragging her towards the water. At first the weight of her body was astounding; once on the move, it skimmed over the mud like a sledge on ice, and slithered into the sea.

The girl leaned over, pressing hard on Sukie's shoulders until she was satisfied that not a flicker of life remained. With the tide sucking hungrily at her own feet, she straightened up and tried to kick Sukie afloat, but she moved barely a yard before drifting back. The girl waded thigh-deep into the water, the undertow pulling her off balance, and as Sukie's lifeless fingers wrapped themselves around her leg, she gave the body a vicious shove, watching with elation as it was caught by the current and carried slowly out of sight beyond the overhanging trees.

Shivering violently, her feet and legs numb with cold, she retrieved the branch, walked several yards upstream and slung it far out over the water. Then, triumphant, she retraced her way along the path, but well before she reached the school, her mood crashed, back to the familiar, dispiriting emptiness. She crept up the fire escape, caressing the diamond that nestled at her throat, wondering if all her fortune must be so hard won. As she pushed open the door of the fourth-form dormitory, she consoled herself with the thought that killing was absurdly easy.

I

The wall behind McKenna was adorned with an old railway station clock and a roundel of police dress swords with burnished hilts and polished blades. He had put up the clock when the office became his on promotion, but the swords, like the portrait of a youthful-looking Queen which hung above the door, had been there as long as anyone at Bangor police station could remember. The large oak desk was tidily arranged with an outward-facing nameplate bearing the legend 'Superintendent M.J. McKenna', tiers of stacking file trays and a pristine, leather-backed blotter.

Systematically, he was opening the mail he had gathered from his doormat before leaving home. There were leaflets, pamphlets, bank statements, telephone accounts, a reminder to renew his 'adoption' of four horses and two donkeys at an East Anglian sanctuary, a letter of thanks from Blue Cross Animal Hospitals for his last donation, and a hand-addressed envelope with a first-class stamp and a Carlisle postmark. The only person he knew in Carlisle was the man from whom he rented his house, who had moved there when his company closed their north Wales plant. He slit the envelope and pulled out a single sheet of paper.

Dear Mr McKenna

I'm terribly sorry to say that I'll have to give you notice to quit the house. The council's written to tell me the ongoing problems with subsidence can't be rectified, so they've no option but to condemn the whole terrace, put out compulsory purchase orders, then demolish the lot. The

5

structural engineers reckon one or more of the houses could just collapse without warning. If that happened, they'd fall right on to the High Street shops.

I'll be in touch right away when I've got more to tell you. Like I said, I'm really sorry, and I'm completely gutted myself about losing the house because I was looking forward to coming back when I retire, if not before.

Yours sincerely
David Madoc Jones

Feeling almost queasy with shock, he reread the few terse paragraphs.

'Beautiful day, isn't it?' Jack Tuttle remarked, shouldering open the door. In one hand he carried two mugs of tea, in the other the morning's official mail. 'Going to be another scorcher,' he added, putting his burdens on the desk. Then he saw the expression on McKenna's face. 'What's the matter with you?'

McKenna handed him the letter.

Jack sat down, reading while he stirred sugar into his tea. 'So? It's not before time, if you want my opinion. That street of yours is a complete dump. Even Dewi Prys would turn up his nose at living there, and he's born and bred on a council estate. You should've moved out ages ago.'

'I don't want to move.'

'So you've said before. You'll miss the views, you'll miss the peace and quiet, and your cats'll have to find somewhere else to do their marauding.'

'It's not that—' McKenna began.

'It's not as if you can't afford to buy a house, is it?' Jack went on. '*Your* inflated salary would run to a swish pad in Beaumaris or elsewhere on Anglesey.' He grinned fleetingly. 'Only impoverished inspectors like me have to shoehorn their families into boxes on Bangor's outskirts.' Watching McKenna replace the letter in its envelope, he sighed. 'You knew this was bound to happen sooner or later. That terrace has been clinging to the side of Bangor Mountain for nearly two hundred years and threatening to lose its grip for the past twenty at least. That's why no one's buying the houses when they come empty.'

Injecting a note of enforced cheeriness into his voice, he said, 'Look on the bright side. You're not tied into a chain and you've got plenty of time to look for somewhere.'

'I've got no choice, have I?' McKenna said irritably, flicking the papers on the desk. 'Anything urgent here?'

'Just a missing persons inquiry Divisional HQ routed straight to CID. It's really something uniform should deal with, but I suspect there's a bit of back-covering going on because the missing person happens to be one of the girls from the Hermitage. The headmistress reported it early this morning. The girl, Suzanne Melville by name, was last seen about eleven on Tuesday night, going from the showers to her bedroom.'

McKenna looked up sharply. 'That's almost thirty-six hours ago.'

'Yes, but she's seventeen,' Jack responded mildly. 'Dr Scott, the headmistress, was no doubt giving her time to come back under her own steam, which she may well yet do, with her tail between her legs, before the day's out. So,' he added, 'how shall I handle it? Route it back to uniform, or waste valuable CID resources chasing some rich kid up hill and down dale?'

'Send Dewi. Depending on what he comes back with, we'll take it from there.'

Jack raised his eyebrows. 'Wouldn't it be better for Janet Evans to go? You reckon her being a chapel minister's daughter puts her near the top of the Welsh evolutionary tree, whereas Dewi's knuckles still scrape the ground, as it were. Or, in other words, Janet's posh and the Hermitage is certainly a very posh place.'

'And no doubt it's also full to bursting with girls and women to whom the comely Janet could prove an intolerable distraction.'

2

Some five miles outside Bangor, the Hermitage lay on the old Caernarfon road that had been rendered virtually obsolete when a bypass was blasted through the mountainside. With the disappearance of most of the traffic, the hedgerows and verges had returned to life, and driving along with Raybans obscuring his eyes, the car hood down and the sun blisteringly hot on his bare arms, Dewi thought he could well be on a country lane far from anywhere. His car was an unusual and quite rare Cavalier cabriolet that came into its own on days like this. When it rained, water leaked persistently through some deviously intractable chink between hood and windscreen.

He drew up with a flourish on the gravel patch in front of the school gates, tooted the horn, switched off the engine and waited patiently for admission. The tall wrought-iron rectangles with their internal structure of more rectangles made, he thought, a determined geometric statement amid the unruliness of ivy-clad wall and overhanging trees. On a board fixed to the left-hand wall THE HERMITAGE was written elegantly in pale-blue Roman lettering on a dark-blue background, with the school motto, something unintelligible in Latin, on a furled banner beneath. The other wall bore warnings in bright-red on white: PRIVATE PROPERTY, KEEP OUT and GUARD DOGS ON PATROL.

There was a view through the gates of a cube-like little house, painted white, from which a middle-aged, ruddy-cheeked man emerged, a young German Shepherd at his heels. He eased open one of the gates, sidled through and approached the car. 'How can I help you?' he asked.

'By letting me in,' Dewi replied good-naturedly.

'What's your business?'

Dewi flashed his identification. 'Sergeant Prys, Bangor.'

'Ken Randall,' the other man said. 'How do?'

The dog began circling the car and sniffing the tyres, then reared up and clamped its large, dusty paws on the top of the door, panting happily in Dewi's face.

'Nice dog,' Dewi commented, tweaking the animal's ears. 'Pet or guard dog?'

'Well,' Randall began, smiling fondly at his four-legged companion, 'he's a bit of both, but to be truthful, really more of a pet. Anyway, there's enough of the other around here already with the regular security guards. We just mind the lodge and let people in and out.'

'Who does that when you're not here?'

'There's an intercom. See?' He pointed to a discreet box fixed on to the wall beside the gates. 'The gates can operate either manually or electrically, so at night, or if I'm going out, I just flick a switch and them up there sees to things.' He moved closer to the car and put his hand on the dog's head. 'Don't mind me asking, but have you come about the girl who's gone missing?'

'I have indeed.'

'Have you only just found out?' he asked. When Dewi nodded, he said, 'Well, to my mind, you should've been told yesterday, as soon as they knew she'd gone.' Absently, he stroked the dog. 'I told Dr Scott she should phone the police when she rang down here first thing asking if I'd seen the girl, but she just reminded me to mind my own business, like always. As it is, they wasted a whole day and, I dare say, half the night, footling around looking for her.'

'Do girls go missing often?'

'Don't ask me,' Randall replied acidly. 'I don't get to know a smidgen more than I need to do my job. Dr Scott plays things so close to her chest that if there *is* trouble at the big house, it's done and dusted before anybody hears a whisper.' He made a face. 'She won't like having her hand forced into bringing you here,' he added. 'I'd bear that in mind, if I were you.'

'Thanks for the advice,' Dewi said. 'This girl,' he went on, 'Suzanne Melville. D'you know her?'

'They call her Sukie,' Randall told him. 'I see her around on her horse, so I know what she looks like, but no more than that. We're only allowed to speak to the girls if it's a matter of life and death, as you might say.'

'OK.' Dewi fired the engine. 'I'd better get up there and see what's what. Nice talking to you.'

Randall smiled. 'And you.'

While he trotted to the gates and pushed them wide, his dog continued to hang over the door of Dewi's car. After giving the animal's ears a final tweak, Dewi sent him away and went roaring up the drive, dwindling figures of man and dog, framed by those peculiar gates, in the rear-view mirror.

The drive ran straight for some hundred yards before making a sharp ninety-degree turn to the left. Another straight stretch ended in a ninety-degree switch to the right and after several more such switchbacks he began to wonder if the drive were not a surreal reflection of the gates.

He had passed the Hermitage on countless occasions, but never before seen behind its twelve-foot-high granite walls. In the early 1920s, some of the ancient woodland through which he twisted and turned so perplexingly was cleared to build a sanatorium where the rich, the aristocratic, and even the royal, were incarcerated for protection from their own excesses. During the Second World War, officers destroyed by exposure to war were hidden there by the government, but by late 1950 it was home only to a small batch of husk-like creatures whose reason had been lost in the PoW camps of the Far East. When they made their final exit the Hermitage was effectively abandoned and nature proceeded to reclaim her own. Wind-blown seeds took root in the landscaped gardens, bramble, nettle and creeper snaked across the lawns to embrace the once-white walls, rhododendron ran riot and killed everything within their shade, while the building itself quietly decayed inside and out from cellar to roof. Ten years later a consortium of businessmen bought land and buildings at a knockdown price, refurbished and repaired, and once again opened the doors to the rich, the aristocratic and, occasionally, the royal, but now for their education.

The branches overhead seemed to sag under their burden of

foliage. Birds clacked and twittered, and shook the leaves, sending down little flurries of pollen and seeds that settled on the passenger seat, his shoulders and the gleaming black bonnet. More than once he had to stamp hard on the brake to avoid the rabbits that sprang from nowhere and the grey squirrels that stared at him, immobile, before shinning up the trees. But for all the heat of the day, there was a chill in the woods that raised goose bumps on his bared skin. He concentrated on negotiating the crazy drive and tried not to look too intently at the trees rooted in their purple shadows, in case it was not simply a trick of the light that made them appear to move. A horse chestnut suddenly thrust a great swatch of withering blossoms and leaf fronds in his face and lovingly caressed his throat before dropping the faint, sweet scent of decay on his clothes.

The next ninety-degree bend brought into sight the flirtatiously swishing tail and pretty rump of a chestnut horse walking through the dappled shadows. The girl in the saddle had an equally fetching rear view. She glanced round as he approached and pulled the horse aside to let him pass.

He drifted to a stop. Smiling, he removed his sunglasses and said, 'Hi.'

'Hi, yourself.' She smiled back. Her eyes were a deep violet and the hair coiled beneath her hard hat was like spun silk. Tight blue britches clung to her thighs.

'Lovely day, isn't it?' he offered.

'Isn't it just?' Her thighs tensed and the horse walked on.

He let the car roll alongside. 'Shouldn't you be in lessons instead of out riding?'

'I guess, but this lady needs her exercise.'

Dewi looked appraisingly at the horse, nodding sagely. 'Nice animal.'

'Isn't she? I wouldn't mind her myself.'

'Oh? Don't you have your own horse?'

'Hell, yes, Mr Nosy! I've got a palomino gelding called Tonto.'

'So why are you riding this one?'

'Because there's no one else to do it.'

'I see.' Still keeping pace, Dewi asked, 'Is this Sukie Melville's horse, then? I hear she's gone missing.'

She snagged the reins and the mare halted. 'How d'you know about that?' She frowned down at him.

'Your headmistress reported it. I'm a policeman. A detective, to be precise.'

'Is that a fact? And what do they call you?'

He grinned. 'Apart from "Mr Nosy", you mean? My name's Dewi Prys.'

'Say what?'

'Dewi Prys,' he repeated. 'D-E-W-I P-R-Y-S.'

She mouthed the words, then shook her head. 'I don't understand your dialect.'

'Welsh isn't a dialect, it's a language. But never mind. You can call me David instead.'

She urged on the mare. 'So is D-E-W-I short for David?'

'Yep, but that's my dad's name. I got stuck with Dewi so people knew who they were talking about.'

'David's much nicer, don't you think?' She looked him over. 'Suits you better, I guess.'

Infuriatingly, he blushed. 'And what's your name?'

She laughed. 'T-O-R-R-A-N-C-E F-U-S-E-L-I.' With that, she turned into the woods and was lost from sight within seconds.

He let the car coast along under its own momentum for several yards, then shook off his bemusement and touched the accelerator. Soon he was catching glimpses of the school, while sounds of human activity reached him lazily, as if all their energy had been absorbed by the heat and the trees. There were occasional shouts from girls at play, muted blasts from an umpire's whistle, the chug of a motor mower somewhere ahead. As the drive opened up on to a forecourt, the mower passed across his field of vision, belching diesel fumes from the exhaust. The young man at the wheel was stripped to the waist. His muscles rippled, his tanned skin glistened with sweat and his coal-black hair was plastered to his skull, and he, too, disappeared into the trees while Dewi was still struggling to put a name to his face.

Sitting on a slight rise, the school was a stark, flat-faced structure in dull white stucco, its three storeys defined by regimented rows of windows, its roof hidden by a parapet, its forecourt partially embraced by angular ornamental walls.

Concrete fire escapes leaned against each end, like flying buttresses carrying the building's weight to the ground. He parked the car, picked up his briefcase and walked towards the centrally placed double doors that provided the only visible access.

Inside, the building smelt of stale cooking, mingled with the odour of freshly dried paint. He was in a white-painted central lobby and, looking down the corridors to right and left, saw that they too were white. The parquet floor in the right-hand corridor was dull and scuffed, that in the left polished almost to a mirror finish, while the walls along both were punctuated by heavy wooden door frames and plain wooden doors with iron knobs. Round, wrought-iron chandeliers hung from chains at intervals along the white ceilings, eight candle-shaped bulbs in each.

A wide, shallow staircase with backless wooden treads and more angular ironwork overhung the lobby, and set in the large triangle the stairs made against the wall were the gates to a lift, their design another repetition of those at the end of the drive.

Stepping rather gingerly on the shining parquet, he made his way along the left-hand corridor, reading the plates on the doors as he went: Miss G. Knight, Deputy Headmistress; Miss B. Grant, Senior Secretary; Dr Freya Scott, Headmistress; Miss E. Hardie, Matron. Flimsy-looking basket chairs sat outside every door, each precisely aligned with its neighbour. He passed the Bursar's office and had just reached that of the Admissions Secretary when a sharp English voice cut the air behind him.

'Are you looking for someone?'

He turned to see a lipsticked and befrocked figure outside the Senior Secretary's door. She looked garish in that grimly minimalist setting.

He walked towards her. 'I'm here to see Dr Scott.'

'And you are?' She sniffed.

'Detective Sergeant Prys from Bangor.'

She pointed to one of the chairs. 'You may wait there. Dr Scott is teaching until mid-morning break.' The door shut in his face.

He eased himself into the chair and, staring at his blurred reflection in the parquet, contemplated the school's apparent lack of interest in the absentee. Even the gorgeous Torrance, with her charming smile and quaintly refined American accent, seemed little concerned. But then, he thought, perhaps this particular missing girl was only the latest in a long line. He rose and wandered back to the lobby.

The lobby bisected the building, with another set of double doors at its far end. He pushed through on to a paved terrace overlooking banks of rhododendron, magnolia and azalea, huge formal flowerbeds, and an enormous expanse of lawn that carried the eye to the ever-moving waters of Menai Strait and the shores of Anglesey. Looking up, he saw that this side of the building was gracefully softened by curved, full-height bays, inset with curved windows, and whereas the face of the building he had first seen was dulled by the green-grey reflection of the trees, these walls glistened in the sunshine.

Imagining that the building, chameleon-like, must change its face and mood according to the time of day, the weather, the seasons, he strolled back to his seat, to find he had company. The chairs outside Matron's door were occupied by two girls he thought must be fourteen or fifteen years old, dressed alike in green and white striped shirts and navy-blue skirts. There the similarities ceased. One looked as if she had been taken in off the streets as an act of charity: lank black hair framed a pasty face marked with lines of pain, her limbs were like sticks and her breasts a mere grudging admission beneath the shirt. Her bony kneecaps were almost deformed and, glancing at the hands clenched fiercely in her lap, he saw equally prominent and raw-looking knuckles. The other girl was what he could only describe as voluptuous, with thick, curly brown hair, bee-stung lips, and the bloom of health and wealth from top to toe. 'Chalk and cheese,' he said to himself, as she looked across at him and smiled boldly.

'Hello,' she said.

He nodded.

'My name'th Daithy Podmore,' she added. 'And thith ith my betht fwiend Alith Dewwinger. What'th your name?'

Involuntarily, he flinched, then felt a rush of real pity. Meeting her eyes, he saw they were strangely opaque, as if she sensed the pity and despised him for it.

'I'm called Dewi Prys,' he replied quietly. 'I'm waiting for Dr Scott.'

'We're waiting for Matron,' Daisy told him, before launching into a speech riddled with traps. If nothing else, he thought, it showed her mettle. 'Alice has got one of her awful headaches,' she went on. 'She could have meningitis, you know, or even a brain tumour. She gets asthma, too, especially when she's been near the horses. That's because of the dander on their coats.'

'I don't!' Alice raised red-rimmed eyes. 'I've always had asthma! It's nothing to do with horses!' She looked close to tears, but there was temper in the set of her mouth.

'How many horses are there?' Dewi asked hurriedly.

'Seven,' replied Daisy. 'Five dim-witted geldings and two vicious mares.' Her voice was scathing.

'Don't you like horses?' he asked.

Before she could respond, Alice broke in, a sweet smile transforming her dreary face. 'She doesn't *appreciate* them. Horses are just gorgeous!'

Dewi gazed at her. 'Have you got one of your own?'

'Dr Scott only lets the sixth formers have horses on campus, so I've got to wait another two years.'

Daisy prodded her and giggled nastily. 'Don't bet on it. You could be dead by then.'

'Don't be so horrible!' Alice wailed, her voice rising.

A voice boomed from the far end of the corridor. 'What's all this noise about?' A stout, middle-aged woman stiffly dressed in traditional nurse's garb squeaked towards them in rubber-soled shoes that left smudges on the gleaming parquet. She favoured Daisy with an indulgent smile, then loomed over Alice. 'What's the matter with you this time?' she demanded, taking hold of Alice's chin in one huge red hand and pulling down her lower lids with the fingers of the other, while Alice squirmed. 'Dearie me! Another headache, I suppose?' Rubbing the small of her back as she straightened, she hefted the keys hanging from her belt and unlocked the door to her room, then turned to Dewi. Uniform rustling, she took a few steps towards him.

'I'm waiting for Dr Scott,' he said, pre-empting interrogation.

She consulted the fob watch pinned to her apron. 'She won't be long.' She stood over him, breathing heavily, her gaze dour and steely. There were broken veins on her ruddy cheeks, grey hairs bristling stubbornly and spitefully round her mouth and on her chin, and the puffs of breath issuing from her smelt of chloroform, as if in her quiet, lonely moments, she drank from the brown glass bottles he imagined must fill the cupboards in her room. 'You shouldn't have been talking to the girls,' she chided. 'Dr Scott doesn't allow strangers to have truck with them.'

He reddened. 'I'm sorry. We were just chatting about the horses.' Feeling like a small child caught out in mischief, he added defensively, 'It would have been churlish to ignore them.'

Frowning, she pursed her lips. 'Don't answer back, young man, if you please.' With that she wheeled away to usher the girls into her room. Before the door closed Daisy, her shoulders shaking with mirth, turned to make an obscene gesture.

Dewi was furious: with the woman, with Daisy, but mostly with himself, for letting reserve fall prey to curiosity. The murmur of voices came from Matron's room, punctuated by yelps from Alice. A telephone rang in the secretary's office and was answered within seconds. Still smarting from Matron's rebuke, he once more wandered into the lobby, to stand at the front doors lost in thought.

A light step, a drift of perfume, jolted him back to awareness. Turning quickly, he saw a tall, fair-haired woman in the shadow of the staircase. She wore a dark-grey suit in some silky fabric and a pristine ivory shirt. 'May I help you?' Her voice was warm and cultured, the words accompanied by an enquiring smile.

'I'm Detective Sergeant Prys,' he said. 'I've come to see Dr Scott.'

'I'm Freya Scott.' With a couple of long strides she moved near enough to shake his hand, then gestured for him to follow. 'I'm sorry to have kept you waiting,' she added, unlocking her door. 'I teach most mornings.'

Her study was a large white room with a wide, curved window offering a tranquil view of the gardens and Strait. Carpet, cabinets, chairs, the massive chrome and leather desk were surely artefacts from the building's heyday, he thought. Behind the desk was a large fireplace, a simple hole in the wall, its empty mouth filled with a wrought-iron screen. Above the mantel hung photographs and an impressive array of certificates, with pride of place given to a reproduction of Annigoni's portrait of the Queen. The desk top was clear except for a gold fountain pen, a telephone console and a closed manila file with the name 'Suzanne (Sukie) Melville' printed on the cover in black letters.

'Do sit down,' Freya said, sliding into a leather chair. She pressed a button on the telephone, ordered coffee and biscuits for two, then gave him her full attention.

She was probably in her early forties, he decided, with streaky blonde hair rolled neatly into a French pleat and a beautifully made-up face. Her features were well defined and even attractive, but her eyes commanded attention. Heavy-lidded and of a deep blue-grey, they were startlingly sensual. Her perfectly manicured nails were varnished a brilliant red and she wore sparkling diamond rings on each hand, yet something about her bearing or manner brought military metaphor to mind, and he could easily envisage her dressed in uniform and even armed.

'Thank you for responding so promptly to my call,' she said. 'Tell me, where are you based?'

'Bangor. The Hermitage is on our patch, so to speak.'

She raised her eyebrows a fraction. 'But I contacted the divisional headquarters.'

'And they routed it to us.' He smiled disarmingly. 'Now, I understand you've already searched the grounds,' he said. 'What other steps have you taken?'

'Thus far, we've questioned all the sixth form as well as the few juniors Sukie's friendly with, but no one has the faintest idea where she might have gone. Or, indeed, why.'

'Has she disappeared before?'

Freya shook her head.

'How often do girls abscond?'

'Very, very infrequently. Our aim is to identify and manage any difficulties the girls may have *before* they become problematic.'

'Who's in charge of pastoral care?'

'It's a team effort.' Lacing her fingers together, she leaned

17

forward. 'Let me explain how the Hermitage is organised. All but a few of the teaching staff are resident, as is Matron. On entry to school, a girl is assigned to one of the four houses, each with a captain from the sixth form as well as a housemistress. There are also prefects and a head girl. The system is designed to ensure that each girl is monitored at every stage of her school career.'

'What about security arrangements?'

Amusement flickered briefly in her eyes. 'I see you noticed the absence of electrified fencing, armed guards and snarling Rottweilers. However,' she went on soberly, 'we propose to install closed-circuit television during the summer holidays, to augment existing facilities. We already have internal and external building alarms, staff on waking duty every night, the lodge keeper and his dog, and twenty-four-hour mobile patrols throughout the grounds. That you failed to see them is testament to their effectiveness, I think.'

'Nonetheless,' Dewi persisted, 'they can't possibly be everywhere at once. The water frontage of this site is about two miles, the road frontage is nearer three, and between the two it must be two miles, if not more. Someone bent on escape wouldn't encounter too many obstacles.'

'No, I agree. And—' She broke off as someone rapped on the door and rose quickly to answer. When the door opened, Dewi thought night must have fallen. Every vestige of light was obliterated by a mountainous woman in chef's tunic and trousers, proffering a tray draped with a snowy cloth. Freya took the tray, murmured her thanks and shut the door. 'I was about to say,' she went on, removing the cloth to reveal white china and a plate of mixed biscuits, 'that I'm more concerned with the possibility of Sukie's having had an accident in the grounds.' She poured coffee, her movements steady and methodical. 'We began searching when she failed to show up at the stables yesterday morning to exercise her horse.' Handing him a cup, offering biscuits, she continued, 'By nightfall, every building and most of the woods had been thoroughly scoured.'

'Is there any chance she's gone off with a man?'

'If that were the case I would know.' Her mouth tightened. 'My girls do not associate with the locals and her parents are not aware of any significant relationships in her life.'

'When did her parents last see her?'

'The day she returned here after the Easter holiday.'

'And how did she get back? Train? Car?'

'Their chauffeur drove her up to London, where she caught the express. She's quite old enough to travel alone.'

'She's quite old enough to do a lot of things,' Dewi insisted, 'which is why I said she might be with a man. And with all due respect, ma'am, you're the last person her friends would tell, whether she's missing or not.'

'I'm afraid I disagree, Sergeant Prys.' Her tone was chilly. 'My girls *would* tell me and as they have not, I'm confident there is nothing to tell. So,' she went on, 'how will you proceed?'

'I'm only instructed to take details, ma'am. My inspector will decide on the next step.' Pulling a form from his briefcase, he laid it on the desk. 'Perhaps you'd be kind enough to complete this.'

Freya's nails dragged the paper towards her. She uncapped the pen and, without once referring to the closed file at her elbow, attended to every question.

'A recent photo would also help,' Dewi said when she handed back the form. Sukie, he saw, was seventeen years old, five feet four inches tall, slimly built, Caucasian, with medium-length, wavy brown hair, grey eyes and no distinguishing marks, scars, or tattoos. Her parents had a grand-sounding address near Newbury and her mother, but not her father, had a title.

Freya slipped a photograph from the file and pushed it across the desk. Contemplating another very pretty girl with the sheen of wealth about her, Dewi asked, 'Why doesn't her father have a title as well?'

'Lady Hester's father is a peer of the realm and she therefore has a title in her own right. As she married a commoner, her children remain *un*titled.' She paused. 'I should say "child". Sukie's an only child.'

He stowed form and photograph in his briefcase. 'Are you sure she wasn't worried about anything? Exams, for instance?'

'She has no external examinations until next year. In any case she isn't academically ambitious. She prefers to coast along, taking what life offers. Horses are her current passion.'

'Does she have a mobile phone? Most youngsters do, these days.'

'I don't allow mobile phones at school,' Freya told him. 'Nor do I let the girls have unsupervised access to computers, so I don't think there's any possibility of Sukie's having developed some relationship over the Internet.' Meeting his eyes, she went on, 'I'm very strict, Sergeant Prys, particularly about the possessions the girls are permitted to have here. While they come from backgrounds you would see as uniformly wealthy, wealth is, in fact, just as relative as poverty. I would be very naïve not to recognise that, and stupid not to take steps to preclude, wherever possible, the likelihood of envy and temptation. I try to ensure a level playing field.'

'So,' Dewi said, 'on this scale of relative wealth, where do the Melvilles feature?'

She offered a brief, oddly sardonic smile. 'Clinging to the very bottom with their fingernails. Her father's family has a poor track record of success in any sphere, and I'm afraid he simply runs true to form. He and Lady Hester depend on handouts from her parents.'

'Are they rich?' Dewi asked.

'Extremely so.'

'Kidnapping Sukie could be worth somebody's while, then,' he remarked.

'Barring the odd one or two, abducting *any* of my pupils could be worth someone's while,' she pointed out rather acidly.

'Which, with respect, is why you should have reported her missing as soon as you knew.'

'I'm aware of that now,' she replied quietly. 'Yesterday I thought at first that she might have had an accident. Later I assumed her absence was some kind of prank and I was simply giving her time to return.' Frowning, she added, 'Surely, by now, if she had been abducted, there would be a ransom demand?'

'I can't really comment on that,' Dewi told her. 'We don't have much experience of kidnappings. But you're probably right. Anyway,' he said, getting to his feet, 'thank you for your help, Dr Scott. And the coffee. Either myself or Inspector Tuttle will be in touch very soon.'

Freya too rose. 'See my secretary on your way out,' she said. 'She's put together plans of the grounds and buildings, and some other literature which may be of use.'

When Dewi emerged on to the sun-soaked forecourt Torrance, now on her own two legs, was leaning against the wing of his car, leather riding boots covered in dust. She was not as tall as he had thought, but her legs were long and exceedingly shapely. With the back of her hand, she brushed at a loose strand of glorious flaxen hair, adding a smear of dirt to the smudge of freckles across her nose.

'One of us will get clapped in irons if I'm seen talking to you,' he told her. 'Matron's already given me a rocket for having "truck".'

She laughed again, spontaneously, and he thought she must laugh often. 'She doesn't miss much.'

'She missed Sukie's disappearing act.' He dropped his briefcase on the passenger seat. 'But then, so did everyone else, apparently. How well d'you know her?'

Torrance shrugged. 'Quite well, I guess, but not especially so. I taught her to ride a few months back.'

'Any idea why she's legged it?'

'I'm sorry?' She frowned, again mystified.

'Run away,' he explained. 'Decamped. Absconded. Whatever.'

She flicked at a leaf shard stuck to the car bonnet. 'Dr Scott isn't sure Sukie *did* run away. She thinks she might have had an accident. That's why we spent most of yesterday doing a horseback search. The security guards were out on foot, too. Generally they just tootle around in their little white trucks.'

'Keeping to the drive and tracks?'

She nodded, scuffing her toe on the ground. 'If someone wanted to get out they could, you know. They wouldn't even have to go through the main gate. The walls are full of holes.' She met his gaze; uneasily, he thought. 'You should talk to Sean. He knows every inch of the place.'

'Sean?'

'The groundsman.' Then she smiled. 'Funny, but he looks quite like you. Most of the girls have a dreadful crush on him.'

'Where does he live?'

'In the village down the road. With his ma, I think.'

A woman came round the side of the building, striding purposefully towards them, a dark-green divided skirt slapping against her bulging thighs. Hurriedly Dewi vaulted into the car and fired the ignition. 'She looks as if she means business. I'd better go.'

'Yeah, you better had.' Torrance's smile broadened. 'But I hope you come again.'

Long before he reached the gates he could see Randall, with his dog beside him, sitting on its haunches, waiting in the shadows cast by the trees.

'They rang down to say you were on your way,' Randall explained when Dewi stopped the car.

Dewi looked up at him. 'D'you keep a record of the comings and goings?'

'That depends on who's coming and who's going,' Randall said. 'I book tradesmen and folk on business, and strangers, of course, but I don't keep tally on the school governors, for instance, or the families, or, basically, anybody I've been warned to expect. They'll sign in at the school. There's a visitors' book.'

'What about staff? Who lives out?'

Randall scratched his ear. 'Bar the teachers, Matron and Sally, the head cook, all of them, I reckon. A lot of the domestics and kitchen staff and so forth are contract workers, and the faces can change from month to month. I'll know who they are, though, because they get ID cards off the contractor.' He paused. 'Then there's the two caretakers and the two groundsmen. They're regular employees, like me. We all keep time sheets and the bursar collects them every Thursday.'

'Are you told about people who visit when you're not on duty?'

Randall favoured him with an eloquent look. 'Like I said, I don't know more than Dr Scott thinks I need know and that's not much.'

In response Dewi offered an equally eloquent look. 'Do me a favour,' he said. 'Your front door can't be more than fifteen feet from the gates. Don't tell me you can't at least *hear* the to-ings and fro-ings, especially the night-time ones.' Glancing at the dog, which seemed to be smiling at him, he added, 'Not to mention the fact that German Shepherds are prone to raising Cain at the slightest noise.'

The other man's ruddy cheeks turned purple. 'I could get the sack if Dr Scott knew I'd been talking to you! I'm trying to help and all you can do is make snide remarks!'

Sensing his master's anger, the dog's expression changed in an instant and Dewi heard a snarl growing in its throat.

'I'm just commenting,' Dewi said mildly. 'I'm not implying anything and I'm not suggesting you should be gawping out of the window every five minutes.' Man and dog continued to stare at him, both bristling. 'But you must hear the gates opening.'

'Did *you* hear them?' Randall demanded. 'They run smooth as silk, because it's my job to see to them and I make sure they work properly.'

'OK,' conceded Dewi. 'Point taken. Apology offered.'

'Hm.' The lodge keeper grunted and his dog resumed its open-mouthed smile.

'I'll be on my way, then,' Dewi told him.

'If it's boyfriends you want to know about,' Randall said over his shoulder as he went to open the gates, 'it's no use coming to me.' He hauled on the huge iron latch. 'They'd come in over the wall, or through one of the wickets, the same way the girls get out.'

Dewi touched the accelerator and let the car glide slowly towards the entrance. Drawing alongside, he braked. '*Do* the girls get out?'

'Now and then, I've heard the women gossiping about girls being seen in town when they should be abed. But that's as much as I can tell you.'

Jack's office was empty when Dewi returned to the police station. He found Janet alone in the CID room. 'Where's Inspector Tuttle?' he asked. 'I'm supposed to report back to him.'

'Downstairs in the squad room with Mr McKenna,' she

replied. 'Organising uniform and dog handlers to search the Hermitage.'

'I thought he was waiting for me to report back.'

'There's been a development. Our chief constable had a telephone call from a heavily titled gentleman who identified himself as the missing girl's grandfather, so it's now all systems go.'

'Are they sending a mobile incident room?' he asked, upending his briefcase.

'I've no idea.' She rose and began looking through the plans and brochures spilled across his desk.

'How many officers are going out?'

'Six from here, six from Caernarfon, eight from Anglesey, plus five dogs, including Bryn the Wonder Dog.' Glancing at a plan of the grounds, she set it aside. 'Who,' she added, 'can detect the faintest whiff of humankind from ten thousand yards and under fifty feet of snow.'

'You're not far out,' Dewi replied, picking up the discarded plan and a sheaf of other papers. 'The search team will need these. And I'll get these circulated,' he added, waving the missing persons form and Sukie's portrait. He handed Janet the school prospectus. 'You'll have to make do with this for now.'

As soon as he had gone, Janet sat down with the glossy book and fast became enthralled by a kaleidoscope of images that seemed to come straight from the school stories she had devoured as a child. She gazed longingly at the many photographs of fresh-faced girls against various backdrops: the main building, the new teaching block, the music rooms, the sports hall, the playing fields, the stables, the competition-sized riding arena, the boathouse at the Strait's edge, even the Swiss Alps. Most impressive of all, she thought, was the enormous swimming pool, an untouched relic of the Hermitage's early days.

Each of the school's four houses was named after an English royal dynasty, each had a captain elected by her peers, each was identified by an item of uniform and a sash tied round the waist for sports. Tudor was green, York pillar-box red, Lancaster bright golden yellow and Windsor a deep, rich blue.

So like those pictured in her old story books were these girls that Janet began to search their faces, looking for the villainness always defined in fiction by ginger hair and mean eyes. Blondes, she recalled, would be glamorous but unreliable, brunettes mysterious, with their potential for good or ill only discovered in the denouement. It was the ordinary, mousy-haired girls who proved themselves heroic. Then she laughed at herself and was still laughing when Dewi returned.

'What's so funny?' he asked.

'Is this place for real?'

'It is, believe me. Right down to the battleaxe of a matron.'

'Elspeth Hardie, she's called, and she's a fully fledged nurse.'

'I gathered that from the way she dresses.'

'What's Dr Scott like?'

He took his time replying. 'On the surface, a classy blonde with impeccable manners and sexy perfume. Underneath she's probably hard as nails. She certainly doesn't like criticism, implied or otherwise.'

'She wouldn't be much use in a job like that if she *weren't* tough. According to the prospectus, she's ex-army and, I quote, "attained the rank of Captain before resigning her commission to follow a long-cherished ambition to enter teaching".'

'What else does the prospectus say?'

'Not much. It's primarily designed to persuade parents to part with money.'

'It obviously works, then. They've got two hundred and twenty-eight girls currently on the books and at fifteen thousand a throw, that's roughly three and half million a year in basic fees alone, plus extra for music lessons, art classes, dancing lessons, riding, livery costs, fencing, sailing and winter sports.'

'Aside from the running costs, staff salaries must be enormous.'

'That depends on whether Scott employs the best, or people with little chance of getting a job elsewhere. If I'm not mistaken, she's already got one convicted offender on the books. I think the groundsman is Sean O'Connor. He and his mates got community service for trashing a pub after a drinking binge, and while it was ages ago and he's a sort of mate of mine *and* he's kept out of trouble since, he's still got a record.'

'And that just goes to prove there are records and records,'

Janet observed. 'Anyway, even if half the staff belong behind bars, I still can't wait to see the place. I always wanted to go to boarding school.'

'Did you?' He was surprised. 'Why?'

'Because when I was young, I read a lot of books by the likes of Angela Brazil and Elinor M. Brent-Dyer about the wonderful adventures of boarding-school life.'

'Absolute rubbish, most probably.'

'So my father used to say. That's why I ended up with the hoi polloi at Ysgol Tryfan.' Her dark eyes glinted with mischief. 'Like you.'

'Don't worry,' he said. 'It doesn't show. Everyone at the Hermitage will think you're one of their own.'

3

Almost with the zeal of a crusader, Freya had come to the headship of the school ten years before with certain philosophies fully formed and ready for realisation, foremost among them the belief that personalities must be cleansed of preconception and messy emotion before her educative process could take root. Inevitably, those with most to gain from her mentoring rose to the top; the rest were left to their own devices.

Knowledge, in its broadest sense, was to Freya the currency of power and therefore withheld from those who could not appreciate its value or manipulate its uses. Mindful that her ability to control depended on the breadth of her own knowledge, she insisted the staff kept nothing from her, however trivial. The dissenters and the disaffected faded from the scene one by one, leaving her with a team obedient to her leadership. If, occasionally, a small voice at the back of her mind might hint that in disposing of the spirited she had rendered herself dependent on the weak and inept, she ignored the warning.

In going missing, Sukie had undermined her power base and created a mystery that was already eating into Freya's authority. When Hester Melville learned early that morning of her daughter's absence, she ran for help to her father, whose power far outweighed anything at Freya's disposal. Consequently, shortly before the school sat down to lunch, the police informed her that a full-scale search would commence within the hour.

Standing commandingly on the refectory dais, she explained the situation to the girls and staff, knowing that with whatever skill she chose her words, its gravity would be obvious. Long before lunch was over the scent of hysteria soured the air.

Once the girls filed from the refectory, she gathered the staff about her own table. 'While I am not blaming anyone,' she began, 'unfortunately, neither the police nor Sukie's family feel similarly charitable. I hope Sukie's disappearance is nothing more than a silly prank; however, it may prove to be something far more worrying and we must, therefore, make every effort to contain its potential for serious damage to our school.'

There was little response, except for fretful mutterings here and there, and suddenly she felt terribly isolated. Looking critically at the women around her, she realised they expected her to shoulder the full burden. Already they were retreating, building redoubts in which to hide until the crisis was resolved.

When Freya left the refectory for her study, only Matron followed. Bristling with defensive agitation, she rejected every implicit rebuke in the headmistress's comments to her staff.

'And it's not fair to say I'm in the best position to know if a girl is upset or worried,' she insisted. 'What about the house captains? The form teachers? Anyway, Sukie never said a word about being worried or upset and nor did anyone else!' She took a deep, fortifying breath. 'And I don't like being pilloried in front of everyone for doing my job as I see fit. Why should Mrs Derringer object to me calling the doctor to Alice? I'm perfectly qualified to know when a doctor's needed.'

Watching the older woman's turned-down mouth and disapproving eyes, Freya wondered if, disarmed by the façade, she had made the mistake of excluding her from that quiet early pogrom of staff. 'I merely said you should have told me first.' She fiddled with a leather-bound appointments book, fighting the desire to bully, which Matron always provoked. 'And do stop calling Alice's mother Mrs Derringer. You know perfectly well she reverted to her maiden name of Rathbone a long time ago. Please don't make another gaffe when she next visits.'

'When's that likely to be? Next blue moon?'

'She's a very busy woman.'

'Don't we know it!' Matron said sourly. 'Jetting to America, jetting to the Far East, jetting here, there and everywhere except to see her only child now and then.'

'She pays us to look after Alice.'

'Caretakers! That's all we are. What that wee bairn needs is some proper mothering.'

'The other day,' Freya reminded her silkily, 'you said that "wee bairn" is a "headstrong little madam in need of a good smacked bottom". Do make up your mind.'

Matron flushed beetroot red. 'That was because she cheeked me when I told her off for behaving like a hoyden, but whether I like the way she behaves or not, she's not a well child. Apart from these headaches, her asthma's getting worse.' She pursed her lips. 'It'll be on our heads when something happens,' she added darkly.

'Her asthma is always worse at this time of the year. She also gets hay fever, which results in blocked sinuses. Hence the headaches, no doubt.'

'The doctor didn't think so,' Matron said, reclaiming lost ground. 'She says Alice needs glasses.'

'Something simple, nonetheless,' Freya murmured. 'Have you made an optician's appointment?'

'Naturally.' Patting her collar, Matron elevated her stately bosom to check that the big silver clasp on her elastic belt sat dead-centre. Then she twitched her apron into place across her ample lap. 'Do the police intend to interview the girls?' she asked.

'I imagine that will depend on what transpires from the search.'

'Only if they are, you'd better make sure that young sergeant knows his place. Despite the fact I'd already hauled him over the coals for gossiping to Alice and Daisy, Rosemary Bebb saw him flirting with Torrance on his way out.'

Irritably Freya said, 'I think the possible effect of a good-looking young man on a bunch of impressionable girls is the least of our worries at present.'

'I quite agree,' Matron commented, nodding vigorously. 'Whatever else Sukie might do, she wouldn't run away and leave her horse.' She paused, to give full weight to her next words. 'I've got a bad feeling in my bones about this. I think she's been kidnapped.'

'That would be a most foolish, and dangerous, suggestion to broadcast.' Eyes and face stony, Freya added, 'There is absolutely nothing – *nothing* – to indicate abduction, as I have already told the police. They agree with me that a ransom demand would have been sent by now, either to us or to Sukie's parents. In any case,' she went on, barely able to contain her anger, 'the precarious state of the Melville finances is no secret.'

'What about Lady Hester's parents, though?' Matron insisted. 'They're certainly not—'

Freya cut her off in mid-sentence. 'You will *not* discuss abduction and that is an order! Do you understand?' As the other woman blinked back tears of shock, Freya turned the knife. 'You overreact, you have too much fondness for emotional dramatics and your viewpoints are frighteningly limited, and that is why, for instance, you refuse to see some of the school traditions for the perfectly natural assessment processes that they are. You seem to forget, Matron, that we are paid to make these girls fit to take their proper place at the head of society. Better the weak fall by the wayside here, rather than where it might actually matter.'

Without a word, humiliated and diminished, Matron struggled to her feet. Wrenching open the door, she stumbled blindly into the corridor, asking herself how much longer she could tolerate the ruthlessness behind the fancy notions and long words with which the headmistress beguiled everyone within the school. The answer was always the same; she would bear it as long as she must, for she had no place in the terrifying world outside.

Deaf to the noises from the corridor, Freya stared through the window, but saw nothing of the glorious view or the banks of rhododendron and azalea blossoms, and even the hundreds of early-flowering roses unfolding their petals to the sun might have been but a few withered leaves for all the notice she took. She thought of the absent Sukie, feeling not curious, or worried, but angry and resentful and rather frightened, for if someone in the school knew what had befallen the girl there had been a revolution in the balance of power.

4

Before leaving to co-ordinate the search, Jack dropped a handful of leaflets on McKenna's desk. 'Something to kick-start your house hunting,' he said. 'I got them from the agent round the corner.'

Eventually McKenna responded. 'Thanks,' he muttered.

Jack made for the door. 'Think nothing of it.' By the time he reached the head of the stairs, he was grinding his jaw with suppressed fury.

Without a vestige of enthusiasm, McKenna glanced at photographs, scanned paragraphs of estate-agent-speak and decided very quickly, and with some relief, that not one of the houses appealed to him. He dropped the leaflets into the waste bin.

While he smoked the second of the ten cigarettes of his self-imposed daily allowance, he reread the information sheet tucked inside the box of nicotine patches he had bought last Saturday. The patches made his skin itch, they were expensive, his throat was sore and he had a persistent, nagging headache and, as he stubbed out the cigarette, he wondered why he was bothering. The business of the house was part of the same picture, a dismal rendering of an impoverished life. He recognised his despondency, yet saw no point in trying to alter his state of mind any more than he would voluntarily move from his rickety old house. He had no parents, no siblings, no wife, no children; no one in whom to invest himself and his past for their present or future. He had no one to care for and no one cared for him, and all the emotion left over from the huge amount he lavished on Fluff and Blackie, his two rescued cats, was of necessity sealed inside. Or was it? he wondered. Perhaps it had leaked away and he was truly as drained as he felt.

Towards two that afternoon, Divisional HQ passed on the news that the body of a young female had been washed up in Caernarfon, near the floating restaurant at the mouth of the River Seiont.

5

The floating restaurant was towed downstream from its winter berth every Easter and moored for the summer months in the lea of the harbour walls, and although partly in the shadow of the castle's lofty Eagle Tower, it offered fine views of the Aber foreshore and an uninterrupted prospect across the water to the south-western shores of Anglesey.

Pedestrians and cyclists could cross the river mouth by way of a bridge that swung back and forth on hydraulic capstans at regular intervals to let the yachts, fishing smacks and tourist launches come and go. On the far side of the bridge a narrow road, hugging the foreshore, trailed around a bluff of land and was quickly out of sight, and it was here the body had finally made landfall, tossed carelessly by the incoming tide on to a seaweed-draped litter of rocks that shelved steeply towards the water.

High on the Eagle Tower, the halyard pinged against the flagpole, the fearsome red dragon emblazoned on the flag writhing and lashing its tail as a stiff breeze tugged the fabric this way and that. Making his way across the bridge, McKenna could hear the whiplash snap of the flag punctuating the murmur of voices from the crowd that had materialised on the quayside, drawn by the smell of drama. In the distance a siren wailed and behind him waves slapped rhythmically at the harbour walls, raising spray. When he rounded the bluff he saw another cluster of onlookers, held at bay by a lone policeman. Further down the road cars, motorcycles and the odd camper van were being turned back the way they had come.

The paraphernalia of death and investigation looked insignificant, he thought, against the backdrop of a huge sky and an endless expanse of glittering water. A small white tent lapped by tiny waves sat crookedly on the rocks inside a cordon of blue and white tape, two scenes of crime personnel in white overalls picked over the ground, while several police officers stood about rather aimlessly, waiting to be told what to do. Right at the edge of the water the local superintendent and the harbour master gazed out to sea, speaking in low voices.

Slithering and sliding on the rocks, McKenna joined them.

'You'd think this was the latest tourist attraction, wouldn't you?' the superintendent remarked nastily, staring at the onlookers with his face expressing his disgust. 'Bloody ghouls!'

'It's human nature to be curious,' McKenna said. He nodded towards the overalled investigators. 'Have they found anything?'

'No,' the superintendent said shortly. 'And in the half-hour or so they've got left before peak tide I don't expect they will.' Morosely, he surveyed the activities. 'Aside from that, tipping a body in water is a sure-fire way of destroying evidence, which is something your perpetrator might well know.'

'There might not be a "perpetrator",' McKenna pointed out. 'Where's the body?'

'On the way to the morgue. Like I said, high tide's imminent. Didn't want her washed back out to sea, did we?'

'There was no point in keeping her here,' the harbour master added. 'The police surgeon says she's been dead at least twenty-four hours and, that being the case, it's most unlikely that she entered the water anywhere in this vicinity.'

'Where, then?' asked McKenna.

'Upstream, most probably, and on this side of the Strait.' The harbour master turned to follow the progress of an ocean-going cruiser cutting an arrogant dash through the waves. 'Once I've had a proper look at the tidal charts, I'll get together with the pathologist.'

Before responding, McKenna watched the cruiser change course, preparatory to entering the river mouth. 'She could have come from the Irish Sea,' he said.

'Unlikely.' The harbour master shook his head. 'Those bodies usually make landfall on the Anglesey coast, or down Cardigan

Bay way.' He touched McKenna's shoulder and pointed across the water, where the tidal flow and the vicious undertows that characterised the Strait were clearly visible. 'You can see from here how the tide runs; up and down and round and round.' He paused. 'Coming back up the Strait, it meets resistance from the river, which makes it slow down somewhat, creating an eddy. So, if there's anything heavy in the water, this is where it generally gets dropped.'

'Who found her?' McKenna asked, looking once more towards the watchers.

'Not one of them,' the harbour master told him. 'She'd have been invisible from the road. A coastguard patrol on its way out to Llanddwyn Island spotted her.'

The pathology laboratories and mortuary were tucked away behind the accident department at Bangor's district general hospital. Once inside the innocuous-looking building, McKenna announced himself at the desk in the foyer, and within minutes a gowned and gloved technician poked his head round the mortuary door and beckoned him inside.

Dogged by a photographer, Dr Eifion Roberts, the senior pathologist, was pacing slowly up and down beside one of the autopsy tables on which lay the body so recently given up by the sea. Now and then he stooped low to scrutinise the sodden, filthy garments, apparently oblivious to the stench of salt water, sediments and rotting flesh that reached McKenna almost as a memory after most of its reality had been vacuumed away by the pumps beneath the table.

Roberts glanced round and said, above the dull roar of the pumps, 'If you want to come closer, you'll have to get gowned up. I don't want the body contaminated.'

'I just want to make an identification,' McKenna told him. 'Or not, as the case may be.'

'Isn't that a job for the foot soldiers, rather than the general?'

Staring beyond the pathologist to the autopsy table, McKenna replied, 'Most of the foot soldiers are out, searching the Hermitage and its environs for a pupil last seen around eleven on Tuesday night.'

'How old?'

'Seventeen.'

'Got a picture?'

He handed over Sukie's portrait. 'She was apparently dressed in an oversized white T-shirt that she wore to bed and a striped silk dressing gown. And slippers, presumably. She'd just come from the showers.'

Roberts looked at the portrait. Gently pushing aside the tangled hair, he examined the mottled, dirt-streaked face. 'You'll have to get a formal ID from someone who knew her, but to my mind there's no doubt. The time fits, too. She's been in the water forty-eight hours at the absolute outside and probably quite a bit less.' He fingered the clothing. 'This may well be the same T shirt, but she'd put on jeans and trainers.' Then he raised the hem of the shirt and hooked his finger under the waistband of the jeans. 'She's also wearing underpants, but no brassiere.' Standing back from the table for the photographer, he asked, 'What's the likely score? Suicide, homicide or accident?'

'I haven't the faintest idea. We're depending on you to show us the way.'

'You've a wait on your hands, then. There's nothing like water for messing up evidence.'

McKenna nodded. 'So I've already been told. I'll get Jack to bring in the headmistress to identify her, then you can start the autopsy.'

6

By four o'clock, Jack had called to confirm that the body in the
mortuary was indeed Sukie's. McKenna set in motion the
mechanics of an investigation made daunting by the prospect of
interviewing and protecting almost three hundred potential
witnesses, and of probing an equal number of possible suspects.
Discussing strategy, manpower and cost over the telephone
with the deputy chief constable, he was reminded not to
overlook the extreme sensitivity of this particular situation and
so, harnessing the other man's worries to extract more
resources, he said, 'Until cause of death is known, we presume
homicide, as usual. I need a mobile incident room and enough
personnel to leave a contingent of officers on twenty-four-hour
guard duty. I'd also be grateful,' he added, 'if you'd deal with
both the school governors and the media. As you say, it's a
sensitive situation and the kind of thing that sets the media
salivating. A brief statement about the girl's death and our
continuing enquiries should suffice for now.'

Jack caught the tail end of the conversation as he walked in.
He took off his jacket, slung it over a chair and sat down.

'Where's the headmistress?' asked McKenna.

'I stuck her in the CID room with Janet and a hot drink. She's
very, very shaken. She's also desperate to get back to spread the
sad tidings.'

McKenna glanced at his watch, then reached for a cigarette.
After some moments of silence, he said, 'We'll start as we mean
to go on; in other words take control from the outset.' He
coughed, then put the cigarette in an ashtray. 'When you go
back to the school,' he went on, 'get the staff and girls together,

and tell them *only* that Sukie's been found dead. Nothing else.'

'Questioning them all is going to be a logistical nightmare.' Pausing to loosen his tie, Jack added, 'If I rope in everyone apart from the dog handlers, I'll have twenty-one bodies, which should be enough to start on the staff and sixth formers, with a few spare to keep tabs on the rest. That said,' he went on, 'at least half the officers are due off shift in the next few hours.'

'I've been promised all the help and manpower we need, so just dangle the overtime carrot.' McKenna retrieved the cigarette. 'The most pressing dilemma is how we interrogate over two hundred juveniles while maintaining their right to have the support of an independent adult.'

'Do we need to bother at this stage?' Jack argued. 'We won't be asking anything contentious in the first round and, depending on the autopsy findings, maybe not at all.'

'Yes, we *do* need to bother. We need to be fireproof. The deputy chief is rounding up a posse of social workers and solicitors to sit in with the girls.'

'And after all that, we'll probably find Sukie fell into the water when she was up to some mischief or threw herself off Menai Bridge. Or Britannia Bridge, as it's nearer.' He grimaced. 'Poor kid.'

'How did you leave things?'

'I stopped the search when you called in case we accidentally mucked up a crime scene. We've bagged what personal property was lying about – sports gear and so forth – and sealed her room after taking some of her clothing for the dogs. I've also fixed a hasp and padlock to the door as the lock doesn't work.' He rubbed his chin. 'On the top floor, where the sixth-form bedrooms are, the fire door alarms don't work either. I'm having them checked to see if it's just down to poor maintenance or if they've been disabled.'

'Have the dogs turned up anything?'

'Not so far.'

'Not even Bryn?'

'It was gone three before he arrived. He was out late last night on exercise with Mountain Rescue.' Jack smiled briefly. 'And unless he gets his statutory rest period his nose goes on strike.'

'If he's operational when you get back, tell his handler we

need to know as soon as possible exactly where Sukie entered the water.' After a moment's thought, McKenna continued, 'And it might be better for the other dogs to be stood down temporarily, so they don't interfere with him.' Again he fell silent, before saying, 'We'll have to play this by ear for the time being, I'm afraid, and use our instincts. What's your impression of the school? So far, that is?'

'Let's say it seems to conform to most of the expectations I took with me. It's certainly a world apart, but I'd say dis-located, rather than distinguished, by privilege. It's also extremely claustrophobic, but that's probably because it's sur-rounded by acres of dense woodland. Then again,' he added thoughtfully, 'the main building was obviously designed as a virtual prison and you can still see where grilles were cemented into the window openings. The sixth-form bedrooms used to be cells for the most disturbed patients. The doors are over three inches thick, with massive external locks and peepholes. The holes are covered with plywood now.'

'And the girls?' McKenna asked.

'The few I've seen in passing look the same as most other teenagers: lost and miserable. I felt sorry for them. And yes, I know,' he added, as McKenna was about to speak, 'my view of teenagers relates directly to the way my own are behaving. At the moment they're swotting for A levels night and day. I just hope,' he said with feeling, 'in fact, I'm *praying*, that both of them get exactly the same passes and grades.'

'They're identical twins,' McKenna said. 'Isn't that kind of thing a foregone conclusion? Well, probably not,' he mused, answering his own question. 'I wonder if there are any twins at the Hermitage?'

'There aren't. I've already checked the registers. And I've requested a PNC check on all current staff and those who've left in the last five years.' He grinned rather wolfishly. 'The school secretary initially refused, allegedly on the grounds of con-fidentiality, when I asked for the information, so I pointed out that obstructing the police is a criminal offence. Even then, she argued about getting Dr Scott's permission, but I get the impression they need "Dr Scott's permission" for anything and everything. Initiative isn't encouraged.'

'Perhaps she can't forget being in the army,' McKenna suggested. 'What about the groundsman? Is it Sean O'Connor, as Dewi thought?'

Jack nodded. 'Yes, but apart from the incident we already know about, he's clean as a whistle. Similarly, the lodge keeper, Ken Randall. He's sixty-two and a widower. His wife died from cancer five years ago.'

'Children? Previous employment?'

'Two sons, both married, both in full-time employment, both living along the coast,' Jack answered. 'Randall used to be a Department of Transport driving examiner. He took early retirement when his wife was dying, then probably found afterwards he couldn't cope without something to do. He's been at the Hermitage going on four years and, although his old job must have honed his powers of observation, I wouldn't lay odds he knows much more than Dewi's already wormed out of him. Dewi reckons he's exceedingly disaffected and therefore quite likely to shoot off his mouth at the first opportunity.'

'I wouldn't bet on that,' McKenna commented. 'Disaffected or not, he'll temper whatever he says with the security of his job and housing in the forefront of his mind. Anyway, he'll be formally interviewed, once we're fully organised. For now, the girls and staff take priority. The security guards,' he went on, 'are very much part of your logistical nightmare and not only because they live all over north Wales. The company operates a rolling system where no guard works the same site for any length of time so, for the sake of efficiency, I asked head-quarters to handle the initial interviews.' With a wry look, he continued, 'And, for a change, none of the guards has a criminal record. I expect we'll find they alibi each other.'

'Only up to a point,' Jack remarked. 'They must be very thinly spread. There are four on duty between six in the morning and ten at night, and two overnighters, which is wholly inadequate by any standard in a place as big as that, teeming with the offspring of the mega-rich. Still, I'm sure we'll find a lot more to criticise before we've finished.'

'As long as no one gets sidetracked by prejudice,' McKenna commented quietly. 'Nonetheless, everyone needs to be aware of the fact that the Hermitage is effectively a closed institution and no doubt riddled with institutional neuroses. The school's norms of behaviour and thought will probably seem dysfunctional, if not actually disordered.'

'If my experiences so far are any indication, the school's norms are dictated by the headmistress.' Getting to his feet, Jack shrugged on his jacket. 'I'd better be off. By the way,' he added, face betraying his feelings, 'who's breaking the news to Sukie's parents? Poor devils! This is every parent's worst nightmare come true.'

'Berkshire police. They've also been asked to pass on anything known about the family's background and to find out if there was a boyfriend on the scene.'

'I'd be surprised if there weren't,' remarked Jack. 'Sukie was a very pretty girl.'

The first stupendous shock hit Freya when she looked on Sukie through the window of the mortuary viewing room and in the minute or so she remained there more shocks buffeted her from every direction. When Jack led her from the cool, gloomy building into the heat of the car park, she groped and stumbled like a soldier blinded by mortar fire.

Instead of taking her back to the school, he drove her to the police station and left her in a cluttered but tidy office with a young policewoman whose name Freya immediately forgot. Offered a hot drink, she asked for tea, hoping the errand would force the policewoman to disappear for a while, but she returned, it seemed, within minutes.

Freya tried to ignore her. Beyond the initial civilities, the young woman made no attempt to impose herself, but her presence alone was sufficient distraction. Desperate for time and peace to retrench, Freya began to feel angry. When she could no longer contain her tears she was furious, even though she had no idea why she should weep. Little by little, she had been steeling herself for the worst since yesterday and in a bizarre way its arrival brought relief. Now the mystery of Sukie's disappearance was resolved, she could concentrate on the practicalities of containing whatever had led the girl to her death.

The waiting became an eternity. Because no one had told her

why she must wait, she began to feel intimidated and even afraid, and the bland young policewoman acquired the threatening aura of a gaoler. Freya judged her to be in her mid-twenties and, on the evidence of dress and general demeanour, not the product of a common background. She spoke well, too, without a trace of the raucous local accent. Freya was considering how to reassert herself in this wholly alien situation when the inspector returned.

With barely time to collect her wits, she found herself whisked along a corridor and into a large, airy room where a thin, good-looking man about her own age sat behind a desk. The inspector put her in a chair and left.

'Sukie's family has been informed of her death,' the other man told her. 'I understand her parents are now on their way here.'

'What?' She blinked rapidly.

'I said—' he began, but she cut him short, inhaling threadily. 'I didn't catch your name.'

He gestured to the nameplate on the desk. 'I am Superintendent Michael McKenna, and I'll be supervising the investigation into Sukie's death.'

Trying to push away the thought of that secret, superior piece of knowledge nestling like a grenade in the hand of someone at the Hermitage, Freya said, 'I assume she drowned herself.' Clasping and unclasping her hands, she added, 'And I can only conclude that, tragically, some private misery drove her to commit suicide rather than seek help. Girls of her age are, unfortunately, often prone to hysterical behaviour that has drastic consequences.'

'We don't know if she drowned.'

She screwed up her face into a parody of bemusement. 'But she must have done! She was pulled out of Menai Strait.'

'She could have been dead when she entered the water.'

'I do not believe,' Freya said, putting all the authority she could muster into her voice, 'that a killer is lurking behind the walls of my school.'

Waiting for him to respond, she studied his face. He had unusually fine features but, like the rather beautiful eyes, they were drawn with weariness and, perhaps, even disillusionment.

'What *you* believe, Dr Scott,' he commented, meeting her gaze, 'has become an irrelevancy. *We* proceed on the assumption of suspicious death. Sukie died not long after last being seen on Tuesday night, so if someone did indeed push her into the Strait, that person has had ample opportunity to cover his or her tracks.' For a moment he regarded her wordlessly, before saying, 'While a suicide, from the school's point of view, would no doubt be the preferred option, in that your liabilities would be significantly reduced, please refrain from speculation. I've no doubt that your word is taken very seriously and any theory you care to promote would quickly gain hold, to the detriment of our investigation.'

A flush of anger staining her cheeks, Freya stared at him, realising that her so far limitless influence was now heavily circumscribed and hostage to circumstance. Then, with an enormous effort of will, she pulled herself under control. Dropping her gaze, summoning more tears, she said, with a catch in her voice, 'Please forgive me. Sukie's death has been a terrible shock and, of course, it creates a dreadful crisis for the school.' Gathering up her bag, she rose. 'At such a time my place is with my girls and staff, and naturally I must be ready to receive Lady Hester and her husband.'

'Sit down, please. I haven't finished.' Stony-faced, he added, 'You will remain here until someone has taken your statement and *I* shall be talking to the Melvilles.' He punched a button on the telephone console to summon her escort. 'Tell me,' he asked, 'could Sukie swim?'

'She could stay afloat in the pool, but she wasn't a swimmer.' Trying to regain lost ground, she went on, 'Of course, the Strait and its shores are completely out of bounds and, in fact, fenced off for most of the length. The girls who go sailing are always accompanied by professional instructors and I don't need to tell you no one swims in those treacherous waters.'

He folded his arms and again regarded her steadily. 'Dr Scott, if you seriously expect me to believe the girls stick to your rules, you're taking me for a fool.'

43

7

Once Freya had been taken to an interview room to make a statement about Sukie's disappearance and its aftermath, McKenna set off for the school. Even if the Melvilles had left home as soon as they were told of their daughter's death they would not arrive before ten o'clock that night, for north Wales was a long way from Newbury. It was a long way from anywhere, he reflected, both physically and psychologically, but it was a distance fostering prejudice rather than mystery. The English had a perception of Ireland, where his forebears had lived; they had views on Scotland, albeit mostly engineered by the Scots; they held opinions about the England beyond their own small patch; but somehow Wales, and particularly her remote and mountainous north, was lost in between. People visited for holidays, huddled together for safety, and left more ignorant and biased than when they arrived.

The high granite walls around the Hermitage with their topping of trees laid deep shadows along a substantial stretch of the road, and although the sun was still well above the horizon, the car's automatic headlights blinked on as soon as he hit the shadow.

A driverless white security van, parked close to the wall, partially obscured the school name board and the gates were barred by an area patrol car. Recognising him, the driver backed away with a roar and the policeman manning the gates jumped to attention.

'Where are the security guards?' McKenna asked.

'In the patrol car, sir. I wasn't sure if they're allowed on site. Their boss has told them about the girl's death, but said it would be better if they came on duty as arranged. They both did the evening shift on Tuesday and finished at two in the morning.'

'And where's Randall?'

'He's taken his dog to the vet's for its booster jabs. Inspector Tuttle gave permission.'

'Keep the guards where they are for the time being,' McKenna decided. 'I'll send someone down to take statements from them.'

The way through the woods was a dizzying affair and twice McKenna overshot the sharp bends, his car coming to rest the second time mere inches from the trunk of an old oak. When he finally cleared the trees and the school came into view on the crest of the rise he was disappointed, for the gates, the drive, the tantalising barrier of trees, created an expectation that was not fulfilled. The place resembled a barracks, and the litter of police cars, vans and personnel carriers on the forecourt looked quite at home there. The huge wagon housing the mobile incident room was parked to one side under the trees, dwarfing its canteen trailer.

As he shut the car door he heard the throaty, unmistakable voice of a German Shepherd, then Bryn crashed out of the thickets to his right, his handler a few feet behind. The dog's paws were covered in mud.

McKenna leaned against the car. Bryn sat on his haunches, gazing up at him, eyes alight with fierce intelligence. 'So, what have you found for me?' McKenna asked, meeting the dog's gaze. He was sorely tempted to stroke the animal's beautiful head.

The handler smiled wryly. 'D'you really want to know, sir? Fag packets, used condoms, glue and aerosol containers, bottles and cans by the barrow load, shoes and trainers, various items of clothing plus male and female underwear, a mountain of paper litter and all the other weird things people chuck over the nearest wall, including a flea-infested mattress, two Tesco trolleys, a brand-new duvet cover still in its wrappers and a child's pushchair, minus the child.' Clipping the leash on Bryn's collar, he added, 'And most of it's probably nothing to do with the school. The boundary wall's crumbling in a lot of places, so the site's as leaky as a sieve even without the wicket gates every hundred yards or so along the wall. You can't see the wickets because they're choked with ivy and undergrowth, but believe me, the locals will know about them.' He paused for breath, gazing fondly at the dog. 'Bryn picked up the girl's trail immediately,' he reported. 'Starting in her bedroom, it goes through the top-floor fire escape on the east side of the building, into the stable block for some obscure reason, through the woods and down to the Strait.'

'Can you show me without messing up the scent?'

'We've marked out another way in.' Tugging the leash, he moved off, Bryn at his heels.

As they crossed the forecourt, McKenna asked, 'Any footprints?'

'Hundreds, I'm sorry to say. Except in the clearings, the ground won't ever dry out properly and it'll get so little sunshine there's probably ice on the puddles all summer long. Where the trail ends, it's just a sea of churned-up mud.'

Entering the woods, McKenna glanced from side to side, expecting to see the hazy glory of bluebells, the glow of anemones, but there was only brush and tangled undergrowth. Ribbons of fluorescent tape fluttered gaily from low-hanging branches every few yards, at least one always in sight. Engulfed by trees, he could hear but not see small animals scurrying in that undergrowth, but those sounds died away as they pushed deeper. Soon all he could hear were their own footfalls and Bryn's panting breaths.

'The place stinks like an open grave,' the handler remarked, breaking the silence. 'And it's gone so bloody cold all of a sudden you'd think it was the middle of winter.'

McKenna imagined Sukie, perhaps alone, perhaps not, flitting through these woods at dead of night and shivered. 'That girl must have had a very powerful reason to come here in the darkness,' he said, momentarily losing his footing as the path suddenly reached a steep slope. 'It's a nasty enough place in daylight.'

'To us, maybe, sir, but if the trees could talk, they'd have more than a few tales to tell.' He too skidded then, in the mud lying treacherously beneath a carpet of dead leaves. 'That said,' he added, grabbing a branch to steady himself, 'this is definitely Hansel and Gretel and Three Bears territory rolled into one, and if I saw a goblin peering between the tree trunks I wouldn't be at all surprised.'

He unleashed Bryn. The dog bounded off, waving his feathery tail, while the two men, walking crabwise, covered the last thirty or so yards down to the water's edge. There was no escape from the trees, McKenna thought; they crowded the banks of the Strait, some trailing their branches, others leaning out at impossible angles, all of them stealing the goodness from the air. As he followed the other man along the narrow, trench-like path along the shoreline, leaves slapped him insolently in the face and dropped water on his clothes, even though there had been no rain for days.

When the path dropped once more, the banks on either side began to rise, until men and dog were not only overwhelmed by trees tangled together overhead, but overhung by roots exposed by erosion: long, twisted, sodden tentacles that sprang out here and there to catch at clothes and flesh. Not wanting to feel their touch, McKenna pressed his arms to his side and his balance was immediately compromised, for the mud beneath his feet was the sort he had once heard described as cannibal mud and it was trying to suck him in with each laboured step.

The path debouched without warning into a dank, muddy clearing, from which another trail climbed upwards before disappearing into a dense grove. Clearing and the path were cordoned off, and under the huge, threatening shadow of Britannia Bridge, men and women in overalls literally combed the earth for whatever it might yield, while others made plaster casts of scattered footprints and the long gouges that criss-crossed the mud.

'Short of trying a match with every item of footwear in the school, I doubt if this will get us very far,' Bryn's handler commented. 'And even if we got a match, who's to say it's relevant? This is obviously a well-frequented area.'

'Where does the trail end?' asked McKenna.

'Right there.' He indicated an area bubbling with dirty water and cordoned off with more fluorescent tape. 'When forensics have finished,' he went on, pointing to the carefully marked chunks of rotting wood and broken branch sticking from the mud, 'Bryn's going to sniff through that lot for a possible weapon.' Tongue hanging out, Bryn was sitting near the cordon and, at the mention of his name, swivelled his head attentively. 'I'm sure he picked up another scent on the path, aside from the dead girl's,' his handler added. 'He could probably follow it back.'

'It's rather a long shot,' McKenna said. 'The trail's at least forty hours old by now.'

'But the air hardly gets disturbed because the trees are so dense.'

'I'll make a decision once I get the initial autopsy report.' McKenna looked at the people toiling in the mud. 'They're nowhere near finished anyway, so it'll be a while before Bryn can do any sleuthing there.' He turned, preparing to leave, then said, 'By the way, are the trees interfering with communications?'

'Radio contact's been OK so far, but the mobile phones are getting zapped.' As McKenna began to walk away, the other man stopped him. 'I don't want to push it, sir, but Bryn shouldn't be underestimated. He's already had someone for wearing a skirt that used to belong to the dead girl. That's how good he is.'

'Has he really?' McKenna said. 'How did that come about?'

'We were following the trail from the girl's room and we'd just got to the bottom of the fire escape when I saw a crowd of girls coming up the path, so I held back until they'd passed. One minute he's standing quietly beside me, the next he took off so fast he pulled the leash out of my hand, going straight for the girls at the tail end of the crowd.' The handler smiled crookedly. 'He found the one he wanted within a couple of seconds and frightened the bejesus out of her.'

Within yards of leaving the clearing, McKenna felt like the only human being left alive. He squelched along the defile through the cannibal mud and, in his haste, almost lost a shoe. Like a child, he looked only at the ground in front of him. When it began to rise he dared to glance upwards and saw his way marked by the beribboned branches. As he had descended, he climbed crabwise, digging in his heels at each step. At the top he stopped and leaned against a puny sycamore in near agony while his smoker's lungs struggled to re-inflate themselves. Still with a band of pain tight round his chest, he set off once more, bathed in the deep green light that filled the woods like water. Now and then the sun found gaps in the dense foliage and flung dazzling rainbow spears to the ground, and when he finally broke cover he saw the school's white walls had acquired a blushing, golden hue.

Stepping over the spidery shadow cast by the antenna on its roof, he made his way to the mobile incident room which, littered with paper, cardboard boxes, overflowing waste bins and used paper cups, had clearly not been cleaned out since its last excursion. A fat, middle-aged constable with rolled-up shirtsleeves and his forehead beaded with sweat was lumbering back and forth, dragging behind him a black plastic sack already stuffed with rubbish. There was a strong but not unpleasant smell of air-freshener.

Aside from the constable, the room's only other occupant was Nona Lloyd, one of Bangor's uniformed officers, although Sukie, her portrait greatly enlarged, smiled at McKenna as if still in the land of the living from her place on a whiteboard. Underneath the photograph the known facts of her brief life and mysterious death were neatly written in black felt pen. Eight unattended computers, screens flickering, sat about on table tops, and annotated plans of the grounds and buildings, fixed to cork boards along the walls, bristled with coloured pins.

Nona, measuring the distances between the red-topped pins on a section of ground plan, turned when she heard footsteps. 'Dr Roberts telephoned, sir,' she told McKenna. 'He wants you to call him.'

'Thanks,' McKenna replied, then asked, 'what are you doing?'

'Calculating the actual distance from the school to where Sukie went into the Strait.' She stood back a little from the plan. 'It's not as far as it seems. Like with the drive,' she added. 'In a straight line, it's barely five hundred yards from the front gate to the main school, yet it *feels* like miles. Everything gets distorted because of the way all the tracks twist and turn through the trees.' Pointing from pin to pin, she defined the extent of Sukie's final journey. 'Give or take a few, it's two hundred and ten yards from the school to the stables, then just another hundred and twenty through the woods to here.' Her slightly stubby finger with its prettily manicured nail came to rest on the waterline below the place where Britannia Bridge sprang out across the Strait.

'Why did she go into the stables, I wonder?' McKenna said, half to himself.

Nona shrugged. 'Maybe someone had left some tack lying about and she went to put it away. It's expensive stuff, especially saddles. Then again,' she mused, 'she might have been getting a titbit for her horse. There are bags of apples and pony nuts in there.' She glanced at him. 'I had a good look around when we arrived. Inspector Tuttle said we needed to get the lie of the land as soon as possible.'

Looking from one plan to another, McKenna thought Jack's advice had been sound. The layout of the whole site had been superimposed on to an Ordnance Survey map, each building drawn to scale. The main school sat at the centre of Freya's small realm, flanked to the west by the teaching blocks, sports hall and playing fields, and to the east by staff flats and the riding arena. The stables lay south-west, he reckoned, off the track leading to the sports hall, and beyond stables and pasture were a swimming pool and open-air tennis courts. That great swath of woodland also contained a chapel, workshops, green-houses, electricity sub-station, and two individual houses, with the name 'Scott' written beside one and 'Knight/Bebb' beside the other. A little way upstream from where Sukie had gone into the water was a boathouse.

The large-scale floor plan of the main school showed him that the basement area housed the boiler room and main-tenance and general stores, and the ground floor the refectory, kitchen and domestic offices, administration offices, head-mistress's study, Matron's surgery, staff and pupil common rooms, a computer room and the library. Dormitories, night duty station, Matron's flat and the infirmary were on the first floor, while the attic floor was sixth-form territory. He smiled wryly when he saw the label 'Smokers' Den' on a room adjacent to the sixth-form common room.

Leaving Nona to her measuring, McKenna shut himself in the cubbyhole reserved for senior personnel. As soon as he lifted the telephone receiver, static crackled in his ear.

'I'm sorry to say,' Eifion Roberts began, 'that you'll have to proceed on the basis of balanced probabilities for now, but first things first. She died from asphyxia due to drowning in salt water, but there's also a great deal of mud, vegetable and other debris in her mouth, some of which gravitated to her lungs, indicating shallow water. She ingested a small amount of food about five hours before she died, which was probably no later than the early hours of Wednesday morning.'

'How d'you know?'

'I said *probably*, Michael,' the pathologist reminded him. 'Some fifty hours elapsed between when she was last seen on Tuesday and her being pulled out of the water this afternoon. Taking all known factors into account, including the effect of immersion on the process of decomposition, she's been dead some forty-three to forty-six hours.' He paused and McKenna heard paper rustle. 'The body's free of disease, she didn't smoke, and I found no alcohol and no signs of the use of controlled substances. Oddly, she wasn't particularly well-nourished – in fact, her stomach's a little shrunken. The hymen,' he went on, 'was ruptured, but not necessarily through sexual intercourse. Riding, gymnastics and tampons are other possible culprits. There was no semen present, she wasn't pregnant and hadn't given birth. When the diatom tests are completed I'll be able to tell you approximately where she drowned.'

'She *seems* to have entered the water about two hundred yards downstream of Britannia Bridge. You should have samples from the area within the hour.'

'Why d'you say "seems"?'

McKenna rubbed his forehead. 'Bryn followed her from the school to the water's edge, but that doesn't constitute proof. The scent could be a leftover from another trip, particularly as she went via the stables.'

'He's not stupid! He'd have trailed her back were that the case. She was hardly likely to swim home up the Strait.'

'Are you *sure* she didn't go off one of the bridges?'

'Fallers and jumpers usually look as if they've dropped a hundred and fifty feet onto concrete instead of water. She hasn't got a single broken bone.'

'A man fell off Menai Bridge some years ago and survived with barely a scratch.'

'Quite,' Roberts agreed. 'I look on him as the exception that proves the rule.'

'You're not helping, Eifion.'

'That's what I meant by balanced probabilities.'

'Then tell me what probabilities to balance.'

'Although you don't know enough about her to discount suicide, there are more certain ways of disposing of yourself than lying face down in the shallows.'

'So what about an accident?' McKenna argued. 'Perhaps she fell and stunned herself.'

'But what was she doing there at that time of night in the first place? She wasn't dressed for trysting.'

'Girls don't necessarily, these days.'

'But they *will* dab on the lipstick and perfume, which she hadn't. In my view, she'd thrown on the first things to hand and that suggests she went out in a hurry, probably to do something of a practical nature. Don't forget,' Roberts went on, 'she was ready for bed when last seen. Who saw her, by the way? Did she speak to them?'

'No. Two form mates just caught a glimpse of her.' McKenna fidgeted with his pen. 'Aren't you making a lot of assumptions?'

'I'm creating a hierarchy.' After a moment's silence Roberts asked, 'You say she went to the stables? Any idea why?'

'Not a clue. Her horse was in the paddock with the others on Wednesday morning. Nor was there a single hoof print anywhere near the trail Bryn followed.'

'Right. I'll get back to work and I need to know as soon as possible about any injuries or falls she'd had in the past month or so.'

'How badly damaged is the body?'

'She's had less of a battering than people usually get in the Strait, but there are still plenty of contusions and lacerations, including some to the head. But such are the biochemical changes caused by immersion in water it's a bugger trying to distinguish between ante- and post-mortem injuries.'

'How soon will you be able to report on the injuries?'

'Once I can exclude pre-existing trauma, perhaps twenty-four hours. The harbour master tells me low tide occurred just after one on Wednesday morning, so she wouldn't have moved far until the tide picked her up as it rose. She'd be near unrecognisable had she been carried under the bridges and through the Swillies up to Puffin Island where the tide turns, so she was probably washed out the other way, caught in the currents and brought back.'

8

As McKenna crossed the forecourt to the school the policeman at the doors saluted. 'Inspector Tuttle's kept everyone bar the cooks in the refectory, sir,' he said, holding one door open, 'which is down that corridor to the right. The cooks are still clearing up after the evening meal.'

The subdued roar of many voices reached McKenna long before he had walked the length of the corridor. Opening one of the refectory's heavy double doors, he stepped into a room that looked at first sight as big as a football pitch, seething with girls, staff and police officers. Evening sunshine poured through huge windows, here and there touching silvered epaulettes, small hair ornaments and spectacle frames.

Long tables, simple slabs of unadorned wood on sturdy legs, had been pushed together to form an unbroken length around three sides of the room. At the far end, under a panoply of portraits, smaller tables stood on a dais, with women of varying ages, sizes, and manner of dress grouped around them on plain wooden chairs. In the well below, girls sat in rows on the floor, while others rubbed shoulders with the police officers, social workers and solicitors on the benches at each table. Leaning, sitting and squatting against the opposite wall were still more girls. The noise in the room bounced off the ceiling, humming in McKenna's ears.

Every girl wore a navy-blue skirt, he noticed, but their shirts were striped with the house colours of red, blue, yellow and green. Searching the sea of faces, he located Dewi, in earnest discussion with an ample woman dressed as a nurse. As he threaded his way around the crowded walls, causing a stir of interest, faces turned to look and he felt the scrutiny of many eyes.

'This is Matron,' Dewi said when McKenna reached them.

'Are you in charge?' she asked. The remnants of a Scottish accent quavered in her voice. 'I'd like to talk to you.'

'Is it important?'

Tears suddenly welled in her large, slightly bulging eyes. 'Of *course* it's important! It's about poor Sukie.'

'Give me fifteen minutes or so,' McKenna told her, then drew Dewi out of earshot. 'The security guards who were here Tuesday night are down at the main gates. See what they've got to say about visitors, whether official or not, trespassers and, most important, the girls' nocturnal activities.' He looked at the girls once more and saw an epidemic of yawning breaking out. 'How many have been seen so far?'

'Fifty. Sixty, maybe.' Dewi said. 'We started on the lower-school kids so they could get away to do their homework before bedtime.'

'Any pointers yet?'

'No, sir. Not a thing.' He paused, gazing absently around the room. 'Something might show up when we start collating statements, but even though the girls have been under surveillance since coming out of lessons, I expect there'll be a lot of cross-contamination in what they tell us. Or,' he added with a frown, 'don't tell us. Everyone, from the deputy head to the smallest kid on the block, gives you the feeling she's scared to open her mouth without the headmistress's say-so.'

'Then we need to make them realise that if someone in this room *is* a killer, any one of them could be the next victim.' From the corner of his eye he saw a girl with a long flaxen plait moving through the crowd towards them. 'We've got a visitor.'

Dewi glanced round. 'That's Torrance.' His face mottled with embarrassment. 'She's American. I met her this morning.'

'Hi, there, David,' she said, then looked at McKenna and smiled.

'I'm Superintendent McKenna,' he told her. 'Can I help you?'

'Well, as we'll be stuck here for hours, I guess I should sort out evening stables. Usually we do our own horses, but this isn't usually.'

'Don't horses live out in the summer?' Dewi asked.

Her eyes twinkled. 'They do, but they still need watering and the once-over.'

'Will you need help?' asked McKenna.

She nodded. 'I'd like to take Alice Derringer.'

'You'll have to be supervised, of course,' McKenna said blandly.

'How else?' Torrance replied easily. 'I'll go get Alice.'

McKenna watched her tap the shoulder of a thin, dark-haired girl. 'I'll send someone else to see the security guards,' he told Dewi, 'while you learn what evening stables is all about. You can also find out why she chose some kid to help and not one of the other horse owners, or, for that matter, whoever's in charge of riding.'

Dewi, absently watching Alice's face light up with the same joy he had seen that morning, said to McKenna, 'Have you heard about the clanger Bryn the Wonder Dog dropped? Alice was with the girl he targeted. So was Daisy Podmore,' he added, pointing to the sumptuous-looking girl seated on Alice's right. 'They're all best mates, apparently.'

'His handler mentioned it,' McKenna replied. 'Which girl was it?'

As Alice scrambled to her feet, Dewi gestured to the girl suddenly exposed on her left. She too had dark hair and, like Alice, wore the green shirt of Tudor House. 'She's called Grace Blackwell.' He grinned. 'Her father's a vicar, so her and Janet should get on like a house on fire.'

'How can a vicar,' McKenna wondered, 'afford to send his daughter here? Even if he's got a good stipend?'

Dewi shrugged. 'Maybe he's got a private income.' After a moment's thought, he said, 'Then again, maybe he hasn't. His daughter wears hand-me-downs as a matter of course. After she'd given us an ear bashing about letting dangerous dogs roam loose around the school, Matron told us Grace has quite a few of Sukie's old clothes. They fit her perfectly, apparently.'

'Bryn didn't touch the girl, did he?'

'All he did was cut her out of the group, like he was sorting sheep, and bark once,' Dewi said. 'There was no need for the fuss she kicked up, but she started screaming like a banshee.

Daisy didn't help, either. She added fuel to the flames by calling her a pathetic amoeba.'

Accompanying Matron along the corridor from the refectory, across the central lobby and down the facing corridor, McKenna came to the conclusion that for all the building's spare lines, austere proportions and wealth of windows, it was no less oppressive than the encircling woodland.

Matron's room overlooked the Strait and the lawns, where the massed banks of rhododendron and azalea were touched with gold by the dying sun. She gestured him to a basket chair and squeezed her bulk into another, keeping her back to the window. 'We don't need the light on, do we? Not quite yet, anyway.' Her voice dwindled away. Then, haltingly, she said, 'Do you know, it's been one of my greatest pleasures to watch night fall over the Strait, but never again.' She shuddered. '*Never* again!' Her bosom heaved as she drew a steadying breath. 'I don't want to think about it, but I can't stop myself. I can almost *see* her, being dragged into the depths by that terrible undertow. You can see it running even at low tide.'

'Menai Strait is notoriously dangerous.' He paused. 'I'm surprised there haven't been other incidents.'

'The shoreline's fenced off. It's out of bounds, anyway.'

'So Dr Scott told me, but I'm sure the bounds, and a good many other rules, get broken.'

'Where *is* the Head?' she asked.

'Making a statement at the police station.'

'Does she know what's going on here?'

'Of course.'

'Doesn't she mind?'

'I'm afraid it's out of her hands.' He let her come to terms with the sudden transfer of authority, before saying, 'Why did you want to see me?'

'I want to know what happened to Sukie.' In the deepening dusk her eyes were like those of a hunted animal. 'Please tell me,' she implored.

'She drowned,' he replied bluntly.

'Did she kill herself?'

'At the moment we're not in a position to say.'

She balled her hands into fists and stared at them. 'Well, I think you'll find she did,' she concluded.

'Why should she?' asked McKenna.

'Well,' she said slowly, 'perhaps she thought she was pregnant. My goodness, I've seen more girls panic that way than I care to remember.' Her mouth worked. 'She had looked peaky of late,' she went on. 'And she was off her food. Oh!' she wailed. 'Why didn't she *tell* me?'

'Do you keep a record of the girls' menstrual cycles?'

'Not unless there's a need. They often come on at the same time, anyway. So do some of the staff. That can happen when women live together.'

'I can assure you that Sukie wasn't pregnant,' he said quietly. 'However, she could have had other worries. Tell me,' he went on, 'who were her friends? Who would share her confidences?'

She hesitated. 'Well, she seemed to get on with most people.'

'That's not what I asked you. To whom was she close?'

'Lately, you mean? I can't really say,' Matron replied. 'I'm not being difficult,' she rushed on, sensing his impatience. 'But at my age, you know things aren't always how they look. In places like this, people come together for all sorts of reasons that have nothing to do with friendship or affection.' She drew another deep, firming breath. 'All I know for sure is that she idolised Torrance Fuseli, the American girl who approached you in the refectory. Although,' she commented sourly, 'if you ask me, it wasn't *you* she was interested in.'

'Was it one-sided heroine worship, or something deeper?'

'I don't know!' She sniffed and pulled a snow-white handkerchief from her pocket. 'I don't seem to know *anything* any more. Sukie's death has knocked everything sideways.' She dabbed her eyes. 'It's a terrible thing to say about such a tragedy, but knowing she was dead was actually a relief! There's no more need to fret about what *might* have happened.'

'You must know *something* about her relationship with Torrance,' he coaxed.

'But I don't! I just know she worshipped her. But as for what Torrance felt about Sukie – well, Torrance is the only one who knows that, and *she* won't be telling.'

'No? Granted, we only met briefly, but I found her quite forthright.'

'But that's the trouble, isn't it? If she's got any feelings, she hides them. Nothing ruffles her feathers, not even a death.' Fretfully Matron rubbed her bare arms and he heard the rasp of flesh against flesh. 'Only myself and the deputy head knew Inspector Tuttle had taken Dr Scott to the mortuary. We were on tenterhooks waiting for her to come back, but he came back alone. Then he made everyone go to the assembly hall. I was standing right next to Torrance when he told us about Sukie and she didn't turn a hair. She didn't even seem surprised. She went a bit quiet for a while, but by the time you turned up she was back to normal. As you must have noticed,' she added pointedly.

'Don't you like her?'

'I don't know her. I sometimes wonder if she doesn't run as deep and dark as those wicked waters outside.'

'What's her background?' he asked.

Matron snorted. 'Money, of course. Her family owns half the oil wells in America, I shouldn't wonder. Apart from young Alice Derringer, she's probably got more money coming her way than anyone here.'

'She asked for Alice to help with the horses. Are they particularly friendly?'

'Yes.' She nodded thoughtfully. 'I thought it was odd, too, when I saw them leave the refectory together.' She fell silent and despite her earlier vow, turned to glance outside. 'Mind you,' she said, after a while, 'Alice is a Tudor girl. Torrance is captain of Tudor House.'

'And which house did Sukie belong to?'

'Windsor. Charlotte Swann's their captain and Nancy Holmes is captain of York.'

She seemed to close her lips rather firmly then, but the light was now so dim he could have been mistaken. 'What about Lancaster House?'

'That's Imogen Oliver's.'

'Which of them is head girl?'

'Oh, none of them. Ainsley Chapman's the head girl. She's won a Cambridge exhibition, so she's leaving next month.'

'Who'll replace her?'

'There'll be a secret ballot at the beginning of the autumn term. Dr Scott and the department heads lock themselves in her study until the next head girl's been chosen.' She glanced at him, then looked away quickly. 'I've often expected to see a puff of smoke coming out of a chimney, like it does when there's a new pope.'

'Were you here before Dr Scott became headmistress?' he asked.

'Come September, I've been here sixteen years.'

'Did you prefer the old regime?'

'Yes, I did. The Hermitage was a—' She struggled to find the right words. 'It was a *kinder* place before. I'm not saying we didn't have to contend with spite and jealousy, because girls are always envious, even if it's only about the length of somebody else's fingernails or the colour of her hair. Now, though, they're competing over everything every minute of the day. Dr Scott might be right when she says they're learning to survive, but at times I can't see the difference between the girls and a pack of wolves.' Then her face tightened with anxiety. 'You won't tell her what I said, will you?' she begged. 'She's looking for any chance to get rid of me. When she says true leadership is the ability to pick the right people for the right job, I just know she's telling me I'm *not* the right person.'

'She can't sack you for nothing.'

'Can't she?' Matron demanded. 'She got rid of eight teachers in her first year. Natural wastage, she called it.'

'Which happens in any organisation,' he said. 'How much involvement do the school governors have?'

'Well, Mr Nicholls, the chairman, visits every so often and the whole board turns up twice a year, but we never get the chance to talk to them. They listen to a lecture from Dr Scott, then go away again.' Frowning at him, she added, 'Don't think I haven't tried to say my piece. I know where my duties lie and I'll stand up to Dr Scott if necessary, even if it causes an atmosphere. Still,' she went on, hurriedly, 'you mustn't think she's a bad headmistress. The school's gone from strength to strength since she took over, especially on the academic side. In the old days the girls went to finishing school or did the season;

now they're groomed for university and a proper career.' She paused to draw breath. 'But the most important thing we offer is stability. For instance, without us, I shudder to think where Alice Derringer might end up. The poor bairn doesn't know from one day to the next whether her mother's in the Far East or the Far West – not that they probably don't both come together somewhere in the middle.' She held her head proudly. 'Alice's mother is Martha Rathbone. She's near the top of the world rich list, you know.'

'Yes, I've heard of her. She has a reputation for philanthropy.'

'If you mean she builds schools and hospitals in the Third World while she's exploiting its cheap labour, you might call it that.' Her voice was sharp with disapproval. 'To my mind, charity should begin at home, preferably with her sparing some of her precious time for her daughter.'

'On the subject of charity,' he said, 'are there any scholarship girls here?'

'We don't offer scholarships.' She looked at him shrewdly. 'Were you thinking about Grace Blackwell?'

'I did wonder how a vicar could afford the Hermitage fees.'

''Isn't that *his* business?'

'Not if it might impinge on ours. I understand Grace has a lot of Sukie's clothes.'

'She has some of her *outgrown* clothes,' Matron corrected. 'Dr Scott encourages the girls to pass on their old uniforms and sports equipment, and there's no reason why she shouldn't. It teaches them something about sharing, if nothing else.' Chewing her bottom lip, peering at him again, she said, pre-emptively, 'And, yes, they do need to learn to give and take. Teenagers are notoriously selfish.'

9

The halogen lights glaring from the corners of the building reduced the sunset to a few wan smudges above the treetops and deeply accentuated the darkness beneath. As McKenna returned to the mobile incident room, moving from one set of lights to another, his elongated shadow rotated disconcertingly about his feet.

Jack was at a table in the main body of the room, munching the last of a sandwich. 'Foodwise, HQ's done us proud,' he announced. 'We've got sandwiches, soup, pizzas, burgers, baked potatoes, all-day breakfasts, cakes, biscuits, fruit, ice cream, soft drinks, tea, coffee and chocolate.' He wiped his mouth on a paper napkin. 'We can't complain about personnel, either. I'd have liked a few more women officers, but that said, we've probably got most of the force's contingent.' Picking up a polystyrene beaker brimming with murky-looking coffee, he added, 'Bryn's handler reported in a few minutes ago. The dog's been through every potential weapon in the vicinity without picking up a sniff, so if a weapon was involved, it probably followed Sukie into the Strait.'

McKenna seated himself on one of the rather flimsy chairs. 'How are the interviews progressing?'

'Probably being hindered by the fact that everyone wants to talk to Dewi. They're clustering around him like bees round a honey pot. Dr Scott asked me, very pointedly, to give him "other duties", but I declined, so I won't be getting any gold stars for co-operation.'

'When did she get back?'

'A while ago. I've asked her to remain in her study.'

'Are you making headway with the staff?'

'Depends what you call headway. Some are scared witless, others are openly hostile and the rest are unbelievably bland, so in terms of gleaning useful information the answer's probably "no".'

'Matron allowed herself a few indiscretions,' McKenna offered, 'but quickly backtracked in case the headmistress got wind of her disloyalty.' He lit a cigarette. 'She's convinced herself Sukie thought she was pregnant and therefore committed suicide.' He smoked in silence for a moment. 'And while suicide's the easy answer, it may turn out to be the right one. Unfortunately, we won't know until Eifion's finished with the body, which he doesn't expect to do before tomorrow night. He's had Sukie's file, as well as the accident book, although there's little information in either. The local surgery that attends the school last saw her three years ago, when she had a sore throat.'

'What about her home GP?'

'Eifion's going to talk to him.' McKenna began casting about for an ashtray.

'I'll get you one.' Jack sighed, getting to his feet. 'D'you want a drink as well?'

'Tea, please.'

'Tea, coffee and chocolate all come from the same contraption,' Jack told him, 'so they all probably taste the same.' He disappeared into the canteen trailer, to return within minutes carrying another container of murky liquid and a thin foil ashtray. 'By the way, the handler wants to know if you're willing to let Bryn try backtracking the other scent he detected.'

'I haven't decided. If it wasn't a dead end, it would probably lead him into the school, which would be very disruptive for the girls.'

'They'd probably enjoy the excitement. Life around here seems unnaturally quiet and well-ordered.'

'I'm sure Sukie's death has been a devastating shock for everyone,' McKenna said quietly.

'You'd think so, wouldn't you?' Jack waved away the smoke from the cigarette. 'You'd think it'd be prompting memories, making people suddenly see the significance of something puzzling or unusual, or just having an *effect*. You'd expect people to be appalled and frightened and grieving, but I've never come across such cold detachment.'

'Don't be so judgemental,' McKenna advised. 'Perhaps it's not had time to sink in properly.'

'No?' Jack's eyes were flinty. 'It's had time enough to focus Scott's mind on damage limitation.'

'Arguably, that's simply part of her job.'

'Can I say something?' Jack regarded him thoughtfully. 'This is the last place I'd want my own daughters to be. I don't like the atmosphere, I don't like the staff and I don't like Scott's ethos. She pushes the survival of the fittest, no matter what, and probably no matter who else gets damaged in the process, and that's without taking into consideration what her definition of the fittest actually entails.' He paused, then went on, 'I told you this afternoon that the girls I'd seen looked lost and miserable; closer acquaintance just confirms that opinion. These girls are chronically unhappy and a fair few seem positively frightened, and *not* because of whatever happened to Sukie. There's a very destructive subtext to Scott's philosophy, so I'm not inclined to give her the tiniest bit of quarter. She's clever and manipulative and probably a complete control freak, and right now, with her knowing Sukie's death could ruin her, I think she could be dangerous.'

'You and I both know that people often attack when they feel under threat.'

'But the problem is when *she* attacks, you won't realise until afterwards and it'll be too late by then,' Jack replied trenchantly. He flicked at the heap of statement sheets on the table in front of him. 'Even though I've kept her out of the way, she's still putting the frighteners on people. I'm sure that's why no one's telling us anything and why the security guards, to a man, give the distinct impression that nothing ever happens. I don't for one moment believe that none of the girls ever tries to get out after dark or smuggles in a boyfriend and I don't believe the staff are equally virtuous. It's just not natural.'

'If the girls, or staff, want to get up to mischief, hoodwinking the guards will be top of their agenda,' McKenna said. 'Apart from that, security is very thinly spread at the best of times.'

'Considering what the parents fork out in fees, the security's a joke.' Frowning, Jack added, 'Maybe we should ask where all that money goes, because it doesn't seem to be spent on creature comforts for the girls.'

'Don't overstep the mark,' McKenna warned. 'The school's financial affairs are not really our business.'

Jack regarded him steadily. '*Everything* is our business at the moment, because we don't know what might or might not have had a bearing on Sukie's death. I've no intention of carrying out this investigation with one hand tied behind my back.'

'I don't expect you to, but there's no point in getting side-tracked over possible irrelevancies and even less point in going in with all guns firing at once. If there *is* something rotten at the core of the place, the way to bring it to light is through subtlety.'

Leaving Jack to begin the huge task of collating the information that was to be put into the computers for cross-referencing, McKenna wandered back to the school. As he neared the doors Janet emerged, cradling a bundle of papers to her chest. She looked hot and uncharacteristically dishevelled.

'Come out for a breather?' he enquired.

'Partly, sir. My head's spinning.'

'I'm not surprised. Where's Dewi?'

'Still in there,' she said with a grin, 'literally besieged by females. He probably couldn't escape if he wanted to.' Then she shuddered delicately. 'Some of them were giving *me* the same sort of treatment. It's not pleasant.'

Hands in his pockets, he leaned against the wall. 'It's only to be expected. Is the sudden flood of hormones loosening tongues as well?'

'I'm not sure,' she replied thoughtfully. 'I've just spent a couple of hours with the fourth formers, who all tried to talk at once and didn't shut up for a moment, but still managed, for the most part, to say nothing much. Then again, I got the impression that a few of them were telling me one thing but meant something quite different.' She looked down at the papers in her arms. 'I'll have to think about that once I've read through these interviews.' Glancing at him rather apologetically, she said, 'I haven't quite finished with them, I'm afraid. When I started on

Daisy Podmore, my brain just switched off. The poor kid's got the most horrible lisp and it's almost impossible to decipher what she's saying.'

McKenna remembered the lush-looking teenager Dewi had pointed out. Then he recalled the flaxen-haired American and Daisy's thin, dark friend. 'Dewi was supposed to supervise evening stables,' he said.

Janet nodded. 'He did. He said nothing unusual happened, except that Torrance told all the horses that Sukie was dead and that they must look after her mare. She's called Purdey, apparently,' she added. 'After that character in *The Avengers*.'

A shiver ran up his spine. '"Purdey" is also the name of a very expensive make of shotgun.' After that, he said nothing more for several moments, then asked, 'What did the girls have to say about Sukie?'

'Not many outside the sixth form actually seemed to know her,' Janet replied. 'Those who did admit acquaintance said she was "lovely", "warm", "sweet", "pretty", "a super rider", and various other positive and complimentary things. In short, no one had a useful word to say.'

He pushed himself off the wall and began to walk away.

'Before you go in there, sir,' Janet said, 'I should warn you that I've just seen Dr Scott. She's most unhappy about what she calls our "unseemly occupation of the school" and intends to call in the chairman of the governors, who, according to the *Who's Who* which naturally has pride of place in her study and which she insisted on showing me, has got pots of money and lots of connections, and is not, therefore, someone our chief constable would want us to upset.' She grinned again. 'I think she's hoping you'll shoot the messenger. I'd gone to ask her why the alarms on the top-floor fire exits had been disconnected and if she knew about Sean O'Connor's conviction for criminal damage,' she went on. 'The top floor gets very hot because it's right under the roof, so she allows the fire doors to stand open to air the place, and she of course knows about Sean. He's constantly supervised and has yet to put a foot wrong, so she wants to know why we're creating such a fuss when Sukie clearly committed suicide, which is distressing enough in itself. Needless to say,' she finished, 'the suicide theory's gaining ground by the minute.'

Inside the school the corridor was awash with staff and girls moving like a tide from the refectory. Then, above the sea-like murmur of their voices, someone wailed stridently, 'I'm scared!' Other girls started whimpering and crying, and within seconds the murmur became a storm of sobs, over which the teachers shrieked like gulls.

Hands raised, her palms facing outwards, Freya materialised in the lobby. 'Girls! Girls!' she said, her voice low but carrying. 'Please, just go quietly to your common rooms for supper. Matron and I will talk to each of you before lights out.'

From his vantage point just inside the door McKenna watched, wondering sourly if the unease Matron had revealed would be mollified by her time in the spotlight with the head-mistress. As the girls passed her, Freya touched a cheek here and there or patted a shoulder and, for all his cynicism, he could only admire the way she handled them.

She waited until they dispersed, then walked towards him with long, graceful, hip-swinging strides. 'I'm afraid there'll be many more tears before the night's out,' she commented.

'And some copycat hysteria,' he replied. 'My officers tell me few of the juniors knew Sukie, no doubt because there's a natural divide between upper and lower schools.'

'Actually,' Freya said, 'it's rather that she wasn't a prefect or house captain and therefore had little to do with them. Nonetheless she had her following, especially among those who like horses.'

'And I'm sure they found her glamorous.' He watched her covertly, thinking about the experiences and forces that had shaped her, wondering if Jack's assessment of her was no more than a measure of his own prejudice, or if she were truly as insensitive and self-centred as she appeared. 'Do you foster hero worship, or discourage it?'

'Neither. It's an inevitability, which will run its course, as you must have found in your own profession.'

'Indeed. It's a way of conforming, isn't it? The rookies copy the old hands who know better than to rock the boat, while anyone who doesn't subscribe religiously to the prevailing philosophy gets pushed on to a very lonely limb.'

'I'll disregard your unfortunate mix of metaphor,' she said wryly. 'I'll also try to disregard the implied antagonism.'

'Call it a healthy scepticism.' When he began walking away from the lobby she was forced to follow. 'For all its trappings of money and privilege, the Hermitage is just another school; therefore the girls' behaviour will cover the spectrum from complete compliance, through defiance, to serious delinquency. Your job is to design coping strategies and I'm sure you do it with the utmost grace, but,' he added, turning to face her, 'don't try to faze me with the tactics you use on the parents, the girls and your staff. In other words for the present you *defer* to me, Dr Scott.' He smiled fleetingly. 'Imagine I'm your colonel.'

'That could be rather difficult. My last colonel was a silly old duffer.' Her own smile held more than a hint of seductiveness and he was suddenly both conscious of her sexuality, and intensely and disturbingly curious about the life it led. She touched his arm. 'Come to my study and I'll buy you a quick drink, as they say, before I do the rounds with Matron.'

She strode down the corridor, then stopped. The door to Matron's room stood open and she was fussing over an ashen-faced Alice.

'What's wrong?' Freya asked.

'Alice needed her inhaler,' Matron reported anxiously. 'She's very wheezy. It must be the dust off the horses.'

'It isn't!' Alice said sharply. 'It's shock and you're not to tell Mummy horses give me asthma. She won't let me have one if you do.'

'Have you got another headache?'

'No, Dr Scott.'

'When's your appointment at the optician's?'

'Tomorrow afternoon,' Alice panted. With one hand on her breastbone, she took a deep breath and McKenna heard the air struggling into her lungs. 'Can I keep my inhaler in the dorm for tonight?'

Matron frowned. 'Well—' she began.

Freya cut her short. 'Of course you can, as long as you hand it back to Matron first thing in the morning.' Inclining her head rather imperiously, she moved on to her study, where the lights already glowed and the windows were open to the balmy night.

Draping her jacket over a coat-hanger behind the door, she asked, 'What can I offer you, Superintendent?' The question was riddled with ambiguity.

'Nothing, thank you.'

'No?' Her eyebrows arched attractively. 'Well, then smoke, if you wish. It's not one of my own vices, but I don't object.' As she pushed an ashtray within his reach, the moist red lips parted in another provocative smile.

Matron had condemned Torrance for so rapidly recovering her composure, he reflected, yet here was the school's role model displaying not only a remarkable self-control, but exhibiting behaviour that was, in the current context, bordering on the bizarre. But it was all very simple, he told himself: authority compromised, she was resorting to the most primitive and compelling power of all.

'I noticed the sixth formers have a smokers' den,' he said.

She put her elbows on the desk and folded her arms. 'They do, despite enormous criticism from those staff with a fashionably hostile stance towards smoking.' The bright-red nails splayed against her pale sleeves looked lethal. 'As you so correctly discerned, I have to manage a broad spectrum of behaviour and, as some of the girls are nicotine addicts, a total ban would only force them underground and create a serious fire hazard.'

Yielding to one temptation, McKenna lit a cigarette and waited for her to make the next move.

Freya watched him, her face expressionless. 'Matron,' she began, 'tells me Sukie did drown.'

He nodded. 'As to whether she drowned *herself*,' he told her, 'we can't yet say.'

69

'But I'm sure you have an opinion.'

He shrugged.

'Please, Superintendent, don't play cat and mouse with me. I need to know.'

'You know as much as we do,' he said. 'The available evidence is very sparse and still open to several interpretations. However, as in all such cases, we proceed on the assumption of possible homicide.'

'That,' she commented irritably, 'has already been made abundantly clear.'

'Therefore', he went on, ignoring her remark, 'identifying the possible killer takes priority.' Shifting in his seat, he put the cigarette in the ashtray. 'Most homicides are committed by someone close to the victim, often a member of the family. While Sukie had blood relatives, we would regard that "family" as being here.' He paused. 'An act of homicide is always preceded by detectable antecedents. There would be warning signals, in her relationship with the killer but, more pertinently, in the killer's own conduct. That's something we shall begin to investigate tomorrow.'

With a small frown she stopped him. 'Have you abandoned the idea that the killer, if such exists, could be a total stranger? An intruder, perhaps? Even a kidnapper?'

'Indeed not.' He retrieved the cigarette, watching her. 'All the signs indicate that she left the building voluntarily, so there might also be a boyfriend in the picture. On the other hand she could have been deliberately lured out to her death.'

Freya clenched her hands. When she spoke, her voice was tremulous. 'I *cannot* believe one of my girls could be a murderess.' After a moment, she added, 'Nor one of my staff.' She stared at him. 'But I'll have to put aside my own feelings, won't I?'

'It would be wiser, and certainly safer, to keep an open mind for the time being,' he agreed. Stubbing out another half-smoked cigarette, he added, 'And to accept that the present disruption is unavoidable. What you described to Constable Evans as our "unseemly occupation" is necessary to protect the school.'

She had the grace to blush. 'I wasn't quite in command of

myself,' she admitted. 'I owe her an apology.'

'Have you spoken to the chairman of governors yet?'

She shook her head. 'He telephoned earlier, while I was still at the police station, and spoke to Miss Knight, my deputy. She tells me your deputy chief constable is keeping him informed of developments.'

'The deputy chief is also handling the media, so please tell your staff not to make any comment.' He glanced at his watch. 'Before I leave tonight I'd like a brief meeting with the sixth formers.'

'Could we do that now?' she asked. 'I know the girls are still being interviewed, but I want to do the rounds with Matron before too long.' She picked up the telephone, told the person who answered to assemble the sixth form in their common room, then rose, making a point of smoothing her well-tailored skirt over hips and thighs as she crossed the room to take her jacket from its hanger. At the door she turned to face him. 'What's happening with Sukie's parents?'

'They've been told to report to the police station.'

One hand on the door knob she asked, 'And then?'

'We'll escort them to the mortuary.'

When Freya entered the sixth-form common room the girls rose as one. Once they had seated themselves she began to speak, talking of the tragedy of Sukie's death, stressing the necessity of the police investigation and pleading with them to assist in any way they could. They hung on to every word she uttered and many gazed at her with undisguised admiration, if not blatant adoration. Watching her bestow a lingering glance here, a special smile there, McKenna was forced to wonder if this power she wielded had driven someone to kill, perhaps for love of her, perhaps out of loathing. Her voice carried well, her words seemed unambiguous and sincere, and he knew she would rarely be misunderstood unless it was intentional, but he was dogged by the feeling that it was all an act, and as calculated and transitory as any performance.

'It would help Superintendent McKenna if you introduced yourselves,' she was saying. Nodding to the girl at the end of the first row of seats, she took a step back.

One by one, they bobbed up and down, and he was struck by the number of foreigners among them: Françoise Dizi, a chic, intense-looking French girl; Justine Salomon, a tall, pretty girl with a faint, attractive accent; Giulia Giucciardi, a fluffy, fair-haired Italian; two of Torrance Fuseli's compatriots, so alike he imagined they had chosen the same face from a cosmetic surgeon's catalogue; the perfectly Aryan Elisabeth von Carolsfeld, with eyes the colour of bluebells, and Therese Obermeyer, also Teutonic, but mousy-haired and as solid as a well-fed carthorse. Before she resumed her seat Therese added, without a flicker of humour, 'And also, I am known as "Lump"!' There was an outbreak of laughter and a few cat-calls, then Ainsley Chapman rose like a new spear of grass shooting from the earth.

Torrance, he thought, watching her closely, had an elusive quality that set her apart from her peers and, despite Matron's doubts, she seemed moved by events, for although her lips curved into a sociable smile when she gave her name, her eyes remained sombre. The girl beside her, Vivienne Wade, carried her own distinction, and her emaciated body inclined towards Torrance's in a way that put a telling distance between herself and the carrot-haired girl to her left, who languidly identified herself as 'Nancy Holmes'. Three black-haired, round-faced, almond-eyed Oriental girls, sitting together, rose together to announce themselves in sing-song voices and, despite their perfect diction, he had to ask them to repeat their names, for a refrain from *The Mikado* was running round and round in his head. Ainsley and Nancy found his confusion immensely amusing.

Ignoring them, he let his gaze return to Vivienne. She was, he thought, exceptional: hair as dark as a raven's wing fell below her shoulders, her skin was semi-transparent, her bone structure exquisite, her eyes the colour of black pearls and she looked like a corpse. The way her eyes slid away from his own was the only sign of life about her.

At first sight these gilded young women had appeared to be different and special, but acquaintance was tarnishing their lustre, and he was beginning to discern in their faces the same meanness, stupidity, humourlessness, weakness and cupidity

72

that plagued the rest of the world. Reminding himself that faults are necessary for the spirit of the individual, he turned his attention to the last row of girls, but was again distracted. He tried to read the looks passing to and fro, the unguarded expressions and unconscious body language, wondering who were the powerful and who the hangers-on, while sensing alliances, hostilities, indifferences. When the last few girls came to identify themselves, he had long lost the ability to match name to face but still smiled broadly at Yelena and Daria because their sculpted cheekbones, pointed chins and wide eyes reminded him of the Madonna in a Russian icon. Charlotte Swann, until then elegantly disporting herself on the window ledge, reminded him of the late Princess of Wales, and he was not the only one so impressed, for at least ten girls turned to look as if she had tweaked their strings. Apparently unmoved by her own effect, she subsided back on to the ledge, and the girl at her side informed him in a toneless voice that she was 'Imogen Oliver, Lower Sixth'. She remained half seated and he could barely see her face above the rows of heads.

'Thank you,' he said. 'I won't keep you long this evening. When Sukie's parents arrive, I have to escort them to the mortuary for formal identification of her body, which was washed up in Caernarfon early this afternoon. She was last seen at about eleven o'clock on Tuesday night, coming from the showers, and we know she died within the next few hours. However, we don't know how or why she died. Did some secret fear or unhappiness drive her to suicide? Or did someone kill her? If she *was* murdered, everyone in this school is at risk until we find her killer. *Most* at risk,' he went on, 'is anyone who might be able to point us towards that person. Tomorrow morning we shall begin questioning all of you in depth and I urge you to be as frank as possible. Whatever you tell us will be treated in the strictest confidence and you may have a solicitor present if you wish.' He glanced at the headmistress. 'Dr Scott has promised the full co-operation of herself and her staff, and there will be police officers in the building throughout the night. They'll be happy to see you at any time, no matter how late.'

As soon as he closed his mouth the exodus began and, without once reminding them of their manners, Freya calmly

73

watched her elite sixth formers push and shove their way out. Nancy passed by in a cloud of expensive perfume, face quite contemptuous, eyes spiteful. Reaching the door, she made a disparaging comment, glancing round to make sure he had heard. Charlotte, making her exit by degrees, undulated rather than walked, her yellow hair glittering when it caught the light, her presence so dazzling she all but obscured the smaller figure limping in her wake. Pale, small-boned Imogen, now in full view, walked with a stick, each step laboured, her left leg dragging heavily.

On the way upstairs Freya had briefly shown him the dormitories, allowing a glimpse of meagre furnishings, ancient linoleum floor coverings and ranks of uncurtained windows, and as this room emptied, he saw more evidence of parsimony. The windows were covered, albeit with cheap cane roller blinds and the floor carpeted in thin hair cord, but the untidy basket chairs looked almost derelict. A television and video recorder stood beneath one window, and on a glass-topped wicker table in need of a thorough scrub were an electric kettle, jars of coffee and powdered milk, an opened bag of sugar and a tray of dirty mugs and spoons.

'In reality,' Freya commented, following his gaze, 'women are no more natural housekeepers than men.'

'I think that depends more on the individual,' he replied. 'Part of the differing behaviours you encounter.' As she began to walk towards the door he said, 'Tell me, have there been suicides in the past?'

She glanced over her shoulder but continued walking. 'Yes. Teenagers are very vulnerable to such acts of desperation.'

'How many?'

She stopped then. 'Several before I came here and one during my tenure as headmistress. That was six years ago,' she added, facing him once again. 'A fifth former whose parents were in the throes of a truly bitter and highly publicised divorce. She overdosed on her mother's anti-depressants.'

'Here?'

'Of course not! We keep the *strictest* control of medicines.'

'And if a girl's using illicit drugs?' he asked. 'How would you control that?'

Her eyes narrowed. 'When you have time, read the section in our prospectus on the management of antisocial conduct. We have access to the best professional services. Now,' she went on, 'if you'll excuse me? I must see to the girls.'

He stood his ground. 'Would you inform the police?'

'You know better than I do that no matter what threats or inducements you employ, the very *last* thing a user will tell you is the identity of their supplier. It can, literally, be more than their life is worth.' Head to one side, she regarded him appraisingly. 'You must wonder, as I do, if there is therefore any point in bringing down the weight of the law on the hapless user, particularly when the law has proved repeatedly that it has nothing constructive to offer.' Turning once more on her heel she added, 'But that said, I would naturally never allow personal misgivings to persuade me to conceal a crime.' She looked back at him, a little smile playing about her mouth. 'I'm not a fool.'

11

Berkshire police sent two officers, a man and a woman, to the Melvilles' luxurious country mansion to break the news that a body, washed up from the Menai Strait in north Wales, had been identified as their daughter's by the headmistress of the Hermitage. For the woman, a young sergeant, this was the eighth time she had been called upon to deliver what her more cynical colleagues described as the 'death-o-gram', while her companion was being newly blooded. Sombre-faced, hats in hand, they delivered their message while standing uncomfortably on the fine Persian carpet in the drawing room.

'Bangor police have asked us to tell you that they need to see you as soon as possible,' the sergeant finished quietly. 'Formal identification must be made by the next of kin.'

John Melville stared at her. 'Do you know, in the old days the bearer of evil tidings would be put to death?' Then, a strange gurgling noise in his throat, he stumbled across the room to an open drinks cabinet, poured himself a huge glass of whisky and emptied it at a gulp.

'My husband is not himself. Please, take no notice.' Uttering her first words since the police arrived, Hester Melville rose from a silk-covered chaise longue in the window bay. Afternoon sunshine slanted through the glass, surrounding her in gauzy light. 'Thank you for coming,' she went on, her voice a clipped monotone. 'The housekeeper will see you out.'

As the police car began to make its way down the long drive, the sergeant turned in her seat, to see John Melville at the window, another vast drink in his hands.

*

76

John was still drinking as he sat in McKenna's office well after eleven o'clock that night. He had arrived clutching an almost full bottle of whisky. Now he held it to his lips, drained the last of it, then dropped the bottle and stared at his balled-up fists, completely sober and praying for oblivion. Hester was talking and, as always, he thought despairingly, she was in control, bred to take without flinching whatever monstrousness life threw her way. Only the common, satisfying transactions of an ordinary existence seemed beyond her.

At the mortuary, gazing calmly on the waxen Ophelia wrapped in a winding sheet, she had said, in her bell-like, always unemotional voice, 'That is our daughter, Suzanne.' John had taken one look at his child and lunged for the window that separated them, beating upon the glass until it threatened to shatter. Someone dragged him away, holding down his flailing arms with surprising strength; perhaps the thin, tired-looking detective with an Irish name; perhaps the other man, big and swarthy with five-o'clock shadow round his jaw. Perhaps even Hester, John reflected. It would not be the first time she had dragged him from the brink.

Raising his eyes when he realised she was no longer speaking, he found the thin detective regarding him expectantly. Well, he thought, let's not disappoint. Let's even surprise him. I might look like a lush, but my feelings aren't pickled. Wishing to God they were, he licked his parched lips. 'A beggar,' he said, with infinite care, 'can live on the alms someone tossed his way maybe a week before, but yesterday's happiness won't help even the richest man get by.' He paused, listening to his own echo. Satisfied his words were as clear as his mind obstinately remained, he rambled on, 'When you lose someone you love, your life turns into a bad French farce. You pull out one drawer, push it back, try another, and another, and another, looking for what you lost. You can't find it, so you start again. You'd like to stop, but the hope of finding what you lost goads you on and on and on, because you can't face not trying, and perhaps not finding what was actually there and only hiding. Did you know,' he asked, peering at McKenna, 'that hope was the last thing to come out of Pandora's box?'

'I doubt if Superintendent McKenna is interested,' said Hester wearily.

'Don't give a bugger whether he is or not!' John thrust out his chin aggressively. 'I want him to know how I feel!'

'Only someone who has lost a child can know how you and Lady Hester feel.' McKenna's voice was gentle. 'I would not presume.'

'Don't bring *her* into it!' He glared, eyes bloodshot and muddy. 'She doesn't figure in this equation. She didn't even cry. Did you see her cry?' he demanded, turning from McKenna to Jack. 'No, you didn't, because she bloody *didn't* cry! But she cried when one of her damned dogs died of old age. By God, she did! She never stopped bawling for days!'

Hester stared at the wall behind McKenna. 'Please take no notice, Superintendent. My husband is not himself.'

'I haven't been my bloody self since the day I married you,' he snarled. 'You've turned me inside out, trying to make a silk purse out of a sow's ear.' Again he addressed McKenna. '*Lady* Hester married beneath her, don't you know? I was the bit of rough she just fancied, but I put a common little bun in her posh oven, so Daddy shoved a shotgun to her head.' Drink was making him maudlin as well as coarse. Tears welled in his eyes and spilled over cheeks livid with the broken veins of alcoholism. 'Poor, poor Sukie. You never wanted her, did you, Hester? 'Cos of her, you've been stuck with me for eighteen years.' He breathed heavily in her face. 'It's been hell, hasn't it? Absolute bloody *hell*!'

Hester ignored him. McKenna was not surprised, for theirs was an old conflict, he thought, looking from wife to husband, fought repeatedly over the same ground and although never before to a death, it retained its fatal energy. He realised he was witnessing now the sporadic gunfire of those who stumbled through the corpses on the battlefield not understanding that the war was lost.

As the silence, broken only by John's stertorous breathing, began to grow oppressive, Jack spoke. 'Did Sukie have any reason to commit suicide?' he asked.

Hester flinched. Her husband guffawed. 'How about having us for parents?' he suggested. '*Two* reasons there, old chap, not just one.'

78

Still gazing beyond McKenna's shoulder, Hester asked, 'Was she pregnant?'

Before Jack could reply, John intervened. 'We know what *she's* thinking, don't we? She's thinking "like mother, like daughter".' With exaggerated effort, he screwed up his face and winked, but the gesture was simply pathetic. ''Spect you know you can always tell when a girl's been dropping her knickers. It shows on her face.' He leered at his wife. 'You can even smell it, can't you?'

With the speed of a cobra she delivered a stinging slap across his face. 'Be quiet!' she hissed. 'Be *quiet!*' She rose, her thin, elegant body quivering with rage. 'Don't you dare speak about my child like that. Don't you dare!' Fists balled, knuckles white, she began to rain down blows on his head.

Moving with his own surprising speed, Jack grabbed her from behind, as he had earlier restrained her husband. For interminable moments she struggled silently, kicking his shins and tearing his hands with her nails, while McKenna looked on helplessly. Inch by inch, Jack dragged her towards the door, reached behind him to open it and pulled her out of the room.

John rubbed his chin, skin rasping on stubble, then ran his fingers through the disarray of his hair, straightened the jacket of his navy pinstripe suit and tweaked his shirt collar. Finally, he rearranged his tie, a shimmering raspberry pink silk affair held down with a tiny diamond stud.

Wondering inconsequentially why the man was dressed as if for a meeting in the City, McKenna scowled at him. 'You should be ashamed of yourself,' he snapped.

'Didn't hear you complaining,' John snapped back. 'Grist to your coppers' mill to let people slug it out, isn't it? Get to hear things that way you wouldn't get to know otherwise in a month of Sundays.'

'I haven't heard anything yet that might explain why or how your daughter died.'

'Already told you. She topped herself because of us and the fighting.'

'Well, now she's dead,' McKenna said nastily, 'you'll be able to stop, won't you?'

'Don't be funny.' John's eyes were dark with pain. 'Sukie

79

alive, Sukie dead, the shame's the same.' His words were beginning to slur. 'Hester married a loser. S'only 'cos Daddy gives her money we haven't turned the corner into Queer Street, but believe me, Mr Superintendent whatever-your-bloody-name-is, we're getting nearer every bloody day.'

'My name is McKenna. Not a difficult name to remember, sober or drunk.'

'Knew it was some Paddy handle.' John blinked hard to keep his eyes open. 'No offence, mate. Best jockeys come from over the water. Never let me down yet and that's saying something. Every other bugger has, and horse-kicked me in the teeth to make sure I *stay* down.' He chewed his mouth. 'Even bloody Sukie, bless her. Got the hardest kick of the lot off her.'

'How?' McKenna demanded. 'What did she do?'

'Cost me a bloody fortune. Cost me an arm and a leg.' He began to laugh uproariously. 'Bloody funny, that is! An arm *and* a leg!'

'I don't find it in the least amusing.'

John stabbed his finger in the air near McKenna's face. 'That's cos you don't bloody know.'

'Then enlighten me, Mr Melville, if you're not too drunk to know what you're saying.'

'Christ! You're an arrogant sod!' Unaware of the dribble at the corners of his mouth, he ranted, 'You should bugger off back to bog-land where you belong. I want to see an *English* copper. Might get some respect off an English copper.'

'That would be rather difficult.' McKenna's words were deliberately ambiguous. 'If you want to get me out of your hair, tell me what Sukie did, then you can go to your hotel and have a nice long sleep.'

'Think I can sleep just like that, do you? What do *you* know? Eh?' He began to whine. 'I'll be opening and shutting every bloody drawer in Christendom for the rest of my life, looking for my little Sukie.' Then, as he drew a deep breath, a sob escaped him. 'Maybe Hester'll start opening a few of her own. Who knows? Who bloody knows anything?'

The scratches Hester had inflicted on Jack's hands smarted like those McKenna's cats dealt out when the mood took them. His shins, unsurprisingly, also hurt, for her stylish patent leather shoes had squared-off toes and high, set-back heels. With them she wore a chic, stone-coloured linen shift and, round her neck, what looked like a cascade of gold. Her wristwatch was also gold, and a stack of gold and diamond rings slithered towards her bony knuckle every time she moved.

With a hastily summoned policewoman in tow, Jack had frogmarched her to his own office and pushed her into a soft chair, where she remained, a cup of black coffee growing cold on the desk in front of her. The policewoman sat behind her, ready to pounce.

'Will I be arrested?' Hester asked, staring at his scratches.

'I've got two daughters of my own. I have an inkling of how terrible you must feel,' he replied, thinking that such empty despair was something the childless McKenna would never understand. 'Shock and grief take people all ways. I imagine that's why your husband's drinking so steadily.'

'Do you?' Her grey eyes flicked over him. 'That's because you don't know him. He needs no excuse these days.'

'But it wasn't always like that?'

'Does it matter?' Her voice was utterly weary.

'Yes, if the conflict between you has a bearing on your daughter's death.'

'Oh, I'm sure it has,' Hester assured him. 'People repeatedly suffer the same things because their own nature determines the atmosphere in which they exist.' After some thought, she said, 'We exist in an atmosphere of misery and misfortune, and of course it infected Sukie. She's listened to our rows since she was a baby. There was nothing she didn't know. Nothing.'

'What was there to know?' asked Jack gently. 'That you were pregnant before you married? Unmarried girls across the social spectrum become pregnant with determined regularity.'

Hester looked down at her hands. 'It broke my father's heart.'

'Did he force you into marriage?'

She nodded stiffly. 'Abortion wasn't an option they would countenance.'

'Why couldn't you just become another unmarried mother?'

'The shame,' she replied, with the merest glint of irony. Then her face assumed an expression that was painful to see. '*Their* shame. They never let me forget, for a single moment.' She met his eyes. 'I could never be proud of Sukie. I had to love her in secret.' After a small silence she added, 'She didn't even have a decent christening. We smuggled her into the family chapel one rainy Monday morning, as if she were a servant's bastard.'

'How old were you when you married?'

'Seventeen. As my husband said, like mother, like daughter. He was eighteen.'

'Sukie wasn't pregnant.'

'No?' Hester frowned. 'How do you know?' Then her mouth fell open and as she clawed at her cheeks, her rings flashed and gleamed.

'Nor had she been raped,' he added.

She shuddered from head to foot.

For a while he let her mourn quietly for the second chance that was now for ever beyond human reach, then asked, 'What does your husband do for a living?'

'This and that,' she replied dully. 'Investment, a stab at merchant banking, a stab at stockbroking.'

'You look relatively prosperous.'

' "Relatively" is very apt. Our finances are bound by the law of diminishing returns. Over the years, John's thrown thousands at various good-looking deals and received hundreds back.'

'Something else for you to row about,' he commented.

'Indeed, yes.' When she looked up, he saw the glaze of panic in her eyes. 'Can I go back now? I promise I won't hit him again.' She gnawed her lower lip. 'He's quite a terrifying person, isn't he?'

'Terrifying?' Jack echoed. 'Your husband?'

'Of course not! I meant Superintendent McKenna. I've always found Dr Scott very intimidating, but Superintendent McKenna makes one feel quite panic-stricken.'

'Why is Dr Scott intimidating?'

'She knows exactly what to do, even in the most difficult situations. She has this tremendous confidence, d'you see? But I suppose that's because she's never wrong.' Hester sighed. 'It must be wonderful to be so *sure*.'

'She seems pretty sure at the moment that Sukie killed herself,' Jack said, 'although she can't say why. Have *you* had any reason to worry about Sukie's state of mind recently?'

'We haven't heard from her since the beginning of term.'

'Weren't you anxious?'

'She didn't get in touch from beginning to end of last term, either.' Hester met his eyes again and he saw how dreadfully tired she was. 'It's like that when your child goes away to school. You rely on the school to look after them. It cuts both ways, you know. When I boarded, my teachers and school friends were far more important to me than my own family.'

'That doesn't explain what I see as a degree of estrangement between you and Sukie.' Jack clasped his hands, leaning forward slightly. 'Lady Melville, I know you're exhausted and distraught, but I think you're hiding something that might be important. Won't you tell me? Please?'

'But why? Dr Scott believes there's nothing to be gained by dwelling on the past and she's right. We must move on and away—' Her voice faltered.

'Always easier said than done,' Jack commented softly. 'Especially when the past won't let you.'

'Dr Scott said it was simply adolescent rebellion that went awry. It wasn't anyone's *fault*. She told us she could contain it and help them both to get through it.' Hester stared at him. 'And she kept her word. She's been marvellous.'

Even though he had no idea what Hester was talking about, Jack saw all too clearly the power the charismatic Freya Scott exercised over both pupils and parents. And if ever a parent were ripe for exploitation, he thought, it was this sad young aristocrat still in hock to the consequences of her own prosaic rebellion. 'Was your husband happy to go along with her plans?' he asked.

'If Dr Scott told my husband to put a loaded gun into his mouth and pull the trigger, he'd do it. He snatches gratefully at any positive suggestion.'

'And what was the problem she said she could "contain"?'

'If she hasn't told you herself, she must think it's unimportant,' Hester replied, with all the firmness she could muster.

'We've hardly had time for more than a brief chat,' Jack lied.

'I still think we should ask her first.' Turning awkwardly in her seat, she glanced distractedly about the room. 'I expected her to be here. Why isn't she?'

'We felt she ought to be at the school.'

'I see.' Hester nodded to herself. 'Yes, you're right. She should be there.'

'So?' he coaxed.

'I don't know—' Again she hesitated. 'It seems disloyal to tell you without her knowing.'

He waited patiently, hoping that the dilemma being worked out behind her gaunt features would resolve itself in his favour.

Hester frowned at him. 'Perhaps you *were* right about her never being wrong. She said Sukie had learned her lesson, but if that were true she would have no reason to kill herself.' While she wrestled with the shackles of obedience, she fiddled with her rings, turning them this way and that. A diamond suddenly caught the light, throwing out tongues of fire. 'We only bought Sukie a horse because Dr Scott told us it would be a "positive reinforcement". We could barely afford her school fees, let alone a horse and its livery. My parents had to chip in yet again.' She paused once more. 'Sukie had wanted a horse ever since Torrance Fuseli brought hers to school.' Suddenly she smiled. 'She adored Torrance. She idolised her. When Dr Scott suggested she have a horse, I wasn't in the least interested in positive reinforcement. I simply thought that if Sukie could only learn to be a little like Torrance, her life needn't turn into one long, miserable, destructive tragedy.' She covered her face with her hands, her fingers hooked like claws into her hair. 'Why?' she moaned, beating her forehead with the heels of her palms. 'Why couldn't she have been with Torrance instead of that other bloody girl?'

'Which other girl?' asked Jack.

'Imogen Oliver.'

'What happened between them?'

'What happened?' Hester let her hands drop to her lap. 'If only to God we actually knew! But how can we, when Sukie didn't know herself?' She looked close to collapse. 'Imogen passed her driving test a couple of weeks before last Christmas, and in anticipation her parents had already ordered her car. She'd wanted a Porsche, so she had one, because they've never been able to say no to her. I watched her grow up, d'you see, getting what she wanted every inch of the way.' Pausing to gather her breath and her thoughts, she continued, 'Imogen and Sukie had always been best friends, so of course, they were out in Imogen's new car all the time and I was worried sick, because Imogen drove like a bloody lunatic. When I asked her parents to pull her up, they told me to stop being neurotic.' She laughed joylessly. 'I imagine they've changed their tune now.'

'There was an accident,' Jack said.

'There was an accident.' Hester nodded. 'A horrible, *horrible* accident.' She glanced at him, her face webbed with downward-drawn lines. 'The day after Boxing Day, they went to see my parents and, once they were inside the estate, Sukie took over the driving. She hadn't passed her test, but that doesn't matter on a private road, d'you see? We expected them back for dinner. When they didn't arrive, I rang my parents. They said the girls had left an hour before.' She fell silent and began to crack her knuckles. Wincing, Jack opened his mouth to ask her to finish the story, but she forestalled him. 'We called the police, of course, but nothing had been reported. Anyway, my parents organised a search party. Two of the gamekeepers found them. The car had ploughed through a fence and ended upside down in a thicket and the girls were lying some way away in the grass. God alone knows how they got out of the wreck. I suppose it was sheer instinct in case the car exploded. Sukie had a massive concussion that kept her unconscious for over a week and Imogen's left leg was so badly shattered it had to be amputated above the knee.'

As ever, Jack imagined one or both of his own daughters hostage to a similarly errant fortune and, feeling both sickened and saddened, he said quietly, 'It was indeed a horrible accident and they were extremely lucky to survive. But accidents happen, so I don't understand why Dr Scott regarded it as a problem and talked of containment.'

'Sukie had *insisted* on driving even though Imogen tried to stop her,' Hester said dully. 'The roads were very icy, d'you see? It was all her fault.'

'But *how* was it her fault?' Jack persisted. 'Was she speeding? Was she driving recklessly?'

'I don't know! She couldn't remember. She was so dreadfully concussed she didn't even recall getting up that morning.'

'So you've only got Imogen's word for everything, haven't you?'

'Don't say that!' Hester shivered. 'She lost her *leg*, for God's sake!' Her mouth worked convulsively. 'But the police took the car to pieces. They *must* have known who was driving.'

'Not necessarily, as neither of them was in the car when it was found. The worst of the injuries to Imogen's leg could have been caused as she struggled out.' He watched guilt and doubt and remorse criss-cross her face. 'But rather than argue with a girl who's just lost her leg, you let Sukie take the blame.'

'Imogen had no reason to lie,' she replied tonelessly, as if the same argument had churned up her own mind countless times and always rolled round to the same simple conclusion.

'No? I can think of several off the top of my head and I don't even know her.' He frowned at her. 'How did *she* explain the crash?'

'My parents keep deer on the estate and Imogen thought one of them might have dashed suddenly in front of the car. Deer have a habit of erupting out of nowhere, you know.'

'She only *thought*?' Jack asked. 'Why couldn't she remember?'

'She was confused!' There was a hint of hysteria in Hester's voice. 'She was utterly distraught!'

'Has she remembered since?'

'I've no idea.' Hester looked past him. 'Our families haven't spoken since the day of the accident. Exactly a week later we had a letter from their solicitor saying they intended to sue.'

'And?'

'We didn't argue. We paid up and shut up. John says it's always the best policy when you're on shaky ground.'

'How much?'

'Six hundred and twenty thousand. It was all we could raise. We had to remortgage the house, but we can't afford the repayments. The bank's threatening repossession.'

'And Imogen doubtless received another payout from her own insurance.'

86

She shrugged. 'I expect she did.'

She looked totally defeated, beaten into the ground by a hail of body blows. She seemed to believe her miserable life was the proof of a self-fulfilling prophecy, yet he wondered if, beset by guilt, she had simply had her capacity for judgement destroyed and let guilt beggar her, metaphorically and literally. 'If you hadn't caved in at the Olivers' first assault, a few more facts might have come to light,' he pointed out. 'Tell me,' he went on, 'what exactly did Dr Scott mean when she talked of containing the situation?'

'Oh, what does it matter? *Nothing* matters now Sukie's dead. I *did* love her, whatever my husband thinks. I loved her so much it *hurt*! All I ever wanted was to bring her up myself, but we don't do things like that. She had to be sent away to school.' Again she fell silent, clasping her hands in her lap. Then, bitterness stalking every word, she said, 'In *my* family, d'you see, your life isn't your own. It belongs to the family and their history. They make all the rules and your children are nothing more than fodder for that great family history.'

'We were talking about Dr Scott,' he reminded her gently.

'Dr Scott.' She nodded her head mechanically. 'Yes, well,' she went on, unknotting her fingers, 'Sukie missed the beginning of spring term because she was still in hospital. I wanted to keep her at home for good, but Dr Scott thought that would be disastrous. She said Sukie needed the security of familiar faces and surroundings after such a traumatic experience, so we took her back. Imogen was already there, bravely hopping around on one leg. We were expected to applaud her "fantastic recovery", but I simply wanted to grab Sukie and run.'

'What did Dr Scott hope to achieve by throwing them together?'

'Oh, she talked of confrontation and reconciliation but most of it went over me. I could only think of two young girls with their lives in ruins being forced to look on the cause of that destruction every minute of every day.'

The cathedral clock struck one as Jack ushered Hester into the back of the chauffeur-driven car. John was already there, slumped in the opposite corner, eyes half closed, breath reeking.

The look she gave him was more eloquent than a thousand words.

Jack watched the car drive away, then trudged back upstairs to McKenna's office to relay the essence of Hester's disclosures. 'I'm sorely tempted to go to that damned school now, drag Scott out of her bed and ask her what *else* she didn't think we needed to know,' he finished.

'So that's what Melville meant.' McKenna's face betrayed sorrow and outrage in equal measure. 'In among his maundering and drunken gibberish, he said Sukie had cost him "an arm *and* a leg", and then began laughing like a lunatic.'

'Didn't you ask him what he meant?'

'No, I didn't,' McKenna said curtly. 'I decided to have him escorted to his car.'

'Probably for the best, in the circumstances,' Jack remarked. 'We shouldn't really interview people when they're the worse for wear.' He fell silent, fiddling with the papers on the desk, trying to find expression for the feelings Hester had evoked in him. Presently, he said, 'What happened between those girls reminds me of a Greek tragedy, but we mustn't assume that it's relevant to Sukie's death.' Stifling a yawn, he rubbed his eyes. 'Even though,' he went on, 'there's a compelling motive for suicide in there.'

'And what's that?'

'Isn't it obvious? Sukie believed she'd destroyed her best friend's future. She must have been eaten up with guilt.'

'I rely on you to keep off the psychological bandwagon,' McKenna told him, grinding his teeth. 'As you said, we've got to keep an open mind, so don't start spouting claptrap just because you got too close to the Melvilles' emotional meltdown. I don't know which of them needs treatment the most.'

'A helping hand springs to mind, rather than treatment,' Jack argued. 'Hester's development was obviously cauterised at some crucial stage. She's utterly pathetic.'

'And her husband's an upper-class English twerp hoping to find his balls at the bottom of every bottle of Scotch he uncaps,' McKenna added, with wholly uncharacteristic vulgarity.

'I imagine he's given to snide remarks about Paddies and so forth when he's in his cups,' Jack ventured.

McKenna's eyes gleamed. 'He wanted to talk to an *English* policeman.'

'He probably only wanted to talk to someone who'd offer comforting answers to the nasty questions his daughter's death has raised, but that's not your style. You'd rather cause an explosion and see what settles with the dust.'

'It must be my Irish genes,' McKenna retorted.

'You Celts do like to flaunt your background,' Jack commented wearily. 'Dewi's so unbelievably Welsh he probably bleeds daffodil yellow.'

'Or leek green,' said McKenna, with a crooked smile. 'He's no longer "Dewi", by the way. He's now "David", because Torrance, our glitzy American with the toothy smile and Rapunzel-like hair, can't get her pretty mouth around "Dewi".' The smile evaporated. 'She seems to have true cross-gender appeal.'

'Why? Because Sukie "adored" her? That's schoolgirl stuff, surely.'

'You said Hester also thinks very highly of her,' McKenna reminded him. 'However, Dr Scott doesn't. Nor does Matron. Interesting, eh?'

'Only up to a point,' Jack said. 'I'm far more interested in the accident and Imogen's paper-thin explanation.'

'Quite.' McKenna began to tidy his desk. 'And if she *has* been lying, she had a first-class motive for murdering her erstwhile friend, especially if Sukie was getting her memory back.' He paused. 'Then again, the motive is equally strong if she's been telling the truth. I'd feel murderous towards someone who lost me one of my legs.'

'But could she have done it without help?' Jack wondered. 'Anyway, we can't go too far down that road until Eifion confirms cause of death. But whatever, forcing those girls back together was the worst thing anyone could do. Hester should have heeded her instincts. Poor bitch! Her daughter would still be alive if she had.'

'Considering she gave you quite a hammering,' McKenna said, eyeing Jack's scratches, 'you're being extraordinarily sympathetic.'

'She expected to get arrested. She finds you terrifying. Pity Scott doesn't feel the same way, isn't it?'

12

After the meeting in the sixth-form common room, Vivienne went downstairs for supper with the others but, sick in heart and stomach, returned almost immediately to her room. At the head of the first flight of stairs she encountered Matron and the headmistress on their rounds. When she gave way, pressing herself against the wall, Matron stalked past as if she were invisible, but Dr Scott paused momentarily to stare coldly into her eyes. Feeling like a sickly fox marked by the hounds, Vivienne scuttled up the next flight and, once in her room, rammed a chair under the doorknob.

She had a packet of cannabis taped behind the bed frame and another stuffed inside a padded coat-hanger but, desperate as she was, dared not open either, for the pungent smoke was sure to alert the policeman guarding the fire exit at the end of the corridor. She collapsed on the bed, wondering where it would all end and, with one of those fearful perceptions her addiction could induce, she realised that the girl she had once been was now only a decaying memory inside the dead thing she had become.

Imogen must feel the same way, she thought. The girl who returned to school early in the spring term to receive Lancaster's house captaincy as consolation for losing her leg had already suffered a sea change in her personality that shocked even Vivienne's blunted sensibilities. The always nice, often kind, sometimes reckless, rich kid Imogen once was disappeared with the amputated leg. Bitter, morose and despairing, her surrogate yawed through the remaining weeks of term on one leg and her crutches while the artificial leg gathered dust in the corner of her room.

Hope seemed to flare briefly the day school reopened after the Easter holiday. Vivienne was in her room when the Olivers' car drove on to the forecourt. As the chauffeur opened the rear door, she watched with something like joy as Imogen put *two* feet and a silver-topped cane on the ground, waved away the chauffeur's helping hand and pulled herself upright. Then she heard the headmistress's horrified voice.

'My dear girl!' Dr Scott exclaimed. She came into Vivienne's line of sight, striding elegantly in high-heeled shoes, and grabbed Imogen's arm. 'Where are your crutches?'

'In the boot,' Imogen replied. She was rock steady on the prosthetic leg.

'Get them,' the headmistress instructed the chauffeur. 'This minute!'

Imogen protested. 'I don't need them.'

'But you do, my dear. You *do*! *I'll* tell you when you can do without them.' Taking the cane from Imogen's hands, she put her arm round her shoulders and began walking her towards the door. 'You shouldn't have done this,' Vivienne heard her say. 'You're not ready. A little at a time, Imogen, a little at a time. *Trust* me, my dear. I know what I'm doing.'

But obstinately, Imogen persevered with her new leg, except when she was in the swimming pool. There, she cleaved the silvery water as clean and fast as ever, and although her wake had lost its old symmetry, her tapering silhouette made her resemble a mermaid. When she hauled herself back into the human environment she became a cripple once more, and she clearly mourned, weeping often both with grief and with a pain that was closer to agony. She also wept with misery, for the headmistress condemned her self-determination as treachery and, under the onslaught of a displeasure as pernicious as a foul smell, Imogen's spirit withered towards another death. Vivienne was not surprised, for only sour and poisonous plants thrived in Dr Scott's greenhouse.

Sukie also grieved. Her friendship with Imogen, an entity in its own right, was suddenly, like Imogen's left leg, not there, but its absence was mystifying. The girls went out of their way to avoid each other and, if inadvertently, they found themselves together, Imogen would hobble away with downcast eyes.

Vivienne perceived guilt in one and raw sorrow in both, but doubting her befuddled impressions, could only ache to help them.

She was jolted from her reverie by scuffles and whispers outside the door. The knob turned slowly, the chair rocked slightly and she heard the vile, vicious, predatory Nancy titter. She clutched her stomach, wanting to vomit with fear.

'McKenna's sussed you out, Dopehead.' Nancy's voice slithered into the room. 'He's after you.'

Then she heard Charlotte's breathy tones. 'When did he say that?' She sounded confused. 'I didn't see him talking to you.'

'He didn't,' Nancy replied. 'Dr Scott told me.' Her nails beat a tattoo on the door. 'You'd better believe it, Dopehead,' she hissed. 'Your days are numbered.'

A dim glow from the outside security lamps lit the cavernous dormitory Daisy shared with seven others. In the next bed Alice muttered, adding her nocturnal voice to the quiet, comforting chorus of grunts and sighs. They were like animals in a den, Daisy thought, loving the familiar sounds. When she was at home, the nights were a lonely torment.

A soft, uncertain wind scuffled among the trees, and she hoped it heralded one of those wonderful storms bursting with the promise of devastation and excitement. During one of last winter's gales she had watched an ancient Douglas Fir snap like a matchstick, and crash to earth in a tumult of flying needles and broken branches. Alice tried to flee its screaming death throes, but Daisy grabbed her arm, dragging her towards the impending disaster simply to relish the experience.

Alice was an odd choice to be her best friend, but in truth, it had never been a matter of choice. The first term was three days old when Daisy arrived, and as Alice was the only first former not already joined in some alliance, leftover and latecomer made their own. Three stultifying years later, Daisy felt trapped in the same kind of oppressive relationship her parents endured, but while divorce was theirs for the taking, even had she been sure that was what she wanted, she did not dare break the bond with Alice. When friendship died at the Hermitage, its body was picked apart, its bones stripped of every scrap of flesh and ounce of marrow, and the one who killed the friendship broken on the wheel. Betrayal, of a certain kind, was still a capital offence in this small, cynical world.

She heard the lift whine at the far end of the building, then footfalls overhead and the thud of bedroom doors. She listened avidly for whatever might come next, as she listened at home for the furious, savage coupling that closed each bitter row between her warring parents, but although she waited until her ears began to hum, nothing arose to divert her agitation. Suddenly she reared up in bed and yelped, dragging the other girls from the shallows of sleep.

'Did you hear that?' she asked, her voice throbbing with horrified excitement.

'Hear what?' someone mumbled.

'That *awful* sloshing noise in Sukie's room. It must be her ghost!'

For a long time Torrance had regarded the arcane traditions of the Hermitage as simply 'quaint', because her New World eyes misread the cosy, wrinkled face of the Old World. Her eventual realisation that brutality and malice were the school's lifeblood brought with it a profound and crippling sense of helplessness, and that feeling returned with a vengeance when she made the rounds of the Tudor dormitories that night. She could actually smell the tension and fear gripping the school, and she searched deep for the brave face she presented and the calming words she spoke. The only light moment in a dreadful half-hour came courtesy of the ever acerbic Alice, when Torrance asked, 'How's your breathing now, little sister?' and Alice, rigid with stress and grey as a corpse, replied, 'Fine, thank you, Torrance, and would you *please* stop calling me "little sister". You may want to run Tudor like a sorority house but, as I've told you before, this is *not* America.'

On the way to her own room, Torrance saw Ainsley going into the showers. She sat on the bed, waiting and counting, and exactly eight minutes later Ainsley returned. Three more minutes passed before she heard the thump of books, the rustle of paper and the click of a lamp switch as Ainsley settled down to one hour of intellectual gymnastics, and Torrance knew that

93

ten minutes after Ainsley eventually went to bed she would be muttering in her sleep, her overstretched brain unable to quiet itself. The prospect made her feel like screaming.

Vivienne's room was tonight as quiet as the grave. There were no soft giggles or heartbreaking sobs, no scraping matches and no cloying scent drifting through the open window. Perhaps, for once, sheer exhaustion had sent her to sleep.

Torrance went for her own shower, and was sitting on the bed, drying her hair, when she heard screams from the floor below, quickly followed by Matron's shouts. Hair flying, she ran from her room and down the stairs, to find Matron hovering over the crumpled figure of Grace Blackwell.

'It's all right,' Matron said, hauling Grace to her feet. 'I'll put her in the infirmary for tonight.'

'What's wrong with her?'

'Daisy was teasing the dorm. I've already told her off.'

'She – she s-s-said she could h-h hear Sukie's ghost!' Grace almost choked on the words. Her eyes glittered.

Torrance recoiled as if she had been punched in the stomach.

'Daisy's a very naughty girl,' Matron was saying, patting Grace's arm. 'You've had enough frights for one day with that stupid police dog, haven't you?' She set off for the infirmary, trudging on leaden feet, with Grace tottering beside her like a drunk.

Leaning weakly against the wall, Torrance watched until they were out of sight and several more minutes passed before she felt strong enough to return upstairs. Once back in her room, she draped a towel round her shoulders and spread out her hair to dry, then sat by the open window. Lights glowed in the police caravan, from where she could hear the occasional voice, and she realised that its presence underscored the sense of menace she felt at every turn. She shivered. '*Damn* Daisy!' she muttered, wanting to throttle the little horror. Matron would have done no worse than chide her gently, for Daisy was one of her particular pets and her mischief, according to Matron, was quite harmless. Was Daisy perhaps retarded, Torrance asked herself, realising that the girl's emotional attachments, as well as her behaviour, were decidedly infantile. She exchanged one idol for another as a child jumps from toy to toy. For a while she had plagued Torrance with her affections and insinuating presence, before dropping her for Justine, who was ousted in favour of Imogen.

A movement outside caught her attention. A figure was crossing the forecourt from the police caravan, trailing an ever lengthening shadow. She stared out as she had on Tuesday night, when the silence was disturbed by the scream of a military jet low overhead and the rustle of trees in its aftermath. Almost immediately, she had heard another noise, as if someone had kicked a stone, then what had sounded like the whisper of voices. She had peered into the darkness until her eyes glazed, but still could not be sure whether what she saw was a trick of the light or a shape flitting among the trees.

Suddenly bone weary, she removed the towel, twisted her hair into a loose plait and fell into bed. Hearing Ainsley's sporadic gabbling through the wall, Torrance remembered that she too had suffered Daisy's attentions for a while, before Sukie became the latest passion. Then thoughts and images of the dead girl that she had resolutely thrust aside all evening flooded her mind and she began to weep.

Alice had not shed a single tear when Sukie's death was announced, nor during the strange, disturbing, dragging evening that followed, when the school's inviolate routines collapsed about her ears. Tea was late, prep was abandoned, and showers and bed turned into a brawling, shouting mêlée that subsided into simmering unrest once Dr Scott and Matron had made their rounds. Alice blamed the atmosphere for her bitchiness towards Torrance, who called her charges 'little sister' only to make them feel protected, not to promote Dr Scott's sinister notions of a surrogate family to which every girl must offer herself like a sacrifice. Dr Scott was a hypocrite, Alice decided as she fell asleep, and she made hypocrites of others, for the Hermitage was, in truth, just a gigantic cardboard box where parents abandoned their daughters as if they were unwanted puppies.

Grace's ear-drilling screams wrenched her awake. She shot upright to see Grace tearing towards the door and Daisy, flapping her arms and howling, in pursuit. She chased her into the corridor, then came running back and dived into bed, giggling like a lunatic. She went on giggling even when Matron burst into the dormitory and began shouting at her. Although Daisy shouted back that she had only been joking and had not heard anything from Sukie's room, her silly, nasty antics set the cauldron seething again, and Matron and Grace were long gone before even a semblance of quiet fell in the dormitory.

Alice tossed and turned interminably, cursing Daisy one moment, the next feeling cold with dread about what the future held for her friend, for sooner or later, she knew Daisy would go a step too far, with deadly consequences. Wanting to warn her, she rolled over, but Daisy, looking quite cherubic, was fast asleep.

With a sigh, Alice tucked her arm beneath her head, sniffing her flesh where the smell of horses still lingered. Wondrous creatures that they were, horses stripped her of all human misery or pretension and made her feel like nothing at all except part of the earth, and she knew Torrance shared that under-standing. Earlier, in the paddock, with the handsome policeman a bemused and silent witness, when Torrance told Purdey and the other horses that Sukie was dead, the electricity in the air had made her hair stand on end. Alice smiled drowsily, for although the memory was heart-wrenching, it was also beautiful.

Faintly, in the distance, she heard one of the horses cry. Thinking it must be Purdey, grieving for her dead mistress, she choked back the sob welling in her throat, but the next one defeated her and she began to weep quietly but convulsively.

Alice's restlessness brought Daisy out of a nightmare where a ravening dog with bloody fangs was chasing her through the woods. When Alice slid out of bed to go to the lavatory she followed, padding barefoot through the dawn gloaming.

Bleary-eyed, still in her other world, Alice emerged from the cubicle to wash her hands and she almost fainted with shock to find Daisy perched on the edge of the sink. 'What're you doing?' she grumbled. 'You frightened me half to death!'

Daisy licked her lips greedily. 'Did you think I was Sukie's ghost?'

'No, I didn't.' Ostentatiously turning her back, Alice washed her hands.

'Bet you did!'

'Oh, shut up!' Alice reached for her towel. 'And grow up, why don't you? You really scared Grace.'

'She's stupid.'

'She isn't, she's just nice. *Un*like you. Sometimes you're really horrible!'

'We are up our own arse tonight, aren't we?' Daisy sneered. 'Could that be because Miss Wonderful picked you to help with evening stables, I wonder?'

'You're only jealous, although I can't think why. You don't like horses.' Her next words tripped out before she had even entertained the thought. 'And horses positively hate *you*. You frighten them.'

'Crap!' Daisy snapped. 'Daddy's going to buy me a horse for my next birthday. So there!'

'So what? *Mummy* would buy me one *before* my next birthday if I asked.'

'I sometimes forget you don't have a daddy to ask,' Daisy put forward thoughtfully. 'I guess he didn't love you enough to stick around.'

Alice flushed. 'You *are* horrible! And stop trying to copy the way Torrance speaks. You sound silly.'

'Better than sounding like a love-struck booby,' retorted Daisy. 'Bet you'd like to marry her, wouldn't you?' she added maliciously. 'You'll be lucky! Miss Wonderful'll probably marry her bloody Tonto. She's weird enough.'

Ignoring her, Alice hung up the towel.

Daisy pinched her arm. 'Did you hear me? I said she's *queer*.'

'I heard. I don't know what you're talking about and I don't want to know.'

'Well, you should! You should steer well clear of her.'

'Horse shit!'

'You think?' As Alice turned for the door, Daisy grabbed her by the hair, and Alice had no option but to stand still and listen. 'Well, you didn't see what *I* saw in the stables a couple of weeks ago.' She paused, head to one side, eyes bright, face flushed. 'I heard Sukie crying, so I went to see why.' She moistened her lips again. 'She was in one of the empty stalls.'

'Well?' Alice demanded. Her neck ached from the pressure Daisy was exerting.

'Miss Wonderful was there, too. She was raping her.' She released Alice's hair and stood back to assess the effect of her words. 'SHE – WAS – RAPING – SUKIE,' she repeated, laying horrible stress on the word 'raping'.

Ashen-faced, Alice gaped, bony chest heaving as she tried to draw breath. Suddenly she lunged violently. 'Liar!' she croaked. 'Liar!'

Daisy stumbled backwards, clutching at air, and fell against a cubicle door, striking her face. As Alice reeled from the room she yelled after her, 'She *murdered* her! Sukie was going to snitch. I *know* she was because she told me. So, there!'

I

Had Fluff and Blackie not been determined to wake him, McKenna would have slept until the alarm clock wailed at seven thirty, but he was driven from his bed long before then. As soon as he was on his feet the cats stopped howling, raced down the first of the steep narrow staircases and skidded around the corner to the second. One day, he said to himself, they'll trip over their own noses and roll over and over like a car gone off a mountainside, then realised they would probably bring him down first. When he was at his groggiest, they would wait halfway down the stairs before shooting under him as his foot was in the air and his balance almost irredeemably compromised. The point of no return had so far been avoided only by a cat's whisker.

By the time he reached the parlour they were at the back door. Once he let them out, they roamed about the little garden, then scrambled across the ivy-clad wall into next door's overgrown patch. Leaving the door open to the fresh morning air, he resolutely turned his back on the enchanting view, which embraced the city, Strait and Puffin Island, as if, like the face of someone once beloved but now dead, it were already a thing of the past.

At seven thirty, gritty-eyed from lack of sleep, Jack plodded into McKenna's office with some papers under his arm and a mug of tea in each hand. 'Berkshire police have sent us a fax,' he said, setting the mugs on the desk, 'to say there's absolutely nothing on the Melvilles. I was expecting a drink-drive on John, at least.'

'They have a chauffeur,' McKenna reminded him. 'So Melville can drink to his heart's content, wherever he is. What do they say about the accident?'

Jack scanned the papers. 'No mechanical faults in the chassis, brakes, steering, wheels, etc. etc. and no post-crash fire to muck things up. Nor was there any ice around, black or otherwise, contrary to what Hester believes. Based on the physical evidence, it appears the car was travelling well in excess of seventy-five miles an hour when it left the road, so they came to the obvious conclusion that the driver simply lost control. Unfortunately,' he went on, 'and I quote, "prolonged and exhaustive forensic examination of the vehicle failed to establish which of the two females present had been driving. Both were wearing gloves and no viable fingerprint evidence was therefore available." So that appears to be that, although as they'd like us to phone, they may want to talk off the record. Will you do that, or shall I?'

'I'll call them after the briefing,' McKenna said. 'I want you to interview Sean O'Connor. You should be able to catch him before he leaves for work.'

'Which hat do I wear? "Nice copper" or "nasty copper"?'

'You know how you function best.' McKenna gave him a lopsided smile.

'I trust Scott will be given the *really* nasty copper routine?'

'I haven't decided quite how to handle that yet,' McKenna admitted. 'I've been indulging in displacement activity and thinking about Sukie's horse. I wonder what will happen to it?'

'If the Melvilles are as broke as Hester reckons,' Jack replied mordantly, 'they'll probably have to sell it to pay for her funeral.' When McKenna winced, he added, 'But I'm sure it'll find a good home. Better than it's got now, most likely, because I don't see how one teacher, with other responsibilities to boot, can look after seven horses properly, even with help from the girls. They need a full-time groom.'

'What "other responsibilities"? According to the prospectus, Miss Attwill is a full-time riding mistress.'

'She might be full-time and she might be the riding mistress,' Jack commented, 'but she also teaches geography and social studies, so she'll be one of the economies Scott grasps at every opportunity. Have you noticed,' he went on, picking up his tea, 'how many part-time staff and contract workers she employs? There's nothing necessarily wrong in trimming excess, but to my mind she's a cheapskate. The prospectus boasts about grand schemes for future expansion, yet in reality the school's a dump.' He grinned briefly. 'I tried to talk to her about the staffing levels yesterday, but all I got was an ear bashing about market forces, market expectations, and market this, that and the other. Trying to get her to stick to the point was like pushing a bus up Snowdon.'

'She's adept at wearing down opposition,' McKenna said, 'as well as deflecting attention elsewhere when she can't. She's very guileful and very clever. Don't forget she's got a doctoral thesis under her belt and to prove *her* particular point, that Shakespeare was the first to record the human capacity for insight, she must not only have jumped forwards, sideways and backwards through a lot of mental hoops, but persuaded a lot of others to follow her blindly.' He took out his first cigarette of the day. 'If she weren't *quite* so clever, I wouldn't mind telling her that her thesis is total rubbish, but she'd misuse the transaction. I'd end up compromised, one way or another.' Gazing thoughtfully at Jack, he smiled slowly. 'Then again, Dewi knows as much as me about the insights to be found in early-medieval Welsh poetry. I'm sure he'd jump at the chance to tell her.'

When McKenna reached the briefing room shortly after eight o'clock, he found it already full, even though many of the officers there had been working at the school until very late the night before, completing interviews, collating statements and putting information into the computers.

'Dr Roberts,' he began, 'is still unable to specify the circumstances of Sukie Melville's death, although he's disinclined to regard it as accidental.' Then he told them of the car crash, discussing its implications and the doubts surrounding the identity of the driver. 'Sukie had no memory of the crash, but believed she was responsible for maiming her closest friend. Day after day, she's been forced to confront the consequences of her actions in the shape of Imogen's amputation. A burden of guilt of that magnitude *could* have made her suicidal. However,' he went on, 'Imogen may have been the driver. If she took advantage of Sukie's memory loss to pass the blame, she would be living in fear of Sukie's memory returning: hence a possible motive for murder. Although she appears to be physically incapable, we mustn't make assumptions about the extent of her disablement. Nor must we assume that she couldn't have had an accomplice.'

Janet held up her hand. 'No one's even *mentioned* that Imogen Oliver and Sukie used to be best friends, sir. No one's commented about Imogen's leg, either.'

'They're remarkable omissions,' he agreed. 'But while we see them as significant, to the school, the friendship and the accident may simply be past history. Nonetheless I shall be asking Dr Scott why she thought fit not to tell us.' He waited for a moment for further questions, before continuing, 'Aside from a natural element of shock, the statements we have to date are uniformly bland and essentially uninformative, including those taken from the security guards and the staff.'

Dewi interrupted. 'I've arranged with the guards to go over their routes, sir, to see if any memories get jogged,' he said. 'They reckon to vary the routes at random, but I'm not sure that means anything. They only do mobile patrols, so they'll end up covering the same ground.'

'And the girls no doubt know precisely where they'll be at any given moment,' McKenna added. 'As they doubtless know a great deal about many other things, which is what I want teased out of them. We don't know, for example, if Sukie had a boyfriend. Dr Scott says not, her mother *thinks* not, but they'd be the last to find out. We must also establish who her friends were. Matron told me she idolised Torrance Fuseli.'

'Sir?' Nona Lloyd raised her hand. 'Do we treat Imogen Oliver as a suspect?'

'We bear her in mind,' he replied, 'pending Dr Roberts's findings.'

Nona held up her hand again. 'A lot of the girls think Sukie killed herself. How should we handle that?'

'Don't encourage the idea,' McKenna told her, 'but don't refuse to speculate about the possibility.' After some thought, he went on, 'Suicide devastates those left behind when they believe they didn't see it coming, but with hindsight the warning signals can become blindingly obvious. The same can be said for murder, which also appears to be an extremely intimate event. Don't forget that the Hermitage is as much a closed society as any prison, with a similar degree of physical and psychological isolation. Dr Scott actively thwarts the influence of mitigating factors from the outside world, and rules the roost in a possessive and even despotic manner. In such a setting emotions become exaggerated and distorted. They will run on a permanent high, and are therefore less easily resolved and dissipated, and a murder could be provoked by something so trivial or incredible that no one took any notice of the antecedents.'

'There's a considerable amount of spite and jealousy,' Janet remarked, 'and the sense of some very unpleasant under-currents.'

'And fear, too,' Nona said. She turned to her colleague. 'Did you sense that, too?' When Janet nodded, she added, 'I'm sure there's a lot of bullying going on and it must be absolutely hellish for the victims. They've got no escape.'

Her remarks triggered discussion among the people in the room and McKenna listened for a while, following the skeins of ideas that were being drawn out. Then he held up his own hand for silence. 'This is the largest investigation we've ever under-taken, we're hamstrung by uncertainties and lack of knowledge, and we're operating in a very complex and complicated environment. Much of what we learn will turn out to be wholly irrelevant: for instance, bullying may be well-established and endemic, but not material to Sukie's death. Conversely, the key could be something which appears completely unimportant, or is so much a part of school life that no one takes notice of it. The potential for us to be sidetracked, either accidentally or deliberately, is enormous. Dr Scott is particularly liable to obfuscate issues because Sukie's death may be the upshot of a level of negligence that could ruin her. So focus is crucial.'

As he waited for more questions, he thought how tired many of them looked, Janet especially. She was very pale and the shadows beneath her eyes aged her. 'A few more things before you go,' he continued. 'First, think very carefully about possible motives for murder, keeping them at the forefront of your mind during the interviews. We've already talked about jealousy and bullying, so consider where they might lead, such as to theft and revenge. Blackmail also comes to mind. Second, you'll be given a recent academic paper on child killers, which outlines risk factors, the trail of warning signs and the detectable antecedents to the event. It should help you to build up a profile of the possible perpetrator without falling into the stereotype trap. Third, in any large group of teenagers, some are bound, by the law of averages, to be abusing solvents, alcohol, or controlled substances and, although Dr Roberts has found nothing to suggest Sukie was a user, the issue could still be very relevant to her death. Girls who *are* involved in substance abuse will be particularly wary and close-mouthed, but they may also be sufficiently disaffected with school life to let a few cats out of the bag. Finally,' he went on, 'remember that a murderer is usually found among those closest to the victim, so while we can't yet exclude outsider involvement, attempted kidnap – although that doesn't seem likely – or a family connection to Sukie's death, we concentrate on the school. Any one of the staff or pupils could know something that places them at risk of becoming the next victim.'

Eifion Roberts telephoned the moment McKenna returned to his office. 'I've had a visitor,' the pathologist announced. 'The girl's mother turned up almost at the crack of dawn, wanting to see her. I spent nigh on half an hour trying to persuade her to go but she wouldn't budge. She said she had a right to see her daughter and if I didn't let her, she'd get her father to get the coroner to *make* me.'

'She was in a dreadful state last night,' McKenna said. 'Perhaps she can't grasp Sukie's death without seeing the body again. You let her, I take it?'

'I couldn't, could I?' Roberts sighed. 'I've got the lass's skull in pieces.' He fell silent. 'In the end,' he went on eventually, 'I had no choice but to tell her I hadn't finished the post-mortem, at which point she literally collapsed.'

'And where is she now?'

'Next door in casualty, waiting to see the psychiatric registrar. I rang the hotel where she's staying but her husband was still abed. I've left a message for him.'

'In the couple of hours he was here last night, Melville consumed almost a whole bottle of whisky and he was drunk when he arrived. I'm not surprised he's still "abed". He must be comatose.'

'You sound like a prissy old virgin at times, McKenna. Puritanical venom literally drips from your mouth. For God's sake, have a bit of compassion! The poor sod's just lost his only child!' With that he disconnected the call.

Expecting to have the benefit, albeit unofficially, of local knowledge and personal opinion from Berkshire police, McKenna was amazed, as well as deeply chagrined, to be told that John Melville was generally well-regarded. 'Doesn't he have a drink problem?' he asked.

'No more so than a lot of others. And he's never made a public nuisance of himself.'

'What about his wife?'

'Considering her mother's a bit of a tartar, Lady Hester's very pleasant. Quiet, mind, but always pleasant.'

'She must be good at putting a brave face on things, then,' McKenna commented. 'Her marriage seems to be a disaster.'

'Her sort are well-trained to keep up appearances and not to frighten the horses.'

Exasperated, he asked, 'What *do* you know about them?'

'Not much, and *that* only courtesy of Lady Hester's parents. This government didn't invent spin-doctoring, you know. The aristocracy's been at it for centuries.'

'So you can't say if Sukie's death might be connected to something her parents or grandparents have done or been involved with?'

'No, I can't, but we've asked our financial people to sniff around. It occurred to us that John Melville could've upset somebody in his many business dealings, even though he always comes out of them the poorer. On the other hand he could have something on somebody, but then you'd expect *him* to be dead, not his daughter.'

'What about inheritance?' asked McKenna. 'Was Sukie in line for a title and fortune that someone else might want?'

'No. Lady Hester's got three older brothers, all of them married with heirs of their own. The title goes to the eldest male, as these things always do. Still, there's no harm in asking her father about the disposition of the estate. He can only tell me to sod off and mind my own business.'

'We'll be grateful for anything you can dig up,' McKenna said.

'I'm sorry we can't tell you more about the car smash. Believe me, we'd like to know ourselves what really happened. In my opinion the Oliver girl's amnesia was just a bit *too* convenient, bearing in mind she didn't even get knocked out. We questioned her doctor about it and he said the psychiatrist reckoned it was down to shock. Can't argue with that, can you?'

'Not very easily,' McKenna agreed. 'Did you know the Melvilles paid her over six hundred thousand?'

'We heard they'd forked out, but I didn't know it was as much as that. She had another fortune off the insurers, too, which, if she *was* driving, means there's been a massive fraud. So, if you do find you've got a murder on your hands, you won't have far to look for a motive, will you?'

2

Mealtimes at the Hermitage were always heralded by the stamp and shuffle of hundreds of feet and the noise of the benches being scraped back and forth as the girls took their seats. Because Dr Scott insisted on group cohesion, the girls were banned from changing places at table and so, at breakfast, Alice had to press her skinny thighs against those of the girl on her left in order to put some inches between herself and the monster Daisy had become overnight.

On the way to her own table, Nancy saw that tiny gulf. 'Lovers' tiff?' She smirked, breathing down Alice's neck.

Fists clenched, shoulders rigid, Alice muttered, 'Bog off, Holmes.'

Laying her right hand on Alice's head and her left on Daisy's, Nancy grabbed a hank of hair from each before taking a step back. '*What* did you say, Derringer?' she demanded.

'You heard,' Daisy whimpered. 'Let go of us before I scream.'

' "Let go of uth befow I thcweam," ' Nancy taunted.

Her neck wrenched almost sideways, Alice struggled to her feet, the bench cutting into her legs. 'Yeth, Nanthy,' she sneered, 'do what Daithy thayth, or elth!'

Ignoring the gaping audience, Nancy held fast, but then she noticed the rapidly bruising weal on Daisy's face. Releasing Alice, she gouged her knuckle into Daisy's cheek. 'What's this, Shitpants?'

Tears of pain sprang to Daisy's eyes. Distraught, Alice launched herself at the sixth former.

3

When McKenna arrived at the school, Matron was the first member of staff he encountered. She was hurrying along the administration corridor as fast as her corsets permitted, mumbling to herself, her face reflecting her inner turmoil.

When she saw him she stopped short. 'Oh!' she panted. 'Oh, it's you. I don't think Dr Scott's expecting you so early.' Making a point of consulting her fob watch, she went on, 'She's very busy and the girls aren't in class yet. Breakfast isn't long done with.' Then she glanced at him, her distress obvious. 'And what a mess that turned out to be! Some of the girls were actually fighting!'

'Over what?'

'I don't know. I doubt if they know themselves. Everything's in a such a dreadful ferment!' She put her hand on his arm. 'How long will you be here? We can't get back to normal with policemen all over the place.'

'Whether we're here or not,' he said, 'I think you'll find getting back to normal isn't possible. You can't restore a disturbed situation to its former tranquillity any more than you can suppress something that's burst free.' He began to move in the direction of Freya's study and Matron turned back on herself to follow.

'I don't understand what you mean,' she fretted.

'Sudden death releases turbulent and often violent feelings in those it touches. You can't screw back the lid.'

'Like an evil genie, you mean, don't you?' Trotting beside him, she shook her head sadly. 'Something like that got into those girls at breakfast.'

'Which girls?'

'Young Alice Derringer and her best friend Daisy Podmore.' She was still clearly worried. 'And Daisy's got a bruise on her cheek. She said she slipped when she went to the toilet in the early hours.'

'She may have done.'

'Well, I didn't hear her and I was up most of the night, what with one thing and another. I had to put several girls in the infirmary because they were that upset, then just when things were settling down, Grace Blackwell came screaming out of the dorm saying Sukie's ghost was about. I tell you,' Matron said, white-faced, 'she fair made even *my* blood run cold.'

Suddenly Freya's study door was yanked open with such violence that McKenna expected it to fall off its hinges. Torrance plunged into the corridor, glared at Matron and him, and strode off. The flash of rage in her eyes was unmistakable.

'Well!' Matron breathed, watching her retreating back. 'Well, really!'

Then Freya herself emerged, a dark, shapely figure, with sunshine streaming through the window behind her.

'Good morning, Superintendent,' she said, inclining her head gracefully. 'Please take no notice of Torrance. I'm afraid everyone's feelings are running a little high at the moment.'

'So I hear,' he replied.

She frowned at Matron.

'I just told him about the fight at breakfast,' Matron mumbled.

'Hardly a fight,' the headmistress commented. 'Simply a ripple in the water.' She looked again at the other woman. 'We won't keep you, Matron. I'm sure you're very busy.' Dismissing her as she would a child, she beckoned to McKenna and closed the door. 'Do take a seat.' He received another of those calculatedly seductive smiles. 'I won't be long.'

'Why was Torrance so angry?' Refusing the offered chair, he leaned against the window ledge.

'Because, despite appearances, she's arrogant and hotheaded,' Freya replied, shuffling papers, 'and while she has a certain amount of charm, I'm afraid she has little else to commend her. When I pointed out that the fracas at breakfast was her fault, she had a tantrum.'

'I didn't know she was involved.'

She stopped what she was doing and, leaning on the desk, gave him her full attention. 'If you *must* have a blow-by-blow account of a very trivial and wholly commonplace incident, you may.' Her breasts swelled under the coffee-coloured silk shirt. 'Nancy Holmes noticed Daisy Podmore's bruised face and, naturally, asked her what had happened. Daisy wouldn't tell her – she was afraid of getting into trouble with Matron for not having told her already – so there was a little argument. Alice Derringer, the girl you saw in Matron's room last night, took it upon herself to intervene, and told Nancy to mind her own business and go away. Or rather,' she added, a little smile playing with the corners of her mouth, 'she told her to keep her "fucking ugly snout" out of other people's busines, and to "piss off". I'm afraid the girls can match their less privileged peers obscenity for obscenity when the mood takes them.'

'And where does Torrance fit in?'

Angling her arms to display her body more temptingly, she said, 'She was very misguided in asking Alice, in full view of the school, to help with evening stables last night. Alice can be wayward and, like Torrance, she's arrogant. She felt sufficiently privileged to insult Nancy without fear of comeback.' She stared at him. 'Sadly, Alice is also weak and given to hysteria, so please bear that in mind when you talk to her.'

'Have you punished her?'

'Naturally. I put the horses out of bounds.'

'For how long?'

'For as long as I think necessary.'

'In the current climate, wouldn't it be sensible to temper discipline? As I told Matron, Sukie's death has released very turbulent feelings.'

'And if I let those feelings prevail the girls will feel even more threatened.' Suddenly she abandoned her provocative pose and sat down. 'I was preparing a letter for the parents. Let me finish, then we'll talk.' She looked up, offering another smile. 'At the best of times I suffer from paper overload, as I'm sure you do.

I need to respond to the media, too. We've been inundated with enquiries from far and wide.'

He moved away from the window to the chair by her desk. 'I would most strongly advise you to direct all such enquiries to our headquarters.'

'I'm perfectly capable of making a simple, reassuring statement, if only to say you and your team are very much in control of the situation.'

Her nerve was admirable, he thought, but her parrying was intensely tiresome. 'The media has a very, very sharp nose for scandal and *you*, it seems, have a lot to hide. Why didn't you tell me about Sukie and Imogen Oliver?'

Her face was unreadable. 'Yes, I should have done,' she admitted quietly. 'I'm sorry.'

'Then why didn't you? You must have known we'd find out.'

Chin on hand, she gazed at him for some time, before saying, 'That accident was indescribably traumatic for both those girls, but I don't believe it has any bearing on Sukie's death.' She paused and when she next spoke there seemed to be genuine emotion in her voice. 'Hester's forced marriage exacted a hellish price, of which her daughter paid the most. For six years I've watched her caught in the crossfire of the dreadful war of attrition her parents wage against each other. If Sukie thought she were pregnant, suicide would be her only option. Don't you realise she could see her whole future staring her in the face?'

'I believe she saw her killer staring her in the face,' he said bluntly. 'Your speculation about pregnancy is completely without foundation.'

'But, is it?' she countered. 'How can we possibly understand what was in her mind?' Frowning, she added, 'Matron shares my feelings and she is, if anything, better placed to recognise when a girl is troubled.'

Refusing to be sidetracked, he said coldly, 'Your *feelings*, Dr Scott, do not allow you to withhold information that may well prove vital to our investigation.'

'I fear that information could well *mislead* your investigation, Superintendent. Both girls were well on the way to a full coming to terms.'

'Are you sure about that?'

'No, I'm not sure. I've studied psychology enough to know there are no certainties in human behaviour, but one must still assume that people have the capacity to gain insight and to move on from the past.'

He was fast losing patience. 'Has it not occurred to you that someone might have decided to avenge Imogen?'

'All anyone knows, apart from myself and my deputy, is that Imogen was involved in a car smash. We relied on natural reticence to stop people demanding the gory details, and we haven't been disappointed. And,' she went on forcefully, 'I trust you'll be equally sensitive with her.'

'You can trust me to do my job, Dr Scott.'

'I've no doubt I can,' she replied rather tartly. 'You seem inordinately efficient. I understand you've had the top-floor door alarms reactivated.'

'Had they been left alone in the first place,' he commented, getting to his feet, 'someone would have heard Sukie leave the building and she might still be alive.' About to make for the door, he stopped and, looking down on her bowed head, asked, 'Wasn't it naïve to think knowledge of the accident could be contained? Sooner or later, someone was bound to come across an old newspaper report.'

'Didn't Hester tell you? There *were* no reports. Her father made sure of that.'

4

Driving past the school gates on his way to interview Sean O'Connor, Jack saw that a media encampment had mushroomed overnight on the opposite side of the road. People with microphones, clipboards and video cameras milled around four mobile broadcasting vans spouting antennae and trailing cables that looked like spilled entrails, while newspaper reporters and photographers sat half out of various cars, ready to move at the first sign of a chink in the watching police defences.

By eight thirty he was knocking on the front door of a house in the long terrace that flanked the village street. The opposite terrace was broken by a Spar mini-market, chip shop, post office, newsagent's, craft gallery and two public houses. Standing back, he surveyed the double-glazed windows embellished with faux leading and snowy net curtains, then looked at the windowsills and the worn slate doorstep, all filthy with dust thrown up by passing traffic.

As the front door opened, a bus roared by in a cloud of diesel fumes, carrying its cargo of underprivileged local youth to school. He felt the ground shake under his feet.

The woman who stood in the doorway wore a fancy knit, short-sleeved black jumper and black skirt, and he thought she must be in her late forties. A thin gold chain bit into her ample neck like a garrotte and her hair looked unnaturally black.

'Mrs Avril O'Connor?' he asked, as the smell of frying bacon curled tantalisingly under his nose. 'Is Sean in?'

'What kept you?' Her voice was heavy with sarcasm. 'Been expecting your lot to come kicking the door in since that poor girl was pulled out of the water.'

'Why?'

'Because,' she said haughtily. Leaving him to close the door, she walked along the spotlessly clean hall towards the kitchen, yelling up the stairs, 'Sean? Cops!'

Jack followed her into the kitchen, looking around approvingly at further evidence of excellent housekeeping. 'Do I know you?' he asked, as she attended to the bacon.

'No.' She kept her back to him. 'But if you're wondering how *I* know *you're* a copper, go and look in the mirror. There's one in the front room.'

'That obvious, is it?'

'It's that obvious.' She nodded. 'D'you want a bacon sarnie and a mug of tea?'

'I shouldn't, really.'

'Why not? A bacon sarnie's not going to get you done for corruption.'

'I had a big breakfast and I'm on a permanent diet.'

She turned to look him over, her pursed lips inside the fat cheeks like a dimple in a big, soft peach. 'I'd say your diet's doing about as much for you as mine does for me, then. Is it worth it? That's what I keep asking myself. Is it worth the trouble and the misery?' Leaving the bacon to sizzle gently, she began buttering thick slices of white bread. Every time she reached inside the packet, the wrapping crackled, reminding him of his childhood when all sliced bread came in greaseproof.

'It's years since I saw bread wrapped like that,' he said.

'I get it from the shop across the road.' She smiled at him. 'Tastes as good as it looks. Our Sean won't eat any other sort.'

'Does Mr O'Connor like it, too?'

'I haven't had chance to ask him lately. He's been six feet under for the past five years.' She put three slices in a row, butter side up, reached for the frying pan and placed two handsome, well-browned rashers on each slice. 'Did you know,' she went on conversationally, topping and cutting the sandwiches, 'that the day our Sean got into trouble was the day we buried his dad?' Two sandwiches went on a sheet of white greaseproof, the other on the plate she pushed towards him. 'There. Eat that up quick before our Sean comes down, then nobody'll know, except you and me.' Her eyes twinkled.

She was washing dishes when her son came into the kitchen, and Jack was licking butter and bacon grease from his fingers.

The scent of deodorant or aftershave had preceded Sean down the stairs and he brought a cloud of it into the kitchen. 'Know you, don't I?' he commented, pouring himself a mug of tea. 'Saw you on telly when the CCTV went up in the city centre. You were saying how it'd stop vandals and muggers.' He looked up. 'Has it?'

'Let's say it's made them a bit easier to catch.'

'You should keep quiet about that,' Avril remarked. 'Else they'll start wearing Hallowe'en masks and balaclavas to stop you getting mugshots.' Glancing fondly at her son, she picked up a tea towel and began drying dishes, smiling when Jack caught her eye.

More used to hostility, if not outright aggression, from overprotective mothers, he felt completely wrong-footed by her easy amiability. Turning to Sean, he said, 'I'm surprised to find you still living at home. You're nearly twenty-six.'

'What's surprising about that?' Avril demanded. 'Young men often stay home these days until they get wed. Apart from the fact that they get their washing and ironing done for free, it saves money.'

'Dewi Prys lives with his mam and dad,' Sean pointed out, 'and he's older than me.'

'And I dare say he could afford to get himself a flat,' his mother added. 'I'm sure the police pay better wages than that Dr Skinflint.'

'Know Prys well, do you?'

'They both went to Ysgol Tryfan, didn't they?' she said. 'They meet up now and then, anyway.' Smiling again, she added, 'Dewi's made sure a few times our Sean got home in one piece.'

'So you still like a pint or two?' Jack remarked.

Sean grinned. 'You look like you do, as well.'

Jack searched for the signs of alcoholism that so coarsened John Melville's features, but saw only a bloom to Sean's face that was clearly a maternal legacy. He was lean and muscular from head to toe, his eyes a soft, dark blue, his hair jet-black, his ancestry unarguably Irish. Wondering if there were not more Irish in Wales than in Ireland, he asked, 'What time d'you usually go to work?'

'Nine,' Avril replied. 'That's why I was making up his lunch box. So if you want to ask him about the school, you'd best get on with it. Dr Skinflint'll only dock his wages if he's late.'

'I wanted to ask him how much contact he has with the girls,' Jack said, responding unconsciously to her.

Sean grinned again. 'That depends on whether the staff are looking. OK! OK!' he said, seeing Jack's expression. 'I was joking.'

Avril glared ferociously at her son. 'He's only here,' she told him, with a nod in Jack's direction, 'because that poor girl could've been murdered. And you've got form, so think twice before you open your mouth.' Turning her attention to Jack, she added, 'And as to whether he has much to do with the girls, he isn't even supposed to *talk* to them. Anyway, what with only the two of them working the grounds, he hasn't got time to spare for any shenanigans. But that's Dr Skinflint for you, isn't it? Get blood out of a stone, she would.'

Sean elaborated. 'We had enough on our hands *before* the horses arrived. Now, there's the arena to look after and the grazing to maintain, and that's still in very poor shape. It was only seeded out last summer and you don't get decent grass after just a few months.' Leaning back in his chair, he crossed his long legs. 'It doesn't help matters,' he concluded, 'that nobody apart from one of the sixth formers knows more about horses than you could write on the back of a stamp. The staff are hopeless.'

'Which sixth former?'

'Torrance Fuseli. Weird name, even though she's American.' Uncrossing his legs, he leaned forward to put his elbows on the table. 'I *do* talk to *her*, when there's nobody about to shop her.' He smiled. 'She's a real stunner, especially on horseback, but she doesn't do anything for me and most likely all I do for her is provide a bit of normal company.'

'Why's that?'

'Because he's already spoken for,' Avril said. 'And even if he wasn't, Torrance wouldn't try to get off with him because she's not one to flaunt herself in front of men. A lot of them do and some of those that don't would rather look elsewhere, if you get my drift.'

Jack gazed at her thoughtfully. 'Is *she* one of those who'd "rather look elsewhere", then?'

'Oh, really!' she exclaimed. 'Trust a copper to think like that. I just meant she doesn't behave like a hussy.'

'How come you know so much about her?'

'Because until Dr Skinflint sacked most of us a couple of years ago, I was one of the cleaners. There were twenty-odd of us doing the school and the classrooms, and now there's four, plus any old Tom, Dick and Harry that comes in with the contract people.'

'It's supposed to "make better economic sense",' Sean told him, perfectly imitating Freya Scott's cultured tones. 'It doesn't, though. They're more trouble than they're worth. They don't know the place, they've no idea what they're doing and, worst of all, they don't care.'

'Autumn last year,' his mother added, 'Dr Skinflint got probation to send a bunch of dead legs to prune the shrubs and they cut down some magnolia trees by mistake. Ruined them, they did. They won't grow again.'

Jack, thinking that Sean, doing his own community service, might have been among an earlier bunch of 'dead legs', asked, 'How did you get the job?'

'I got it for him,' Avril announced. 'He'd just finished at Glynllifon College when the old groundsman died – probably,' she remarked caustically, 'from overwork. The assistant got promoted, so I told Dr Skinflint about our Sean, she said "send him to see me", I did and she took him on. Pays a pittance, mind, even though he's qualified.'

'At least I'm doing what I want,' he said. 'There isn't much in my line of work around here.'

'There isn't much in any line of work,' Jack commented. He watched Sean's eyes. 'Did you know Sukie Melville, too?'

'We'd pass the time of day when she was out on her horse, but that's about it.' He shifted again in his seat. 'Look, even if the girls *try* and talk to me, I avoid them. Torrance got into trouble the other day because she was seen with me.'

'Did she?' Jack frowned. 'I mean, did she actually get into

trouble, or did she just get reminded about the rules?'

'Matron gave her an ear bashing, on Scott's orders, and told her if she didn't toe the line she wouldn't be allowed to stay on another year to try for Oxford, which would make her father livid. Last time, Scott threatened to send her horse away.'

'Are you *sure* you're not coming on to her? Because if you're not, the headmistress is overreacting, to say the least.'

'She just won't let those girls have any truck with the locals,' Avril broke in. 'Doesn't want them contaminated, does she? It was the same when I worked there. We weren't allowed to talk to them and if they tried to talk to us we were under orders to tell the teachers.' She took the kettle off the cooker, stuck the spout under the tap, then switched on the gas. 'She could easily take day girls, but she won't, in case they muck up her ideas about keeping her girls "pure". And I don't need to tell you,' she went on, rinsing out the teapot, 'that she wouldn't let a *Welsh* girl through the gates, no matter how much family money there was. Nor an Irish one, come to that, though there's been quite a few Scottish girls over the years. So that's why Torrance got the big stick waved in her face.'

'You must have known Sukie,' Jack said to her. 'What was she like?'

'Nice enough,' Avril replied. 'A bit flighty and not very bright, in my opinion, but no harm in her.' She sat down at the table while the kettle boiled and folded her arms. Her skin was as pink and clean as a baby's.

'Did she have any particular friends?'

'The Oliver girl, the one who lost her leg, poor thing. They were closer than two peas in a pod. Went everywhere together and did everything together.' As she dredged her memory, her face creased into a frown. 'She looked up to young Torrance, as well. Mind you, a lot of them did. That must be how she got to be house captain – Torrance, I mean. The house captains get voted in by the girls. At least, they did when I worked there.'

'Why d'you say Sukie was flighty?' asked Jack.

'Well, you know. The way she came over.' She smiled. 'I found some dirty books under her mattress one day when I was changing the beds.'

'What did you do with them?'

'Put them back, of course. They were harmless enough. What?' she demanded, seeing the expression on his face. 'You think I should've snitched? If I had she'd have been held up to ridicule in front of the whole school.'

'I doubt that,' Jack said. 'Teenagers and mucky books go together. Dr Scott must know that.'

'She probably does,' Sean said, getting up as the kettle began to whine, 'but that wouldn't stop her making a meal of something.'

'Don't you get on with her?'

'I make a point of keeping out of her way, but it doesn't always work.' He brewed the tea and put the pot on the table, topping it with a cosy. 'She interferes. She messes with everything.'

'I don't see how she can interfere with the grounds,' Jack said.

'The job involves long-term planning and you're always at the mercy of the weather. At the moment we're up to our ears trying to catch up on ourselves after all last month's rain and before the next lot comes. On Tuesday Scott decided she wanted the field mown where the marquee goes up on Open Day, which isn't for another three weeks. I told her the grass would've grown again by then, but she said if I didn't do it there and then, I'd be looking for another job.'

'She actually said that, did she?'

Sean smiled crookedly. 'What she *actually* said wasn't what you expect from any lady and I wouldn't repeat it in front of Mam.'

Avril patted his arm. Her eyes looked moist.

Looking from mother to son, Jack asked, 'What do you and Torrance discuss? It must be important if she's willing to risk getting into bother.'

He shrugged. 'The horses, mostly. The state of the grazing. Things like that.'

'Does she talk about the school?' Jack persisted. 'And what goes on there?'

Sean's eyes flickered and his sudden unease was almost palpable.

Avril grabbed his arm. 'If you know something you'd better

tell,' she ordered. 'You can't afford to get mixed up in other folks' troubles. Not when there's been a death.'

'I'd only be causing trouble for Torrance.'

'If you *don't* talk,' Jack pointed out, 'you'll cause a lot more for yourself. And for your mother,' he added, playing on the relationship. 'Dr Scott won't know, I promise.'

'What's a copper's promise worth, though?' Sean asked wryly. He stared into Jack's face for several moments, before letting out his breath in a long sigh. 'What the hell! You've probably sussed her out already.'

'Who?'

'Viv Wade in the sixth form. She's a user and Scott knows all about it but she won't lift a finger to help her.' He paused, mouth tight. 'Or try to stop her. Torrance asked me to find out where Viv's getting the stuff from so she could force Scott's hand. You know? Do something about it, or we'd tell the cops she was deliberately covering up a criminal offence.'

'*We'd* tell the cops?'

Sean nodded. 'I said I'd back her up. Go with her to Scott or the cops. Whatever.'

'I see.' Jack watched Avril look at her son as if he had slain a dragon.

'When Viv went out, Torrance let me know,' Sean went on. 'So I could follow her.'

Jack stopped him. 'How did Torrance let you know?'

'She's got a mobile, of course. So has Viv. That's how she orders her taxis. They pick her up near one of the wicket gates on the Treborth Road side.'

'I see,' Jack said once more. 'Then what?'

'Usually she does a few pubs, but doesn't speak to anybody, then gets a taxi back. But last Tuesday week, after she'd done the rounds, she walked up High Street and sat on a bench outside the cathedral. Ten minutes or so later this car arrived, she got in and they drove off.'

'Did you follow?'

'I couldn't, could I? I'd parked behind Boots.'

'What make of car was it?'

'A green Astra,' Sean told him. 'It definitely wasn't a taxi.'

'It may be a minicab,' Jack pointed out, 'or just a friend's car.'

'Well, I've got the number, so you'll be able to find out, won't you?'

'Indeed, yes.' Jack gazed at him. 'Do you think Vivienne noticed you?'

'She's seen me a couple of times, but we just acted like it was a normal outing.'

'We?'

'Me and Paula, my fiancée. I'm hardly likely to tail some schoolgirl round town at night on my own, am I?'

'Right,' Jack said. 'I'll have that car registration off you and just for the record, where were you *this* Tuesday?'

Avril, her face stony, gave her son no chance to reply. 'He was here, all evening, apart from when he and Paula went across to the pub, and they were back by nine. Paula wanted to go to bed early because she had to be up for the early train to London.'

'She lives in Porthmadog,' Sean added, 'so she always sleeps over when she's going to London. I drive her to Bangor station.'

'Why does she go to London?' Jack asked.

'To get to Heathrow,' Avril said. 'She's cabin crew on the air liners and she's just gone off to New Zealand. So if you want to talk to her, as I've no doubt you will, you'll have to wait.'

5

When Jack stopped the car for the school gates to be opened, flashbulbs began popping in his eyes. He growled at the hungry faces swarming around him, then accelerated up the drive, reaching the forecourt in time to see McKenna leave the mobile incident room. He slammed the car door and waited, rubbing his forehead. His skull felt tight, the portent of a thunderous headache.

'Eifion Roberts called not long after you went out,' McKenna said, stopping by the car. 'Hester Melville turned up at the mortuary wanting to see Sukie. When he told her she couldn't, because he was still doing the autopsy, she collapsed.'

'Shit!'

'He rang again about ten minutes ago to say Hester's being kept in hospital, at least overnight. Meanwhile, her lush of a husband knows nothing about the whole sorry mess. He was still in bed when Eifion first called the hotel and now he's gone off somewhere.' His mouth twisted. 'Probably to find some drink.'

'It wouldn't hurt you to be a bit more charitable,' Jack commented. 'I'd be doing more than hitting the bottle if it was one of my girls. I'd be suicidal.'

'Maybe so, but you wouldn't leave your wife in the lurch,' McKenna said. 'That's why Melville doesn't warrant sympathy. At a time like this, they should be together.'

'It doesn't work like that.' Jack sighed. 'Times like this show up a relationship in its true colours and I reckon the Melvilles can't stand the sight of each other.' He paused, before asking, 'Is Eifion any further forward?'

'He's found a contusion at the base of the skull consistent with a blow, but he's not sure how old it is.'

'She hadn't fallen off her horse recently.'

'No, but she could have banged her head plenty of other ways. In the gym, for instance.' McKenna took out his cigarettes. 'She seems to have been prone to getting knocked about. There's a lot of subcutaneous bruising to the torso, thighs and buttocks, most of it probably ante-mortem.'

'I wonder if the killer actually *knew* immersion in water would virtually wreck the evidence?'

'Perhaps they simply thought that once a body went into the Strait, it never came out,' McKenna said. 'At least, not as a recognisable whole. If there *was* a killer, that is,' he added, blowing smoke towards the bright-blue sky. 'How did you fare with Sean O'Connor?'

'I think,' Jack replied thoughtfully, 'that it might be a good idea to talk to him when his mother isn't there to answer for him. They're quite a double act. She alibis him for Tuesday evening, along with his fiancée, who left on Wednesday for New Zealand, so she's probably still in the ether somewhere over the Pacific Ocean.' Scraping his shoe on the ground, he went on, 'Pity Dewi can't add his weight this time. Apparently, it's not unknown for him to make sure Sean gets home safe to Mam when he's in his cups. Still, that's Dewi's way with the locals, isn't it? He doesn't see them in black or white, just varying shades of grey.'

'Sean's got a reputation for honesty and hard graft,' McKenna pointed out, 'even among our own brethren. One adolescent kick over the traces doesn't bespeak a criminal.'

'I'm not saying it does and I'm not saying his mother's covering for him,' Jack admitted. 'The thing is, Sean's been conspiring with Torrance to find out where Vivienne Wade gets her dope. Now I'm sure his mother knew nothing about it, so I was just wondering what else he hasn't told her.'

'Then get Dewi to ask him,' McKenna replied.

6

The previous night, in the sixth-form common room, Ainsley
Chapman had made McKenna think of a new blade of grass
springing from the earth, but now, seeing her for the first time
at close quarters, she brought winter to mind. Clad in a white
shirt, a long, dark-brown skirt and matching waistcoat, her
skinny legs weighed down by clumpy black shoes, she looked
spare and sombre, like a denuded branch, and exhausted, as the
year would be come December. They sat face to face by the
window of the visitors' room and, although she was in the eye
of the brilliant morning sun, her skin was ghostly pale. Suffused
by the light, the downy growth on her cheeks and forearms had
the effect of a halo. 'Did you not sleep very well, Miss
Chapman?' he asked.

'I didn't get to my room until much later than usual and there
was some reading I had to do.'

'Aren't your exams over?' He smiled. 'Congratulations, by
the way. I hear you've won a Cambridge exhibition. You must
be very pleased.'

Without a trace of pride or pleasure in her voice or on her
face, she said, 'Thank you. I am.'

'So,' he went on, 'why are you still swotting?'

Her forehead creased and her hands clenched and unclenched
with a life of their own. 'Oh, I can't rest on my laurels,' she said
breathily, jerking her head. '*Getting* a place is one thing.
Keeping it is an entirely different matter.' Then she clasped her
hands together and leaned forward to peer at him. 'When I go
up, I'll be competing with the best brains of my generation. I
can't relax for a moment.'

'You'll drive yourself into the ground if you don't.'

She hesitated briefly before responding. 'Dr Scott says we must learn to cope with stress and competition.' She mumbled to herself, as if making sure she were correctly relaying thoughts and words that were not her own. 'Mathematics is different from other subjects. One must stay constantly up to date but, more important, one's *mind* must keep the keenest edge.'

'Don't you take part in any sports?'

'Oh, yes.' She nodded stiffly. 'The head girl must be an all-rounder. I captain the tennis and lacrosse teams.'

'Do you compete with other schools?'

'Yes.'

'Where?'

'Schools like ours in England and Scotland.'

'Not Wales?' he asked.

'Is there such a one?' She looked utterly perplexed. 'I don't know of it.'

Trying to foster some enthusiasm, he smiled. 'Tell me, then, what does being head girl actually entail?'

Her eyes closed like traps, then opened wide and her brittle tension was alarming. She jerked scrawny shoulders. 'Well, you know . . .' Her voice was reedy, her eyes glittering with the light of panic.

'As head girl,' he went on quietly, 'your insights could be of considerable help. So what can you tell me about Sukie?'

Swallowing hard, Ainsley shook her head once more. 'I didn't really know her.'

'She wasn't one of your special friends?'

'No.'

'Several people have said she was very attached to Torrance.'

'Yes.'

'Were they actually friends?'

'Torrance taught her to ride.'

'And?' She simply stared and he added, 'How did that come about?'

'Sukie asked her to.' She half moved from the chair. 'Can I go now? I've got a maths class in fifteen minutes.'

'You can leave when you've answered my questions, Miss Chapman. Put your mind to that and you'll make your class.'

He tried another smile, but that too fell on stony ground. 'You girls live cheek by jowl,' he carried on patiently, 'so you'd have been bound to hear any rumours about Sukie's being pregnant. *Did* you hear any?'

'Dr Scott says she must have been. That's why she killed herself.'

'Dr Scott is saying that *now*,' he stressed. '*After* the event. Was anything said beforehand? Did Sukie appear upset or worried?'

She made an enormous effort to concentrate. 'I assume,' she began, 'she wouldn't want breakfast if she had morning sickness.' Then, frowning, she said, 'But I know nothing about that. The girls who keep horses don't breakfast with the rest of the school. They eat in the kitchen after morning stables.' She looked up at him. 'Fat Sally would know.'

'Fat Sally?'

Startlingly, she giggled, then clapped a hand to her mouth like a child. 'You know!' she said, between her fingers. 'The head cook.'

'That's not very gracious.'

'But she *is* fat!' Ainsley protested. 'She's absolutely gross! She eats too much. Dr Scott should force her to diet. She should tell her to lose at least eight stone if she wants to keep her job.'

'I think that would be outrageous.'

'I disagree.' Her nose literally in the air, she crossed her legs, the left dangling over the right. Hardly any muscle shaped her calves. 'Someone as fat as she is bad for the school's image.' Shuddering delicately, she went on, 'She's like those obese and ugly slum women one sees in Bangor, who live on state welfare, breeding like rabbits and draining the economy.' Her face became suddenly animated. 'Do you realise that the simple expedient of compulsory sterilisation for such women – and, of course, for the children they've already produced – would largely resolve the problem of the underclass within a generation?'

He gazed at her wonderingly. 'You study eugenics?'

'Dr Scott and a select few of us debate the issue,' she told him. 'Behind closed doors, of course. People can be so silly and sensitive, can't they?'

'Not necessarily,' he said. 'Eugenics have a very dirty reputation. Do you know why?'

'Naturally, Dr Scott has explained how the subject is always linked deliberately and emotively to Nazi Germany.' Dismissively, she flapped her thin pale fingers. 'It is *so* irrational! People must be made to accept that uncontrolled and indiscriminate breeding enfeebles the genetic pool.'

'As a matter of interest,' he asked, 'if Sukie had been pregnant, how would your preferred order deal with it?'

She turned her dead eyes full on him. 'I don't quite understand.'

Returning that empty stare, he asked himself if she were capable of attaching ideas to consequences. 'What would be done about it?'

'I imagine Dr Scott and Lady Hester would arrange an abortion.' She paused. 'Now, of course,' she went on, with utter callousness, 'there's no need.' Impervious to the flash of anger he was unable to hide, she glanced at her watch. 'I can only spare you a few more minutes. Was there anything else?'

He could almost hear the echo of Freya's voice, and see her hands shaping this girl. 'You haven't told me whether there were rumours about Sukie.'

'There were whispers,' she admitted with another shrug.

'About pregnancy?'

'I don't know.'

'What else could they concern?'

'The break with Imogen Oliver. They'd been best friends for years, but they wouldn't even talk to each other.' She squirmed in the seat, control beginning to desert her. 'As nobody knew why, the rumours became more and more – well – silly.'

'How? What was said?'

Studiously, she averted her eyes. '*You* know.'

'No, I don't!' he snapped. 'You're the one with her finger on the school's pulse.'

'Am I?' Once again that weird light flickered in her eyes. Convulsively, she twisted her hands together, staring at her watch. 'I must *go*!' She uncrossed her legs, ready to rise.

'I haven't finished with you yet,' he said sharply.

Ignoring him, she shot from the chair and ran for the door.

127

By the time he reached the corridor she had disappeared. Furious with her, he was on the verge of pursuit when Justine Salomon, hands in pockets, sauntered into view from the lobby.

'Have you seen Ainsley?' he demanded.

'Indeed, yes,' she said. 'In floods of tears and going like the proverbial bat out of hell towards the classroom block.'

He swore under his breath.

'She'll be fine once she has her head stuck in a book,' Justine added, 'but if you prefer to make sure, the head's secretary can telephone for you.' She indicated the room next to Freya's study and, as he was about to knock on the door, said, 'I'm free until after morning break. Shall I wait?'

'Go to the visitors' room. I won't be long.'

With narrowed eyes and pinched lips, the secretary heard him out, then spoke to someone in the classroom block. 'Fortunately, Superintendent,' she reported, 'no harm was done *this* time. However, Dr Scott does not feel it appropriate for our girls to be subjected to intensive police questioning without support from the staff.' She spoke slowly, clearly and correctly, as if he were a half-witted foreigner incapable of understanding the vernacular.

'And where *is* Dr Scott?' he asked, biting his tongue on a more trenchant response.

'She is engaged.'

'When she becomes *dis*engaged, tell her to come to the visitors' room.' Ignoring her lemony face, he added, 'Ainsley Chapman will be given one more opportunity to speak to me. If she refuses she'll be taken to the police station to be interviewed under caution, as will anyone else who fails to co-operate with my investigation.'

He returned to the visitors' room to find Justine leafing through a glossy magazine from the stack on a console table. 'Have you seen this?' she asked.

He sat down and, taking the magazine from her, began turning over page after page of photographs depicting the wedding of a raddled-looking middle-aged woman to a florid-faced man of advanced years and hideous countenance. In one picture, bride and groom were dwarfed by the baroque wedding cake into which both were sticking a long-bladed knife, while a mêlée of garishly dressed guests pressed around them, desperate to catch the camera's eye.

'Venetia,' she told him, pointing to the bride, 'is Charlotte Swann's mother and I *think* that's husband number five, although he could be number six. I expect even Charlotte's lost count.' Smiling, she replaced the magazine. 'She can ask if she ever gets to meet him. The last two stepfathers came and went almost without her knowing. Venetia does serial monogamy, you see. She beds many, but only weds the super-rich, who usually happen to be ugly. Her latest looks like a frog, doesn't he?' she commented. 'And I can't see a kiss from Venetia turning him into a prince.'

'Nor can I,' McKenna agreed, amused by her wit. 'Are you close to Charlotte?'

'No, but she has problems and sometimes she tells me about them. But then, she talks to anyone who'll listen.'

Slouching a little, she rested her elbows on the chair arms and linked her fingers, mood and manner worlds apart from the neurotic Ainsley's and, in contrast to the head girl's dour garb, she wore a finely tailored navy skirt barely skimming her knees, a gold and white striped shirt cinched at the waist with a leather belt, and elegant navy sandals.

'Why does Ainsley dress differently?' he asked.

'Dr Scott dreamed up that ghastly outfit to distinguish the head girl from the rest of us.' She grinned then. 'I suppose it's marginally better than a label round the neck.' Her well-modulated voice, almost perfect colloquial English and faint, attractive accent were quite beguiling and he suddenly saw her as one of those rare people whose presence could make others feel instantly happier.

He smiled at her. 'Where are you from?'

'A small village near Bonn in the Rhineland.' She returned his smile without a hint of coquetry. 'But we aren't German. To be frank, we don't know what we are. For centuries people have moved through the Low Countries to the Rhineland from all over Europe, so we could have originated anywhere.' Rearranging her long, well-rounded legs, she went on, 'But we're in good company. Beethoven's family came to Bonn from Malines in Belgium, but before that they may have migrated from Spain.' She thought for a moment. 'Perhaps it is the Spanish influences that make his music so insistent.'

'One of his friends was called Salomon,' he remarked. 'Johann Peter Salomon.'

'Yes, I know,' she said. 'He was born in the same house in Bonn where Beethoven later came into the world. He was a musician too. He died in London in 1815 after being thrown by a horse and he's buried in Westminster Abbey, and I know all about him,' she added with another smile. 'because my father would love to claim him as an ancestor, but unfortunately he can't find the proof.'

'What does your father do?'

'He's a translator. We're all fluent in French, German and English, and he also has Italian and Spanish, as well as Classical Greek, Latin and several of the ancient languages. I suppose he *should* be called a scholar.'

'And are you an only child?'

'Yes, like many of us, Ainsley included. Both her parents are high-flying academics, so she had a lot to live up to *before* Dr Scott decided to set her new standards. Unfortunately for Ainsley, she keeps moving the goalposts.' She paused, her forehead creased into a frown. 'I *try* to give Dr Scott the benefit of the doubt, but she's very capricious and extremely over-bearing. When she took away my house captaincy, for which I've yet to forgive her, she flatly refused to listen to any objections either from myself or the girls who had elected me.' Seeing his puzzlement she asked, 'Did you not know? She gave Imogen the captaincy of Lancaster after she lost her leg, saying it would provide her with a "positive focus". So, in simple terms, she was foisted on the house, whether she or they wanted it that way or not. To me, Dr Scott's reasoning was crassly insensitive.'

'How did Imogen feel?'

Justine shrugged. 'I don't know. These days she says little. She's a shadow of the person she was.' She bit her lower lip. 'But if *I* couldn't be annoyed about something as trivial as the house captaincy, what chance has Imogen to express the appalling anguish *she* must feel?' With another frown, she unlaced her fingers and folded her arms. 'Dr Scott constantly messes with the school's dynamics. She experiments, without caring that her actions have consequences, and she only got away with the house captaincy business because no one had the heart to cause Imogen more sorrow. She deliberately exploited our feelings for her own ends.'

'Tell me where Sukie fitted in,' he said.

'What's that saying in English?' she asked, eyes as bleak as snow. 'Happy as a pig in muck? That was Sukie, until early this year, and then she was so sad you wanted to weep for her.' She crossed her legs, swinging her right foot. 'I'd never taken much notice of her before. She coasted along without causing trouble and although she wasn't outstandingly good at anything, she didn't find it hard to keep up. I'm sorry I can't be more specific, but the only remarkable thing about her was her friendship with Imogen.' She moved again, uncrossing her legs, refolding her arms; talking of Sukie clearly disturbed her equilibrium. 'You may hear some very silly rumours,' she went on. 'When they stopped speaking to each other, some said it was an affair turned sour, which is absolute rubbish. You can sense such relationships and I'm convinced there was nothing like that between them.' Staring despondently at her hands, she fell silent.

'How much do you actually know about Imogen's accident?'

'Just that she'd been in a car smash. Dr Scott told us on the first day of spring term.'

'How was Sukie's absence explained?'

'A bad case of food poisoning.'

'Were you satisfied with those explanations?'

Again she shifted uncomfortably. 'They failed to account for the broken friendship that was so obvious once they both returned, or for the terrible grief that troubled them.' Miserably she went on, 'And because we didn't know we couldn't help them, and it's been very, very hard for us, too. You see, there's the same cross-section of personalities here as there would perhaps be in a small village and the same mix of problems. So Imogen's accident was an event . . .' Suddenly, she looked lost.

'Are you trying to say,' he asked quietly, 'that when a member of a small community is maimed it has implications for everyone?'

'Yes!' she exclaimed, nodding vehemently. 'But we had to behave as if nothing had happened. Dr Scott told us the bare facts, set in motion her plans for Imogen and expected us to fall in line, but people cannot be so easily directed. I think Imogen needed to dwell on the past until she was strong enough to leave it behind . . . as with her false leg. Do you understand? She couldn't use it until what was left of the old one had healed.' She began to weep, almost bewildered by the powerful backwash of emotion. '*She* hasn't had the chance to heal! When I first saw her after the accident the shock was like a punch in the guts. For Sukie, it must have been absolutely devastating. Imogen looked after her, she was her buffer and she made up for Sukie's bloody horrible home life, and then, suddenly, they can't even bear to be in the same room. I'm not surprised Sukie was pregnant,' she added wretchedly. 'She must have been desperate for affection. And now she's dead.'

'Whatever Dr Scott would like you to believe, Sukie wasn't pregnant,' he told her.

'No?' Tears coursing down her face, Justine looked up at him. 'But she was still desperately unhappy and I should have done something.' She choked back a sob. 'I'm ashamed of myself and my parents will be ashamed of me.'

'There's no call to blame yourself,' McKenna said gently.

'There is!' Reddish blotches discoloured her creamy complexion. 'I was taught never to turn a blind eye or take the line of least resistance, but I've done both.'

'Your own welfare must come first. Taking up someone else's cause can be risky.'

'That,' she retorted contemptuously, 'is how people always justify letting evil prosper.'

'You're not engaged here in fighting evil and you have no more than a civil duty towards your fellow pupils.'

'You're wrong!' He held his breath in anticipation of some dramatic disclosure. She stared at him, her face a picture of misery, but simply said, 'Some people are stronger than others, so the greater responsibility must fall on them.'

Watching her scrub away the tears with the heel of her hand he felt, for the first time since he had entered the school gates, something bordering on optimism, for he was sure that the bitter lessons Justine had learned at the Hermitage would one day help to mould her into a formidable force for good.

For a while he let her be, then put to her some of the other pressing questions that Sukie's death had raised, but she had little to tell him.

As she rose to go, Freya suddenly appeared at the door. 'Why have you been crying?' she demanded, scrutinising Justine's face.

'Because I'm upset,' Justine replied. 'I'm upset about Sukie and I'm upset about Imogen.'

'My dear.' Freya patted her arm. 'Everyone is upset. Tragically, Sukie is beyond our help, but we're doing everything in our power to guide Imogen through this dreadful period.'

Justine's face betrayed her doubt. 'I don't think I believe you.'

'As you said, Justine, you're upset.'

Freya turned away and, the exchange terminated, Justine had no choice but to leave, but more than once she glanced back as she walked away.

'She's a remarkable young woman,' McKenna said.

Standing ramrod straight by the window, Freya threw a stern shadow towards him. 'Many of my girls are remarkable, Superintendent, and although I can't remember the last time I saw Justine cry, she'll be able to cope with whatever you said to *make* her cry.' Her eyes glittered like the diamonds on her fingers. 'Ainsley, however, is delicate and highly strung, as is common with an intellect such as hers, and I'm *appalled* by what you did to her.' Her fury was like an entity. 'Now, I'm told you're threatening her with arrest.'

'It was Ainsley's own decision to absent herself from the interview,' he pointed out. 'She, like everyone else, is obliged to answer my questions.'

'She assures me she has nothing to tell you.'

This was an argument about territory, he told himself, and about power, and for the time being, it was his lot to appease. 'People rarely appreciate how much they know,' he said, 'so we tease it out, strand by strand. When I talk to her again, she can have someone with her, but not, for obvious reasons, a staff member or a fellow pupil.' Her shadow pointed like an accusing finger across the polished floor, and he felt incredibly wearied by this battle of wits and wills. 'Perhaps *you* should tell her why she can't be let off the hook,' he suggested. 'A word with Imogen might also be a good idea. I appreciate her fragility, but she was closer than anyone to Sukie and whatever happened last Christmas won't have wiped out a lifetime of friendship.'

'Why do you say "whatever happened"? You know what happened.'

He shrugged. 'A figure of speech, Dr Scott.'

As she moved away from the window her shadow seemed to impale him. 'Imogen's counselling is at a critical stage. Please bear that in mind and make sure you say nothing to disturb her very hard-won balance.' Then she stopped herself. 'I'm sorry! That sounded offensive. I'm afraid I've had a very trying morning, which the unexpected arrival of Alice Derringer's mother, all the way from Quebec, did nothing to help.'

'Like other parents, she must be very anxious.' He smiled at her, deliberately and disarmingly. 'I'm sure you set her mind at rest.'

When Freya smiled back the gesture transformed her from martinet to minx. 'I didn't, as a matter of fact. She wants to see *you*. Our Martha never deals with the monkey when she can collar the organ grinder just as easily.'

7

Torrance's first lesson of the morning was a double period of chemistry. Her mood, like the chemicals she handled, was unstable and unpredictable, veering from anger about the unjust way Dr Scott had blamed her for the upset at breakfast to an ominous uncertainty about Alice, for although Torrance knew Alice was good with animals, and sensible and efficient, she knew little else about her. She might well be recklessly arrogant, as the headmistress insisted, and perhaps, Torrance thought despondently, that explained why Alice was now deliberately and pointedly ignoring her. Or possibly, she argued with herself, Alice had been persuaded that any association with her would only lead to trouble.

At any other time Torrance would have faced Alice and demanded an answer, but suddenly even something simple and reasonable appeared hugely daunting, set about with ambiguity and riddled with dangerous possibilities, and with an appalling sense of shock she realised that the confident, optimistic person she had always believed herself to be no longer seemed to exist. She felt terribly insecure and terribly threatened. When she dropped a retort holding nitric acid and merely watched the smoke rise as the acid burned into the wooden bench, she realised she also felt frighteningly helpless.

She downed tools and left the laboratory quite some time before break. Emerging from the classroom block into a brilliant day as yet unmarred by rain clouds massing behind the distant mountain peaks, she strode off, head down, scuffing gravel. Dewi, a passenger in one of the security vans, saw her as she crossed the forecourt and the policeman on duty outside the main block nodded to her. Another policeman, posted at the second-floor fire exit, also nodded as she opened her bedroom door. Within five minutes she was back out, booted and breeched, hair coiled inside a snood, hard hat swinging from her fingers, wearing a white T-shirt with a horse's head printed on the front.

When she reached the paddock she found Tonto and Purdey grazing muzzle to muzzle, well away from the crabby skewbald mare that dominated the herd, and she leaned on the fence for quite some time observing the ebb and flow of their silent interactions. Briefly Tonto lifted his head to acknowledge her presence, then returned to pulling at the thin grass. Hoping the grazing in the adjoining field would be fit by the autumn, Torrance went to the tack room for a leading rein and, slipping through the gate, approached Purdey. The little mare stood quietly as she clipped the rein to the head collar and followed Torrance amenably into the yard. To handle, she was as docile as a rabbit; it was only under saddle that she showed her true colours, when her fine breeding and outstanding speed turned her into a handful that had often proved too much for Sukie's limited capabilities.

'Poor baby,' Torrance said softly, stroking her neck. 'What'll happen to you now?' she wondered, imagining the horrors that might befall an unwanted horse. As she buckled up the girth, it occurred to her that there was nothing to prevent her from buying Purdey. She vaulted gently into the saddle, resolving to approach the Melvilles at the earliest opportunity.

She took Tonto to the foreshore when the tide was out, and let him gallop to his heart's content up and down the mile or so of safe sand. At other times they went into the woods, going round and round the endlessly interweaving tracks. He seemed to find the arena, large as it was, claustrophobic and had several times decamped by taking a flying leap over the fence, so she schooled him now on the rides.

Purdey, in contrast, loved the disciplined environment of the arena. Usually Torrance would ride her through the woods for a while to let her limber up, then head for the arena, but today she went up the tarmac path towards the school's main block. Daisy's nasty story about Sukie's ghost had spread through the school like wildfire after Grace screamed in the night and although she had convinced herself it could only *be* a story, Torrance still dreaded encountering a ghastly, dripping figure in the strange green gloaming that washed through the trees.

Knowing Purdey would sense her mood, she made a superhuman effort to force the thoughts away. As she passed him, she gathered another nod from the dutiful policeman and then, looking neither to right nor left, she squeezed Purdey into a trot, listening intently to the rhythm of the hoof beats on the hard ground.

8

After Freya introduced him to Martha Rathbone, McKenna waited until the headmistress had closed the study door behind her, with something of a thud, before saying, 'Shall we find somewhere more private? There's a nice pub down the road.' He steered her out of the school, slowing his pace so that she could keep up with him, for she limped heavily. From somewhere near at hand but out of sight, he could hear the regular clip-clop of hooves.

'Could we go in your car?' she asked. 'I'm so tired I'm not even sure which day it is.'

He had parked his car, a sapphire-blue Jaguar, under the trees and its bodywork was spattered with pollen. 'How did you get here?' he asked, gunning the engine and turning in a wide circle to face the drive.

'I hired a car at Manchester airport. My chauffeur's on holiday because I wasn't planning to return to Britain until the end of term.'

Once the guardian police moved out of the way, he drove out through the gates. The photographers and reporters craned forward to peer through the car windows, then backed away, faces dull with disappointment.

'I don't think they've recognised me,' Martha remarked. 'Thank heavens for small mercies, eh?'

He was not surprised. She bore hardly any resemblance to the newspaper photographs he had occasionally seen. In an old suede jacket, denim jeans and cotton shirt, she looked homely and ordinary, distinguished only by the fine, clear eyes and obstinate mouth Alice had inherited. Curly brown hair flopped around a lined, unmade-up face and even her voice lacked any pretension.

'I noticed you limp,' he commented.

'I'm rheumatic,' she said. 'It runs in the family. So far, it hasn't caught up with Alice, but she's got her own problems. Asthma can be very nasty.' Surreptitiously, he looked at her fingers, devoid of rings and as gnarled as exposed tree roots. 'We're not from very good stock, I'm afraid,' she went on. 'Had we been animals, we'd have been put down at birth.'

He was further surprised when the landlord at the pub greeted her warmly.

She asked for coffee and biscuits, then followed McKenna to a table by one of the small, deep-set windows. 'I bring Alice quite often,' she explained, draping her jacket over a chair back. 'She likes to have lunch here, much to Freya's disgust, I may add.'

'Alice must find ordinary experiences hard to come by. A pub lunch can only be good for her.'

'I only wish there could be more of them. Our way of life is totally unnatural.' She nibbled a biscuit, dropping crumbs on the table.

'The Hermitage is full of girls in a similar position.'

'And look at them!' she exclaimed. Scooping up the crumbs and dusting her hands over the ashtray, she added, 'They're no more than fodder for Freya's crude psychological experiments. If Alice weren't relatively settled, I'd send her somewhere else, but that said, to my mind one boarding school is very like another. There's too much of a marketplace mentality about them these days, as if they're supplying a product rather than helping children to grow into useful citizens.' Suddenly she grinned. 'Freya's quite Jesuitical in her approach, you know. "Give me the child, and I will give you the man", except that she gives you the woman, moulded as much as possible in her own image.' Her face clouded. 'I'm sorry. I shouldn't talk about her like this.'

'Her philosophies must go down well with most parents,' he ventured, lighting his fourth cigarette of the day. 'She's got what you might call a full order book.'

She nodded. 'Yes, just like a double-glazing salesman with a superb sales pitch. She mainly targets the nouveau riche, playing on elitism and good old English snobbery, forever dropping names and titles and past successes, and people buy into the image. They believe the school *must* be good because the fees are so high, the same way they think a swanky dress shop won't sell you tat. And yes,' she added, pre-empting comment, 'I *did* fall for it. My second husband was the one who opened my eyes. Five minutes with Freya was enough to convince him she is, as he put it, "full of shit", if you'll excuse the language.'

'I'll bear that in mind,' he said, nonplussed.

'Oh, I'm sorry! You've got far more important things to do than listen to this.' She picked up her cup and took a large gulp. 'Freya did her best to convince me Sukie Melville killed herself, but if that were the case the school wouldn't be crawling with police. Do you actually know how she died?'

'Not yet.'

'I see.' She chose another biscuit, which she broke into four neat pieces. 'On the way back, I worked myself into a near frenzy thinking about homicidal maniacs and kidnappers.' Worry was drawing more lines on her face. 'I don't bother over-much about my own security, but Alice has been surrounded by what I call the negative trappings of extreme wealth since she first drew breath, simply because the world's full of lunatics and she's an obvious kidnap target. As she well knows,' she added ruefully. 'A couple of years ago she started fantasising about being kidnapped and deprived of an ear or thumb to be enclosed with the ransom note I'd get. Naturally, Freya wanted to consult a psychiatrist. Oh, do excuse me!' She yawned then, covering her mouth with those crooked fingers. 'Anyway, I flatly refused. I suspect it was primarily a plea for my attention, although Alice claimed she was just bored.'

'How did Dr Scott know? Children usually keep their imaginary lives to themselves.'

'Alice made the mistake of sharing hers with that horrible Daisy Podmore, who, allegedly, is her best friend. I've never liked Daisy and I liked her even less after she went sneaking to Freya "for Alice's own good", which is always the rationale of someone out to cause trouble. When her little bomb turned out to be a damp squib, she was very put out.'

'Why don't you like Daisy?'

'Have you met her?'

'I've seen her,' he said, 'but not spoken to her.'

'You'll get a shock when you do, then,' Martha said. 'She's got the most awful lisp I've ever heard, despite years of speech therapy. It's so bad she almost reinvents pronunciation and, worse still, you feel virtually compelled to copy her.' She met his eyes. 'Yes, I know it's not her fault, but I'm sorry to say I find her utterly repellent. It's nothing I can put my finger on, it's just there. Her parents are a total nightmare as well. Her mother's a braying tart and her father's an absolute slimeball. I say that even though I've only met them once and then only briefly, but with some people you know what they are as soon as you set eyes on them.'

'How did Alice react to Daisy's betrayal?'

'She was really hurt. I told her to ditch Daisy and either make do with Grace Blackwell, who hangs around with them at times, or simply keep to her own company, but that caused an argument. As she pointed out, I'm not famous for my ability to choose wisely.'

'How many times have you been married?' he asked, thinking of Charlotte Swann's fragmented background.

'Twice,' Martha replied. 'I was thirty-two the first time and the marriage was dead in the water before Alice arrived three years later. I made the not unusual mistake of hoping a child would bind us together. Alice was eleven when I remarried and that marriage lasted two years.' She fiddled with her cup. 'I think there's a sort of blind spot in my character and I'm afraid Alice has it too, if Daisy's anything to go by.' After a long pause she said, 'To be honest, I'm not interested in being married. Alice is my whole life. I've never even wanted another child.'

'Are you an only child, too?'

'I had an older brother called Danny.' She gazed at him, a distant look in her eyes. 'Because of him, I tried not to love Alice too much, but it wasn't possible.' Taking a deep breath she went on, 'Until Grandad died when I was ten, we lived a perfectly unremarkable life. My father was an accountant, Mother stayed at home, and Grandad had a small but absolutely rock-solid precision tool and instrument business. After he died the business went to my mother, and she discovered this wonderful flair for innovation and development. Everything just took off.' She picked up another biscuit. 'Danny wanted to go into the business once he'd taken his degree, but he died. He caught meningitis and died in the space of a few hours, so that's really why I've so little patience with the trappings of security. Disease is a much greater hazard than a kidnapper or psychopath.'

'How old were you?'

'Sixteen. I dreamt about him the other night, you know, and I haven't done that since just before my father's last illness.' She sighed. 'But they do say that to dream of the dead is a sign of trouble with the living.'

'Is your mother still alive?' he asked.

She shook her head. 'That's why I'm awash with money, and why Alice will be one day.' Munching the biscuit, she fell silent. 'It's odd,' she went on after a while, 'how many Hermitage girls stand to inherit through their mothers. Apart from Alice, there's a French girl whose mother owns half Marseilles, I shouldn't wonder, a German girl who looks like a carthorse whose mother owns an enormous sausage factory – what else? – and the ghastly Daisy will get some fine Home Counties properties, not to mention a couple of dozen very profitable retail outlets when her mother goes to heaven.' She peered at him, questioningly. '*Should* I do something about extra security?'

'We'll be maintaining a strong police presence at the school, day and night, for the duration, and its very isolation helps us to ring fence the place.' He chose another biscuit, eating instead of smoking. 'However, we can't ignore the possibility of kidnap and as it's not an area where we have much expertise, our chief constable has asked for assistance. That, initially, will be an assessment of risk, based on intelligence.'

'I read somewhere,' Martha said, 'that murders are usually committed by someone very close to the victim.' She stared at him, face again webbed with anxiety. 'I don't know whether that makes me feel better or worse!'

9

Nona Lloyd, with some of her colleagues, was interviewing fifth formers in the library when the bell rang for morning break. The girls began to fidget immediately, several stood up, and as soon as one made for the door the rest, without a word to their interrogators, followed. They were just like Pavlov's dogs, she thought, sticking her pen down the spine of her notebook.

As she was walking down the corridor, Janet came up behind her. 'Any joy with your lot?' she asked.

'Not really,' Nona replied. 'How about you?'

'A few interesting odds and ends,' she said, turning into the lobby, 'but nothing that's likely to tell us who might have blood on their hands.' At the door she stopped. 'I was planning to escape for half an hour. Fancy a trip to the Antelope?'

'It would be nice to breathe some fresh air, wouldn't it?' Nona remarked. 'But shouldn't we ask Mr McKenna first?' Then she noticed the gap where his car had been. 'Oh, he must have gone out,' she added.

'And what he doesn't know won't hurt him,' Janet said lightly, leading the way to her own car.

Although she was a few years older than Janet and a married woman, Nona always felt inadequate in comparison, even if the comparison existed only in her own mind and her presumed shortcomings mostly related to matters over which she had never had any control. Janet owned a physical elegance quite uncommon in Welsh women and her face, when not in the throes of a mood, could be beautiful. Her voice was unusually attractive too, Nona thought, as she listened to her talking about the morning's interviews with the fourth formers.

The Antelope was a bare five minutes' drive from the school and, following Janet to the terrace overlooking Menai Bridge, Nona began to wonder how she could improve her own pitch and diction. For the first time since she had joined the police six years before, she also started to consider her future. Janet, as a fast-track graduate entrant, would forever be at least ten steps ahead and she would always be somewhat upper-crust, at least by local standards, but there was nothing to stop Nona bettering herself where she could. Rather than let envy corrode her will, she should let it be a spur.

'Coffee, tea or a cold drink?' Janet asked, preparing to go to the bar.

'Black tea, please.'

Watching her walk away, Nona realised that while the elegance was innate, the style could be borrowed and resolved to overhaul her own wardrobe at the first opportunity. Unlike Janet, she was condemned to wearing uniform at work, but it would take only a day in Chester's exclusive dress shops to transform her off-duty wear. *And* her bank balance, she reminded herself ruefully, as Janet returned with their drinks.

Janet lit a cigarette, hungrily pulling smoke into her lungs. 'This is the first I've had since breakfast,' she said, noticing the frown Nona was unable to hide. 'I need it.'

'I'm not preaching, but cigarettes really are lethal,' Nona said. 'My uncle lost one of his lungs to cancer and now they've found a shadow on the other. Why don't you try nicotine patches? They seem to be helping Mr McKenna to cut down.'

'Yes, I'd noticed he wasn't smoking so much,' Janet mused. 'That must be why he's more miserable and bad-tempered than usual.'

Nona shrugged. 'Better that than dead.'

'How do you know, anyway?' asked Janet. 'About the patches?'

'I saw the packet on his desk the other day.'

Janet grinned. 'He's probably got them stuck on every available inch of skin.'

'Well, there's not too much of that these days, is there? He's gone terribly scrawny-looking.'

'He's always been thin.'

'Yes, but not emaciated, like he is now.'

'Don't you think he's still attractive, though?'

'I suppose,' Nona said slowly.

'But then, if your husband's anything to go by, Mr McKenna's not your type, is he?'

Laughing, Nona said, 'When Mam first met Gwynfor she said he was built like a young bull.'

'And is he?' Janet asked roguishly.

'Janet, really!' Nona's face was bright pink. 'It's not like you to be crude.'

'Blame that hormone-crazed atmosphere at the school.'

'Those girls *are* a bit OTT, aren't they? I don't remember being quite so obsessed with sex at that age.' Nona thought for a moment. 'Then again, we went to school with boys, so that probably explains the difference.' After another pause she asked, 'Have they been quizzing *you* about boyfriends? They've tried it on me, even though I told them I was married.'

'In their circles I don't imagine being married stops people playing away from home,' Janet commented. 'Actually, they were more interested in Dewi's love life. Not a few of them blush even at the mention of his name, so he could no doubt have a new career as a bit of rough for the posh girls if he wanted to. So could Sean O'Connor, come to that.' She grinned again. 'And Mr McKenna's firmly fixed in Freya Scott's sights, whether he knows it or not. She was trying to find out from me earlier what makes him tick. I told her I'd let her know when I find out myself.'

'Have you heard anything about Sukie having a boyfriend?'

'I've heard a great deal about her supposed pregnancy,' Janet said, 'but not a word about who could have helped her to get into that condition. Grace Blackwell, for one, was wittering endlessly about the pregnancy, but said repeatedly that Sukie wasn't "like that" – in other words that she wasn't one for the boys. I was tempted to ask her if she thought there'd been another immaculate conception, which probably isn't the best remark to make to a vicar's daughter.'

'She's the one Bryn nabbed for wearing Sukie's old skirt, isn't she?' Nona asked.

Janet nodded. 'I think Bryn quite scared her. She's also

worried about the rest of the hand-me-downs she's got; she thought we were going to take them away. When I said not, Daisy started taunting her, saying she couldn't wear Sukie's clothes now in any case because next time Bryn smelled them on her he'd tear her to bits. So according to Daisy, Grace is back to wearing sackcloth and ashes.'

'Daisy's rather horrible, isn't she? She makes my skin crawl, even though I've barely passed the time of day with her.'

Janet stubbed out one cigarette and reached for another, saying, 'My last until after lunch. OK?' Then, she went on, 'I'm not sure Daisy *is* as nasty as she seems. Deep down, I think she's really unhappy and there could be much more to her relationship with Grace than appearances suggest.'

'Why d'you say that?'

'Well,' Janet began thoughtfully, 'as you'd expect, after Daisy's little outburst, Grace got very snivelly. Daisy said she was only blubbing for my benefit, because she was always the first to preach about "the truth hurting". So,' she added, with a slight shrug, 'I don't know quite what to make of either of them, particularly as I'd already sat through a diatribe from Grace on the various sins that abound at the Hermitage.'

'Sins?' Nona echoed. 'What kind of sins?'

'The kind *my* father, as a man of the cloth like Grace's father, is also inclined to condemn out of hand, even though they might only demonstrate the confusion and irrationality of the human spirit.'

Nona pressed for an answer. 'But what did she actually *say*?'

'She claims some girls get punished for nothing, yet others get away with murder – she actually said "murder". That led to a lecture on the inevitability of divine retribution, as interpreted by her father, and a further discourse on the issue of sacrifice, again by reference to her father and the sacrifices he has to make to keep her at the school. Some sort of religious trust pays part of the fees, but he has to make up the balance.'

'Well, then, nothing of what she says is unreasonable, is it?'

'I suppose not,' agreed Janet. 'I'm just not keen on the subtext, because I think she's sanctimonious and very envious. She had a lot to say about Sukie's grandparents and their bottomless purses while in the same breath listing what *she* has to do without, including music lessons, even though she's got a wonderful singing voice and leads the church choir at home.'

'You should've asked her if she was jealous of Sukie.'

'I did.' Janet blew a plume of smoke skywards. 'She admitted to being jealous of quite a lot of the girls at one time, before going through a process of resignation which has, she said, led to enlightenment. She now realises that an excess of worldly goods can corrupt the spirit; poverty, on the other hand, is positively uplifting.'

'I see what you mean about her being sanctimonious,' Nona remarked. 'But she sounds a shade pitiful, for all that. I'd defy most people not to go a bit peculiar when they're getting *other* people's wealth rammed down their throats day and night.'

'So would I,' Janet said. 'But I'll still have a look at that paper we've had on child killers to see if she fits the profile. Jealousy can be very, very corrosive.'

'But in her case it's too vague a motive,' Nona argued. 'Why pick on Sukie, and not one of the others?' She frowned. 'And isn't she a bit puny? She wouldn't have the strength. By the way,' she went on, lowering her voice conspiratorially, 'did you know some of our less sensitive male colleagues have opened a book on the killer? I hope Mr McKenna doesn't find out. He'll crucify them.'

'You're joking!' exclaimed Janet.

'I'm not.' Nona swallowed the dregs of her tea. 'And guess who's odds-on favourite at the moment.'

'I've no idea. Who?'

'Daisy.'

'Why?'

'Because she acts like a psycho, I suppose.'

'So do plenty of the others.'

'Yes, but Daisy's got that awful lisp, and you can't help thinking a flaw like that means there's something bad about a person.'

'What about Imogen, then?'

'She wasn't *born* that way. Anyway, think about it,' Nona urged. 'Daisy looks strong enough to dispatch a grown man.'

'Every girl I've spoken to so far has calluses on her hands, as a result of wielding tennis racquets and lacrosse sticks. When I first saw them I felt quite nostalgic, because I used to get them, too. Then I remembered what sports did for my muscles, as well, so, barring a few of the very young ones, I'd say they're *all* strong enough.'

'You're probably right,' Nona conceded, getting to her feet. She unhooked her holdall from the back of the chair, eyeing Janet's chic leather shoulder bag as she did so. 'So if anyone asks me about having a bet,' she went on, 'I'll tell them to put their money on a rank outsider. There are two hundred plus to choose from, without including the staff.' As they left the terrace, she tried surreptitiously to match Janet's long, easy strides, but it was hard, for although Janet was only a couple of inches taller, her legs seemed endless. 'Haven't you read that paper yet?' When Janet shook her head, she said, 'The theories are very interesting, but I'm not sure they hang together. Maybe they don't go deep enough.' Then she corrected herself. 'No, they go astray because they're based on the innocence of childhood when there's really no such thing.'

'You think not?' asked Janet, unlocking her car.

Nona slid into the passenger seat. 'People who commit murder as adults were just as capable when they were children,' she said. 'They don't suffer some great moral collapse on their eighteenth birthday. Quite frankly, I'm surprised *more* children don't kill, because they've had less exposure to socialisation processes.' As Janet turned out of the car park into Treborth Road she added reflectively, 'Mind you, the Hermitage girls get subjected to completely abnormal socialisation processes. In a way, they're actually *designed* to bring out the worst, so not only is everything going to be exaggerated, but nobody can escape.' She twisted round in her seat. '*We* couldn't wait to get out of there, could we? Why was that? What did we *actually* feel?'

'In a word,' Janet replied, 'threatened. At least, I did.'

'Me, too,' Nona told her. 'But not by anything specific. It's just a general feeling of menace, like thunder clouds that won't blow away. Not only that, I literally find it hard to breathe, although that might be because of the trees.'

'So, going on from that,' Janet mused, 'someone could feel *so* threatened that they're compelled to kill, even if they weren't in *real* danger.'

'Yes, but it would still spring from a recognisable motive,' Nona said. 'Like envy, for instance, or greed, or gain.'

'What about love, hate, and revenge?' suggested Janet. 'And what about just for kicks? That's *more* than likely in that place.'

'On the other hand,' Nona observed, as the school gates came into view, 'perhaps Sukie just got into a fight with someone and her death was completely unintended.'

'Tipping her into Menai Strait was far from accidental.'

'Not if the other person thought she was already dead and just panicked.'

When next Dewi saw Torrance she was inside the arena, leaning far out of the saddle to latch the gate.

The security guard beside him needed no persuasion to park for a while and pulled up on the grass beside the rough wooden fencing. 'Big, isn't it?' he commented, surveying the vast expanse of sand. A row of jumps was lined up on the far side.

'Horses tend to need plenty of room,' Dewi replied, with barely concealed sarcasm.

Torrance took Purdey through one circuit at the walk, then round again at the trot, before coaxing her into an elegant extended trot across the arena's diagonal. Once at the far corner, she set the mare cantering fluidly in figures of eight.

'Why does she keep looking at her watch?' the security guard asked, as Torrance and her mount thundered past at the gallop on the other side of the fence. The mare was snorting and kicking up sand, her neck dark with sweat.

Dewi thought for a moment, then took a wild guess. 'It's all to do with discipline,' he said. Hoping that was enough to cover his ignorance, he saved himself the bother of further invention by getting out of the van.

Torrance had stopped near the jumps. She dismounted, lashed the reins to the fence and began hauling the striped poles across the arena.

'D'you want some help?' he called.

'If you're offering,' she shouted back.

Leaving the guard to stare, he vaulted the fence and, under her instructions, moved uprights and dragged poles. She shifted the things as if they weighed next to nothing, he thought, ploughing ankle deep in the sand that had already filled his shoes. Ten minutes hefting left him puffing and ruddy-faced, while she still looked as fresh as a daisy. When she remounted he leaned against the fence, arms spread out, right leg crooked behind him, watching what was arguably poetry in motion.

Purdey owned the rare ability to adjust her stride to the distance between the jumps, and she took them effortlessly, flying over one after another with her ears well pricked. If I buy her, Torrance said to herself, setting her at the last line of fences, we could take up hurdling. The first, a four footer, disappeared underneath and the second, six inches higher, rushed towards them. The mare took off, forelegs tucked well under, hindlegs flowing. In mid-air, something happened. Torrance felt herself rocket skywards and the reins were torn from her hands. Then, in a jumble of sensations and colours, she plummeted to earth and the world went black.

Dewi saw her ejected from the saddle. He saw her tumble, seemingly in slow motion, to the ground. He watched her crash head first into one of the uprights, yet still remained by the fence, immobilised by shock. Only when Purdey skidded to a halt a foot from his nose did he recover his wits. Showing the whites of her eyes, the mare was trembling from head to foot and lathered with sweat. He picked up the ends of broken rein, knotted them around a fence post, then ran to Torrance, yelling over his shoulder to the guard.

She was in a heap by the shattered fence, a blue and white striped pole across her body, her left foot trapped in the stirrup iron and her right twisted sickeningly beneath her. He threw the pole to one side with the strength of Hercules and as he laid his finger on her neck, she let out a groan that sounded like the last breath expelled by the newly dead. There *was* a pulse, but it was very slow and her flesh was already growing clammy.

The shadow of the guard fell over him. 'I've called for an ambulance,' he said, kneeling down. 'Shouldn't we get her into the recovery position?' he urged.

'When I've checked her back.' Dewi was already kneading each vertebra. 'It seems OK,' he said at last, 'but that's not to say she hasn't broken her shoulders or ribs or pelvis. Let's turn her on her side. You hold her head and for God's sake, don't let it twist.'

Once she was rolled into position, the guard eased open her mouth and probed inside with his finger. 'Her airway's open,' he reported and at the same moment Torrance emitted another groan.

Surveying the tangle of boot and stirrup iron, Dewi said, 'We'd best leave her leg until the paramedics get here.' He touched her neck again. 'She's very cold. Have you got a blanket in the van?'

'There's my jacket. It's behind the seats.'

Running to and fro through the sand was, Dewi thought, like trying to run in a dream. He draped the jacket over Torrance, then held her wrist. Her pulse was still slow, but regular, and he could hear her breathing: deep, slow inhalations that lifted his leaden heart a fraction.

The guard was on his knees examining the saddle. 'Seen this?' he asked, holding up the girth. Two buckles and two snapped leather straps dangled from its end. 'You fasten the girth to these buckles and the buckles are stitched to the saddle under here.' Taking care not to nudge the saddle, he lifted the flap. 'Somebody's cut partway through the straps and left just enough to keep the girth in place until it was put under real pressure, like when the horse was jumping. This was no accident. In your book it was attempted murder.'

The blood-chilling howl of a siren brought people running from the school, but they simply milled around at a loss on the forecourt as the ambulance went from view behind the trees.

Red-faced and puffing, Matron set off in pursuit, but Freya stopped her.

'What's happened?' she demanded.

'I don't know!' Matron squawked.

Freya turned to the policeman by the door. 'Do *you* know?' she demanded, breathing in his face like a dragon.

'There's been an accident, ma'am,' he told her, listening with one ear to the exchange on his radio. 'A girl called Florence was thrown from her horse. Sergeant Prys is going with her to the hospital.' Freya opened her mouth to speak but he held up his hand to silence her. When the radio message finished, he said, 'Superintendent McKenna is on his way back as we speak. His orders are that no one is to attempt to leave the site and he wants everyone to assemble immediately in the refectory. And you need to get a vet here fast to check on the horse.'

II

Torrance's crashing fall was common knowledge almost before the ambulance had cleared the grounds. Accounts were embellished with each new telling and, quite deliberately, McKenna played his own part in intensifying the drama.

Standing on the refectory dais to address the whole school, he reminded them that one of their number was already dead, before saying, 'For the past three days, Torrance Fuseli has been exercising Sukie Melville's horse. Now she has had a terrible fall. If she lives – *if* – she could well be brain-damaged and crippled.' He paused, his gaze raking over the sea of faces below. Many of the younger girls were already weeping. 'Torrance's fall was no accident. Someone wilfully sabotaged the saddle, intending this to happen. That person,' he added, his words slow and measured, 'intended to kill her.'

Beside him on the dais Jack, still with a blinding headache, thought that McKenna was making scant impression in several quarters. Freya had been relegated to the floor of the refectory and the staff, obviously more intrigued by her sudden demotion, watched her constantly while whispering to each other. Among the girls he could detect boredom on many faces, as if one death and one attempted murder were of no consequence.

Charlotte had devoted half the morning to preparing for her interview with McKenna and in anticipation of the summons she skipped the lesson before break to rifle her wardrobe. Now, almost beside herself with disappointment and resentment, she remembered the agonies of indecision she had suffered before selecting the soft grey linen slacks and silvery-coloured silk vest she eventually donned, and the further dithering that preceded the choice of a light, floral scent to mist on neck and wrists. Only the jewellery presented no difficulties, for she had already decided to wear her newest diamond earrings and the matching bracelet. What an awful waste of her time, she thought angrily, watching McKenna's mouth open and close without hearing a word he said, and all over some silly horse and its stupid rider. Everyone knew Torrance rode like a demon, so she had only herself to blame for being injured. Then, wondering at last what that injury might entail, Charlotte began to sweat and tremble, for when Imogen had dragged her maimed and hideous body back to school after the accident, Charlotte had been violently sick. Since that time she would run in the other direction rather than face Imogen, but bloody images of twisted metal and mutilation nonetheless filled her head and the dread, dead clump of Imogen's false foot was never far from her ears. Although Matron gave her sleeping tablets to vanquish the nightmares, Charlotte soon discovered that the demons haunting her days were all the mightier for their enforced idleness during the hours of darkness. Oh, God, she beseeched, while McKenna droned on, if only Sukie's death could release her from their hold.

Sitting directly behind Charlotte, engulfed in her perfume, Imogen felt sick and was frantically casting around for a means of escape from the claustrophobic press of bodies. Should she struggle upright they would, she knew from experience, ostentatiously edge aside to let her hobble past and, in so doing, make her the focus of hundreds of pairs of eyes. Bile rose and fell in her throat, her guts heaved stormily and her leg hurt so brutally that she wanted to scream, as if her splintered bones were still rammed under the dashboard of the car or a butcher were smashing a cleaver relentlessly through her thigh. The pain was inconceivably vicious and, because it emanated from something that no longer existed, utterly ridiculous. Her leg was dead before it was severed from her body and, like other mysteriously dead flesh, it had gone first to the pathologist, and then to be reduced to smoke and ashes in the hospital incinerator. How could it *still* hurt?

She tried to listen to what McKenna was saying and wrestled

again with her attention when his dark-haired companion took up the lecture, but her mind was consumed with images of Torrance, the latest hostage to fortune, with both legs shattered, even now being set upon in the aseptic atmosphere of the operating theatre by masked men with knives and saws. She wanted to weep and howl and scream until the festering grief drained from her; instead, she must be stoical and sensible and philosophical, because Dr Scott – ignorant, insensitive, *cruel* Dr Scott – demanded the sacrifice of her feelings for the sake of her teachers and fellow pupils.

The accident was a defining experience that had acted upon Imogen's personality like an earthquake, causing destruction of seismic proportion and exposing unsuspected and terrifying fault lines in her parents and in herself. Albeit with something artificial and inadequate, her leg could be replaced, but the friendship with Sukie was annihilated and Imogen soon knew for which she would grieve most. The hope she had nursed of repairing that terrible rift perished on Wednesday morning when she learned Sukie was missing, for they had been too close for too long not to know, even after the accident, when the other was in peril.

Imogen's sob jolted Vivienne from her torpor. She glanced along the row, to see her rocking jerkily back and forth, the false leg rising of its own accord before thumping back to the floor. Heads turned, necks craned and faces mottled with embarrassment as others watched, but no one offered help. Angrily, Vivienne stood up and, bruising knees and treading on feet, pushed her way towards Imogen. She picked up the silver-topped cane from the floor under the bench, tucked it under her arm and, hefting Imogen upright, half dragged and half pulled her towards the doors, trampling many more toes as she went. With Imogen's arm slung about her shoulders, she walked her out of the refectory without a backward glance.

'Thanks,' Imogen muttered, while the lift creaked upwards. She knuckled her eyes, but the tears persisted.

'No problem,' Vivienne said, leaning against the handrail, ankles crossed. 'Charlotte's perfume was knocking me out, anyway.'

'Me, too.' Imogen tried a wan smile.

'Will McKenna send a posse after us, d'you think?'

'There's no need. He's got uniforms by the fire exits.'

'Has he really?' Vivienne said, as the lift ground to a stop. 'I've not been upstairs since breakfast. I thought they'd have gone.' She hauled back the two gates, then waited for Imogen to unlock her door, but her hands trembled so violently that the heavy iron key rattled out of the huge old mortise and fell to the floor.

It lay there, Vivienne thought, rather symbolically. With the cruellest clarity she remembered the day Dr Scott presented that key to Imogen to safeguard the painkillers she kept in her room. Another bloody consolation prize, she said to herself, as she bent to retrieve it.

'I'll make coffee.' She headed for the common room.

Mystified, Imogen looked after her. As she held a fixed impression of Charlotte as a vacuous but dangerous nincompoop, so did she of Vivienne as someone damned by her own weakness. Her friendliness was unexpected, but the sudden decisiveness she had shown in the refectory was remarkable.

The policeman at the fire exit rose when he saw Vivienne approaching. 'Shouldn't you be in the refectory, miss?'

'I had to come up with one of the girls,' she told him with a smile. 'She isn't very well. I'm making her a drink.'

When he saw her approaching, the policeman had thought she looked positively sullen, like so many of these rich girls, but the smile she gave him transformed her. He followed her into the common room. 'Which girl would that be?'

'Imogen.' She switched on the kettle. 'The one with a false leg.'

'Oh. I see.'

'Are you allowed a drink?'

'I wouldn't say no. I'm parched. It's a hot day.'

'Isn't it?' Lining up three clean mugs, she said, 'We're all terribly worried about the girl who fell off the horse. I probably shouldn't ask, but is there any way you could find out how she is?'

'Hasn't Superintendent McKenna said?'

'I'm not sure he knows,' she replied innocently. 'He's still downstairs, talking to people.'

He nodded, walked to the window and, head inclined, spoke into the radio clipped to his shoulder. After several minutes' silence and more mutterings, he came back to take the steaming drink she held out. 'Much obliged,' he said, leaning on the back of a chair, which creaked under his weight. 'Superintendent McKenna will tell everybody when he's ready, so keep it to yourself. And you didn't get this from me – OK?'

'OK.'

'Your friend's going to have a very sore head for a few days and she's sprained her ankle. Apart from that she's fine.'

Surprising both of them, she kissed him on the cheek. His beard was a little scratchy, but he smelt nice and not at all like the proverbial pig. Before he could recover his wits, she picked up the other drinks and went.

Imogen was in a chair by the window, clutching a half-empty glass of water, her face grey with pain. Her leg was propped against the bed like part of a shop-window dummy, the stump to which it had been fastened a lump beneath her skirt.

Vivienne put Imogen's coffee on the counter. 'Have you just taken some pills?'

Imogen nodded.

'How many have you had today?'

'Two at breakfast, two now.'

Scrutinising the label on the brown plastic bottle, Vivienne said, 'That was your midday dose. You can't have any more until supper, then that's it until the morning.'

'I'm allowed more if I need them.' She snatched the bottle, as if Vivienne were likely to fling it through the window.

Holding her mug in both hands, Vivienne put it to her lips. 'It's a slippery slope, Imogen. Take care you don't find yourself at the bottom, like me.'

'I want it to stop hurting.' Her voice was barely more than a whisper.

'Even prescribed medicines can turn your whole existence into a miserable cycle of scoring, consuming and getting stoned one way or the other.' She paused. 'What'll you do when the doctors realise you're addicted and cut off your supply? They will, you know.'

At a loss for an answer, Imogen said, 'You can smoke if you

want, only lock the door first.' When Vivienne failed to move she added, 'Lock the door, anyway. Scott's sure to send someone to pry and I don't feel like talking.'

'I'll shut up, then.' Vivienne walked to the door and turned the key in the lock, then reached into the pocket of her skirt, where she kept her cigarettes and lighter during the day.

'I didn't mean you.' Imogen watched her. Vivienne had very elegant legs, she thought, with savage envy, and she made a cigarette seem like a smart accessory.

Smoke dribbling from her nostrils, Vivienne returned her look. 'By the way, Torrance will be fine. She just sprained an ankle and bashed her head.'

'How d'you know?'

'I'm sworn to secrecy, but it's official.'

'You bribed that copper, I'll bet.' Suddenly, Imogen shuddered from head to foot. 'Thank God she wasn't really hurt!'

'Not like Sukie, you mean?' Ignoring Imogen's sharp intake of breath, she asked, 'Had any thoughts about that?'

Imogen tried to shake her head, but her neck was almost rigid.

'Well, I doubt it was an accident.' Vivienne sank on to the bed and, picking up the false leg, began to examine it from the toes upwards, the cigarette stuck at the corner of her mouth. 'And I don't believe the pregnancy story, whatever Scott's putting about, but that said, there's no denying she'd been pretty down in the dumps lately, so she might well have topped herself.' Speculatively, she gazed at Imogen. 'What do *you* think?'

Imogen made no response. As the ash on Vivienne's cigarette grew longer and began to droop, she leaned awkwardly from her chair to offer a tin holding the remains of a scented candle.

'Ta.' Vivienne took it from her. Still investigating the artificial leg, she enquired, 'What *was* making Sukie so bloody miserable? You knew her better than anyone. You've got to have some idea.'

'I don't!'

Vivienne stared at her. 'Maybe not,' she agreed thoughtfully. 'You hadn't had much to do with her lately, had you?' Again, there was no response. 'Why was that? What went wrong between you?'

'I can't say!' Imogen sounded as if she were being throttled.

'No?'

Turning away from Vivienne's penetrating gaze, Imogen muttered, 'No.'

'Shame about that,' Vivienne observed. 'If you and Sukie hadn't been split asunder, so to speak, you'd probably be able to point the coppers in the right direction.' She upended the leg to peer into the cup, then rotated the knee joint through its limited articulation. 'Personally, I never was much sold on the suicide option and after Torrance's cleverly engineered accident it's lost whatever credibility it had. So,' she went on, 'it looks like we've got a killer hiding in the woodwork. Not a happy thought, even if you don't know anything about Sukie's death. Rather makes one feel like one of those ducks in a fairground shooting gallery that people take pot-shots at.' Putting the leg on the bedcover and taking the cigarette from her mouth, she added, 'There's dried blood in the cup.'

'What?' Imogen started, taken aback by the abrupt change of subject.

'I said there's dried blood in the cup. Is there therefore *wet* blood on your dressings?'

Slumping once more in her chair, Imogen nodded reluctantly. 'Some,' she admitted. 'It chafes, like a badly fitting shoe. Dr Scott says my skin won't toughen up for ages.'

'D'you know, I never realised she was an expert on prosthetics and amputations as well,' Vivienne remarked acidly. 'Why on earth don't you just take the damned thing back?'

'It was made to measure.'

'So? It won't necessarily be a perfect fit first time round.'

'I can't just take it back, anyway. It's not like a dress I might have bought. I don't even know where it was made.'

'But you do know where it was fitted,' Vivienne said. 'After the Easter hols, I thought you were getting your act together, but you've gone straight back to square one. What's Matron had to say about it?'

'She wants me to wait for my next home appointment.'

'When's that?'

'August.'

'So you're happy to suffer for another couple of months, are you? Still, the drugs should keep you quiet.'

'Stop it!' Imogen cried. She squirmed around on the chair. 'Torrance wouldn't say things like that!'

'I know she wouldn't,' Vivienne replied. 'She's too kind-hearted. She never hauls me over the coals, either. She just sorts me out, as best she can, the way she does with you. I'm not out of my head *all* the time,' she added, watching Imogen with exasperated anger. 'I'm well aware of what she does for you, but I don't understand why. Why don't you go to Bangor hospital for physiotherapy?'

'Dr Scott said their physios wouldn't be much good.' Imogen's eyes were beginning to glaze. 'It's National Health.'

'Oh, for God's sake! They're all the same!'

'And Dr Scott said Sukie *did* kill herself,' Imogen said in a rush. 'She's sure of it.'

'The police obviously don't agree with her.'

'That doesn't mean she isn't *right*!' Imogen paused, gnawing her lip. 'I heard her telling Ainsley it must be Sukie's fault the girth snapped on Torrance. She never looked after Purdey's tack very well.'

'That copper said the surcingle straps had been cut.' She stubbed out the cigarette and immediately lit another. 'And believe me, they wouldn't be lashing out all this money investigating a suicide, whatever Scott thinks. She's in denial.'

'She's what?'

'She's in denial,' Vivienne repeated. 'About your accident, about Sukie's death and now about Torrance. When you first came back after the accident, she milked the drama for her own ends, but since you insisted on looking like you've got *two* legs she's pretending nothing much happened. Don't you see?' she asked urgently. 'While Scott can push it away she doesn't have to admit she might be responsible for some of the mess, so she doesn't need to bother sorting it out. She's lazy and selfish, and she's making your life hell on earth.'

'What else can I do?' Imogen wrung her hands.

'Stop acting like a bloody moron. Call your parents, or at least, your doctor.'

'He'll be angry. He fixed up treatment at Bangor for me and he doesn't know I've broken the appointments.'

'Then you'll have to lie about it. Say you thought you were getting on OK.'

'But I can't! Dr Scott will know if I call the hospital.'

'Yes, she will,' Vivienne agreed. 'If you like, I'll come with you while you tell her.'

'Would you?' Tears, of misery and gratitude, welled in her bloodshot eyes.

'And until you can get to see the experts, I'll help with your physio.'

Imogen's face was chalk-white. 'You'd have to look at the stump,' she croaked.

'I'm not Charlotte. I won't throw up. Anyway, I already know what stumps look like.'

'How?'

'When I had my appendix out, I met a kid who'd had her leg cut off because she had a tumour in her knee.' Appraising the length of Imogen's stump, she added, 'She'd lost a lot more than you.'

'How old was she?'

'Ten.'

'Poor little thing.'

Vivienne shrugged. '*She* didn't think so. She said being alive with one and a bit legs was much better than being dead with two.'

The moment McKenna gave his consent and without bothering
to seek Freya's permission, Martha dragged her stunned, ashen-
faced daughter out of the school, bundled her into the hire car
and drove to the pub from where McKenna had been so
peremptorily summoned. 'Torrance will be fine,' she said,
watching Alice push her food around the plate until the fat,
golden-brown chips threatened to slide off the edge. 'You heard
what Superintendent McKenna said. Apart from a badly
sprained ankle, she'll just have a nasty headache for a few days.
She was very lucky.' She smiled encouragingly. 'And there
wasn't a scratch on the horse, thank goodness.'

'Somebody tried to *kill* her!' Alice wailed.

The nearby diners raised their eyes.

'Keep your voice down. And stop playing with your food,'
Martha added, as Alice's face adopted a mutinous scowl.
'Someone tampered with *Sukie*'s saddle, not Torrance's.'

'But everyone knows Torrance rides Purdey. Everyone!'

'But no one knows *when* the saddle was sabotaged,' Martha
pointed out, starting hungrily on her own lunch. 'Are the
stables and tack room kept locked?' she asked, trying to divert
Alice's attention from the near miss of another tragedy.

'Nope,' Alice replied. 'I mean,' she went on, chewing a
mouthful of chicken, 'they can't be locked when the horses are
in during the cold months in case of fire and I guess nobody
bothers once they're out. There's nothing to steal except the
tack and a few odds and ends.'

'How many people know they're not locked?'

'Everybody, I should think.'

Relieved to see the food on Alice's plate disappearing, Martha said, 'It strikes me that whoever cut the saddle had to know what they were doing. I wouldn't know where to start.'

'Well, *I* would,' Alice asserted. 'You don't *need* to know much.'

'You need to know enough,' Martha asserted, then the implications of Alice's remark struck her and she went cold. Careful to keep her voice level, she said, 'Dr Scott told me Torrance asked you to help with evening stables yesterday. I hadn't realised you and she were quite so pally.'

Alice stared at her plate, her mouth clamped shut.

'D'you think,' Martha went on, 'that Torrance might have sabotaged the saddle herself? If she knew she was likely to be thrown, she'd have been ready for it, so she'd have fallen carefully.'

'That's absolute *bollocks*!' Alice snapped, her voice cutting.

'Dr Scott also told me,' Martha said, trying to stop herself from bursting into weary, angry tears, 'that you've been punished for swearing at one of the sixth formers this morning.'

'So?'

'Is it true?'

'I told Nancy Holmes to "bog off". That isn't swearing.'

'It's extremely rude,' Martha told her. 'Why did you do that?'

'She asked for it.' Hatred glinted in her eyes.

Martha dropped her knife and fork and grabbed a glass of water. Ravenous as she was, the food was sticking in her throat. Her child was turning into a stranger and, worse still, a stranger from whom she would want to keep her distance. 'You know, Alice,' she said slowly, 'you've always had a tendency to look at things rather negatively. You get that from your father, I suppose. None of his family was ever *happy*. They were always beset by some woe, even though they had no reason.' She took another sip of water. 'I always felt they were living inside a thicket of miserable obsessions. Occasionally they saw some light, but they never tried to break out. Maybe they were scared – I don't know. Maybe they simply preferred the safety of being in a place they knew with boundaries they could see.'

'So?' Alice demanded once again, when Martha's voice tailed away.

'I hoped you'd be different. I want you to understand happiness.'

'Whenever I've done something *you* don't happen to like, you blame it on Daddy! All my bad points *have* to come from him, don't they? That's the only way you can justify divorcing him!'

Finding that her hands were trembling, Martha put the glass on the table. 'I've told you countless times that we were simply unsuited. I didn't suit him, he didn't suit me. It was nobody's fault.'

'You should've realised all that *before* you got married. You were old enough,' Alice said nastily. 'You put him through all that for nothing!'

'Is that what he told you?' When Alice remained silent, she asked again, '*Is* it?'

'I haven't seen him for years, have I?' Alice retorted.

'That wasn't my doing.'

'How do I know it wasn't? You could have told him not to see me.'

'But I didn't,' Martha insisted. 'I wouldn't do that to you. Anyway, I've no quarrel with him and I shouldn't imagine he has one with me.'

'I guess Daisy's right, then, isn't she? She usually is.'

'Daisy?' Martha frowned, wondering what that monstrous brat had to do with her family concerns. 'Why? What has she said?'

'She said Daddy didn't love me enough to stick around.'

Alice's sorrowful bewilderment enraged her. 'Don't you think that was very cruel of her?' she asked, working hard to keep her fury under control.

'Not if she's right.'

For some time Martha sat in silence, before saying, 'When parents separate, children usually stay with the mother, because they need a mother more than a father.' Wondering how deep was the hole she could be digging for herself, she went on slowly, 'But that doesn't mean the father doesn't love his children. It's just the way things work out.'

'Did Daddy love me?'

'Yes.' Martha put all the conviction she could muster into her voice. 'He did. He *does*.'

'Then why doesn't he ever come to see me?'

'Perhaps he's just not sure you want him around.' She paused. 'Why don't you ask him? You've got his address, so there's nothing to stop you writing, or even telephoning. If you like, I'll get in touch with him for you, although I think you're quite old enough not to need an intermediary.'

'But what if he *says* he'll see me when it's the last thing on earth he really *wants* to do?'

Realising that she had made things worse rather than better, Martha said, 'Alice, all human transactions involve what you might call the oil of dishonesty. We dissemble because there's always a two-way traffic of cause and effect and no one can ever be sure what someone else thinks or feels. At best, we make assumptions; at worst, we delude ourselves with wishful thinking. In the end, we have to rely on instinct and our experience of a particular person. *My* instinct about your father,' she concluded, 'tells me that he's an honest, decent man who'd never intentionally hurt you.'

'But you don't *know*,' Alice said dully. 'You don't know if he'd be lying or telling the truth if he said he wanted to see me.' Then her voice began to rise. '*Nobody* knows when someone's lying or telling the truth.' Her food came rushing back to her throat. She clamped a hand over her mouth and made a dive for the toilet door.

13

By lunchtime Torrance had been moved from the hospital's accident department to a small private room on the second floor. Perched on the window ledge, Dewi watched over her while he waited for the first of the round-the-clock guards to arrive. Every so often, he checked the monitors on a trolley beside the bed.

She lay on her back, snoring gently, her chest rising and falling reassuringly. The cage over her injured ankle made a hump at the foot of the bed and an ugly welt was developing on her forehead. Although her face had been cleaned, revealing grazes on cheek and chin, her arms were still streaked with dirt, with more dirt embedded under her short, square fingernails, and her tangled hair was riddled with grains of glinting sand. The bruises, grazes and dirt took nothing from her; if anything, he thought, they suited her, for she was an earthy young creature, as bold and sweaty and natural as the horses she rode with such panache and which she so clearly loved. As the ambulance was hurtling towards the hospital, she had suddenly roused herself to ask about Purdey, before sinking once more into a stupor as soon as he reassured her.

He felt a little strange; light-headed and slightly sick from shock. Never before had he seen anyone thrown by a horse, and he could still barely believe she had survived, let alone with only minor injuries. Whoever had cut the surcingle straps must feel intensely disappointed, he thought, and was probably already planning their next attack, for whether she was aware of it or not, Torrance knew something about Sukie's death. Why else should someone try to kill her? he asked himself. So why had

McKenna, when he called him from the hospital, continued to counsel caution about assuming that Sukie had been murdered?

A shadow fell across the glass panel in the door, then Janet walked in. 'I've brought her pyjamas and things,' she said, placing a soft leather travel bag on the floor. She peered at the sleeping form. 'She looks OK, considering.'

'She's tough. The medics said she's got muscles all over.'

'Horses do that for you,' Janet replied. 'When they're not trying to kill you, that is.'

'You *like* horses.'

'They're still dangerous at both ends and uncomfortable in the middle.' She walked around the bed to join Dewi by the window. 'What actually happened? All I've heard are wild stories about sabotaged saddles, horses turning turtle in mid-air and Wonder Woman here being impaled on broken jumps.'

'Don't be catty. It doesn't suit you.'

'I swear it's getting hotter.' Unfastening another shirt button, flapping the garment against her skin, she added, 'I wasn't being catty. I was commenting on the fact that Torrance's importance seems quite disproportionate to her status.'

'She's obviously popular. She was elected house captain, remember?'

'Yes, but why is she so *significant*? Nobody's got a clue what to do with the horses now. The school's in utter turmoil.'

'Don't exaggerate,' Dewi chided. 'They've got Miss Attwill. She must know what to do.'

'You think? If you ask me, she'll be hard put to work out which end needs feeding.' Janet grinned. 'And no way is she going to exercise Tonto or Purdey. Tonto's a lunatic and Purdey, she told me, "has all the typical and worst qualities of a horse of that colour". In other words she's a stroppy redhead.'

'Then the horses will have to go to a livery stable.'

'I shouldn't think that's even occurred to them. They can't see further than the boundary walls.'

'It's far more likely that Scott's destroyed their capacity for joined-up thinking. People are so worried about upsetting her they forget what they're supposed to be doing.'

'In what way?' she asked, almost hypnotised by the blips proceeding without interruption across the monitor screens.

'By doing the rounds with the security guards, I was hoping to loosen a few tongues,' Dewi told her, 'and perhaps dig up something on the ones on duty Tuesday night. I thought they might only alibi each other because they've got a vested interest, but the only vested interest they've got is appeasing Scott. If they don't pass her house at exactly the right intervals, she reports them to their boss. Bebb and Knight do the same, too.'

'Spending the nights on watch can't do much for *their* relationship,' Janet remarked spitefully.

'Don't make two and two add up to five simply because they live together.'

'Come on! I admit Knight just looks as though she feeds on wasps, but Bebb's the archetypal dyke type.'

'They're sisters,' Dewi told her. 'Miss Knight and *Mrs* Bebb. She's a widow.'

'That *is* a surprise,' she said slowly. 'How d'you find out?'

'From the guards. It's a pity Scott didn't think fit to tell us, but I'm sure she'd much prefer us to jump to the wrong conclusion, like you did. Keeps us off balance, doesn't it?'

Janet nodded thoughtfully. 'Yet another example of something being completely different from the way it appears.'

Suddenly Torrance groaned and began to thresh about under the light blanket. Janet started towards her, scanning the monitors, but there was nothing to indicate impending crisis. She hovered over the bed. 'Has she said anything?' she asked, straightening the blanket about Torrance's shoulders.

'Only about Purdey, but she wasn't properly conscious.'

Janet pushed Torrance's tangled hair away from her face. 'Mr McKenna isn't sure Torrance's fall is connected to Sukie's death, because there's probably any amount of skulduggery going on at the Hermitage.'

'He told me much the same when I rang,' Dewi said.

'He's fairly certain Sukie *was* murdered, but until Dr Roberts comes up with the goods, he's hedging his bets.' Janet turned away from the bed then, to resume her seat on the window ledge. 'Talking of which,' she went on, 'I hear some enterprising colleagues have opened a book on the killer. Who's *your* money on?'

'It isn't,' Dewi replied flatly. 'I don't approve of gambling at the best of times, but that's just sheer bad taste.'

'It's human nature,' Janet said. 'I expect there's another book open now, as well, on the next likely victim.'

14

When he finished addressing the school, McKenna had stepped down from the dais and had stood for several minutes by the refectory doors, watching the girls rearrange the benches beside the tables before setting out crockery and cutlery. They functioned like well-drilled army units and in the corridor behind him another platoon, this one made up of domestics and kitchen staff, waited beside their enormous hot trolleys, with Fat Sally in the vanguard. As she led the way into the room, her flesh wobbled grotesquely and indecently with every movement and, for a moment, he had been won over by Ainsley Chapman's seductive argument. This obese cook, the homely Matron, the lesbian games mistress he had met that morning were, he thought, such stereotypes, while Freya Scott's whole objective turned on never fitting into the scenarios she created.

Spinning on his heel, he made for the lobby, where he came upon Jack, who was lounging against the door jamb, hands in pockets.

'Can you tell what they're getting for lunch?' he asked. 'From the smell of the food?'

'No,' McKenna replied. 'Institutional cooking always smells the same. It could be anything.'

'Why is that, though?'

'I don't know. Does it matter?'

'Not really.' Jack followed him on to the forecourt. 'But if you want, you could partake of whatever it is in Scott's study. She asked me to extend the invitation.'

'I don't want,' McKenna said shortly.

'She suggested it when we were waiting for you to get back after Torrance's accident.'

'Torrance didn't have an accident. She had a cunningly contrived fall, which could easily have killed her.'

'Scott didn't like that explanation at all,' Jack commented. 'She tried to convince me the surcingle straps had rotted because Sukie didn't look after the tack properly, so I told her there were clear cut marks, from something like a Stanley or Swiss Army knife, or even a scalpel. Once she'd taken *that* on board she was very quick to let me know that Sean O'Connor keeps Stanley knives in his workshop, which he doesn't always lock, despite her explicit orders.'

'There'll be knives of one description or another all over the place,' McKenna said. 'And Matron, who looks the type to harbour the tools of her trade, may well have the odd scalpel in her room.' He mounted the steps of the mobile incident room. 'Once forensics give us a lead, we'll start looking, although I shouldn't imagine the saboteur is stupid enough to leave the thing lying around. It's doubtless at the bottom of the Strait or buried deep inside a muck heap.'

Jack frowned. 'There *aren't* any muck heaps when the horses are living out. The stables are empty.'

'As Sean would tell you, because it's yet another of his jobs, droppings have to be cleared from the pastures to keep the grazing free of parasites.' He glanced over his shoulder. 'But don't panic. You won't find yourself elbow deep in horse manure. We'll set Bryn scouting if necessary.'

Jack dogged his footsteps into the senior officers' cubbyhole. 'If we take Scott's lead, we won't bother. She's already fingered Alice Derringer for the saddle, on the basis that she's one of a handful with the necessary know-how, and the *only* one with a motive for hurting Torrance.'

'What motive is that?'

'The way Scott tells it, Alice is eaten up with resentment because the fight at breakfast wouldn't have happened if Torrance hadn't wanted her to help with evening stables yesterday, which is another thing that's bothering Scott because she reckons it smacks of bestowing a special favour.' Jack sat down and tweaked the creases on his trousers. 'I pointed out it could mean anything or nothing, or just perhaps that Torrance knows Alice is efficient because she fags for her.' He smiled then. 'She really doesn't like the term "fagging". She says doing a bit of housework teaches the girls something about duty, they all serve their time at it, there's no likelihood of the seniors coercing the juniors into providing other, less innocent services, and it isn't free labour, whatever Avril O'Connor might have told me. She got very voluble on the subject of Avril. She sacked her because she was lazy and slipshod, and a gossip to boot, and Scott will not, and I quote, "have the school's affairs bruited abroad by anyone". Needless to say,' he went on, 'I asked what "affairs" she meant. Very condescendingly she informed me that the Hermitage is a family and in all families there are not only things people *prefer* to keep private, but things which *should* be kept private.'

Chin on hand, McKenna gazed across at him. 'Denting her armour isn't easy, is it?'

'I did my best,' Jack replied. 'I said a girls' boarding school must attract a fair number of lesbian teachers, the way paedophiles congregate around children's homes, so she informed me that although women aren't bound to betray trust just because they're that way inclined, undesirables would be flushed out and removed. She doesn't run a laissez-faire establishment sympathetic to perversions.' He smiled again. 'And, of course, if any of the girls got too close, she'd deal with it. Managing people, whatever the circumstances, is her forte. She's even got certificates to prove it. They're hung up behind her desk.'

'I've seen them,' McKenna said. 'Are they kosher?' he asked. 'Or the sort you can buy mail order from places in the Far East and America?'

Jack laughed. 'Oh, they're definitely genuine. So are all the aristocrats, models, political wives and other high flyers in the photos of old girls she's got in her study. I recognised quite a few of them.'

'I didn't know you read the society pages,' McKenna remarked.

'The twins like to keep up with what the A list is doing so they spend my hard-earned cash on fripperies like *Hello!* magazine,' Jack said. 'If Scott's right, Charlotte Swann might be gracing its pages before long. She's set her heart on modelling now the bottom's fallen out of the Princess Di lookalike market.'

'That girl's a tragedy waiting to happen,' McKenna said, his voice suddenly gloomy. 'God knows what her childhood was like. Justine Salomon showed me some pictures of Charlotte's mother getting married for the fifth or sixth time, before telling me the woman was no better than a tart.'

'I wouldn't know about that,' Jack commented, 'but Charlotte *is* illegitimate. Scott told me, when she was giving me the Hermitage-is-a-family spiel. In other words this is the only family Charlotte has, despite her legions of relatives by marriage. Dysfunctional backgrounds, irresponsible parents and promiscuous mothers are par for the course, apparently.'

'I wonder how Hester Melville would have turned out if she hadn't married that dipsomaniac?'

'Well, she did. There's not much point in that sort of speculation.' Jack paused, before saying quietly, 'But it would help to know where we're going with Sukie's death. After what happened to Torrance, I don't understand why you've still got doubts about her being murdered.'

'I haven't, but as we can't be sure when the saddle was tampered with, we can't say Sukie wasn't the intended victim.'

'I overheard somebody saying Torrance was jumping Purdey yesterday. Surely the girth would have given then.'

'Perhaps,' McKenna conceded. 'It would depend on how deep the cuts were.'

'Scott told me she couldn't understand why Torrance didn't notice them when she saddled up,' Jack said. 'And much as it pains me to agree with her, I must say she's got a point.'

'No, she hasn't. She's trying to pass the buck, so that Torrance gets all the blame for being careless.' Lighting a cigarette, McKenna added, 'The girls here, like a lot of people, have a habit of undoing the girth only on the left-hand side. The right side's left attached to the saddle, so next time it's used, it's buckled up again on the left. Whoever messed with Purdey's saddle knew that and made the cuts on the right-hand side, knowing they were most unlikely to be noticed.'

15

As Martha followed Matron into her office-cum-surgery, she thought the woman's steps were beginning to drag almost like her own. Her brisk, puffing efficiency had all but evaporated.

'Alice was sick, you say?' Matron frowned. 'She actually vomited?'

Martha nodded, easing her aching bones into a chair. 'Halfway through lunch.'

'Hm. Could be a tummy upset from the heat, I suppose.' She stood with her back to the window, chewing her lower lip. 'Where is she now?'

Where indeed? Martha thought. When she drove into the forecourt, Daisy was leaning against the ornamental wall, smirking like an evil pixie. Without a word to her mother, Alice dived out of the car and hastened away with her and, as they reached the trees, Grace Blackwell, the other side of their triangle, came to meet them. The three of them moved as if joined by an invisible bond and, watching them, Martha wondered, somewhat fearfully, if they had persuaded themselves that life was a riddle whose solution they could only find together.

Dragging her attention back to Matron, she said, 'She went off with Daisy and that other girl they knock about with.'

'Well, she'll be all right, then,' Matron said, in a rush of relief. 'Daisy would tell me *immediately* if Alice were poorly. She looks after her like a sister.' She offered Martha one of her tight-lipped, uncertain smiles. 'Daisy's such a nice girl, isn't she?'

'Is she?'

'She is indeed! Always happy, always smiling! If there were more like her my job wouldn't be half the trial it is.' Squeezing behind her desk to sit down, she added, 'She doesn't even get upset when she's teased about her lisp.'

'Perhaps you only see one side of her,' suggested Martha, to whom Daisy's ever ready smile was not a meaningless social gesture nor a true smile, but more a baring of teeth.

'Oh, I don't think so.' Matron was adamant. 'Everybody likes her. I've never heard a bad word said about her.'

'But wasn't she involved in the fracas at breakfast?'

Matron shook her head. 'Dear me, no. That was between Alice and Nancy Holmes, and I must say you could have knocked me down with a feather when I heard. Alice *swearing*, of all things!'

'I suppose the tension's getting to her. It must be hard on everyone.'

Matron kneaded her hands. 'It's dreadful,' she admitted. 'One thing on top of another! I shudder to think where it might all end.'

'At least Torrance wasn't badly hurt.'

'Not this time, but who knows what'll happen next?' Fear deadened Matron's voice. 'First poor Sukie, then Torrance. Who's next? I ask myself. Who's next?'

16

Vivienne used cannabis because other people had told her it numbed the capacity to feel and although they were yet to be proved entirely right, until today she had believed it took the edge off her pain. Now, utterly wretched after the emotional Armageddon of an hour with Imogen, she knew better, but perversely, the only hope of respite still lay in her addiction and so, as soon as lunch was over, she sidled out of the refectory.

She was about to set foot on the staircase when Jack Tuttle almost pounced on her. 'Superintendent McKenna asked me to see you,' he said.

She swallowed hard. 'Why?'

'You all have to be interviewed. Had you forgotten?' He began herding her up the stairs, chatting amiably. 'If you don't mind, we'll go to your common room. Somebody's using the visitors' room. Would you like to have a woman officer with you?'

'What?' She half turned.

'Shall I ask a woman officer to be present?'

'No.' Taking the second flight of stairs two at a time, she hurried along the corridor towards the smokers' den, with his footsteps thumping determinedly in her wake. The room stank of stale tobacco. She threw open the window, perched on the ledge, pulled cigarettes and lighter from her pocket, and started to speak even before he had found himself a seat. 'You know I smoke dope. My parents did too, but they grew up and took to drink instead.' Fingers shaking, she cupped her hands round the lighter flame. 'I don't know if they ever got busted because we're not hot on communication, but they won't be surprised when I do. I doubt if they'll even care.'

The bluish tinge to her skin made Jack think of the undead in a horror film. She was just as pitiful, too, he realised and probably just as doomed. He smiled gently at her. 'From our perspective, nailing the suppliers is more important than prosecuting users.'

'Dream on!' She grinned fleetingly, with the mirth of a death's head. 'I don't fancy being crippled by a baseball bat.' Then her mind's eye was filled with a picture of Imogen's terrifying stump, with its glistening scars and raw calluses, and her hands remembered the feel of taut, angry flesh and knotted muscle. She was afraid the touch of that mutilated limb would stay with her until the day she died.

'People worry about you,' Jack said.

Vivienne knew it was important to concentrate, in case he trapped her into a dangerous admission, but she felt dreadfully dislocated; part here, part still with Imogen, part elsewhere and, as ever, out of reach. 'Yeah, I know,' she said at last. 'And look what happens to them.'

'Are you referring to Torrance?'

'Who else?'

'If there's a connection between your drug taking and what happened to her, there must be a pusher in the school.'

'You're twisting my words. I just meant that bad things happen when people bother about me. I kept telling her to leave me alone, but she wouldn't. She's a stubborn cow.'

Jack regarded her hungry eyes and jittery limbs. 'You've got youth, looks and brains, and you must have money or you wouldn't be here. So why take drugs?'

The death's-head grin flickered once more. '*Because* I'm here.'

'Most girls would give an arm and a leg for an education like this. I know my own daughters would.'

'Stop talking about missing limbs, will you?' she pleaded.

Baffled by the surreal turn of the conversation, he stared at her.

'I smoke dope because it helps pass the time,' she went on tonelessly. 'There's an awful lot of it.'

'You subscribe to the view that life is pointless, do you?'

'Isn't it?' Shifting uneasily on the window ledge, she dragged hard on the cigarette. 'What was the point of Imogen losing her leg? What was the point of Sukie being born?' She turned to blow smoke through the window. 'And please don't tell me they're being punished for something they did in another incarnation.'

Somewhere, Jack remembered, he had read that the pain and grief of youth were pleasurable, because they were no more than a rehearsal for the real thing, but this girl's grief and pain would be her dark escort to the grave. 'That would be very crass,' he said. 'But the fact that apparently pointless things occur doesn't make *life* futile.' In an effort to reach her, he added, 'Even if you feel you're just filling in time between being born and dying.'

The smoke from her cigarette wriggled in the draught. 'You must be a good father. You take the trouble to think.'

'I'm not sure my girls would agree with you.'

'They wouldn't be normal if they did. You always think your parents are the world's worst.'

'Are yours?'

She shrugged. 'Dunno. They're so laid-back their heads bump on the floor.' She ground out the cigarette in an ashtray overflowing with stubs, knotted sweet wrappers and balls of tinfoil. 'Anything goes, as far as they're concerned.'

'Taking drugs probably destroyed their capacity to care.'

'I wonder why they don't do the same for me?'

'Perhaps they never will. You could save yourself a lot of money and no end of unhappiness by giving them up as a lost cause.' He met her wary eyes. 'I can't condone lawbreaking, but you need help rather than punishment and some constructive occupation.' He paused then, hoping for comment on the school's much-vaunted pastoral care and its impact on her own welfare, but she said nothing. 'So,' he asked eventually, 'what will you do when you leave here?'

'I've no idea.'

'No plans to follow in Ainsley Chapman's footsteps?'

'Don't be funny! I flunked two A level papers. I won't get into the reddest redbrick, never mind Oxbridge.'

'What's to stop you doing resits?'

'Where? Scott can't wait to see my rear view.'

'You could find a crammer.'

'Maybe,' Vivienne agreed, sliding off the window ledge and into a chair in one liquid movement. 'How old are your kids?'

'They're twins, the same age as you. They've both got places at Bangor University.'

'So you're stuck with them for another few years.' When she smiled, her face lit up. 'But I don't expect you mind, do you?'

'If anything, I'm glad.'

Elbows on knees, she leaned forward, staring at the floor. The cheap hair-cord carpet was spotted with coffee stains and holed with cigarette burns. 'I went to prep school at seven, like my brothers, then came here. We see our parents during the holidays, but we hardly know each other. The people at school are really your family.' She grimaced. 'Tough if you don't get on.'

'You must have *some* friends.'

She shook her head. 'I wasn't allowed to have them. I arrived here with a reputation, so Scott was afraid I'd be a bad influence.' She groped for another cigarette. 'Torrance is the nearest I've got to a friend, but that's only because she won't let Scott push her about.'

'Surely you weren't on drugs when you came here?'

'Nah, but my brothers were. Their public school chucked them out in the end.' She watched him through a haze of smoke. 'I can almost hear your mind working. Do I do drugs because it's in my genes and Scott knew that, or do I do them because she isolated me with her cruel little games? I don't know the answer, so I can't help.' Crossing her legs, she draped her right arm over her left, the cigarette dangling from her long pale fingers. 'I don't want to sound more bitter and twisted than I actually am, but Scott marked me out from the start. I got excluded and ostracised in all sorts of ways, but you could never put your finger on *how*. She's too subtle for that.'

'Does the same thing happen to others?'

'If Scott thinks you're likely to ruffle her atmosphere, you get the treatment, and you keep on getting it until your spirit breaks.' Rearranging herself into another unconsciously elegant pose, she added, 'The teachers won't interfere because they're scared of her. They know if they side with the underdogs they'll end up joining them. She doesn't just victimise people, though. She has favourites, but the trouble is you're never sure who's in and who's out of her good books, or why.' With another smile she said, 'You should talk to Torrance as soon as her head's together. She's got some really wild theories.'

'Like what?'

'Oh, nothing very startling.' Her smile died and her body slumped, along with her mood. 'Only that Scott's emotionally retarded, sort of locked in her own adolescence. She's very fickle, you see. She'll be all over someone one week and dropping them like a hot brick the next. She *plays* with people. Unfortunately, no one but her knows the rules of the game.'

'Might Torrance know something that would help to explain Sukie's death?'

When she glanced at him, her eyes were narrowed, but perhaps only because of the smoke wreathing about her face. 'I doubt it.'

'But they were close, weren't they? Lady Melville said Sukie adored her.'

'Lady *Hester*,' Vivienne corrected him politely. 'There's a protocol to be observed, you know, not that it makes the slightest difference. "Lady Hopeless" would suit her better.' She puffed on the cigarette. 'She was barely out of rompers when Sukie was born and she stayed that way because her own mother locked her in a time warp by constantly harking back to the upset she'd caused. And of course, none of them ever missed an opportunity to tell *Sukie* how much misery and disgrace she'd brought on the family.' Jack's face clearly betrayed his feelings, for she went on to say, 'Yes, they are cruel and unreasonable, but so are lots of people. Sukie coped with it by kidding herself she was a changeling. She was always wishing her real mother would come and take her away.'

'Did she tell you that?'

'She told everybody, and people sympathised to her face and sniggered behind her back, as they do if you let your dreams be known, although Torrance didn't, ever. She once gave me a hell of a slap when she overheard me giggling with Charlotte about it.'

'Did she slap her as well?' Grappling with the dynamics of

Sukie's changing allegiances, he suddenly realised that Torrance's casual gesture of support would be enough to provoke the lonely Sukie to shift her complete loyalty, particularly in the wake of her ruined friendship with Imogen.

'Dunno,' Vivienne replied. 'Probably not. She'd know it was a waste of energy.'

Gradually, silence fell about them, and at first it seemed pleasant and agreeable. Lolling gracefully in her chair, Vivienne continued to puff at the cigarette. Absently, he rustled papers. Outside, birds twittered, leaves whispered in the breeze and the motor mower chugged as Sean O'Connor went about his business. But for all its tranquillity the atmosphere was lethargic, and Jack began to understand how it could so easily become stultifying and oppressive, as if becalmed in the middle of a huge ocean. The questions he wanted to ask jostled in his mind, but he sensed she was near the edge of a precipice and was afraid of pushing her over. Settling for something innocuous, he said at last, 'Why did you take Imogen out of the refectory earlier?'

'Jesus!' The cigarette fell from her hand and began burning another hole in the carpet. When she bent down, he saw shivers rippling down her skinny back.

'I'm sorry, I didn't mean to upset you.'

Her fingers shook as she picked up the butt and when she looked up at him she seemed to have grown old in the space of seconds. 'I brought her upstairs because she wasn't well and nobody else was bothering.' The death's-head grin returned. 'My brief reunion with the human race.'

'Your bitterness is painful. If not to you, to others.'

'Not half as painful as Imogen's stump.'

'Why?' he wondered, almost talking to himself. 'Why is her accident more important than Sukie's death? Whenever we try to talk about Sukie, the conversation drags itself round to Imogen.'

'I don't know. Maybe they're one and the same.' Her voice was weary. 'Maybe because Imogen's still here. Sukie's pain is all over.'

17

Sukie's room had been sealed shut since the day before and when McKenna pushed the door, stifling, foetid air belched in his face. As he opened the window, he nudged a parched spider plant on the ledge and almost sent it crashing down on to the forecourt.

There was one chair in the room and he placed it so that he caught the breeze through the window. He sat down, the chair wobbling under his weight, and contemplated the sparse, shoddy furnishings, the disarray of clothes on bed and floor, the soiled jodhpurs slung over the radiator, the dusty riding boots, the untidy piles of magazines and schoolwork, and the thread-bare teddy with a frayed blue ribbon round its neck which was tucked up in the bed. Sunlight falling on the counter that ran the length of the wall showed up a layer of gritty dust and talc, sticky rings left by innumerable mugs and cups, and even fingerprints on the silver photograph frames that vied for space with a china beaker crammed with pencils and ball pens, used bottles of pink, silver and glittery blue nail varnish, tubs of talcum powder, sticks of lip colour, a box of tissues, an empty letter rack painted with lotus flowers and dipping swallows, a stationery casket to match, a slender gold wristwatch, which had stopped at ten twenty some unknown morning or night, and a tangle of fine gold chains beaded with oval pearls.

Scenes of crimes personnel had ransacked this room yesterday, but had come upon only the superficial residues of a young girl's life. There were no letters, diaries, scrapbooks, notebooks, personal organiser, or mobile telephone, or even a calendar. Crammed higgledy-piggledy on the shelves over the counter were various school books, a clutch of popular novels, well-thumbed catalogues for tack, riding wear, stable equipment and horse feed, several *Vogue* magazines, a score or more horse magazines, a clutch of teen publications and the ubiquitous *Hello!*. When he checked under the mattress, there was none of the pornography Avril O'Connor had once found. The school-work files harboured no cryptic jottings that might yield insights, and the doodles defacing almost every sheet of paper were composed of stirrups, naïve depictions of a horse's head and the meandering scrawls of boredom.

He reached for the gold chains and, idly shaking out the tangles, imagined how their delicacy would have suited her. Then he picked up the watch, turning it in his fingers. The back of the case was hallmarked and it should have been put into safekeeping. The wallet and purse found in the bedside cabinet were already in the police station safe, along with ninety-seven pounds in cash and four platinum credit cards on the Melvilles' accounts.

One by one he lifted the photographs, taken unawares by the weight in the frames. A haughty grey-haired woman in country tweeds, whom he took to be a grandparent, stared at him unsmilingly, as did Freya, surrounded by her current sixth formers. The pictures of Purdey showed her with Tonto in the pasture, displaying her pretty head in a portrait and, with Sukie in the saddle, posing before a Victorian Gothic mansion that featured in its own right in another picture, its unprepossessing architecture softened by evening sunlight and the shadows of nearby trees in full leaf. The two remaining photographs faced each other in a double frame. In one Sukie and Imogen, arm in arm and laughing, screwed up their eyes against some blistering foreign sun. They were still laughing in the other picture and, wearing coloured sun tops and cotton shorts, were both on bicycles, their legs splayed out as they zoomed down a hill towards whoever held the camera. He stared at them for a long time, feeling almost as his own the terrible sense of loss.

Rapping gently on the partly open door, Janet broke his reverie. 'I've finished with Charlotte Swann, sir. Who shall I see next?'

'Alice Derringer, when she gets back from the optician. In the meantime, perhaps you'd list and pack Sukie's belongings. We'll need to get the Melvilles to check if anything is missing.' He left his seat to stand by the window and lit a cigarette. 'How did you fare with the Princess Diana lookalike?'

'Don't ask!' She picked up the topmost garment from the heap, a dress fashioned from two layers of gauzy grey chiffon suspended from shoe-string straps. 'The claws were out the moment you turned your back.' The rolled-up garment was put on the end of the bed. 'She was expecting you to interview her.'

'I know. Dr Scott said she'd spent half the morning making sure she looked her best.' He dropped ash out of the window, where it disintegrated in a sudden gust of wind. 'That aside, did she tell you anything useful?'

'Depends on your definition of useful.' Holding a skimpy sweater by its hem, she lined up the side seams. 'She gave me no end of "useful" tips on how the right make-up, hairstyle and clothes could do wonders for me, and even snare me a rich boyfriend if I went where the beautiful people hang out, which is, I hasten to add, a very long way from north Wales.'

'I'm sure you'd rather stay where you are and as you are,' he said. 'Charlotte's like a blown egg covered in jewels and enamel. She's no family to speak of and no inner resources, and she's besotted with the superficial. I almost feel sorry for her.'

'You wouldn't if you'd actually spoken to her,' Janet said waspishly. 'She's shallow and spiteful, and talks a load of incontinent drivel.' Absently placing the folded sweater on top of the dress, she took hold of a jacket. 'I think she could be really dangerous. She's got no moral sense whatsoever and, given the wrong sort of company, could incite others to do the most outrageous things.'

'Come on,' he chided. 'That's a very harsh judgement on the briefest of acquaintances.'

Janet shook her head. 'No, sir, it isn't.' Looking then at what was in her hands, she laid the jacket on the bed to fasten the buttons. 'She said it would have been better for everyone if Imogen had died in the accident, because not only have her injuries made her repulsive, but her ugliness is incredibly embarrassing and very difficult for people. Charlotte was sick the first time she saw Imogen without her leg and even now, she says, her gorge rises every time she sets eyes on her.'

'Perhaps she's only voicing what others think but are too inhibited to say.'

'Or too sensitive,' she added. 'Charlotte's very cruel and even if that's not her fault, it doesn't make her any the less dangerous.'

'I suppose not.' At the small sink set into the far end of the counter, he doused his cigarette under the tap, then filled a toothpaste-smeared glass with water. As he dribbled the water around the spider plant it pooled on the dried-out soil and popped with air bubbles before being absorbed. 'I'm going to see Imogen,' he told her. 'She should know if Sukie kept a diary of any description. When you've finished here, ask Matron for Sukie's luggage. There'll probably be a trunk stored somewhere.'

The spiky leaves of the spider plant tickled his chin as he waited for Imogen to open her door. Bedsprings creaked in the room beyond, then there was silence. He knocked again, heard the bedsprings again, then a thump and imagined her stick hitting the floor. As another thump was followed by a dragging noise, he could almost see her hauling her maimed body towards him. A key rattled in the lock and the door was inched open, Imogen's fingers like claws round the edge. Her face was grey and lined with pain. 'That's Sukie's plant,' she whispered.

'I know.' He smiled. 'I wondered if you'd mind looking after it for now. It was dry as a bone.'

She hopped backwards a few feet then stood in the middle of the room, leaning heavily on the silver-topped stick, her body twisted, the stump of leg hanging uselessly. Her eyes were like huge black holes.

As he put the plant on the counter, he accepted that however Sukie had parted with her life, it had not been at this girl's hands, for her balance and equilibrium were totally destroyed. If I push her, he thought, she'll simply topple. She backed further and collapsed on the bed, leaving him the chair. The artificial leg lay on the floor on a heap of discarded clothes.

Lifting herself on her hands, she wriggled across the bed until she was leaning against the wall. The single foot in a fluffy pink mule, barely twelve inches from his knees, was disturbing. While his reason told him the quest was futile, his instinct was to search for its companion. She watched him, her face reflecting his own confusion.

'I've been looking through Sukie's things,' he said eventually, 'but there was very little of a personal nature. Would you know if she kept a diary?'

'I – She –' Words seemed to stick in her throat. She swallowed hard and tried again. 'She sort of did, a long time ago. She wasn't very good at keeping it up to date.'

'Was she not inclined to commit her thoughts to paper?'

Imogen shook her head. 'Not really. She preferred to talk.' She wrapped her arms round her waist and hunched her shoulders, staring at her foot.

What could you do with only one leg? McKenna considered all the new impossibilities forced on this girl, beyond the obvious, and began to hurt for her. 'Has Dr Scott spoken to you about me?' he asked.

'No.' Another head shake.

'I thought she would have done by now.'

'Why?'

'Because, as I said last night, I must interview all of you.' He waited for her to respond and when she continued to sit in silence added, 'She impressed upon me that I must be sensitive to your feelings.'

A noise between a snort and a sob escaped her lips. '*She* isn't!'

'You know, Imogen,' he said, leaning forward and clasping his hands, 'I'm getting very mixed messages.'

The corners of her mouth turned up, then down. 'So you can't tell whether you're coming or going? Join the club.'

People had been dangerously soured by lesser misfortunes than hers, he told himself. It was unfair to condemn her, yet her air of angry self-pity was so intense he could scarce believe she had not shared her anguish with someone in the school, who then, convinced Sukie was to blame, had settled the score by killing her.

'Have you had lunch?' he asked.

'Vivienne brought me a sandwich.'

'I noticed she helped you from the refectory earlier. Are you particularly friendly?' Vivienne, with the ethical structure of her personality undermined by drugs, might well have dispatched Sukie, he thought.

'No,' Imogen replied. 'Our paths hardly ever cross.'

She could be lying, he decided. He gazed at her speculatively, but before he could speak, she added, 'I was surprised myself.' She met his eyes and shrugged. 'It was probably because Torrance isn't here. She sort of looks after me.' She shuddered, just once, but with frightening violence.

'Torrance wasn't badly hurt,' he said quickly.

'I know. Vivienne told me.' The pink-clad foot began to wave from side to side. 'Will she be staying in hospital?'

'For a while. And she's under twenty-four-hour guard.'

'Good.' Imogen nodded, as if to herself, then said, 'I'm sorry, I'm not being a very good hostess. You can smoke if you like. There's a tin on the shelf you can use for an ashtray.' Apologising again, she added, 'And I'm sorry I can't offer you a drink, but you can make yourself one in the common room.'

'Thanks, but I don't want one. Do you?' When she shook her head, he went on, 'I expected your rooms to have better facilities. A kettle, at least.'

'Dr Scott thinks we'd be less inclined to mix if we were too comfortable. I expect you've noticed how her ideas invade every corner.' She glanced about her. 'Even in these poky little cells.'

His eyes on the enormous old key hanging from the door lock, he said, 'Matron told me these rooms housed the most violent patients in the old days.'

'That's why the locks were on the outside. Sean had to turn my door and cut a new keeper. He's good with things like that.'

'D'you have much contact with him?'

'Not as much as some would like, but a lot more than Dr Scott knows about!' She smiled spontaneously and it was as if a light had come on behind her eyes, returning her fleetingly to the girl she should have been. 'Don't misunderstand. He doesn't mess with us. He's too nice to take advantage and anyway, he's engaged.'

'Nonetheless, he must get plenty of offers. He's the only young man in the vicinity. Ken Randall at the lodge is in his sixties and so is Sean's boss, and the guards and the caretakers are determinedly middle-aged.'

'That's no accident. It's all part of Dr Scott's grand design.'

'And where do you fit into that?' His voice was quiet. 'What's she got in mind for you?'

'Nothing,' Imogen said. 'Absolutely nothing. She's done her bit as far as I'm concerned. Now it's up to me.' The light in her eyes flickered wildly, but did not quite gutter. 'There's a certain logic in there, I suppose. I can't rest on my crutches for ever.'

'Would you want to?'

'I can't get off them. Whenever I try, I fall over.' She paused. 'I'm speaking metaphorically.'

Knowing he was probably tearing at an open wound, he said, 'Now Sukie's gone, you might be able to stand on your own. The past won't be dragging you back.'

'I didn't even feel that,' she told him.

'I beg your pardon?'

'You expected to hurt me, but you didn't and you won't. No one could hurt me as much as I hurt myself.' Again she paused, but this time the silence was oppressive with the unspoken. 'I'm speaking literally *and* metaphorically.'

Playing for time, he lit a cigarette, then searched for the tin. 'Was your estrangement from Sukie as absolute as everyone seems to think?' he enquired at last. 'Or did you sometimes still get together?'

'We hadn't spoken a word to each other since the crash.'

Sensing from her tone that the shutters were coming down, he asked, 'Had she taken up with anyone else?'

'No.' Her certainty betrayed the passion with which she had watched and listened for news of Sukie. 'I don't think anyone wanted to be her friend, except Daisy Podmore from the fourth. She pestered her day and night, wanting to be best friends, wanting Sukie to teach her to ride, wanting this, that and the other.' She stared vacantly beyond her foot. 'But it didn't mean anything. Daisy always jumps in when people split up. She picks over the bones like a vulture.'

'I don't understand why Sukie should be ostracised.'

Momentarily, her eyes met his, and she looked both guilty

and terrified. Then her glance flicked away. 'I didn't mean that,' she mumbled. 'I don't think *she* wanted another friend. I don't think she could believe it was over between us.'

'And you?'

'What about me?' Her voice was harsh.

On the point of asking if she had shared Sukie's disbelief about the death of their friendship, he saw the look on her face and closed his mouth.

18

Afternoon classes had finished some ten minutes before McKenna made his way back downstairs. As he turned into the administration corridor he all but collided with Daisy. She gave him a look that mingled rage with furtiveness, then dodged out of sight.

Matron, lips pursed, forehead creased, was standing just outside her room. 'I don't like to say this, Superintendent,' she began, 'but all these questions you're asking, not to mention having police everywhere, are bringing out the worst in these girls. They're quite unlike their usual selves. Even young Daisy, bless her, is all put out and irritable because Alice isn't back from town yet.' She stopped for breath. 'And she's normally the last to let a little disappointment get to her. She's one of the sunniest children I've ever come across.'

'She's hardly a child,' he said. 'She's fifteen.'

She adopted an indulgent expression. 'They're all children! They might not see *themselves* that way, but believe me, they are.' Weighing him up, she apparently found him wanting. 'I can tell you've none of your own by the way you talk. All *you* see in Daisy is a well-developed teenager who obviously takes pride in her appearance, but I see the other side of her. I see the other side of all of them.' Her bosom heaved under the starched uniform. 'Teenagers are very confusing,' she went on sagely, 'especially to themselves. One minute, they're all grown up and wanting their freedom, then, in the twinkling of an eye, they're crying like babies or having a tantrum. They don't know whether to cling to childhood or grasp being an adult.' Her lips pursed once more. 'To my mind it's a long, hard road to maturity, but one they've got to travel alone, whereas Dr Scott says children are just little lumps of clay to be moulded, forcefully if need be. Then they get fired like so many pots in what she calls the "crucible" of the school. I can even think of a few she's decorated to her own design.'

Her breath began to wheeze and he hoped she had finally run out of steam, but as he was about to speak, she commenced another diatribe. 'I dare say you want to see the Head, don't you? Now, she's another one letting things get to her.' Concern for a fellow being now transformed her face. 'She's worried, you see, and with good reason, if you want my honest opinion, not that she needs *me* to show her the writing on the wall. Parents have been ringing up non-stop all day and some of them are talking about taking their girls away. But what else can you expect?' Chewing her mouth, she added, 'And I shudder to think what'll happen when news of Torrance's accident gets out.' She paused, staring at him. 'The girls want to know if she can have visitors yet.'

'That's something I was going to discuss with Dr Scott,' he said, seizing an opportunity to escape.

'Then let's see if she's still in her study.'

He trailed in her wake the few yards between the two rooms, waiting at her side as she rapped at the study door. When Freya appeared, he thought she looked quite unruffled, although her mouth tightened with annoyance when she saw Matron. Handed over, as he imagined the two women transacted children, he let her draw him in. 'I think Matron hoped to be part of the discussion,' he commented.

'Do you?' She busied herself angling two chairs in front of the open window and, taking one herself, offered him the other.

Glancing outside, he was struck by the change in the weather that had crept up unawares. Purplish cloud hung over the Strait, turning the waters dark and the lawns and flowers lividly bright. A wind snapped spitefully now and then at the trees, lifting the leaves to show their pale undersides.

She followed his gaze. 'There's rain on the way. And thunder, too, if the number of people complaining of headaches is any indication. Matron's been inundated with requests for painkillers.' Surveying the tossing leaves, she added, 'I hope the wind dies down. High winds can make people very edgy, if not violent.'

'Did you learn about the effects of weather in your psychology studies?'

'No, in the army. One must be aware of anything likely to affect the mood and morale of the troops.'

'Your current crop of recruits is less than happy in any case, according to Matron.'

'Oh, really!' Freya exclaimed. 'What else does she expect?' She rose, rather quickly, took the ashtray off her desk and slapped it down on the window ledge. 'She's simply terrified of change, in whatever guise it comes, even if it's only a ripple in the waters of life.'

'Sukie's death is more of a tidal bore.'

'I'm aware of that.' She crossed her legs elegantly and he was forcibly reminded of something else that Imogen could no longer do. 'Unfortunately,' she went on, 'Matron's perceptions are wholly self-centred. Her life is completely bound up within the school and she finds upheavals of any kind immensely threatening. If the unexpected happens she goes to pieces.' She regarded him thoughtfully. 'I make endless concessions, partly because she's quite good at her job and partly because of her age, but we still end up crossing swords far too often. Only the other day I asked her to consider an alternative to that ghastly nurse's uniform she lives in, but she wouldn't hear of it.'

'It's harmless enough, surely?'

'Not necessarily.' Freya shook her head. 'I must accommodate all sorts of parental whims, staff presentation being one of them.' She made a face, somewhere between apology and challenge. 'And talking of parents, many of them are expressing the gravest concerns for their daughters' safety.'

'I trust you referred to the constant police presence?'

'They'd prefer a resolution, as I would. I hate to criticise, but you seem to be doing little beyond talking to people.'

'The days of wearing a deerstalker hat while peering through magnifying glasses are long gone,' he told her, 'and in any case, until the pathologist can tell us exactly how Sukie died, we're in something of a limbo.'

'When do you expect to know?'

'Perhaps later today.'

'And then what?'

'That will depend on whether it was suicide or murder.'

Turning her head to gaze at the turbulent waters, she said, 'I remain convinced it was suicide. Since the accident, she'd become increasingly unstable and unhappy, and because there was no hope of settlement to the situation, that made her extraordinarily vulnerable and fragile.'

'Was that why she wasn't eating properly?' he asked, unable to take his eyes from the beautiful profile of her chin and neck. 'Her stomach was shrunken.'

For several moments Freya remained silent, before saying, 'Queen Victoria's physician first recognised anorexia in 1874, and for long afterwards it was described as a compromise with suicide. That, I think, is very relevant to Sukie.'

'Is Ainsley Chapman another victim?'

'Ainsley was born skinny, as others are born fat. She's somewhat neurotic, too, as you've no doubt gathered, but in any group of adolescents there will be those with problems. These girls are no different from their peers anywhere in the world.'

'Oh, but they are,' he said. 'Their wealth alone creates a huge divide and they live in a rarefied atmosphere which is designed for containment. Without normal outlets, their feelings, whatever they are, will turn in on themselves.' He paused, watching her face. 'Sukie's distress was obvious, but no one knew what had caused it. Similarly, no one quite understands why Imogen's personality is now as maimed as her body, although everyone unwittingly reacts to the pathological situation their ruptured friendship caused.'

'You're reading far too much significance into that event,' she countered. 'Relationships between adolescents are always in a constant state of flux.' With a sigh, she added, 'And I'm afraid you're crediting Sukie with too much importance. Before she died, she was no more and no less significant than the others. Life would fast become unbearable if every girl had to be singular. The Hermitage reflects the outside world, Superintendent, where people subsume their individuality to the needs of their particular group.'

For many, he thought, her constant parrying must have the

same effect as water dripping on stone. He felt quite wearied and only stubbornness stopped him from leaving. Reaching for his cigarettes, he said, 'I intended to ask Imogen to tell me about Sukie, but quite frankly, it seemed too risky. She looks close to a breakdown.'

She folded her hands in her lap. 'Inevitably, you would have found her at her most defenceless. What did you wish to know about Sukie?'

'The sort of person she was,' he replied shortly, unable to hide his irritation. 'Weak, strong, loyal, dishonest, kind, malicious, hard-hearted, generous, mean, easily led, a leader, a bully, a victim?'

'She was an ordinary teenager, with strengths and weaknesses like everyone else.'

'You said this morning she bore the brunt of her parents' marital strife. That must have made an impact.'

'In years to come,' Freya said, 'I think it would have derailed her, certainly as far as her own relationships with men were concerned. However, harsh though it may sound, that's no longer relevant.' She met his eyes, her expression unfathomable. 'I'm afraid I can suggest no reason why anyone should want to kill her. I'm equally mystified by Torrance's fall.'

'Have you told her family?'

She nodded. 'They weren't surprised she'd had an accident.'

'Do they think that's what it was?'

'Was there any point in telling them otherwise? You have her well-protected. She shouldn't come to further harm.'

He felt like slapping her out of her complacency. 'The harm's been done, Dr Scott. Enough of it to ruin you.'

19

As the afternoon wore on, the sky grew darker, riven now and then by the unearthly blue of a lightning storm far out to sea. Shortly before six o'clock the rain began to fall, at first in spatters, but soon in a downpour, hammering so hard on the roof and bodywork of the mobile incident room that McKenna could barely hear what Eifion Roberts was saying. He clamped the telephone receiver against his ear, trying to cut out some of the din.

'As I said earlier,' the pathologist reminded him, 'I found a lot of ante-mortem contusions to the body, the nature of which suggest regular and repeated assaults, so I called in a colleague who's autopsied a few boxers in his time. Like me, he reckons young Sukie's been used for a punchbag, although she wasn't beaten to death. We estimate the last battering occurred around ten days ago.'

'Would her injuries have been visible?' asked McKenna.

'Not unless she'd stripped off. Mostly, they're on the torso and thighs. Career bullies don't generally advertise their handiwork, which makes it all the harder to identify their victims.'

'Quite,' McKenna said quietly, making notes for the next briefing meeting.

'The head injuries,' Roberts went on, 'are relatively superficial, in that none would be fatal and they probably occurred in the main when she was being knocked about in the water. However, the laceration at the base of the skull I mentioned before is more consistent with bludgeoning than random injury. Its dimensions, which are quite regular, indicate something not too thick and not sharp-edged.' He paused.

'Anything from a broken branch to the shaft of a hockey stick.'

'Or a crutch or walking stick.'

'Possibly,' Roberts agreed, 'although I'd advise against going mob-handed into the school and confiscating every blunt instrument in sight. Wait until the wound debris come back from analysis. I'm expecting to hear later this evening.'

'At least we can finally discount accident or suicide.'

'That you can. The way I read it now, she was stunned by that blow, hauled into the water, then left to drown.'

'She may have fallen in when she was hit.'

'She was dragged. I found fresh abrasions on the toe ends of both trainers.'

'How much strength was required?'

'No more than average. She didn't weigh much and, unconscious, wouldn't put up any resistance.'

McKenna made some more notes. 'Was there anything under her fingernails?' he asked. 'Tissue, fibres, perhaps?'

'No,' Roberts replied. 'Just dirt.' He stopped speaking and McKenna could hear the sound of a pencil tapping against teeth. Presently he went on, 'Far be it from me to tell you how to do your job, Michael, but I don't think you should let on you know Sukie was murdered. That knowledge gives you the only real advantage you've got and the longer the killer thinks you're fumbling in the dark, the more off-guard they'll hopefully become. There's absolutely no forensic evidence on the perpetrator, nor is there likely to be, unless they were daft enough to hang on to whatever Sukie was clouted with, which, to my mind, is the last thing they'd do. You're dealing with somebody very clever and very cunning.'

The evening's briefing was scheduled for seven and as soon as McKenna finished his discussion with Eifion Roberts he sat down with Jack to collate the information that had been accumulated during the day. After relaying the pathologist's finding, he said, 'What we need now is a credible motive.'

'Imogen Oliver's got motives by the bucketload,' Jack said irritably. The headache that had plagued him for hours had miraculously disappeared once the scent of thundery rain began to energise the air, but was now returning with renewed vigour.

'She might not be capable herself, but what's to stop someone doing her dirty work for her?'

'My instinct tells me she's not a killer, even by proxy. And if she confided in someone about the accident and set up an emotional chain reaction, which resulted in a kind of punishment killing, then I'm sure she doesn't suspect.'

'You know nothing about her. You've barely spoken to her.'

'She was hardly in the mood to cope with challenging and provocative questions,' McKenna commented. 'Saying she's on a knife edge is the understatement of the year.' Regarding his colleague rather accusingly he added, 'You let your compassion get the better of you with Vivienne Wade, even though her drug problem could be connected to the killing.'

'*Your* interviews weren't a roaring success, either,' Jack snapped. 'Ainsley Chapman ran out on you, Justine turned on the waterworks and Torrance got clobbered before you could get to her. In other words, what we *do* know about these girls would fit on the back of a stamp, and what we *don't* would fill an encyclopaedia, because people are deliberately hiding things from us. First it was Imogen's accident, then Vivienne's addiction and now the bullying.'

'And Sukie's death might not be connected to any of them.'

'No?' Jack sounded intensely sceptical. 'Sukie's death *feels* like a murder that was waiting to happen. Bullying could well be the motive.'

'I know,' McKenna admitted, 'and we'll look into it. But we'll be treading very delicate ground, because it's probably so much part of the school ethos it's a virtual tradition and as these girls will have to live with the bullies long after we've gone, they won't be keen to grass them up. It's not our job to make a bad situation infinitely worse, but that said, Freya Scott needs reminding there's a very thin line between promoting survival of the fittest and encouraging criminal assault.' He paused. 'I can't help wondering how far she'd go to protect her reputation and the school's image, and I'm sure plenty of girls would be willing to do anything for her if she gave them the nod. Sukie only had to open her mouth to ruin her.'

'I don't like conspiracy theories,' Jack told him, kneading his forehead. 'If Scott was as bothered as that about the bullying, she'd put a stop to it. Look, we're fairly sure Sukie went out voluntarily on Tuesday night, which means she'd no idea she was walking into a death trap. She *trusted* whoever she was going to meet, or more likely, whoever lured her out; therefore, she wasn't planning a midnight picnic with the bullies.'

'That's not to say they weren't waiting for her.'

'But would they need to go to such lengths? When they've obviously had no end of opportunity in the past to persecute her?'

'Perhaps it was imperative to neutralise her. She could have been on the verge of breaking ranks, reporting them to Childline, or even to us.' McKenna toyed with a cigarette, then with his lighter. 'Although I think that's doubtful,' he concluded reluctantly. 'I've heard nothing to suggest she was inclined to make waves. All in all, she seems to have kept a low profile. I get the impression she was just a nice kid who didn't make enemies and didn't attract passionate feelings.'

'And therefore had no apparent reason to get murdered,' Jack said. 'So, it's back to basics: who *benefits* from her death?'

'Or loses out if she remains alive.' McKenna lit the cigarette, then glanced at his watch. 'Time's getting on,' he said. 'What else have we got?'

'Not much,' Jack replied, shuffling through his papers. 'HQ haven't come back with any intelligence on abduction; none of the staff – past, present or contract – has form, apart from Sean O'Connor; Berkshire police haven't called back, so I assume there's nothing new to report; and the school's financial affairs are in sound order and all above board, so Sukie can't have stumbled on an embezzlement scam.' He smiled. 'I asked the chair of governors for the name of the school's accountants. He was livid, but he couldn't very well refuse.' Then the smile died. 'I also rang John Melville, poor sod, to find out if Sukie had a mobile, but she hadn't. Still, he's given permission for us to have details of her credit card transactions for the last six months. The card companies promised to fax them tomorrow.'

'What about the car Sean saw Vivienne getting into?'

'It belongs,' Jack told him, extracting a sheet of flimsy from his papers, 'to a mate of a well-known drug pusher from Manchester who, since the A55 opened along the coast, has made use of the facility to extend his operations right across north Wales – him, and a load of other undesirables,' he added trenchantly. 'Manchester police are about to land on the pusher and his minions from a great height, so Sean could find himself in court giving evidence. So could Vivienne, but it wouldn't be a good idea to tell her because she'd be off like a rocket into the far blue yonder. She reckons informing on the pusher would earn her a kneecapping with a baseball bat.'

'Don't underestimate her,' McKenna said. 'She's got a lot more guts than you'd expect. Imogen told me she'd given her stump a massage, because the muscles were knotted up. Torrance does it for her usually. She seems to do an awful lot the professionals should be doing.'

'Yes, well, I told you Scott's a cheapskate, not that physiotherapy for Imogen would cost her anything, except perhaps a dent in her know-it-all arrogance.' Rubbing his forehead again, Jack yawned. 'I've sealed Torrance's room, by the way, so her things don't get pinched. I took the SIM card out of her mobile as well.'

'That's something else we should tell Dr Scott,' McKenna remarked. 'About the mobiles.'

'So she can confiscate them? And make a big deal of it into the bargain?' Jack shook his head. 'That isn't a good idea. Those mobiles could be a lifeline.'

'I think that's a bit of an exaggeration,' McKenna commented. He smoked in silence for a while, then said, 'It occurred to me that thieving could be behind Sukie's death.'

'Janet went through her things with Matron when she packed them. Nothing seems to be missing even though her room was open for nearly two days after she disappeared. The cash would have gone, surely?'

'I suppose,' McKenna conceded. 'There could have been a lot *more* money, of course. And jewellery.'

'We'll ask Torrance when she's fit. She's got to know *something*. She wasn't half killed for no reason.'

'Then why hadn't she already told us? Anyway, we don't know she *was* the intended victim of the saddle sabotage and even if she was she probably won't remember a thing after the concussion she's had.' McKenna ground out the cigarette, and pushed the little pile of ash and tobacco shreds into a cone. 'There's little hope of uncovering actual evidence to identify whoever was out of school on Tuesday night, so we'll have to look for something that jars or strikes a false note.' He made a crater in the cone with the stub end. 'Imogen said Daisy Podmore was pestering Sukie. It sounds as if she had a crush on her, so maybe Sukie spurned her advances and Daisy took it too personally. Daisy, incidentally, is not only hot favourite in the killer stakes, but Martha Rathbone's least favourite person, despite being her daughter's best friend.' He glanced in Jack's direction. 'I take it you've heard about the bookmaking? It's been organised by central division, apparently.'

'Dewi told me a short while ago. It's an absolute disgrace.'

'Something like it was bound to happen. Still, you never know what that line of thinking might provoke. We could do with some inspiration.'

Jack's headache, coupled with the day's interminable frustrations, finally bettered his patience. 'It's not inspiration we need,' he said through gritted teeth, 'it's some good, solid policing. We've done nothing but footle around and we'll never know if there *was* any hard evidence because your softly-softly approach has given the killer any number of opportunities to get rid of it, not to mention taking a crack at Torrance and anyone else who gets in the way. We should be going through that school like a dose of salts, *frightening* the truth out of them if necessary.'

'We have enough personnel on site to prevent further incidents,' McKenna said stiffly. 'And I happen to agree with Eifion's assessment of the situation.'

Jack's chair screeched along the floor as he rose. 'Well, I don't. He's the pathologist; *we're* the investigators. Horses for courses, or had you forgotten?'

As more and more officers filed into the mobile incident room for the briefing, the temperature inside climbed until, by the time McKenna stood up to speak, the place was a veritable sweat box. After posting two uniformed officers outside in case any of the girls or staff were minded to eavesdrop, he had all the windows opened.

Jack had placed himself in the front row, and sat with his legs crossed, arms folded and his chin sunk in his chest, but the expression on his face remained all too visible. McKenna looked over his head, but it proved much harder to ignore the implication of negligence in what he had said. That nagged persistently at the back of his mind, threatening to distract him even further.

'Dr Roberts has now confirmed that Sukie's death was a homicide,' he began, 'and although we can't exclude anyone at this stage, she was probably killed by one of her fellow pupils. How, then, can we distinguish that person from the rest? The paper you received this morning presents a series of factors, antecedents and warning signals that help to build a profile of the potentially murderous child, who usually bears a very close resemblance to the murderous adult. The difference lies in the fact that we don't *expect* children to kill and we therefore tend always to be in denial.'

Glancing quickly at the key points he extracted from the paper, he went on, 'One important factor is a family background inhabited by violence, alcoholism, mental illness and characterised by poor parenting and serious emotional deprivation. Material poverty also features very frequently. Children take their lead and learn how to behave from the adults within their orbit, and although this is not the place for a debate on nature versus nurture, it would be a rare child who did not react and respond to such an environment. The need for personal and psychological survival forces the development of coping strategies, which may manifest themselves in various ways: truancy, substance abuse, violent mood swings, aggression, extreme timidity, perpetual conflict with those around them, coldness, absence of empathy and social responsibility, intellectual deterioration, confusion, depression, apathy, unnatural secretiveness, habitual dishonesty and lethargy. At a certain point, disentangling coping from copying becomes impossible, for the onlooker and for the child, who is effectively trapped in a profound and unreachable state of complete disaffection where life's normal transactions mean nothing. That is when the child turns into a ticking bomb.'

He waited for questions, but none was forthcoming; his

audience seemed both bemused and close to exhaustion. Fighting with his own fatigue of the spirit, he said, 'The Hermitage girls have a natural family and a school family, of which the latter probably exerts the greater influence on the majority. This school family appears to border on the classically dysfunctional. Our presence here inevitably adds to existing stresses, but we're seeing them at their worst because their worst exists and is, I suspect, barely below the surface at the best of times. So the effect of the school's ethos, functioning and personalities is crucial to our profiling process. Unfortunately for that process, many of the girls will be at least a reasonably good fit, partly because of the law of averages, partly because the school has made them so. I hesitate to say we should be on the lookout for someone who could be described as a natural-born killer – aside from the difficulty of recognising such a person, murder is usually motivated by mundane, rather than esoteric, considerations: loss or gain, love or hate, revenge—'

At that moment, every telephone in the room began to ring. McKenna picked up the one on the table beside him, to hear Freya, her voice very subdued, saying, 'Would you come to the school immediately? There's been an incident.'

20

She was waiting for him in the lobby. 'Please come upstairs.'
There was no ambiguous invitation in her manner, only
undisguised anxiety.

'What's happened?' He followed her into the lift.

'Imogen lashed out with her stick at Nancy. She almost
brained her.' Freya stared at him unblinkingly. 'Is that what
happened to Sukie?'

The lift whined jerkily upwards. 'You know I can't tell you.'

Without warning, her knees buckled and she fell against him.
'Dear God!' she moaned. 'It *was* Imogen!'

His hands fluttered about her shoulders and, despite himself,
settled there. She was trembling from head to foot. Then the lift
jolted to a stop and they heard Matron, shouting hysterically,
in the adjoining room.

Freya lifted her head to look into his eyes. 'How great *is* your
need, I wonder?' she murmured, her lips quivering. Then, she
broke away, dragged open the lift door and stepped into the
corridor.

For long moments he remained in the lift, the rational and the
physical at total war, before he was able to pull himself
together. When he walked into Imogen's room, he found a
different kind of battle in progress.

She was threshing about on the bed, the shoeless artificial leg
thumping the quilt, while Matron, red in the face and puffing
furiously, tried to hold her down. The silver-topped stick lay on
the floor. When she noticed McKenna at the door, half-hidden
behind Freya, she stopped struggling, but her eyes were alight
with rage.

Freya's voice shook. 'Why on earth did you hit her?'

'Because she's a bloody bitch!' Imogen seethed. She fought free of Matron's weakening hold to drag herself upright, then stood beside the bed, swaying alarmingly. Her body contorted itself grotesquely when she bent to retrieve her stick.

'Don't touch it!' McKenna warned.

She twisted her head to look at him. 'Why not?'

'You know why.'

Falteringly, she straightened up, still swaying. 'I didn't kill Sukie.' 'How could I?' The anguish in her voice and expression betrayed her completely.

He glanced around the room. 'Where are your crutches?'

Freya touched his arm. 'Must you? She needs *some* support.'

'The hospital will lend us replacements.' Hoping Matron would take the hint, he added, 'Perhaps Matron would ask Inspector Tuttle to arrange it.' He took a pair of surgical gloves from the inside pocket of his jacket, snapped them over his hands and picked up the stick. 'The crutches, please,' he said to Imogen.

'They're under the bed.' As he knelt down, she watched intently, and when he rose again, she said, 'You won't find any blood. She saw it coming and dodged.' She was still swaying and he began to feel dizzy, then a little nauseous. 'Never mind, eh?' She leered fiendishly. 'There's always the next time.'

Holding her face in her hands, Matron rocked back and forth, looking as if she had been literally crushed by events. 'Dear God!' she lamented, echoing Freya. '*Dear* God!' The bedsprings screeched beneath her.

He leaned the stick and crutches against the wall, put his hands under her elbows and dragged her off the bed. Harrying her from the room, he pushed her into the lift, again instructing her to go straight to Jack.

'What shall I do then?' she wailed, grasping the lift gates to stop them closing.

'Whatever you would normally do at this time of the day,' he said curtly.

She seemed to collapse with relief. Her bosom drooped over the wide elastic belt, her jowls relaxed and her mouth fell open, and his last view of her before the lift gates closed was of the swags of tartar staining her lower teeth.

As he stood in the corridor, analysing his own contribution to the spiralling tension within the school, he heard Imogen's sharp, well-bred voice telling Freya that she wanted to be left alone.

Freya demurred. 'What if Nancy comes back?'

'I'll lock myself in,' Imogen snapped.

When he moved the few paces to her door, he found she was no longer swaying but clutching the back of a chair for support. 'I'd rather you didn't,' he said. 'I'll make sure Nancy keeps her distance, although I'd very much like to know what provoked you.'

'And whatever your differences with anyone,' Freya added, 'violence is not the solution.'

Imogen glared at them. 'I lost it! OK?' She inched around the chair and sat down, muttering something unintelligible.

The reptilian Nancy was in the sixth-form common room, entertaining a large audience with the lurid details of her encounter. Charlotte, bearing an even greater resemblance to her deceased role model, crouched at her side, clutching her hands.

His eyes like flints, McKenna stared at them. 'If any of you goes within twenty feet of Imogen Oliver you'll regret it. Do I make myself clear?'

Haughtily, Charlotte threw back her head, eyes flashing. 'Why haven't you arrested her?' When he made no response, her pencilled eyebrows disappeared under her blonde fringe. 'Are you actually letting that sick freak get away with what she did? Nancy could have been killed!'

When Janet described Charlotte's utterances as 'incontinent', she had been right, he thought, sorely tempted to take Imogen's lead and set about her with the stick.

Then Nancy sniggered. 'Yeah, like Sukie,' she remarked. 'D'you think he's made the connection yet?' she asked conversationally. She looked him over, deliberately and insolently, then her gaze came to rest on the stick and crutches in his hand. 'Well, goodness me, as Matron might say. Perhaps he isn't just a thick-headed Irish plod after all.'

*

When McKenna reached the lobby, he found Jack there and he felt as if he had walked blindly into another ambush.

'What the *hell*'s going on?' Jack demanded. 'Matron came staggering into the MIR, looking all set for a heart attack and squawking fit to bust about Imogen.' Then he noticed McKenna's freight. 'What are you doing with those?'

'What does it look like?' McKenna snarled.

Jack bit back the riposte he was about to make. 'I gathered from Matron that Imogen took a swipe at Nancy – with her stick – and you want us to borrow a stick and crutches from the hospital.'

'Yes.'

'Why?'

'Why d'you bloody think?' McKenna marched out on to the forecourt, strode over to his car and, opening the boot one-handed, took out three large evidence bags.

After a moment Jack followed. He watched him fill and seal each bag, then said, 'Imogen might have tried to clobber Nancy, but there's a world of difference between bashing the school bitch in the heat of the moment and the cold-blooded murder of your one-time dearest friend.'

In the act of stowing the bags in the boot, McKenna rounded on him. 'Not an hour ago you said Imogen's got "motives by the bucketload".'

'And *you*,' Jack reminded him, holding on to his temper with the greatest difficulty, 'were sure she isn't a killer.'

McKenna tore off his surgical gloves, threw them into the boot and slammed down the lid. 'I *had* to take her stick and crutches. I had no choice.' Bleakly he added, 'Anyway, it's done now. It's too late to backtrack.'

'Yes, it is, isn't it?' Jack stared at him. He felt furious, confused and sickeningly afraid for Imogen. 'By now,' he said, 'it'll be all over the school not only that Sukie was murdered, but that Imogen did it and they'll be waiting with bated breath for the big finale, when we clap her in irons and chuck her in the back of a Black Maria. Maybe, though, you should arrest her now,' he went on, his voice steely, 'while she's still relatively in one piece. You've left her at the mercy of a bunch of pack animals and I don't rate her chances overmuch.'

'I've already warned Nancy and her hangers-on to keep away from her and I intend to place a guard outside her room.' Deliberately McKenna avoided Jack's eyes. 'While I attend to that,' he went on coldly, 'perhaps you'd finish the briefing. You know what to say.'

'I've said it. I discussed the effects of persistent and vicious bullying in a place where kids are shut up with the bullies for months on end. Then I told most of them to go off duty. Everyone's had enough for one day – more than enough, in fact.'

'Have you sent someone to the hospital?'

'Not yet.'

McKenna opened the car boot once more, removed the three evidence bags and thrust them at Jack. 'When you do, tell them to take these to the pathology lab.' He closed the boot and strode off without a backward glance.

Jack stayed where he was long after McKenna had been swallowed up by the darkness of the lobby. Close to despairing of the man, he looked heavenwards, where the sky had cleared to a washed-out blue after that summer downpour. The forecourt and drive were already drying into a patchwork of light and dark as the water soaked away to the parched soil beneath, although the drainpipes gurgled still and raindrops slid persistently from the trees, plopping to the ground or ballooning on the well-waxed bodywork of McKenna's Jaguar.

Miss Attwill suddenly came into view, trudging head down from the direction of the stables. Her clothes looked sodden and her paddock boots were caked in mud. She stopped by the door to kick off the boots, then she too disappeared. He was about to turn away when a movement caught his attention and he looked up to see Daisy at the dormitory window. She was staring at him fixedly.

21

Much of what McKenna had said at the briefing meeting went over the heads of most of the police officers; it was Jack's terse statements about bullying, about the girls having no safe place, that made an impact. Even that, however, Dewi recalled, was nothing in comparison to the effect Matron's dramatic arrival achieved.

Jack had shunted her into the senior officers' cubbyhole, but her words flowed out in an agitated torrent, and long before she had finished relating her story and pronouncing on its implications, the officers in the adjoining room, listening in total silence, should have been persuaded that it was now a matter of 'suspect apprehended, case closed'. Some clearly were; others remained intensely sceptical. Dewi heard someone, who must, like Janet, have had the benefit of a university education, say that Imogen's attacking Nancy and therefore proving herself a killer was 'just *too* serendipitous'. Roughly interpreting the remark to mean 'too good to be true', he stared at the two officers who had organised the betting. They looked almost as agitated as Matron sounded.

'What's the matter?' he asked. 'Did you miscalculate the odds?'

They ignored him. Gathering up their papers and belongings, they hurried out of the room and started a general exodus.

'Imogen's down at twenty to one,' Nona told him. 'She's going to cost them an awful lot of money.'

'I hope she bankrupts them,' Dewi snapped. 'Have you placed a bet?' he demanded.

Nona flushed bright red. 'No!'

'How come you know so much about it, then?' Without giving her a chance to respond, he walked away.

Through the trees he could see brake lights flashing on and off as the drivers in front of him negotiated the bends in the lunatic drive. Nearing the gates, he found a queue of cars; Ken Randall, with his dog beside him, was checking each one as it left. Dewi waited his turn, and was about to move up when he saw Martha Rathbone's anonymous hire car trying to nose its way in. As he pulled over on to the verge to let her pass, she gave him a brief salute. Alice, sporting a pair of spectacles, was hunched sullenly in the passenger seat.

The dog trotted up to the car, sniffed the tyres, then put his paws on the door, panting and grinning. Dewi unwrapped a bar of Kit Kat and slipped it between the wicked-looking teeth. Chewing fiercely, the dog watched him intently and Dewi thought it was almost as if the animal were trying to speak to him. He stroked its head, tweaked its ears and ran his fingers through the soft brindled coat, wondering how his parents might respond if he broached the subject of having a dog of his own.

Once out of the gates, he stopped again, surveying the raggle-taggle of media vehicles on the opposite side of the road. Cups, sandwich wrappers, crushed cans and cigarette packets littered the grass, torn paper and ribbons of plastic bedecked the hedges. Concluding that it was fast coming to resemble a travellers' camping ground, he left the car and sauntered across, hands in pockets.

A woman in a dark-grey suit ran up to him, avid for news 'You're Detective Sergeant Prys, aren't you?' she asked, with a smile that made no impression on her empty blue eyes. 'So, what have you got for us?'

'A bit of advice,' he said. 'Get this lot cleaned up before I decide to move you on.'

He returned to the car, gunned the engine and swept away in the direction of the village and Sean O'Connor's house.

22

As she drove to the hospital, with Imogen's custom-made stick and crutches on the back seat of the car, Janet came to the conclusion that an effect need not bear an authentic or verifiable connection to a cause. She was astounded that McKenna had let one incident, that in context was both reasonable and completely comprehensible, overturn the direction of his investigation and set him on a path she was sure would prove to be disastrously misguided. Imogen could have wielded the stick because she was defending herself from attack; it was Freya Scott who, aided and abetted by Matron, had implied that Imogen's behaviour was tantamount to guilt for Sukie's murder. McKenna had allowed himself to be swept along by their deeply flawed and injudicious assumptions, apparently without once considering that for them, such a neat solution was immensely expedient.

Jack had left her in charge of Matron when he went over to the school in search of McKenna and it had been remarkable how quickly Matron's near hysteria gave way to what Janet perceived as something akin to callous satisfaction. 'Mind you,' she had said, 'why Imogen should have wanted to kill Sukie is a mystery. But then, who knows what might've gone on in the past?' Favouring Janet with a complicitous look, she had added, 'They'd been so very *close*.' Those few words contrived to sully what Janet would always believe had been only an innocent friendship. 'Still,' Matron finished, 'we won't have to wonder for ever. It'll all come out at the trial.'

'Aren't you getting rather ahead of yourself?' Janet had asked.

Matron had smoothed her apron and rather smugly replied, 'I think you should let Superintendent McKenna decide what's right and what's not. He wouldn't have taken away Imogen's stick and crutches unless he had the very *best* reasons. Now, would he?'

'There are plenty of other potential weapons lying about the school,' Janet had told her. 'Hockey and lacrosse sticks, tennis racquets, cricket bats—'

Matron had interrupted her. 'Maybe so, but he hasn't confiscated *those*.'

She left the stick and crutches in the pathology department, then went to collect their replacements – utilitarian NHS equipment with holes for height adjustment drilled through the metal shafts, and preformed grey plastic handles and underarm supports. After putting them in the car, she returned through the low-ceilinged reception area to the lifts and thence to Torrance's room. One policeman sat outside the door, another at the bedside, thumbing through a car magazine. Torrance, still comatose, was now wearing navy and cream striped silk pyjamas instead of the hospital-issue gown that had been put on her in the accident unit.

'Any change?' Janet enquired.

The policeman looked up from his magazine. 'She's been mumbling now and then about this and that, but she's not making any sense.'

There was a drip by the bedhead, releasing measured doses of some clear liquid down a plastic tube into a vein on the back of her hand. Janet peered at it. 'What's that for?'

'To stop her getting dehydrated.'

With a last glance at Torrance, she made for the door. 'It might be a good idea to write down what she says,' she remarked. 'Even if it does sound like gobbledegook.' As she left the room, something someone had said in the long hours since they invaded the school suddenly nudged the back of her mind. Who was it? she wondered, meandering past the nurses' station. *What* was it? One of the nurses bade her good evening and drove the memory back into obscurity.

23

At the best of times Miss Attwill was out of her depth with the horses. Justine, realising the woman was fast approaching the point of being overwhelmed by her increased responsibilities, took pity on her and helped out with evening stables, staying behind to clean and check the tack when Miss Attwill returned to school. She was glad of the peace, and the routine occupation, for since McKenna wrecked her equilibrium earlier in the day, she had found herself as restless as the proverbial cat on hot bricks.

English was a wonderfully rich language, she thought, minutely examining, for the third time, the surcingle straps on Tonto's saddle. Neither French nor German lent itself to such a wealth of metaphor or analogy, nor the silly little puns and aphorisms Matron proudly presented as insights. Justine wondered if she were the only one who felt at times like screaming at Matron. She recognised her rage for what it was, a reaction to the abnormal and claustrophobic conditions in which she lived, and knew it was not intrinsic to her nature, but she also understood how, in others, that rage might take root in the inner void, and with nothing to check its growth, make monsters.

She replaced Tonto's saddle on the rack, took down the next one, subjected that to an intense scrutiny, then moved on. Once she was satisfied no more nasty surprises lay in wait, she turned her attention to the bridles that hung on pegs below the saddles; they too were in proper order. Head collars and martingales were shaken out and rehung next, alongside the carefully looped lead and lungeing reins. Then, she rearranged the feed sacks, tidied an already neat stack of empty buckets, checked each horse's grooming kit to make sure the dandy brushes, curry combs, hoof picks, mane combs, scrapers and body brushes were all there, counted brushing boots, overreach boots and similar horse paraphernalia, looked at the turnout rugs and sweat sheets in case any were dirty or mouldy, and almost panicked when she could not find the electric clippers, before she remembered that Dr Scott, having had to pay over two hundred pounds for them, insisted on keeping them in her study. With nothing more she could conceivably do, Justine reluctantly switched off the lights and shut the stable doors behind her.

The horses were on the far side of the pasture, in a group beneath the trees. Elbows on the fence, she stood watching them, her gaze wandering over the thin grass, the semicircle of trampled earth in front of the gate and back to the animals. In the dusky light, they looked as insubstantial as ghosts and seemed to cast no shadow. She stared, perturbed by a sense of something amiss with the natural order of things, before she understood, for the first time in all the years she had been in this place, that the overpowering presence of the thousands of trees surrounding the school created its own light, and one which seemed to flout the laws of nature.

Suddenly beset by crude terror, she took flight up the path. The school was no haven, she thought, bursting into the lobby and leaving a trail of filthy footprints in her wake, but it was at least the devil she knew.

She turned for the stairs and met another devil, Daisy, on the way down. She appeared to be prodding Alice in the back – probably with a pitchfork, Justine said to herself. Clinging to the rail, Alice crept from stair to stair as if blinded, every so often lurching forward when Daisy urged her on. At every move her new spectacles slid further down her nose.

'Glasses are supposed to *help* you to see,' Justine said witheringly.

Alice peered at her, watery-eyed and looking rather sick. 'I haven't got used to them yet.'

'What are they for?'

'Reading.'

'Then why are you wearing them *now*?'

'Like she said,' Daisy lisped, 'she's getting used to them.'

'Oh, for heaven's sake!' Justine was tempted to slap both of them. 'Act your age!' She pushed past, stamped up to the first landing, then remembered she was still wearing her dirty boots. Crouching down to remove them, she chided herself for being so irritable. No harm had been done; Alice was merely being asinine, which was nothing unusual, despite her undoubted intelligence, and Daisy was only running true to form. Daisy, she reflected, picking up the boots and going on her way, caused problems wherever she went, using her considerable powers of imagination to create trouble out of nothing and taking enormous delight in the mayhem that followed. But perhaps, Justine thought, as she reached the top landing, the girl had no awareness of her faults. They might lie too deep for recognition, for all that they compelled her progress through life.

She stopped in her tracks when she saw the policeman outside Imogen's door.

He heard her gasp and raised his head. 'There's nothing to worry about, miss.'

Hand to her breast, Justine asked, 'Then why are you sitting there?'

'Orders.' With that he clamped shut his lips.

Dropping the boots outside her room, she ran along the corridor to the common room and found the whole of the sixth form congregated there, listening to what she thought at first was an impromptu lecture from Dr Scott. As she stood by the door, looking for a vacant seat, she quickly realised her mistake.

'And so,' the headmistress was saying, 'Superintendent McKenna was forced to the conclusion that Imogen killed Sukie. It's a terrible, *harrowing* situation and I pray you will all, despite your own distress, do your utmost to guide the younger girls through this dreadful time. Inevitably, they're already aware that something is horribly amiss and I intend to call a special assembly before lights out to tell them what has happened. It will be immensely difficult for them to grasp the brutal facts, but it would be very dangerous to allow rumour and hearsay to gain the upper hand.' She paused, looking down at the floor, then threw up her head. 'Now we know how Sukie died, the school can move on and away from the tragedy. Nonetheless, we must pray for Imogen. She is in torment, whatever her sins.'

Justine reeled into the corridor, astounded by the woman's appalling cant: she had looked triumphant.

Convulsed with shudders, she stumbled back to Imogen's room. The policeman leapt to his feet and tried to bar her way, but she dodged round him and threw open the door.

Imogen used the window end of her wall counter as a desk. She was seated there, writing, the bottle of painkillers and a clean glass at her elbow, and when Justine erupted into the room she looked up, placing her hand over the paper.

Questions tripped over each other in Justine's mind: How do you address a murder suspect? Is this another of those stiff-upper-lip occasions when the British behave as if nothing is wrong? What can I say? Why do I want to shrink away as if she's carrying the plague?

The policeman, breathing down Justine's neck, reached out to put his hand on her shoulder.

Imogen spoke. 'It's OK,' she told him with a smile that was ludicrously serene. 'Justine's a friend.'

Muttering about having to leave the door ajar, he backed off. Justine heard his chair creak as he sat down.

'I take it you know,' Imogen said quietly.

'I don't understand.' Justine's eyes filled with tears. 'Dr Scott is saying you probably killed Sukie.'

'It's a logical assumption.'

'I don't believe it!'

'That's sweet of you,' Imogen said, 'but I expect you're in a minority.' She turned the writing paper face down, then, leaning her elbow on the counter, levered herself round to face Justine. 'You see, I tried to hit Nancy over the head with my stick, so Superintendent McKenna decided I must have done the same to Sukie.'

'But we don't *know* what happened to her!'

'*We* might not,' Imogen reminded her gently, 'but the police obviously do.'

216

'Oh, God!' Justine put her hands to her face.

'In a strange sort of way I'm glad,' Imogen went on. 'About Nancy, I mean. Things are out in the open now. Everything's so much clearer.'

'Why did you hit her? What had she done?'

Imogen shrugged. 'Nothing much. Just the usual needling and bitching. But all of a sudden I wondered why we put up with her, so I thought I'd give her a taste of her own medicine.' She looked up at the other girl. 'Don't upset yourself. They won't find Sukie's blood on my stick or the crutches.'

Justine gaped. 'McKenna took your crutches, too? How in God's name does he expect you to manage?' she demanded angrily.

'They're borrowing some from the hospital.' After a moment Imogen added, 'Would you see if they've got them yet?'

'Yes, of course,' Justine replied vaguely, still trying to grasp the enormity and the sheer horror of what had transpired while she was killing time in the stables. 'Do you want anything else? A drink? Some food?'

Imogen smiled yet again. 'Later, perhaps.'

Muttering to herself in every language she knew, Justine walked very slowly down to the ground floor. Her body was numb, her flesh stone cold, and her capacity for thought and reason had deserted her. She felt in the midst of such horror she feared the school was about to be swamped by a tide of blood.

Matron was in the lobby, standing foursquare in front of Janet Evans, a pair of crutches and a cheap-looking walking stick in her hands. Justine sidled around the side of the staircase to linger in its shadow, eavesdropping.

'I'll take these up to Imogen later,' Matron was saying. 'She won't need them just yet.'

'Suppose she wants to go to the toilet?'

Matron sniffed. 'I'm sure I can be relied upon to look after her, whatever she's guilty of.' With a frown she pursed her lips. 'Why don't you go home? Most of your colleagues are long away.'

'I was hoping to finish with the fourth formers tonight.'

'Isn't it a bit late to be asking questions?' Matron consulted her fob watch. 'And what, may I ask, is the point? You know what happened to poor Sukie.'

'Even so, we must finish taking statements from everyone,' Janet replied evasively. 'I've got about ten girls left from the fourth, including Grace, Alice and Daisy.'

'You can't talk to Grace. I said she could spend the night in the infirmary again.' Matron paused. 'And I don't think you should bother Alice. She's complaining of another headache, even though the optician's prescribed reading glasses.' She allowed herself a brief smile. 'She looks quite the little intellectual when she's wearing them, though I dare say she'll get teased unmercifully until everybody's used to seeing her like that. But then,' she added indulgently, 'girls will be girls, won't they?'

'Girls will be *spiteful*,' Janet said, 'and people underestimate how much harm spite can do, especially in a closed community like this. I'm quite sure Nancy provoked Imogen's attack through sheer spite.'

'Whatever gave you that impression? Imogen's not been herself since the accident. It almost unhinged her, in my opinion.'

'All the more reason for her to be sensitive to spite.'

'You *do* repeat yourself,' Matron remarked. 'I don't think you've any idea how the Hermitage functions. After all, you just went to the local comprehensive, didn't you?'

'Yes,' Janet replied, anger staining her cheeks. 'But oddly enough, we managed not to kill each other.'

'You should learn to control your tongue, madam!' Matron snapped. '*And* your temper! Before you find yourself in the same boat as Imogen.' She wheeled away and began clomping up the stairs, her breath coming in furious, noisy gasps.

Justine waited, listening intently for those unmistakable footfalls, but more than thirty seemingly interminable minutes elapsed before Matron returned downstairs and bustled along the corridor towards her room, just as the headmistress emerged from her study. They spoke briefly, their voices too low for Justine to overhear the conversation, then Matron went into her room and slammed the door. Freya Scott locked her own door and, briefcase in hand, strode across the lobby and out through the double doors into the twilight.

Wondering what had become of the special assembly the headmistress had planned, Justine took herself back to Imogen's room, each step laboured and leaden. This time the policeman opened the door for her.

Imogen was in bed, the duvet up to her chin, auburn lights glinting in her dark hair from the soft glow of the bedside lamp. She had not removed her leg. She looked whole and for a split second Justine forgot the nightmare of the past six months.

24

Freya's house in the school grounds, isolated within a grove of old oaks, was perpetually in shadow and always cold, for the trees stole the warmth, even at the height of summer. Like the school a model of its time, the square, uncompromising building was also painted white inside and out, but here luxurious rugs softened the polished floors and fine furniture and dazzling abstract paintings were carefully arranged in every room. Yet for all their elegance, the spaces were bereft of vigour or genuine purpose.

Two enormous couches upholstered in dark-blue leather squatted on each side of the sitting-room fireplace. Seated in the middle of one, Freya dug in her long red nails and the leather yielded like still-live flesh, for all that it was as dead as it was cold. She shivered, unable to throw off the sense of evil portent that seemed about to intercept her future. When Sukie and Imogen returned to school after the accident, it was if they had been dragging behind them the shadow of death and now, she thought, viciously jabbing the leather, Sukie, in defiance of the law of God that stated the dead shall have no further part in the world, was creating havoc.

It was impossible to think of Sukie without thinking of Imogen; they were indivisible, even in death. It was reasonable to suppose that Sukie had died because of her, and the whys and wherefores were immaterial, despite those being the issues that so troubled McKenna. But not any longer, Freya told herself, still amazed by his compliancy, by the ease with which her little show of frailty had brought him to his knees. Those few moments in the lift, the way his mouth had loosened with desire when he felt her touch, would be memories to savour for years to come.

Reluctantly, she pushed herself off the couch and went upstairs to shower and change before returning, as she must, to the school, to make a show of leadership and compassion. It was the last place she wished to be, for although she had devoted ten years of her life to the Hermitage, it had let her down.

As she hurried up the path through the near dark, her feet twisting on the uneven surface, a raindrop splashed on her hair and she jumped. She started again when an owl screeched close by, only relaxing once lights were visible behind the phalanx of trees.

The place was teeming with police officers, each offering a brief salute as she passed. She unlocked her study, checked the telephone for messages, then left the room. Therese was standing in the lobby, her unmistakable bulk silhouetted in the light from the other corridor. 'Did you want something?' Freya called.

Therese advanced, every action slow and ponderous. The nick-name 'Lump' suited her perfectly, Freya thought, for the figure coming towards her looked as if it might be made from yard upon yard of the fat, greasy sausage Frau Obermeyer's factories spewed out by the mile.

The girl stood to attention with her hands by her side. Her face, its lineaments distorted by superfluous flesh, was devoid of expression. 'You told us there would be a special assembly,' she said. 'With prayers for Imogen.'

'And I asked Matron to let you all know I'd decided to wait until the morning,' Freya said impatiently. Then she made an effort to soften her tone. 'How is Imogen?'

'She was asleep when Justine last went to look. One of us will go again soon. She will want supper.'

'Where's Matron?'

Therese shrugged her massive shoulders. 'I don't know.' Then the girl Freya dismissed as stolid and stupid astounded her. 'You are wrong not to hold an assembly tonight, Dr Scott. The school is disintegrating. If you do not take control a new order will emerge that you *cannot* control.' She paused, her lower lip trapped in her teeth, looking uglier than ever. 'We are near to being the monsters human beings become when constraints are lost.'

'Are you?' Suddenly, Freya's mouth was dry. 'In what way?'

'Nancy and Charlotte caused Imogen's anguish, so they must suffer.' She spoke like vengeance personified. 'I should like to lock Nancy in the cellar with the spiders that terrify her. All night, I would stand outside the door listening to her screams.'

'And Charlotte?'

'Ah, yes.' Therese gnawed her lip. 'Charlotte the harlot. It would be good to cut her face,' she added chillingly, 'but I contented myself with throwing nail varnish on her clothes.' She offered what was meant to be a smile. 'They are ruined.'

Eventually, her mind consumed by implications and consequences, Freya asked, 'Does she know yet?'

'Do you hear her screaming yet?'

Enraged, Freya went upstairs, cursing the shiftless, spineless individuals around her, but above all, cursing Sukie. The girl she had judged in life as a nonentity had in death grown into a malign, dangerous presence, so powerful she could reach out from the mortuary to jerk so many strings it was as if the Hermitage had become her very own puppet theatre.

Therese's words chanting remorselessly through her head, Freya strode along the corridor to the sixth-form common room. But for the light flickering from the television, it was in darkness. She stood at the door, counting heads. Charlotte's blonde halo shone like a beacon. She went next to the smokers' den, wrinkling her nose at the stench. Vivienne and Françoise Dizi were, as ever, wreathed in clouds of smoke. Surprisingly, several others were with them, including the two Russian girls, Elisabeth von Carolsfeld and Justine, who offered Freya a brief, civil nod that implied all was relatively well with the world.

What, Freya wondered, was likely to happen when they had finished watching television, talking and drinking coffee, and Charlotte went to open her cupboard and drawers to find her luxurious garments streaked and splattered with nail varnish as if with the blood of a score of murders? How, she asked herself, could she pre-empt the inevitable? Slowly retracing her steps, she decided the problem was far from hers alone and resolved to share it among those who had helped to provoke its creation. She knocked on Ainsley's door and turned the handle. The lights were on but the room was empty. Then, from the corner of her eye, she saw Vivienne coming along the corridor. Rather than speak to her, she took to the stairs and went in search of Matron.

25

Cigarette in hand, McKenna paced his office; desk to window, window to door, door to desk; berating himself at every step for being such a damned fool – a *blind* fool, he muttered savagely. He had believed himself in control, convinced he had Freya Scott's measure, yet he walked headlong into the trap she had the wit to fashion from a chance incident and the penetrating insight that alerted her to his famine years without the warmth of a woman's flesh. She could make whatever she wished of those few, contrived moments in the lift and, no matter how much he protested, the doubts would stick to him like greasy smoke. At best he would be judged a willing party; at worst guilty of a deliberate assault. Jack had warned him to be on his guard and he had been right, but McKenna would never be able to tell him.

When the fax machine hummed, he stopped in mid-stride. Paper bearing the heading of the hospital's pathology laboratory began to roll out and curl up. He waited until the guillotine severed the last sheet, gathered them together and dropped into his chair, grateful for anything that might distract his attention, even this densely written and jargon-laden scientific report on the residues from Sukie's body.

To the naked eye, apart from the few dead leaves and spears of grass clinging to her corpse, her hair and clothing had appeared merely saturated with dirty water, but the microscope had revealed the secret, teeming life of that water and the traces her killer could not destroy. He pored over minute detail of the fungi, algae, seeds, leaves, grasses, petals, chemicals, fish scales, bio-organisms, fish, animal and human excreta and hazardous waste in her clothing and hair, and the traces of soap, powder, deodorant, perfume and cosmetics on her skin, then turned to the analysis of the blow that stunned her before she was consigned to the Strait. Again, her skin had seemed barely broken, but the hugely magnified photographs included in the report showed a complex of tiny wounds at the back of her skull in which were embedded the splinters of wood her thick hair had protected from the water. Reduction of those splinters into their constituent elements proved that she had been attacked with a length of rotting beech that had lain in the cannibal mud for many years.

The telephone rang as he was completing a second reading of the report.

'I take it you've got the scientific analysis?' Eifion Roberts began. 'It's probably not as much as you hoped for, but it's certainly enough to let that young amputee off the hook. She can have her fancy stick and crutches back. And you won't need to trouble yourself confiscating every stick-like object within two miles of the school.'

'Imogen Oliver could still be the killer,' McKenna said wearily. 'What's to stop her using a broken branch instead of the stick or a crutch?'

'Likelihood,' the pathologist replied tetchily. 'In most cases people use what's nearest to hand and especially so when they've only got one leg. Think about it; she'd have been flat on her face in the mud the moment she dropped her supports to try to pick up anything.'

'So, we're back to square one.'

'Are you? What the devil have you been doing for the last couple of days, then?'

'Looking for non-existent facts. We can't focus on anyone, we can't eliminate anyone.'

'Rubbish!' Roberts exclaimed. 'You're just not putting your mind to things. What's happened to your famous lateral thinking?' After a long pause, when there was no response, he asked, 'What's the matter with you?'

'Nothing,' McKenna said tightly.

'You're fibbing. I know you too well, Michael.'

McKenna stared blankly at the Queen's portrait over the

door. 'I've got to move house,' he said at last. 'The council's condemning the whole terrace.'

'There's a surprise!'

'And Jack thinks I've completely fouled up the investigation.'

'Have you?'

'I don't know. I seem to have lost focus.'

'And I've seen it coming for months,' Roberts told him. 'You've been hiding in that poky slum of a house, but now it's crunch time and you've got to move out, you're going to pieces.'

'Don't be ridiculous!' McKenna snapped. 'And don't start lecturing me!'

'You've only got to put down the phone if you don't want to listen.' The other man's voice was suddenly gentle. 'But who else, apart from me, can you turn to for a bit of advice, unwelcome though it may be?'

'I don't need advice. I need facts.'

'All the facts you need are probably staring you in the face, but you're too screwed up to see them.'

'Stick to pathology, Eifion. You're not a psychiatrist.'

'See? You always get nasty when someone strikes a nerve. I'm your friend and I don't like what's happening to you.'

'Nothing's happening to me!'

'A moment ago you admitted you're not even doing your job properly. What's the next step?'

'I'll resign and go and work for the RSPCA. You've often said I care far more for animals than people.'

'That's true and you're not really a natural policeman. You're more of a crusader; a deliverer, even,' Roberts remarked. 'But does your preference for animals stem from knowing they won't *deliberately* hurt you? I mean, even if you happened to be dying from Cat Scratch Fever, you wouldn't blame whichever little moggie had delivered the fatal blow because there wouldn't have been any malice behind it. Similarly,' he added, 'if you got chucked off a horse and your head smashed to smithereens, you'd exit this vale of tears praying the horse wouldn't be shot for having killed you.'

Despite himself McKenna had to smile. The pathologist's next words erased that smile completely.

'The thing is, Michael,' he said, 'bar that bloody journalist who somehow got hold of your divorce petition earlier this year, who but me knows your ex-wife used to batter you to hell and back?' He waited, but the silence lengthened. 'You wouldn't tell Jack,' he went on. 'You think he'd judge you badly, although you're doing him a disservice to assume he's so lacking in understanding. And you aren't close enough to anyone else.'

'So?'

'So while you might have got rid of your wife, you haven't got rid of the damage she did and until you face up to that it'll go on festering inside you.'

McKenna could find nothing to say.

'As you haven't hung up on me, I assume you're at least willing to listen.' Again, Roberts waited. 'Right, then,' he began. 'Symptoms first. General loss of focus, capacity and perspective; apathy, bewilderment, chronic fearfulness, insomnia, lethargy, mental exhaustion, fatigue, blunted sensibilities, increasing depression. Next, the coping mechanisms. You found a bolthole and dug in, devising all sorts of convoluted strategies to keep the demons at bay. But now the real world's reared its ugly head again and the demons are back with a vengeance, vivid as the day they were born. Time hasn't tarnished them one little bit. So,' he continued, 'you don't know which way to turn. The progress you thought you'd made was nothing of the sort. You're virtually paralysed, almost too bloody scared to put one foot in front of the other, because you can't see a way forward. Or,' he added thoughtfully, 'because you expect to get slapped down again as soon as you budge.'

McKenna remained silent.

'I'm not getting much feedback, am I?' the pathologist asked. 'Still, the fact that you're *not* jumping down my throat must mean something.' He paused, then said, 'If the marital boot had been on the other foot, as it were, this would be a classic case of battered wife syndrome. There's a corresponding battered husband syndrome, which, as yet, people aren't too keen on recognising, especially if they happen to be a victim. Goes against the macho grain and suchlike crap.'

With growing despair, McKenna realised he had not moved a muscle since Roberts began his observations, as if he were indeed paralysed, as his friend suggested.

'You need help, Michael, and fast, before everything collapses about your ears. You're hanging on by your fingernails.'

'I can't walk out in the middle of an investigation.'

'Why not? Jack's more than capable. What if you got knocked down by a bus?'

'That would be different.'

'Only in the detail. Listen, whatever you do or don't do has a direct impact on your colleagues and, by your own admission, you're barely functioning at the moment. D'you want a disaster on your hands?'

'I admitted nothing of the sort,' McKenna insisted obstinately. 'I simply said I seem to have lost focus.'

'Oh, suit yourself! You usually do.'

'And,' McKenna went on, ignoring the outburst, 'I'd hoped you'd give us something that might help.'

'You're back in denial,' Roberts commented tersely, 'but it won't work. You're facing the inevitable, just like Hester Melville, who has, by the way, discharged herself from hospital. Against advice, I might add.'

'She has that prerogative.'

'And you obviously think you've got your own prerogative,' Roberts said angrily, 'despite the possible consequence. Well, don't say I didn't warn you!'

26

Dewi drove up and down the village street twice, looking for a parking space near the O'Connors' house, but in the end had to leave his precious car in a narrow alley.

Avril welcomed him like a long-lost relative and all but dragged him into the hallway.

'Actually,' Dewi said, 'I was looking for Sean. Inspector Tuttle thought it might be useful to have another chat with him.' When he saw the naked fear on her face he added, 'Just to see if he can fill in a few blanks.'

'What sort of blanks?' she demanded.

'The great big ones about the school that no one else is willing to talk about.'

'Oh, *those*!' Avril breathed a sigh of relief. 'The problem is,' she added presently, with a grim smile, 'will our Sean be able to find enough time to tell you? Or you to listen, for that matter?'

'Well, if I don't see him we'll never know.'

'He's gone for a drink with his mates, like he always does on a Friday after work.' She looked at the old wooden clock on the wall, pursing her rosebud lips. 'They usually start off at the Harp, but by now they could be anywhere.'

When Dewi retrieved his car, he found it mercifully unmolested by local louts, although not by passing seagulls. The black fabric hood, but not the easily washed metal bodywork, was splattered, rather artistically, with chalky white droppings. Telling himself it was supposed to signal good fortune to come, he set off for Bangor and its multitude of taverns.

Knowing where Sean liked to drink, he left the car in the

covered parking area opposite the cathedral and, after checking in the Harp, walked down High Street to the White Lion. Sean was all alone at a corner table with a half-drunk glass of Guinness. A gaggle of half-naked girls nearby were unashamedly making eyes at him.

Dewi bought himself a pint of shandy, then sat down at Sean's table. 'Your mam thinks you're getting bevied up with your pals,' he remarked.

'Yeah, well I don't feel like it tonight.' He stared at Dewi. 'Are you *on* duty, or off?'

Dewi shrugged. 'Depends.'

'What on?'

'Whether you feel like telling me things you wouldn't necessarily want to talk about in front of your mam.'

'What sort of things?'

'Dunno, do I?' Dewi commented. Quaffing shandy, he added, 'Unless you tell me.'

'By that,' Sean said, 'I assume you're expecting me to help you break down Scott's wall of silence.'

'It's not so much a wall of silence as a cloud of confusion.'

'And what makes you think I can see through it any easier than you?'

'How long have you been working at the Hermitage?' Dewi asked. 'It must be four years, at least.' He took another long drink. 'Four years of unconscious observation, not to mention all the other stuff you picked up by being as nosy as some curtain-twitching old maid.'

Briefly, Sean grinned. Then, wrapping his strong labourer's hands around the glass, he said, his face serious, 'Nothing for nothing, *Sergeant* Prys. You tell *me* something first.'

Dewi nodded. 'Fair enough.'

'Am I under suspicion?'

'Your mam might worship the ground under your feet,' Dewi replied, 'but I know she'd never lie for you. So, provided Paula doesn't drop you in it, you've got a solid alibi.'

'Have you arranged to speak to her?'

'Yes, when she lands later on tonight.'

'Right.' Sean picked up his drink. 'What's Jack Tuttle done with that car number I gave him?'

'Checked it out and that's as much as I'm saying.'

'Right,' Sean again said. When he put down his Guinness, the glass was less than a quarter full. 'So what d'you want to know?'

For the next hour, the girls at the neighbouring table, whispering and giggling, played up to the two gorgeous young men, but neither took the slightest notice of their antics. With a collective toss of their garish young heads the girls eventually flounced out into the street, but not before the brashest of them had leaned over to ask, 'What's the matter with you two, then? You queer, or something?'

27

Vivienne had been on her way to her room for a fresh pack of cigarettes when she saw Dr Scott outside Ainsley's door. Involuntarily she stopped short, as if her reluctance to meet the woman, a reluctance rooted in years of chronic fear, had taken physical form and were pushing a hand in her chest. Then something utterly remarkable occurred. The headmistress took a step towards her, hesitated and suddenly turned on her heel to hurry down the staircase. Vivienne, trying to put a name to the expression that had flickered briefly across her face, walked slowly along the corridor, nodding absently to Ainsley as she emerged from the showers with a towel slung about her shoulders and her hair plastered wetly to her bony skull. She was in her room tearing off the cellophane from a cigarette packet when she realised what that expression betrayed. Dr Scott was afraid, she thought jubilantly, and not only because Therese's fantastical, apocalyptic schemes for retribution must by now have reached her ears. She was in fear of the unforeseen and ungovernable consequences of her latest opportunism, of being exposed for the ruthless, manipulative sham that she was. No one, not even Nancy or Charlotte or their hangers-on, truly believed Imogen guilty of Sukie's murder, and the expedient resolution Dr Scott contrived and thrust in the face of the police might yet prove her Achilles' heel. There was a groundswell of resistance to the injustice and as Vivienne closed her door she had the strangest feeling. She pictured herself and the headmistress joined in a battle that the woman already knew she would lose. Telling herself that hallucinations were part and parcel of her condition, she went to check on Imogen, but her new, if fragile, clarity of mind persisted, astounding her with the sense of something approaching cheerfulness.

The policeman on guard in the corridor opened Imogen's door for her, then stood aside. The room was, as usual, tidier than most, with Imogen's possessions neatly ordered along the counter, her clothes folded, her books on the shelf, the borrowed stick and crutches in the corner, an unstamped letter propped against the spider plant newly installed on the window ledge and a rinsed-out glass upended on the tray next to the bottle of painkillers. Imogen was still asleep. Scratching her cheek, Vivienne stared at the recumbent form under the duvet and, although she wanted so much to talk to her, knowing how exhausted Imogen had been at lunchtime, she thought it might be kinder to leave her undisturbed.

Imogen lay on her left side, face towards the wall. Vivienne imagined the inflexibility of the artificial leg beneath the good one, then cringed when she remembered the feel of the stump. Debating with herself whether to come back before or after supper, she wondered absently how anyone could lie so absolutely still.

'Oh, Jesus!' she whispered. Snatching up the pill bottle, she found it was empty.

28

When McKenna arrived home, his two hungry cats had their noses pressed to the glass panes in the front door. Wailing plaintively, they circled him every step of the way from the door to the downstairs kitchen, where from long conditioning he immediately set about filling clean dishes with food and water. Then he filled the kettle, dropped four teabags in the pot and slumped at the table. The cats purred as they ate, glancing up at him every so often to make sure their world was still in order.

From the spread of Fluff's body on the floor, he had to concede that she was indeed becoming what the vet had described as a 'cat and a half', but he attributed her girth to her history as a starving vagrant that now compelled her to eat everything in sight. Fatter or not, she was agile as ever. Blackie remained sleek, despite dietary supplements of field mice, birds and, possibly, rabbits. One overcast spring day, McKenna had found four rabbit paws on the patio flagstones, but not a drop of blood nor a wisp of fur. Later, he was accosted by the embryonic juvenile delinquent from next door but two, who reported that Blackie had been 'copped' tottering through the back gardens with the hapless animal squirming in his jaws.

Once the kettle boiled, he made the tea and put it to brew on the cooker. Fluff came to sit at his feet and began grooming herself. Blackie was still eating. He looked from one to the other, seeing his life before their arrival as a time in abeyance, like the blankness Jack had said preceded the birth of his daughters. McKenna loved his cats with the ferocious, protective vigour others bestowed on their children, and knew only a child of his own could ever invoke a similar devotion;

but with each passing year the prospect of fatherhood receded, in inverse proportion to the hope. Perhaps hope was all that Freya Scott had represented, he thought, forcing himself to confront his momentary folly; perhaps less than hope, merely a biological imperative.

Fervently wishing he could so neatly unravel the welter of emotions and impulses that had killed Sukie, he turned his attention to his own meal and was cutting bread for toast when the telephone rang. Praying that it would not be Eifion Roberts, he dusted the crumbs from his hands and lifted the receiver, to be told that Imogen was fighting for her life after overdosing on painkillers. She had left him a letter.

Sunset still glowed bright in the western sky but once inside the school gates, the total darkness of the woods closed about him. Water dripped from the trees, and the reek of wet earth and rotting vegetation was everywhere. As he negotiated one or another of the crazy bends, his headlights caught the startled eyes of small animals, and intermittently, he heard the owl above the trees, although dusk had silenced the thousands of birds that filled the day with their song. There were no nightingales in Wales, he recalled, turning slowly round the last bend, but why, no one knew.

The school was lit up from end to end and faces were pressed to the glass at almost every window. Matron was one of those on watch and she advanced across the forecourt as soon as he stopped the car. The harsh white fluorescence of the outside security lamps was grossly unkind to her ageing face, turning her into a hag. She wrung her hands, stared at him, then led him in silence into the school and to her room.

'Who found her?' he demanded. 'When?'

'Vivienne Wade went to see if she wanted supper. She was all right when I took up the stick and crutches you'd borrowed, and I know several people looked in on her later, but no one else noticed.' She blinked rapidly. 'Isn't that strange?'

'Noticed what?'

'I'm not sure.' She frowned. 'Maybe that she was sleeping too deeply—'

He interrupted her. 'Where's Vivienne now?'

'She insisted on going to the hospital. Dr Scott's gone, of course, so I don't see why Vivienne thought *she* should, but she wouldn't be put off. I suppose she feels she's got a stake in the matter. She *did* find her, after all.' She collapsed into a chair and her whole body seemed to deflate. 'It was awful! Françoise came tearing downstairs, screaming there was an ambulance on its way, then Dr Scott rushed up and found Vivienne and your policeman dragging Imogen around the room trying to wake her up.'

'How many tablets had she taken?'

'Thirty-odd? She gets forty-two every Wednesday and she's allowed six a day.'

'Did it never occur to you that she might overdose?'

'Why should it?' Matron snivelled and grabbed the handkerchief stuffed into her belt.

'Because she'd lost her leg, she was clearly in extreme pain and her lifelong friend had just died!' he replied savagely. 'What's in the tablets?'

'Dihydrocodeine.'

He had no idea what an overdose might do, but wanted to wound. 'Then don't expect her to survive. Where's her letter?'

Matron's whole face began to quiver. She levered herself upright and faced him. 'Don't speak to me like that! Who are *you* to criticise? Eh?' She panted stale breath in his face. 'It's *your* fault this happened!' He backed away and almost fell over a chair. 'Your *fault*!' she screeched. Dragging a crumpled envelope from her apron pocket, she flung it at his feet. '*There*'s her letter! Dr Scott opened it. This is *our* school!' She began to sob, helplessly flapping her hands. '*Ours!*'

Crouched miserably and uncomfortably on the edge of a chair in the visitors' room, McKenna told himself he must read the three pages of Imogen's rather cramped script slowly and calmly. When he first unfolded her missive and saw how she had begun, the words rabbit-punched him in the belly. He still felt sick.

Dear Superintendent McKenna

When you took away my stick and crutches, I realised how

helpless I really am. I can't even get to the bathroom on my own. I know you're getting me another stick, and I know Vivienne and Justine will look after me, but I hate being a burden and dependent on the kindness of others, and I despise weakness – so that's partly why I despise myself so much – but I don't want to be pitied, either. I just want to be what I was before the accident, and that's impossible.

When you brought Sukie's plant to my room, I saw you looking at my foot and I knew exactly what was going through your mind because the same things go through mine, day and night. I can't wear high heels, or frocks, or sandals. I can't sunbathe, or have lovers, or run through the streets after a party, and if a rapist comes after me I can't run away, because I've put myself in the grim, freaky world of the maimed and ugly and helpless.

People tell me I'll get used to having a false leg and eventually get my independence and they could be right, because I've actually seen models on the catwalk with <u>two</u> false legs. People learn to live without limbs, I know. In some places they've got no option. They can go for a walk, step on a landmine and get their legs blown off, or have their arms chopped off because they belong to the wrong tribe. It's a wicked world and when I see pictures of people like that I want to die, because they all look so <u>brave</u>. I'm not. I'm a coward and a fraud.

When you have a limb amputated, you know it will hurt, but you can never imagine how much it hurts until it happens. Nobody will talk about the pain, so you can't know if it might become tolerable, or even go away altogether, and for me the prospect of waiting to find out is too hard, too daunting, too <u>uncertain</u>. When Vivienne found me taking extra pills this morning, she said I was on the slippery slope to becoming a junkie, and she was quite right, but what else can I do? The pills make me feel sick and dizzy, and give me blinding headaches and constipation, but all that put together is better than the pain.

~~I'm writing to you so that~~ Even if I'm not dead when you get this letter, you must start to right the terrible wrong I did to Sukie and her parents. <u>I</u> was driving the car. I was driving too fast and just lost control. Sukie was stunned in the crash, but she wasn't knocked out. She pulled me out of the wreck in case it blew up. Then she passed out.

My parents know, but I pray to God Sukie really couldn't remember and that she never knew how dreadfully I betrayed her. We loved each other like sisters, and I haven't got words to tell you how horrible it was after we came back here but couldn't be together – couldn't even speak to each other. My parents forbade me ever to speak to her again, in case I let something slip by accident, or my conscience simply got the better of me. Sukie believed she'd lost me my leg and I wanted to tell her that wasn't true more than I actually wanted my leg back, but I couldn't. I let myself get caught up in one lie, but it went out of control far faster than the car. My father put me on his own insurance when he bought my car and he was absolutely incensed about how much the crash was going to cost him. The lying started when the police told us Sukie couldn't remember anything. We swore those dreadful lies were God's honest truth just to save some money, because my parents are both mean and greedy. But then, in my experience, very rich people usually are. I went along with them because I'm weak and I knew my father would punish me if I disobeyed. I felt sorry enough for myself as it was.

My parents had always despised the Melvilles. They called Hester silly and immature, and John a born loser. My father laughed about ruining him – 'only sooner rather than later,' he said and thought it was 'piquant' for the Melvilles to be beggared by the people they believed were their closest friends.

My insurance money was put into trust – I was supposed to have it next year. The money my parents swindled out of the Melvilles is in one of my father's accounts. I'm relying on you to make sure the Melvilles get back their money and my parents get what they deserve. Don't let me down, because I could come back to haunt you.

I can't tell you how much calmer I feel already. I just wish and wish I'd found the strength to tell Sukie the truth. I wish that so hard it hurts more than my leg, because if we'd still been close, I would have known something was wrong

238

and I could have kept her safe. When I realised you thought I'd killed her, I felt like going mad with grief, but I don't really believe you're stupid enough to fall for Dr Scott's conniving. She won't care who you arrest as long as you solve the problem for her, although she'd probably prefer it to be me because I've become quite a burden to her and I know she'd like to wash her hands of me. Unfortunately for her, she can't do that without showing her true colours.

Sukie was the sweetest, kindest, bravest person I've ever known. She was brave in all sorts of ways, not just because she pulled me out of the car. She was never nasty either, or bitter, though God knows, her family gave her plenty of cause. She shouldn't have died. She didn't deserve to die. She'd never hurt anyone, so she must have died because of something I began by lying and that's unbearable. That's why I want to die, as well. I wouldn't even think of killing myself if she was still alive.

When you were talking to me earlier I wanted so much to ask you how she died, but I couldn't pluck up the courage. Do you know? Did she suffer? Did she know? I pray not, I really, really do.

Imogen Oliver

PS Last Christmas, Sukie gave me a beautiful necklace. I'm positive I haven't lost it because it was too precious – it was the last gift I'd ever have from her – but I can't find it. The drugs affect my memory, you see, and I forget where I've put things, especially the small ones and I can't crawl around on the floor or move the furniture to look in case I've just dropped something. Since the accident, I've become a lot tidier, because it makes life a little easier, but things still seem to disappear of their own accord. Please find the necklace for me. I want to wear it to my funeral.

Folding the letter with shaking hands, he pushed it back in the envelope and damned every single person who had crossed her path since that tragic December day, beginning with her murderously avaricious parents and finishing with himself. Had he returned after taking away her crutches, she might have told him the truth, but the complete mental disarray that followed his insane capitulation to Freya Scott gave Imogen time to make an irrevocable decision. Harrowed, enraged and even close to tears, he left the school, after first arranging for Imogen's room to be locked and sealed. When he arrived at the police station, he contacted Berkshire police and faxed a copy of her letter. Realising that Jack also needed to know, he scribbled a covering note and sent that, with the letter and, as an afterthought, the report from pathology, by messenger to his house. Then he drove to the hospital.

29

Matron felt worse rather than better after she had lost control and screeched at McKenna, as if letting the cauldron of emotion boil over had spilled fat on the fire beneath. Grimly hauling herself upstairs by the banisters, she promised herself that ugly, obese Therese Obermeyer was the next in line for a lesson she would not forget in a hurry. She had been utterly appalled when the headmistress told her what Therese had done to Charlotte's clothes. Dim-witted and thoughtless Charlotte might be, but she was harmless and surely more to be pitied than condemned.

Therese was not in her room. Matron marched and puffed up and down the top floor, throwing open one door after another. Only a few of the girls were asleep; most were wakeful, intensely troubled by the second ambulance drama of what had been a truly horrible day.

Ainsley was head down in one of her books, pretending as usual that the world beyond the written page had no importance. For several moments Matron watched her in silence, before stalking away.

Yelena and Daria were closeted together in one room, gossiping in Russian. 'Speak English,' she snarled at them. 'D'you hear me? You must speak *English*!'

Without even registering their bafflement, she made her way to the sixth-form common room. Nancy was there, in the midst of a small group of admirers, still watching television.

'Where's Charlotte?' Matron demanded.

'Showers,' one of the girls replied, not taking her eyes from the screen.

'How long has she been there?'

'Dunno.'

Then how much time was left, Matron agonised? Once she had showered, Charlotte would choose her clothes for the morning, wanting to look her best for her public even though she had nowhere to go. Very soon, now, she would be pulling from her wardrobe one ruined garment after another. So frightened that she could barely draw breath, Matron stomped into the smokers' den. Françoise was almost invisible behind the cloud of acrid smoke that wreathed around the other three occupants before drifting towards the open window. When Matron made out Therese, the cauldron bubbled over again. She walked up to her, lifted her huge hand and hit her across the face with every ounce of her strength.

'You *monster*!' she screamed, as Therese reeled back. 'You fat, evil, ugly *bitch*!'

30

There was little respite in the accident and emergency unit at Bangor hospital any day or night of the week, for if the locals were not at each other's throats after downing yards of ale, holidaymakers were falling into the sea or off the mountains. McKenna fought his way through the swollen crowd of Friday night disasters to the reception desk, only to be elbowed out of the way by a man with blood pouring from a wicked gash on his right cheek. Eventually he managed to catch the receptionist's attention, but had to wait while she twice searched the computer records before telling him that Imogen had been moved to the intensive care unit on the third floor.

The hospital was a labyrinth of intersecting corridors, each with a broad line of colour painted on the floor, but too distracted to remember which colour would take him where he needed to go, he zigzagged back and forth interminably, until a young nurse extricated him from his confusion and pushed him into a lift. As he rounded the corner by the unit he almost fell over Vivienne's feet. She was seated in a flimsy-looking chair, long legs stretched out, lovely face more bruised-looking than ever.

He stood over her. 'How's Imogen?' he asked.

'Not good.'

'But how *bad*?'

'Nobody's saying. They've done what they can, so it's in the lap of the gods.' Wearily, she gestured towards the unit's door. 'You could ask the doctor. Dr Scott's in there, too.'

'Would you know if the Olivers have been told?'

'Matron was supposed to do that.'

Lost for words, he uttered in the end the obvious cliché: 'If she pulls through, she'll have you to thank.'

'You think she'll *thank* me? If I were in her shoes – or shoe, to be more precise – and somebody rescued me I'd be distraught.'

'Don't!'

She sat up straight and regarded him levelly. 'Imogen's overdose was virtually a foregone conclusion. *We've* known it for months, even if Dr Scott and Matron preferred living in cloud-cuckoo-land.' Putting her hand to her mouth, she coughed and it sounded like a bark. 'Torrance has been doing a lot for her that should have been done by professionals, including keeping track of the pills she was shoving down her throat. If my wits weren't addled I'd have realised sooner that she'd emptied the bottle. I gave her a bollocking at lunchtime for taking an extra dose.'

'Why did she have so many tablets in her room?'

'Because – and I quote – "she had to learn to take responsibility for her medication". In actual fact,' Vivienne went on, 'Matron couldn't be bothered doling out a day's supply at a time, or making sure she wasn't stockpiling.'

Grasping at straws of comfort, he said, 'The fact that she hadn't locked her door suggests she wanted to be found.'

'Does it?' She gazed at him speculatively. 'Perhaps she just couldn't make it that far after you pinched her stick and crutches.'

He left her and took the stairs down to Torrance's room. She was now 'sleeping', rather than 'unconscious'.

He sat in the car, chain smoking, letting memories of the day roll past his eyes like a cavalcade of disasters peopled with the wounded and battle-weary, so absorbed in his reverie that he did not even see Freya emerge from the building, scan the car park to find him, then wave.

31

On her own initiative, Justine had assumed responsibility for the absent Torrance. She toured the Tudor dormitories, answering questions and calming fears where she could, but refused to let Daisy interrogate her about Imogen's stick and crutches, and their removal by the police.

'If you won't tell me,' Daisy had said, trying to goad, 'I'll have to come to my own conclusions.'

'You will, anyway,' Justine replied shortly, before switching off the dormitory lights and closing the door.

Barely five minutes later, Daisy had heard Françoise scream. She shot out of bed and ran for the door, but rushed back into the dormitory when a siren wailed in the distance. Shouldering her way through the girls now crowded at the window, she found herself a prime viewing slot and so missed nothing of the ambulance's arrival nor of Imogen's sensational departure. When McKenna's Jaguar slewed to a halt on the forecourt, she watched Matron waddle out to meet him and waited then for the next instalment of the drama.

Nothing happened. One by one, almost numbed by shock and weariness, the other girls drifted back to bed. Daisy stayed at the window, desperately afraid of missing something that might let her see which way the wind blew, and perhaps show her what else there was to fear, but McKenna's own departure was all that took place and in the end she too returned to her bed.

She could not sleep. Memories, thoughts and imaginings scuttled round and round her brain like rats in a maze, until she lost all sense of the boundaries between truth and fiction, romance and reality. In turn, she sweated profusely and shivered uncontrollably, first jettisoning the bed covers, next wrapping them about her like a shroud, but whatever she did she continued to burn and freeze. Then that hot, horrible itch began its assault, as if her groin were infested with insects. She groped in the locker for her diary, although there was no real need to check. Since she was eleven years old, and two days short of beginning her first term at the Hermitage, her periods had come upon her with such regimented regularity that she often felt her body was possessed of a demon and no longer her own.

She heard a door slam overhead, then shouting, then thundering footsteps and more shouting. Thrusting the unopened diary back under a pile of clothes in the locker, she disentangled herself from the bedding and sat up.

'Alice!' she hissed across the few feet that separated their beds. '*Alice!*'

Alice mumbled and jerked her head, but remained asleep.

'Sod you,' Daisy muttered. She found her slippers, padded to the door and eased it open and, one foot in the corridor, one still in the dormitory, listened avidly, trying to work out who was yelling what, for Therese's stentorian proclamations virtually drowned out Matron's hoarse song while Elisabeth's angry soprano counterpointed both. It reminded Daisy of an operatic trio, hectic and discordant, and when Justine took up the recitative it became a quartet teeming with Wagnerian overtones. Therese had done something to Charlotte – no, to Charlotte's beautiful clothes – but she had not. She had only *said* she had, but Matron could not know that when she smacked Therese in the face. Daisy quivered with the delight of violence done and the prospect of more to follow. Therese was cruel and dangerous and arrogant, Matron shrieked, and obviously did not care that Dr Scott was already beside herself with worry. This was the last straw. It was *terrible*!

Too bad, Daisy said to herself, paraphrasing Therese's scornful rejoinder. The voices were growing louder as the skirmish proceeded to the head of the stairs, so rather than be caught, she closed the dormitory door behind her and slipped along the corridor to the infirmary.

Five of the twelve beds in the long, narrow room were occupied, four of them with weedy youngsters not yet tempered by school life.

Grace was in the last bed on the right, hunched against the bedhead with the duvet up to her chin. When she saw Daisy slithering along the linoleum towards her, she scowled. 'What do *you* want?' she muttered.

Daisy sat heavily on the bed, and started bouncing up and down. 'You-can't-hide-for-ever,' she said, the words sprung with the rhythm of her body. 'Did-you-do-what-I-said?'

'I'm *not* hiding and yes, I *did*!'

'Liar!'

'I did!'

'When?'

'Earlier, so shut up about it.'

'I'll-find-out-if-you-haven't.'

Still scowling, Grace snapped, 'Oh, give it a rest!' Then, wiping her face of all but innocent curiosity, she asked, 'What's all the noise upstairs about?'

Daisy stopped bouncing. 'Imogen's been carted off in an ambulance. I think she's dead. Charlotte must have done something to her, because Therese was going to do something to *her*, so Matron clouted Therese.'

'You do love trouble, don't you?' Head on one side, Grace stared at her. 'I've never known *anybody* who can make things up the way you do. Imogen probably took an overdose. She's absolutely *full* of self-pity.'

'I'm-not-imagining-the-noise,' Daisy replied, bouncing again.

Grace dropped the edge of the quilt and grabbed Daisy's bare arms. 'Stop that!' she seethed. 'You're getting on my nerves!' When Daisy tried to pull away, she tightened her grip like a vice.

Daisy yelped. 'Let go! You're hurting me!'

Grace pulled her down. 'And if Imogen *was* dead, they wouldn't bother putting her in an ambulance,' she said. 'She'd be in a mortuary van.' Then she pushed her so hard that Daisy tumbled off the bed.

'Cow!' Daisy scrambled to her feet, rubbing herself. 'Fucking cow!' she added savagely, backing away towards the door. Grace watched, her mouth a thin line.

Daisy's flesh stung and under the bright light in the corridor outside the infirmary she could see the livid bracelets Grace's fingers had left around her forearms.

32

Hester had informed the ward staff that she intended to leave, argued with them and the hastily summoned psychiatric registrar, scrawled her signature on the release papers, made herself presentable and left the hospital all without any conscious awareness of having made a single decision, driven by a compulsion to act that was generated by her husband's late-afternoon visit.

After they left the police station in the small hours and went to their hotel, he had acquired a new bottle of whisky and spent the rest of the night slouched in a chair in their room, silently and steadily drinking, not once uttering a word. At some point she had fallen into a fitful but dreamless sleep. When she awoke he was on the bed, curled up beside her, his arm a dead weight across her hips, the empty bottle wedged under his cheek, his foul breath filling the room.

So that he would not know where she had gone, she ordered a taxi. When she arrived at the mortuary, she was asked to wait and sat on a leatherette bench in the chilly, gloomy foyer for what seemed a long time. The place stank of death. Eventually the pathologist with the kind eyes and gentle voice came to tell her it would not be possible for her to see Sukie. He touched her shoulder comfortingly. Glancing at that pink, well-scrubbed hand, she realised what it must have been doing and fainted.

At some time during this interminable day her husband discovered where she was and came to see her, but not before making an effort to keep up the ever essential appearances. He wore a clean shirt, a different tie, his suit was brushed and his face washed and shaved, but he could do nothing about the stench of whisky seeping from every pore. As he leaned over her, puzzled and even distressed, she turned away her head. He was so drunk that his usual belligerence was beyond him and he left within fifteen minutes. Watching his retreating back, Hester knew that never again did she wish to set eyes on him.

Once she had discharged herself she took another taxi into Bangor. The taxi driver directed her to a café-bar, where she sat unnoticed among the students and tourists. She ordered black coffee, swallowed it without tasting a drop and left.

At twilight, she was standing in the middle of the Menai Bridge, her fingers tight around the tall iron railings, the wind ruffling her hair and humming through the suspension cables. By now she had acquired a raincoat and umbrella but had little recollection of their purchase. She could only remember the summer rain falling like shards of glass on her bare arms. The silky raincoat felt warm, but she shivered nonetheless.

The walkways projected from each side of the bridge and once she had moved into the lee of the towers she was standing on air. Behind her, the tide ran towards Puffin Island and beneath her the floodlit reflection of the bridge shimmered in the dark waters far below. She looked only downstream, her gaze fixed on the dense, dark shadows of the woods that surrounded the school. Had she raised her eyes even a little, she would have caught the full glory of a summer nightfall, but she could see nothing beyond the terrible contours of her new world. Grief slung about her like a shroud, she contemplated the anguish of her child's lonely death and the horror of it threatened to stop her heart.

I

On Friday night, sheer nervous exhaustion had kept Alice in the grip of sleep throughout the rumpus on the sixth-form corridor. She missed Daisy's exit from the dormitory, but for some unfathomable reason, was roused briefly by her stealthy return. Within minutes of sliding into bed, Daisy had begun snoring gently, and despite sporadic noises and raised voices from the top floor Alice too went back to sleep.

When she woke again, clawing her way out of a nightmare with her heart thumping wildly, the sky was blue and freshly washed. The outside security lights had already switched themselves off. She scrambled into a sitting position and looked across at Daisy, whose hair was a tumble of curls on the pillow, framing a face innocent of all expression. Alice despaired. Try as she might to disbelieve Daisy's terrible accusation about Torrance, the poison had done its work. Was Daisy simply a wicked liar, or was Torrance truly a monster? She knew Daisy, knew how deeply she felt her parents' neglect, saw the hurt behind that ever ready smile, the brutal disappointment when neither of them showed for Sports Day or Open Day, but what did she *really* know about Torrance? Everyone wore a false face at times. Alice had shown hers to her mother when, instead of hugging her as she so desperately wanted to do, she had wounded her with one barbed comment after another.

Why did some people say Torrance was devious? Did she beguile with her kindness? Alice asked herself wretchedly. Had her detractors seen a face Torrance only exposed to the secret, perhaps passionate transactions that took place in those dingy sixth-form bedrooms under the roof? The girls in the dormitories below heard everything but saw nothing, and so constructed their own context around the laughter, arguments, slamming doors, running footsteps, creaking bed springs, the thump of Imogen's false leg and the mystery of nocturnal meetings, when voices were suddenly quenched, when whispers drifted through an open window to hang tantalisingly in the still air of a summer night, or someone sobbed with such deeply felt heartache that the eavesdroppers wanted to weep themselves.

Some time after five o'clock, Alice crept to the bathroom. Turning the cold tap full on, she held her wrists under the gushing water, then doused her face. With a towel to her chin, she stared into the mirror, searching for the outward signs of her inner turmoil, bemused by the familiar, ordinary reflection that returned her gaze. Daisy looked her usual self, too. She had scoured her friend's face for the tell-tale marks of dishonesty and dishonour and found nothing. Would to God Daisy had her mother's transparency, she thought bitterly.

She traipsed back towards the dormitory and, knowing madness borne of uncertainty lay behind the closed door and in Daisy's bed, she stopped dead, changed direction and slunk up the top staircase. Dirty handprints smeared the walls and there were chips in the woodwork, like the marks of beavers' teeth and claws she had seen outside Canadian houses. Expecting to see policemen on guard, she peered round the corner, but the corridor was empty, so she scuttled to the sixth-form common room holding her breath and letting it go only when the door was safely shut behind her.

The room smelt revoltingly stale. She pulled up the blinds and opened both casements. Then her eyes lit on the kettle. Squinting at the water level indicator, wishing she had not left her new spectacles in her locker, she flicked the switch, spooned coffee granules into the only clean mug she could find, made her drink and draped herself on the window ledge, staring at a less familiar aspect of the suffocating treescape and a sky now criss-crossed with the vapour trails of high-flying jets. A car drew up on the forecourt and two of the kitchen staff emerged, stopping on their way into the building to chat to the policeman at the doors. Alice jumped off the window ledge, afraid of being seen if they glanced upwards, and sat instead in a chair in front of the silent television. Putting the coffee mug on the floor, she leaned forwards to push the switch and stark images of the human conflict hit her in the face. She looked at pictures of charred remains, shredded limbs stuck in filthy boots, dead heads with strategic bullet holes and fly-blown corpses, then the dead disappeared and a procession of the living shambled across the screen, looking somehow familiar, as if all refugees wore the same dismal rags and faces. Two teenage girls, arm in arm and smiling, suddenly appeared, clad in ill-fitting, out of date hand-me-downs. Feeling a painful, sorrowful kinship, she turned up the sound, to hear talk of the unknown number of adolescents who had been raped and mutilated and murdered in the wars that raged relentlessly across the world.

Sickened, she was about to switch off the television when a tranquil picture of the Hermitage, where life was also cheap, unrolled before her.

2

Rubbing sleep from his eyes, Jack blinked at the portable television on the kitchen counter. A half-consumed mug of coffee stood on the table before him, while at the cooker his wife Emma, equally sleepy, was preparing a mushroom omelette for his breakfast.

'I fully intend to go back to bed,' she told him. 'At least until ten.'

'Lucky you,' he grumbled. 'Some of us have murders to solve.'

'One murder, one attempted and one unconnected attempted suicide,' she corrected.

'How d'you know Imogen's suicide isn't connected?'

'It's obvious. That letter she left for Michael says it all.' She turned the toast under the grill. 'Poor kid! Fancy losing your leg then being made to lie about your closest friend.'

'Maybe she wasn't made to lie. She could just hate her parents.'

'Or she could be off her head, but I doubt it.' She tipped the omelette on to a warm plate and placed it on the table.

'If she's not around to back up her allegations,' he began, picking up knife and fork, 'her parents look safe from prosecution. They're hardly going to confess.'

Emma piled the toast into a rack, topped up Jack's coffee, poured her own and, stifling a yawn, seated herself. Covertly, he watched her tumbled dark-brown hair shining in the early morning sun, her glowing skin, her firm yet voluptuous body under the thin cotton nightshirt, and wished he could return to bed with her, instead of spending another day in the foetid atmosphere of the Hermitage.

The television screen flickered with hideous images that fascinated and repulsed in equal measure. The newscaster droned quietly, before the talking political heads took over, justifying the unjustifiable in every camp. He stopped listening and the picture of the Hermitage, taken by some enterprising photographer making an incursion into the grounds, was gone before it registered. The next shot was of Freya Scott, in a taxi, waiting in the flashbulb glare for the gates to be opened, while the voice-over catalogued the disasters that had recently befallen this exclusive enclave for the daughters of the rich. As she was replaced by another talking head, he returned to his breakfast.

'Listen!' Emma said urgently.

Sitting at Freya's desk, wearing a grim expression, the chairman of the school's governors stated that the headmistress was completely devastated by events and had requested a period of extended leave. While she considered her future, the deputy head would assume control. The matron, who had given sterling service for many years, had also signalled her intention of retiring immediately. 'Once the police have completed their inquiries into Suzanne Melville's tragic death,' he continued, 'I am confident the Hermitage will be able to return to normal.' The American girl, thrown from a horse the day before, was 'well on the road to recovery', but he refused to be drawn on the identity or condition of the girl rushed to hospital late last night, except to remark that it was regrettable how these three unconnected incidents, following hard on each other's heels, had given rise to such sinister and misleading conjecture.

3

'Lies,' Freya muttered to herself, cradling a glass of water. 'Lies, lies and more damned lies!' She drained the glass and hurled it at the television. Neither glass nor screen shattered. The glass ricocheted off, fell to the floor and rolled into a corner, and the man on the screen continued telling lies.

She had stayed at the hospital until long past midnight. When she returned to the school, the ground was cut from under her before she crossed the threshold. She found the man purveying these bland untruths seated in *her* chair behind *her* desk in *her* study, from where he had already made the pronouncements being broadcast. Rage at his dissembling she might, but he was merely oiling the facts to make them easier to swallow, as she had done without a second thought on countless occasions, for hard-edged truths stuck in the craw and inflamed emotion, as Matron, in outer darkness after being bettered by her own, could well testify. Freya had governed her school by controlling people's feelings, by contemptuously dismissing each and every criticism; today she faced the ugly consequences of that arrogance, and the destruction of all she had striven and connived to achieve.

Nicholls had been brutal. Gone was the face she had known, for it was a mask, like one of the many she herself assumed, and she was confronted by the ruthlessness that had made him rich enough and powerful enough to be her champion in the first instance. Now her accomplishments and triumphs were as nothing; only her failures mattered. Staring at the glass, from which a few drops of water had dripped on the polished floor, she began to calculate her losses: power, prestige, respect, money, loyalty, devotion and hope. McKenna had represented her last chance of escaping unscathed from the mess, but he too had deserted her. When Vivienne told her he had been and gone, she hurried out to the hospital car park, and in the banks of lights that turned night almost to day, picked out his car immediately. She raised her hand, took a tentative step forward and realised he was looking through her without a flicker of recognition, as if she were an importunate stranger.

4

Alice's exit from the sixth-form common room led her virtually
into the arms of a policeman. When he demanded to know
what she was doing there, the lie sprang almost gaily to her lips.
'I was tidying up,' she assured him. 'It's one of our jobs.'

He frowned at her, scratching his chin. 'Bit of an early bird,
aren't you? It's barely half-six.'

The next lie was even easier. 'Saves doing it later.' She ran off
before he could respond, savouring her precious knowledge.

Creeping into the dormitory where the others were still
asleep, she realised she was one of only a tiny elite as yet aware
of the momentous fate that had befallen Dr Scott and Matron.
She sat on her bed, wondering whether to wake Daisy but,
distracted by voices from outside, went to look out of the
window. Miss Attwill, dressed for riding, was walking across
the forecourt with the remaining horse owners in tow, Justine
an elegant addition to the depleted group.

Watching them disappear into the trees, Alice imagined the
sight that would greet them when they reached the stables.
Hungering to be there, she suddenly found there was nothing to
stop her for Dr Scott, with her stultifying controls and
demeaning diktats, was history, if only for a few blessed hours.
She threw off her pyjamas, dragged on knickers, jeans, trainers
and T-shirt, snatched her glasses from the locker and made for
the door.

5

Jack left home not long after six, after offering his wife a kiss brimming with promises. As he waited at the school gates for admission, in the rear-view mirror, he saw reporters and cameramen spill across the road, so eager to accost him that not one of them bothered to check for oncoming traffic. Not far behind him, Dewi, gangsterish in black sunglasses and the raked-back black convertible, had to brake sharply to avoid ploughing into them.

Looking wearied and dishevelled, Randall trudged out of his little billet. His dog wriggled through the gates and faced the media, hackles up and fangs on show. They began to retreat, shouting.

'Bastards!' Randall leaned a hand on Jack's car door. 'They were climbing over the walls during the night. I had to get your lot to shift them.'

'They're a bit like vampires,' Jack said. 'They don't sleep at nights.'

'Well, there's the scent of blood around and no mistake,' Randall commented. 'How's that lass they took away?'

'So-so.'

'What a mess, eh? The place is coming apart at the seams.'

'What time did the chairman of governors arrive?'

'About eleven, I think. There was so much coming and going, I lost all track of the time.' Randall paused and, leaning into the car, lowered his voice. 'Did you see the morning news on TV? Well,' he went on, when Jack nodded, 'it was a pack of lies. He's sacked both of them.'

'How d'you know?'

Randall tapped the side of his nose. 'I'm not saying. Wouldn't want to get someone else into trouble, would I? But you see if I'm not right.' With a lift of the hand he moved away. He waited until Jack had moved on and Dewi was through, shut the gates forcefully on the crowd outside, then returned to his house, the dog at his heels.

Almost bumper to bumper, Jack and Dewi made their way along the crazy drive. Once they reached the forecourt, Dewi locked his car, lovingly patted the wing and slid into the passenger seat beside Jack, sunglasses still in place.

Jack yawned. 'What's the point of locking a convertible if you leave the hood down?'

'It's got an immobiliser.'

'I'm still surprised no one's tried to pinch it. Especially where *you* live.'

'Apart from the fact that everyone knows it belongs to me, it's too conspicuous.'

'There's logic in that, I suppose,' Jack said. 'Martha Rathbone's adopted the same philosophy, but reversed it,' he added. 'She told me yesterday she'd realised years ago that fancy limousines get the wrong sort of notice, so she only ever uses ordinary motors.'

'Sensible lady.'

'She's a nice lady, too; very down to earth, for all her millions. Pity her daughter's turning into a snotty little rich bitch. She's giving her mother a really hard time.' Jack sighed. 'Still, I suppose the tension's got to come out somehow. I wonder how they'll all react to the latest crisis.'

'What crisis?' asked Dewi.

Jack turned to look at him. 'Don't you watch morning telly in your house? Following last night's drama, the chairman of governors was on the box first thing saying Scott's "considering her future" and that Matron's retired forthwith. However, according to Randall, they've both been turfed out on their ear and not before time, in my opinion.'

'*What* drama?' Dewi demanded.

'You'd gone before it happened, hadn't you?' Jack remembered. 'Imogen Oliver overdosed on painkillers; bleak prospects and a bad conscience apparently got the better of her. She was found about nine thirty, along with a letter addressed to Mr McKenna, in which she claims *she* was at the wheel when the car turned over and she then entered into a conspiracy with her parents so the insurance company wouldn't give them a clobbering.'

'Hell!' Dewi exclaimed. 'The bodies are mounting up.'

'She's not a body. She's another near miss, like Torrance. I rang the hospital first thing and they said she's fairly stable, although not by any means out of the woods yet.' Glancing across at the school as Miss Attwill and her entourage emerged, he added, 'Forensics reported on Sukie's head wound. She was whacked with a piece of rotting beech and that suggests the killing was opportunistic rather than premeditated. It also widens the field of suspects again.' He drummed his fingers on the steering wheel. 'Talking of which, did you find Sean O'Connor last night?'

'Eventually,' Dewi replied. 'I called at the house first, but his Mum said he'd gone pubbing. I ran him to earth in the White Lion.'

'And?' Jack asked. Still looking at the riders, he thought how smart Justine was in her breeches and boots.

'He asked me about the car registration he'd given you, so I said you'd got it in hand,' Dewi replied. 'Then he wanted to know if he was actually under suspicion. I hedged – couldn't do much else, really – and changed the subject. I pointed out that he must know a lot more about the school than he realises, then stood him a few rounds to loosen his tongue.' He stopped speaking and followed Jack's gaze. 'I hope Justine isn't planning to ride Purdey,' he said next. 'It smacks of tempting fate after yesterday.'

'It wasn't Purdey's fault Torrance came off,' Jack reminded him. 'And you probably got more of a shock than she did. She must be used to hitting the deck.' Glancing at Dewi's worried face he added, 'If you really believe bad luck's bundled up in threes, we're up to speed with Imogen.'

'I suppose,' Dewi conceded.

'But you can still keep your fingers crossed,' Jack said. 'Now, what about Sean?'

'I came to the conclusion he's already told us everything,

although he did say Randall isn't a closet paedophile, just in case we were thinking he might be. He also said Matron argues with Scott quite often over the way things are done, but always loses the argument and suffers for opening her mouth. He's seen her in tears on more than one occasion and he's heard Scott slagging her off to various people, but he warned us not to feel sorry for her, because when she falls foul of Scott, she takes it out on the girls.'

'Now why doesn't that surprise me?' Jack remarked bitingly. Presently he said, 'It might be worthwhile having another chat with Sean's adoring mum, because in the main, most of what I learned yesterday came from her, no doubt because women are infinitely more observant.' A flock of starlings erupted shrieking from the treetops as Alice burst on to the forecourt. 'What's *she* up to?' He jumped out of the car, shouting to her, 'Alice! Where are you going?'

Her head jerked and he was sure she had heard, but she refused to heed. Glasses halfway down her nose, she loped away and soon disappeared round a turn in the path.

'I'll go after her,' Dewi said. 'She's probably making for the stables.'

As he headed off, to be engulfed in turn by the trees, Jack strolled into the shadowy foyer. Other than police officers, there was no one about; either the girls were allowed to sleep in at the weekends or the whole school was taking advantage of the headmistress's unforeseen absence. He sensed a difference in the atmosphere already, as if inner night had rolled away.

With her glasses now hooked into the waistband of her jeans, a bridle hanging over her shoulder and a saddle clutched to her chest, Alice approached Purdey, put on the borrowed tack, stroked her neck, whispered in her perky ears, lashed the reins to the fence and returned to the stable. Admiring her quiet efficiency, Dewi watched her emerge with another saddle and bridle which she slung over the fence beside Tonto who, snapping his hooves, rolling his eyes and snorting, was yanking at his tether.

Alice noticed him when she turned round. Her face went

bright red, but defiance glittered in the eyes. Ignoring her, he sauntered across to Justine.

There were the dark shadows of a sleepless night under her eyes. 'How is Imogen?' she asked, with undisguised anxiety. 'Have you heard?'

'She's still with us.'

'Thank God for small mercies.' She removed Tonto's head collar, put on the bridle and, once the chin strap was buckled, turned her attention to the saddle. Alice lurked a few feet away.

'Are you planning to ride that animal?' Dewi asked.

'Yes.' She bent down to reach for the girth. 'He has to be exercised.'

'Then make sure you double check everything *before* you get aboard,' Dewi warned.

'Everything *has* been double checked!' Alice gave him a withering look. 'We're not stupid!'

Cuttingly he said, 'No, but *you're* out of bounds. Dr Scott told you to stay away from here.'

Alice raised her chin. 'She's not in charge any longer, so what she said doesn't count.'

Justine stared at her. 'What do you mean?'

'How d'you know?' Dewi asked Alice.

Justine caught her arm. 'What are you *talking* about?'

In the narrow confines of the stable yard their exchange was easily overheard; heads began to turn and activities were suspended.

Miss Attwill hurried over. '*I* said Alice could stay,' she told Dewi, her eyes skittering fearfully back and forth. 'We need all the help we can get. Dr Scott doesn't *really* need to know,' she finished pleadingly.

'Dr Scott's been suspended.' As Alice spoke, she felt her heart lift. 'Well, she's actually on extended leave, but I expect it's the same thing.' She looked at the dazed faces around her. 'It was on television this morning. Matron's gone, too.'

Every room along the administration corridor was empty, so Jack went to the kitchens. Some of the domestic staff sat around a table, drinking tea and gossiping, others were cooking breakfast or preparing vegetables for lunch. Fat Sally lumbered out of the huge walk-in refrigerator, a sheep's carcass hanging over her shoulder, her white overalls dark with blood.

'In case you haven't heard yet,' Jack began, 'I thought I'd better tell you that Dr Scott has gone on extended leave.'

'We know,' one of the cleaners said. 'It was on telly.'

'Well, then,' he went on, 'you'll also know about Matron.' There was a loud thump behind him as Fat Sally dropped the carcass on the butcher's block.

'Yes, we do,' the cleaner said. She looked around. 'And good riddance, too!'

Voices murmured agreement and one woman, elbow deep in a mound of potatoes by the sinks, said she blamed Matron for Imogen's overdose. Fat Sally simply took up a cleaver and began butchering the carcass with clean, deadly strokes. He glanced at her as he made for the door and was shocked to see tears coursing down her pendulous cheeks.

'Hey!' the cleaner shouted. He stopped in his tracks and turned. 'Tell that boss of yours to pull his finger out before somebody else gets hurt!'

Janet was pursued up the drive by a massive, chauffeur-driven Bentley Continental in British racing green. The ultimate convertible, she thought, as it parked disdainfully beside Dewi's prized car and made it look like a cheap tin toy. The chauffeur leapt out, whisked open the near-side rear door and saluted the tall, sleek man with silver hair and hand-tailored clothes who emerged.

He stared at her, appraising her from head to foot, then moved forward, hand outstretched. 'Good morning,' he said, with a flash of teeth. 'I'm Nicholls, the chairman of governors.'

'Yes, I know,' Janet said, offering her own hand. 'I saw you on television. I'm Detective Constable Evans.'

His flesh was warm, his grasp firm. When his thumb began to caress the back of her hand, she pulled free. A spasm of anger crossed his face. 'Superintendent McKenna doesn't seem to have arrived yet,' she told him, 'but Inspector Tuttle is here.'

'I don't think I need to bother either of them.' His eyes were steelier than his hair.

Despite telling herself that people who fooled with wolves

were bound to get savaged, she felt a passing sympathy for Freya Scott. 'I think you should let Superintendent McKenna be the judge of that,' she advised. 'It's unfortunate that we had to find out about Dr Scott and Matron from a television news bulletin.'

'What *I* decide to do at *my* school is *my* business!'

'In normal circumstances, perhaps,' she conceded, 'but not in the middle of a police investigation.' She started walking away. 'If you'd like to come with me, I'll take you to Inspector Tuttle.'

Twice, Justine tried unaided to get into Tonto's saddle, but he turned his head one way and swung his hindquarters another. Finally, while Alice held the bridle, Dewi gave her a leg-up, before dodging out of reach of the suddenly clattering hooves. Leaning on the fence, as he had yesterday in the arena, he watched Tonto lead the others, at a cracking pace, towards the track that passed the classroom block. In the sunshine his coat was as dazzling as Charlotte's hair. Alice sat on an upturned bucket, her envious gaze following his.

'They're going to the foreshore,' she said. 'The tide's out.'

'I hope Justine will be OK.'

'She's ridden him before. You *should* be worrying about Miss Attwill. Purdey goes mad when she starts galloping.'

'So why is she riding her?'

'Someone has to. Justine could, but Miss Attwill can't handle Tonto at all.' Alice rubbed her eyes, leaving dirty smears on her face.

'You look tired,' Dewi observed, thinking how plain she was.

'That's because I've been awake for hours.'

'Where did you see the news on TV?'

'In the senior common room.'

'What were you doing there?'

'Minding my own business.'

'There's no need to get stroppy,' he said mildly. 'I'm entitled to ask.'

Instead of responding, she stared glumly at the ground, then raised her eyes to look again after the horses, now tiny figures in the tree-hung distance. 'They won't go in the woods any more,' she said with a violent shiver. 'They're afraid of seeing

Sukie's ghost.' Slowly she met his gaze. 'Do *you* believe in ghosts?'

'I suppose so.' He regarded her thoughtfully. 'Have you ever been to that old house in Conwy called Plas Mawr?' She shook her head. 'I've never actually *seen* anything, but it's certainly got a creepy atmosphere.' He grinned wryly. 'To be honest, I wouldn't want to spend the night there, especially not alone.'

Alice mulled over his words. 'My mother says people are never *really* honest. She said it's not possible.'

'Did she?' He was taken aback by the abrupt change of theme. 'Why's that?'

Trying her hardest not to reinterpret and redefine, she said, 'It's impossible to know what someone else truly *feels*, but that's behind what they say, even if they don't know it themselves.'

'In my experience, when people tell you lies it's deliberate.'

She frowned. 'But you only deal with criminals.'

'Alice, criminals are simply the ones who got caught.' He smiled down at her. 'And if they stood out from the crowd, we wouldn't be turning the school upside down looking for the person who sabotaged Purdey's saddle.' His smile faded when he saw her tormented expression. Moving away from the fence, he crouched beside her. 'What is it? Do you know something?'

'No!' she exclaimed violently. 'I don't know *anything*!' Tears streaming down her dirty cheeks, she jumped up and fled in the direction the riders had taken and was yards away before he was even upright.

Cursing himself, he took off in pursuit, but she soon stopped. Doubled up, she leaned against a huge beech tree for support, and he could hear her rasping breath long before he reached her. Pausing only to glance at her ashen face and blue lips, he slung her over his shoulder and headed back to the school at a fast trot.

6

Gauzy morning sunshine suffused Torrance's hospital room and she could see the light through her closed eyelids as she climbed hand over hand up the side of the bottomless well of unconsciousness. Every so often, always looking upwards, she stopped to gather her strength and when she finally reached the top her eyes snapped open on a bright, white horizontal expanse.

Without moving her head, she found first one, then all four, of the sharp lines that enclosed the expanse, which her brain quickly rearranged into a rectangle that she was viewing from a particular perspective. The four vertical expanses suspended from above became walls, and she knew there must therefore be a door and a window to let in the light that had roused her.

She flexed her fingers and wiggled her toes. One foot was very stiff, with a dull pain gnawing at the bones. Sharper pains bit elsewhere about her body, and when she tried to move her head, agony speared her neck and shoulder. Her mouth was utterly parched and her throat too stiff to move her tongue, but she could feel every complaining inch of her body, so the crashing fall she remembered with complete clarity had not crippled her. She also remembered lying in the ambulance, clutching David's hands, and his gentle voice telling her that Purdey was unhurt. When the memory made her smile, her face threatened to crack.

Her senses told her she was not alone. Steeling herself to withstand the pain, she very carefully moved her head to the left. A plump young woman in uniform sat by the bed with her nose in a copy of *OK* magazine. Then she turned her head to the right. A gaunt, dark shape stood at the window, a black hole in the haze of light. Believing Death was waiting to carry her away, she opened her mouth to scream.

7

Nicholls leaned on Freya's desk, well-manicured fingers splayed under his weight, waiting for Jack's response.

Jack met his angry, imperious look. 'You may address the school to explain that the deputy head is now in charge,' he said. 'And if you *must* sustain the fiction, I won't even stop you repeating the nonsense about Dr Scott's extended leave and Matron's voluntary retirement.' He paused. 'However, you will say nothing about Imogen Oliver or Sukie Melville. Is that clear?'

'No?' Eyebrows raised, Nicholls said, 'Imogen Oliver attacked Nancy Holmes with her stick. Your superintendent removed both stick and crutches for forensic examination.' He looked over Jack's shoulder for a moment, then his gaze swivelled back. 'Shortly afterwards, Imogen Oliver all but killed herself. Suicide,' he went on, 'is regarded by the experts as a homicidal impulse turned inwards; more pertinently, it is often the next act of someone who has committed murder. Cripple she may be, but I am convinced Imogen Oliver is the killer.' Regarding Jack with narrowed eyes and a narrower smile, he added, 'So why don't you simply pack up that hideous contraption you have parked in the grounds and be on your way? I will deal with the loose ends. If the Oliver girl survives it will be made clear to her parents that she is not welcome to return. That, I think, should solve the problem. It will also put a stop to your frittering away any more public money.'

'You and Freya Scott are two of a kind, aren't you?' Jack remarked. 'You both see the Hermitage as some kind of parallel universe, where you can upend the rules to suit yourselves. But shall I tell you how it really is?' he asked, as Nicholls's mouth contorted with fury. 'You're living inside your own dangerously warped version of reality and that's at the root of everything that's gone so horribly wrong.'

'Your chief constable will hear about this!' the other man seethed.

Jack shrugged. 'Feel free. And while you're talking to him, ask about Imogen's letter.'

'What letter?'

Jack smiled wolfishly. 'The letter she left for Superintendent McKenna, which Matron and Dr Scott took it upon themselves to open.' He moved round the desk, crowding the other man towards the door. 'Now, Mr Nicholls, I have a lot to do, but before you go I'd like to know how you got in here last night, as the caretakers wouldn't have been around to unlock the door.'

'I have my own keys.'

Jack held out his hand. 'Then if you wouldn't mind? You'll get them back eventually.'

Only moments before, Jack had put down the telephone after telling Martha about Alice's asthma attack when McKenna walked into the mobile incident room, dropped his briefcase on the floor and sat down heavily. 'Randall's just brought me up to date on Matron and Dr Scott,' he said. 'How did that come about?'

'Matron phoned Imogen's parents to tell them about her overdose,' Jack replied, 'and they called Nicholls. He came here while Scott was still at the hospital and made his executive decision. However, as he didn't think to tell us, I've given him a good trouncing.' After a small pause he added pointedly, 'In your absence, that is.'

McKenna's face was pinched with fatigue. 'Yes, I should have said I'd be late.' The silence stretched then, broken only by the click of his lighter. 'I've arranged for those two who started the betting to be formally reprimanded,' he went on at last, blowing smoke towards the open window. 'I also spoke to Berkshire about Imogen's letter, but they can't interview her parents yet. They left at the crack of dawn to come here.' Staring at the glowing cigarette end he said, 'And in a way, rather like Freya Scott, I was considering my position. I should have foreseen Imogen's overdose.'

'No one else did.'

'That's no excuse.'

'Well, none of us is infallible,' Jack admitted. 'Alice had an almighty asthma attack because of something Dewi said to her, although he's no idea what. She recovered after a couple of puffs from her inhaler, but I've let her mother know.' He yawned. 'Maybe we should let her take Alice away for the weekend. The kid's nerves are like piano wire – hence the attack, I imagine.'

'Everyone's nerves are strung to breaking,' McKenna commented shortly. 'I called at the hospital on my way in. There's no change in Imogen, but Torrance has come round.' He smiled fleetingly. 'When she woke up, Vivienne was standing at the window with her back to the light, looking like the Grim Reaper.' Then his face fell once more. 'Hester Melville's been readmitted. Someone walking their dog found her late last night on Menai Bridge, lying in a heap on the walkway. I haven't spoken to her, though. She's stuffed to the gills with sedatives, which is probably for the best.'

'Does her husband know?'

'I've no idea. You could don your social worker hat and get in touch with him, couldn't you?'

'And *you* could get your bloody act together!' Jack retorted angrily, his patience on the verge of exhaustion. 'Even the kitchen staff have got your measure. The message from them to you is "pull your finger out before somebody else gets hurt"!'

'I see.' Cigarette quivering between his fingers, McKenna folded his arms tightly, almost visibly shrinking into himself as if Jack were about to strike.

McKenna's response was a reflex, beyond his control, and with a sickening jolt Jack saw how they must look: he the bully, McKenna the victim. That insight made so much that had baffled him fall instantly into place and he understood at last why Emma's long friendship with McKenna's former wife had foundered so suddenly and mysteriously. For months after McKenna walked out of the marriage, Emma had been Denise's champion, even when she took up with another man, and then, without warning, she refused even to speak to her. When Jack asked for an explanation she would only say, 'I made a dreadful mistake. Some people are not what they seem to be.'

Staring intently at the papers in front of him he said, 'I'm sorry. I was out of order.'

McKenna's tension lessened a fraction. 'Arguably, it's a fair comment. I haven't been conspicuously successful.'

'None of us has got past first base with this pig of an investigation,' Jack said, 'because Scott made sure we wouldn't.' His voice tailed away, his mind awash with images of Denise, no longer the wronged wife, but the evildoer, who had so diminished her husband that he lived in fear of his own shadow. He lifted his head and, looking into McKenna's eyes, saw there the darkness that dwelt in so many of the Hermitage girls, as if the light of life were guttering. How often, he thought despairingly, had the man been black and blue under his clothes, as Sukie must have been?

'Freya Scott is a tyrant and a bully,' McKenna remarked quietly. 'And unfortunately, despite your warning me about her on Thursday, I let her get the better of me. A psychologist would say she creates a psychic drama with everyone in her orbit to ensure she stays in control, but transactions of that kind have a devastating effect because they expose people's deepest insecurities.' He dropped the remains of his cigarette in the ashtray, and rose to his feet rather unsteadily, his chair rocking. 'Bullying *is* a transaction, you know,' he added, 'even though the victims are coerced. For some, their pain satisfies a diffuse and deep-rooted sense of guilt. Others are simply too scared of more pain to resist.' His mouth twisted, perhaps in a wry smile. 'The devil-you-know syndrome.' Bending down for his briefcase, he said, 'I'm going to see Matron.'

Bereft of words, Jack watched until he was out of the door, then put his head in his hands. He wanted to weep.

Walking through the school on his way to Matron's flat, McKenna encountered signs of the new order at every turn – uncharacteristically noisy girls, the thump of pop music from behind closed doors, a pervading sense of freedom – but underscoring the buoyancy was a strident unease and there was little laughter, although he recalled reading somewhere that children and teenagers were supposed to laugh hundreds of times each day. The few staff he saw resembled shell-shocked survivors of some dreadful battle and he wondered if they understood that the war was far from over, or how easily the school could collapse about their ears once the novelty began to dissipate and fear of the unknown took its place.

He climbed the stairs to the first floor, passed the junior dormitories and rapped on Matron's door. Putting his ear to the wood, he knocked again, much more loudly, and long before he heard her dragging footfalls his imagination had her already dead by her own hand.

'Who is it?' Her voice was full of tears.

'Superintendent McKenna.'

The tumblers fell in the lock, then she inched open the door. Her appearance was soul-destroying.

'May I come in?' he asked.

Without a word, she turned and plodded away. He shut the door and followed her into a small sitting room that overlooked the gardens and Strait, and allowed a distant view of Anglesey. By the window there was a tub chair with squashed chintz cushions where she seated herself. She still wore her uniform, but not the belt with the silver clasp. That lay on the floor, the clasp winking where sunlight caught its intricate workings, the overstretched elastic rippled along both edges. Her clothes looked as if she had slept in them and her hair was in total disarray, but it was her collapsed face that shocked him.

'I've only just heard,' he began. 'I'm truly sorry.'

She looked at the hands clasped in her lap. 'I don't expect anyone else is.'

As soon as she opened her mouth, he realised that the tartar-stained teeth he had noticed yesterday were missing. Without them, she hissed like a serpent.

'Why were you forced to retire?' he asked.

'I wasn't. I've been sacked. Summarily dismissed with forty-eight hours to quit the premises.' She clamped her lips together to stifle a sob.

'But why?' he persisted.

'I hit Therese.'

'You hit Therese?'

'Nicholls arrived in the middle of it. He sacked me on the spot.' Her eyes glistened. 'Then he lay in wait for Dr Scott.' A tremor shook her and her breath came in short, sharp gasps. 'Oh, but he's a hard man! A *cruel* man! I'd heard one of the little ones in the infirmary crying not minutes before, but he wouldn't let me go to her.'

He waited for her to regain a little composure. 'What made you hit Therese?'

'She told Dr Scott she'd thrown nail varnish on Charlotte's clothes. She was going to lock Nancy in the cellar, too. Nancy's terrified of spiders and the cellar's crawling with them.' She stopped speaking, but her lips continued working. Raising blood-shot eyes, she found more words. 'After Dr Scott had gone off in the ambulance with Imogen, I went looking for Therese. I shouldn't have done. I lost control of myself.' She breathed in deeply, and her lips sucked on the toothless gums. 'And d'you know what? It was all for nothing! Therese hadn't done *anything* to Charlotte's clothes. She only *said* she had, to frighten Dr Scott, because she blamed Nancy and Charlotte for Imogen lashing out.' She shuddered. 'Thank God she didn't know then about the overdose – she'd have killed both of them. She's perfectly capable of it, I'm sure, and now I've had time to think, I'm just surprised it didn't happen sooner. There's been so much—' she stopped in mid-flow, surreptitiously glancing at him. 'Friction,' she said rather lamely. 'Friction and bad blood.' Shaking her head des-pondently, she added, '*Far* too much of it. I've warned Dr Scott over and again, but she just wouldn't listen.' Her body shook with another violent tremor. 'And now look where it's got her! "Considering her future" indeed! She's had the sack, too. Well,' she added, her malice like a live thing, 'it serves her right! So much for all her fancy ideas, eh? Why wouldn't she be told?' Wringing her huge red hands, she stared at him. 'Do *you* know? Do *you* understand? For as sure as God's in his heaven, *I* never did.'

Not understanding her questions, he had no answers, and while her mouth continued working and her face flushed with emotion, he remained still and silent.

'She thought she could control people.'

'Did she?' he responded.

'Yes.' She nodded wildly. 'She thought she could mess about with people's feelings and get away with it. Well, you can't. You can't force people to feel what you want them to, but Freya

Scott thought she could. She said people never know what they really want, and it was up to her to show them. She was forever spouting suchlike psychological claptrap, but I'm not sure even *she* knew what she was talking about half the time. I know no one else did.'

'A little knowledge is often more dangerous than none at all.'

'That's what I kept trying to tell her.' Frowning, Matron looked hard at him and, even in the throes of her misery, he discovered her native wit had not deserted her. 'She tried it on with you, didn't she? She tried *something*, anyway,' she added, when his face betrayed him. 'That's why you're still floundering over Sukie's death. You were too taken up being bamboozled by Freya Scott.'

He dropped his gaze and let the silence grow, afraid to meet her eyes in case he caught the knowing gleam in hers.

'It's not *fair*!'

Her outburst broke his tension. 'Shouldn't you contact your union?' he asked.

'I can't,' she replied dully. 'It's Saturday.' Gums grating on each other, she leaned forward. 'Nicholls said it was my fault Imogen overdosed. Do you believe that, too?'

This was not the time to remind her that she had laid the blame at his own feet only a few hours earlier. 'If Imogen's telling the truth about the accident, she must have been under intolerable stress. Something was bound to give, especially after Sukie died.'

'And if she wasn't telling the truth?'

'She's still clearly disturbed. I don't see her overdose as attention seeking.'

'It wasn't! She *meant* to kill herself, and she would have done if I'd heeded Dr Scott. She was hell bent on making Imogen responsible for her own medication and told me repeatedly to give her *all* the tablets. But you see,' she added, touching his hand, 'I knew that was asking for trouble. She gets prescriptions for three months' supply at a time, but I only ever gave her a week's worth so she never had enough to do herself any *real* harm.'

'There was always the risk of her stockpiling.'

'Oh, no, there wasn't! She was in too much pain.'

8

Almost shoulder to shoulder, Janet and Martha stood at the foot
of the long sloping lawn bordering the Strait, with the noise of
two hundred-odd girls clattering around inside the school
coming to them in sporadic bursts.

Martha found the fast-flowing water only yards away quite
hypnotic. She fixed her gaze on a racing whitecap and tried to
follow its progress. When she lost it she tried another, but lost
that, too. They were forever elusive, she thought glumly, like
hopes and dreams, and her daughter, who had fled the moment
she saw Martha in the refectory corridor.

'It's a lot cooler since yesterday's rain,' Janet observed. 'I'm
not keen on very hot weather. It's too tiring.'

'Alice prefers cool, windy weather as well.' Martha shuffled
her feet, for the grass was still damp. 'She even enjoys the
rain.'

'Your life really does revolve around her, doesn't it?'

'That's why my marriages never worked,' Martha said ruefully. 'Maybe marriage and motherhood are mutually exclusive
states.' She paused, then went on, 'Or perhaps marriage is just
the means to the end, although what that end *is* is anyone's
guess. I thought it was about having a child, but the way my
child's behaving at the moment makes me dread to think what
the outcome will be.'

'Alice is in an invidious position,' Janet pointed out. 'Her
loyalties are split between you and school.' She smiled. 'More
pertinently, she's at a notoriously difficult age. Teenagers don't
make much sense, even to themselves.'

Staring across the water unseeingly, Martha said, 'Children

are yours for so little time before the process of natural separation begins, and you only realise that's happened after the event, when it's too late.' She glanced at her companion. 'Your mother would know exactly what I mean. I'm sure she's been moved to tears, too, at times, by the sight of another woman with a small girl in tow, remembering how it was when you were little.'

'She's never said anything like that,' Janet told her, surprised by such a personal disclosure.

'She wouldn't. Mothers learn when to shut up.' Martha smiled then. 'Well, *some* do. I've never been able to keep my opinions to myself. But nor can Alice. That's why the fur flies between us so often.'

'What do you argue about most?'

'Her choice of friends,' Martha replied, once again staring out over the water. 'I can't stand Daisy Podmore and I'm not enamoured of Grace Blackwell, for all Matron's little wisdoms.' Her eyes flicked back to Janet. 'Haven't you heard her? Whenever Grace is mentioned, she says, "Grace by name, grace by nature" and gives you that sickly smile of hers.'

'I wasn't particularly taken with Grace,' Janet admitted. 'She's a bit of a prig. But I felt rather sorry for Daisy.'

'Why? Because she lisps so horribly?'

'No.' Janet shook her head. 'Because, deep down, I think she's terribly unhappy, for all her smiles.'

Martha stared at her thoughtfully. 'You may be right. And perhaps that's why Alice is so miserable and moody – she's being infected by her. But then,' she went on, '*everything* these girls do or feel affects the others. Your job must be an absolute nightmare, sorting out what matters from what doesn't.'

'It is.' Janet fell quiet, mulling over how much she should disclose. Eventually she asked, 'Have you ever worried that Alice was being bullied?'

'Yes, frequently. By Daisy.' She paused. 'I've watched them until I was almost cross-eyed, trying to work out what their behaviour says about the way the power falls in their relationship, but I'm none the wiser. One minute Alice is calling the shots; the next it's Daisy.'

'Where does Grace fit in?'

Martha scuffed the wet grass. 'Wherever Daisy will let her, I suppose.'

On his way downstairs from Matron's flat, McKenna saw the two women, their still figures like grey daubs on the sweep of lawn. He stood for a moment behind the front door, watching them. What were they talking about? he wondered. Anything and nothing, he decided: ideas, impressions, snatches of this and that, passed back and forth until something struck a chord or made a connection, as ever when women were together.

Reminding himself he must tell Martha that so far there had been no feedback on the likelihood or otherwise of kidnap, he turned away.

9

In the mobile incident room's cubbyhole of an office, Jack was dozing over the stack of papers on the desk. When Nona rapped on the door the sound, like gunshots in the confined space, catapulted him into wakefulness. Guiltily running his hands over his face, he blinked at her.

'I know how you feel, sir,' she said.

'Yes, well,' he muttered. 'We're all getting sleep bankrupt. What did you want?'

'I've finished going through Sukie's credit card statements.' She dropped more paper on the pile. 'It didn't take long, though. She wasn't exactly a big spender.'

'From what her mother told me, there isn't much *to* spend,' Jack commented. 'They live hand to mouth, albeit in a posh kind of way, but maybe not for much longer in a mansion, as the bank's threatening repossession.'

'I can't understand why people should want to spend a fortune just keeping a house going. If I were in their shoes, I'd sell up and buy a little terraced cottage.'

'People like that would rather shoot themselves.'

Nona frowned at him. 'I thought you liked them, sir. Lady Hester especially.'

'I do and I feel desperately sorry for them, but I can still recognise them as a breed apart.' He looked through the statements, his tired eyes making little sense of the facts and figures, although the escalating debit balances leapt off the page.

'I'm really surprised how quickly these turned up,' Nona was saying. 'Considering today's Saturday and we only asked for them yesterday anyway.'

'Once in a while, organisations are not only helpful but actually efficient.' Jack noticed a bright red asterisk against a name he recognised from the magazines his daughters left about the house.

Nona craned over the desk. 'They're jewellers, sir. Based in Bond Street.'

'I know and I assume the seventeen hundred and odd pounds Sukie spent with them last December was for Imogen's Christmas present.'

'Probably. It's the biggest amount by far that she'd ever spent. The next biggest is with a saddler's, earlier this year.' She turned to a new page, pointing to another asterisk. 'See? Just under a thousand. The rest of her money went on magazine subscriptions and stuff for her horse, plus the odd fifty quid or so in department stores, mostly during the Easter holidays.' Taking a step back, she added, 'I called the jewellers to find out what she bought, but they can't say until they've looked up their records. They promised to get back, if not today, by Monday at the latest.'

'OK.' Yawning and stretching, Jack said, 'You'd better go and search Imogen's room for the necklace – she may have simply mislaid it, as she said. While you're there, list her belongings, then get them packed. Whatever happens, I doubt she'll be coming back.'

'If I can't find the necklace, we could ask her parents what it looks like. They'll be here soon, I expect.'

'I'd rather try to find out from John Melville,' Jack told her. 'We may interview the Olivers about Imogen's letter and I don't want to create any distractions, however innocuous.'

Nona was barely out of the door when the telephone rang.

Eifion Roberts announced himself by barking out, 'Where's McKenna?'

'Talking to Matron.' Wincing, Jack held the receiver away from his ear. 'She's had the sack.'

'Yes, I know, along with the headmistress. I heard it on the radio.'

'I saw it on early-morning television.'

'Well, then, by now the world and his wife should know, so I wouldn't be surprised if parents start turning up in droves to remove their offspring.'

'Some might, but a lot of them seem to be abroad, congregating in various fashionable places.'

'Does that include the next of kin of the latest catastrophe?' the pathologist asked. 'The kid with one leg who downed enough painkillers to fell a horse?'

'No. They're on their way here.' Jack related then the claims Imogen had made in her letter, adding, 'Is she likely to survive, d'you think? Because if she isn't around to back up her statements there's no prospect of taking them further.'

'I can't say. Depends on how she fares in the next few days.' Roberts paused, tapping something against his teeth. 'Most of what she swallowed was washed out quickly enough – in fact, we've got the stomach contents here for analysis – but it still had time to get into her system and add to what was already there. The cumulative effect of months taking the stuff, plus a hefty overdose, could result in organ failure.'

Jack said nothing, feeling the pain of these wasted lives as if the girls were his own flesh and blood.

Roberts coughed. 'Tell me,' he said, rather hesitantly, 'is McKenna all right?'

'Why shouldn't he be?'

'Just give me a straight answer!'

'I can't. He's not been "all right" for a long time. I sometimes wonder if he ever was.'

'That's very perceptive of you.'

'Why are you asking, anyway?'

'We had a barney yesterday and, not by any means for the first time, ended up at loggerheads. He wanted me to sympathise because he's got to shift from that slum he lives in and got into a temper when I wouldn't.'

'Yes, well, it's his bolthole,' Jack commented, uneasy with the direction of the conversation.

'So, perhaps it's time his friends helped to prise him out of it,' Roberts replied quietly, 'even if it means taking the bull by the horns then hunkering down until the storm blows itself out.' He waited for a moment, before saying, 'There's a place coming up for grabs I know he's always fancied, but it's strictly a word-of-mouth affair. If he doesn't get in now, he won't have a chance.'

'Where is it?'

'That ancient cottage right by the pier,' Roberts said. 'No neighbours aside from gulls, cormorants and the odd seal, and some of the finest views going, but until he's got over his sulks, he won't be speaking to me, so I can't tell him. *You* could, though. I'll fax over the info, shall I? And you can let him know I've got something off Sukie's body I wasn't expecting – pressure marks on her neck and shoulders from where she was held down in the water. We may, but *only* may, be able to lift prints from her T-shirt. There's also a faint imprint of what looks like a trainer on the seat of her jeans.'

Nicholls's beautiful car had still been gracing the forecourt when McKenna crossed on his way to Matron's flat, but some time within the last hour, both man and car had departed. He walked along the administration corridor, the keys that Jack had taken from Nicholls in his hand, ready to give him access to whatever secrets Freya might have hidden in her study. Reaching her door, he found it wide open, with the deputy headmistress seated stiffly behind the desk.

'Can I help you?' Miss Knight asked, her face as vinegary as her voice.

'I see Mr Nicholls has gone,' McKenna said. 'I thought he intended to address the school.'

'He changed his mind.' She sniffed. 'The task has been delegated to me.'

'And when do you propose to do it?'

'I haven't yet decided.'

'I don't think you should leave it *too* long,' he advised. 'The girls, and the staff, have a right to the facts.'

'I'm perfectly aware of their rights, thank you.'

'I hope you're equally familiar with the facts,' he remarked. 'Please ensure that no one is left with the misapprehension that Imogen killed Sukie.' Nodding to her, he retraced his steps back to the lobby, where he stood by the double doors deciding what to do next now one set of plans had been thwarted.

Therese and Justine came into view, from the direction of the stables. Justine's boots were crusted with sand, Therese's shapeless jeans and scruffy shirt bespattered with dirty splashes. As they neared the doors, he could almost see the stamp of

Matron's huge hand in the ugly welt on her left cheek.

They were speaking to each other in German. When he asked Therese if she had been to the stables, unconsciously she responded in that language. '*Ja*,' she said and began to say more, still in German, before switching to English. 'I have been grooming. Picking out hooves, washing tails and manes. A *child* is less demanding of time than a horse, I am sure.'

'I didn't realise you had one,' he remarked.

'I do not have a horse *here*,' she told him. 'At home, I have a Hanoverian stallion, but I am not allowed to bring him to school.'

'Why not?' He fell into step beside them, his nose assailed by the pungent smell of sweating horse that clung to Justine's clothes.

'There is no stallion pen,' she replied, giving him a look that questioned his common sense. 'He would cover the mares if he ran with the others.'

Justine stopped at the foot of the stairs, her face drawn. 'Is there any more news of Imogen?' she asked. 'Sergeant Prys told us earlier only that she is still alive.'

'No,' he said. 'That's all we know. But Torrance has regained consciousness.'

She shrugged. 'Torrance is tough.' With a huge sigh she added, 'Imogen is not. She's very, very fragile.'

Therese turned towards her. 'We thought Vivienne was weak, but look how she has surprised us all.' Then, with a frown in McKenna's direction, she asked, 'Where *is* Vivienne?'

'Still at the hospital,' he said. 'Sergeant Prys may be able to tell us more about Imogen when he comes back. He's gone to see Torrance.'

'That will please her,' Therese remarked. 'She is a little in love with him, but not as much as she is with Tonto. She has the T-shirt to prove *that*!' A wicked grin momentarily transformed her, then her habitually lugubrious expression was back in place. 'That is a joke,' she went on. 'A play on words. A horse's height is measured in hands. Her T-shirt has a horse's head on the front and on the back, the words "I like 16 hands between my legs".' She stared at him, a keen and surprising intelligence in her somewhat piggy eyes. 'It is vulgar, yes, but I am not telling you this to suggest she is unwholesome.'

'Are you sure about that?' he asked softly. 'This is a very unnatural environment with little room for proper outlets. Things must get quite overheated at times.'

'But not with Torrance. She isn't interested.' Therese paused. 'She is truly more interested in horses. It may be what people call displacement, but I do not think so. She loves to be with them. Perhaps they help her to forget being human.' Again, she stared at him. 'And here, that is good. It keeps her sane. It is a pity Imogen had no such safety valve,' she finished meaningfully.

'Why say that?' he asked. 'Do you believe she killed Sukie?'

'No!' Suddenly, Justine sat down on the stairs, collapsing like a puppet with broken strings. 'We do *not*, however much Dr Scott tried to persuade us.' She looked up at him. 'I'm *glad* she's gone and I very much hope she never comes back. I'm not sorry about Matron, either.'

He turned to Therese. 'How did Mr Nicholls know Matron had hit you? Did you tell him?'

She shook her head. 'It was Daisy Podmore. She was loitering on the landing when he arrived. She must have heard Matron shouting at me about Charlotte's clothes. But then,' she added, 'she is *always* snooping.'

'Matron told me,' he began, 'that you were after Nancy and Charlotte simply because there's friction and bad blood between you. Is that all there was to it?'

'No, it isn't,' Justine exclaimed. 'She deliberately misled you. We were going to punish those two because they'd driven Imogen beyond endurance with their bullying. It was the last straw.'

'Were they also using Sukie as a punchbag?' McKenna asked. 'Someone was. The pathologist found the evidence when he cut her up.'

At that bald, brutal statement, Justine put her hand to her mouth as if she were about to vomit.

Mournfully, Therese nodded. 'But she was not alone. Ainsley has suffered; Daria too, before she hit back, and Vivienne. Many of the little girls are also their victims.' She gulped, and a tear slid down her cheek and dropped from her chin. 'We have done what we could to stop them, but whenever we complained to Dr Scott, she would simply tell us that "the wheat must be sorted from the chaff".'

Justine let her hand fall to her lap. Her face was ashen. 'If you remember,' she said to Therese, 'she *also* accused us of deliberately misconstruing the natural follow-on to her damned "Make or Break".' Her gaze rested on McKenna then. 'Every year, the seniors put the first formers through this test of physical and mental endurance, and grade their performance. Dr Scott took the idea from military training.'

'And I suppose Nancy and Charlotte passed with flying colours?' he asked.

'No, they didn't,' Justine replied. 'They were bullied mercilessly for a long time. They learned the hard way how to survive.'

'Do you know why Sukie was being bullied?'

'Because she was there. Because it was her turn, just as it might be her turn to be Daisy's crush. These things go round and round for ever.'

'Why "Daisy's crush"?' McKenna asked.

'Oh, she has a new crush every few weeks. She's famous for it.' Justine smiled wanly. 'Her passions are almost like phoenixes. The old bird consumes itself as the new one rises from the ashes.'

'And is Daisy another bully?'

'I don't think so; not yet. But she's taunted about her lisp and the size of her breasts, so I expect she'll turn the tables when she gets the chance.'

'What about Alice Derringer?'

'*That* one!' Therese rolled her eyes. 'Everyone leaves her alone. She is a little scorpion.'

'Tell me what happened to Imogen,' he urged. '*How* had she been driven beyond endurance.'

'With utter wanton cruelty,' Therese replied curtly.

'You see,' Justine said, 'Imogen was always a brilliant swimmer, and when her stump had healed enough and the weather got warmer, she started going to the pool. She'd leave her crutches on the side.' She stopped and brushed a hand across her eyes. 'Nancy, or Charlotte, or one of their gang, used to run off with them. Imogen would flop about like a dying fish while they danced in front of her, calling her "Peg Leg" and "Cripple", prodding her with the crutches but making sure they kept just out of reach. Yesterday,' she added, her voice trembling, 'she decided it was time Nancy had a taste of her own medicine. If only she hadn't missed!' she finished bitterly.

'Did Dr Scott know?'

'Of *course*, she did!' Therese said contemptuously. 'We *told* her! She said, "Imogen must learn to accommodate her new situation and its implications."'

There was little he could do but leave them with their grief and guilt and anger. He returned to the mobile incident room, wondering if the grief would stay with them long enough to become almost a friend and thought it probably would, although the guilt would not be so kind.

'Is there a motive in there?' he asked Jack, when he had finished relaying the story.

'Only if Nancy or Charlotte were lying at the bottom of Menai Strait with a dented head.'

'You don't think Sukie's death could be simply bullying that went too far?'

Jack thought for a moment. 'You're suggesting manslaughter at most, whereas I'm positive it was far more deliberate. Eifion's found pressure marks from where she was held down in the water, as well as a probable trainer imprint on her jeans.'

'I see.' McKenna pulled out a cigarette, then carefully put it back in the packet. 'Nonetheless, the contemptible Nancy and her detestable sidekick warrant interrogation, but as they're both over eighteen, we'll do it at the station. Just make sure there's a nice big audience when you take them away.'

'I was planning to visit Avril O'Connor.'

'There's nothing to stop you. Those two can cool their heels in the lock-up for a couple of hours. It might do them a world of good.'

11

Shivering, Martha trudged along the bank above the foreshore, where the uncut grass was sodden from yesterday's rain. Cold crept through the soles of her shoes, the wet hems of her trousers slapped against her ankles and she ached from head to foot, with the bone-deep pain that seemed to have been her lot for ever.

The trees ahead grew so close to the water she could barely make out the bruised passage through the grass. Pushing aside the drooping branches, shying when the cold leaves slapped her in the face, she inched forward, scared of sliding helplessly into the Strait. She searched the ground before each step to make sure there was purchase in the squelching mud, while the water rushed past on her right. The tide was coming up in a hurry, driven by a thin north-westerly that had stolen all the warmth from the morning and was harrying more rain clouds about the mountains. Ever distrustful of her body and the sudden spasms that might afflict knees or hips or ankles, she crept gingerly forward, eyes firmly on the ground. The racing tide on the periphery of her vision made her dizzy and she staggered alarmingly more than once.

'Why am I doing this?' she muttered. 'Why the *hell* am I bothering?'

Alice was a little ingrate, a spoiled, silly, nasty brat who had clearly decided to throw in her lot with the others of her kind infesting Freya's proving ground.

'And what else did I expect?' Martha demanded, without expecting a response from the alien forces of nature that surrounded her. 'She was seven when I sent her away. What right have I to expect her to feel anything for me?' Because I feel so much for her, she thought, answering her own questions. She's my child and I *won't* abandon her.

She bore on through the trees, with the same dogged persistence that made her fight the constant pain, sagging with relief when the tangle of mossy trunks and smothering foliage fell away to expose the entry to a small glade and a golden sandbank, where the furrows ploughed earlier by the galloping horses were not yet obliterated by the swirling tide. When she heard Alice, from somewhere near at hand, she stopped in her tracks. Carried by the wind, the words came to her with total clarity.

'Of course,' she was piping, 'I knew immediately what had *really* happened to Dr Scott. When Mummy sacks someone on the spot, she says so-and-so is "considering their position". The guff about extended leave is just to explain their sudden disappearance.'

'Jeez!' Daisy exclaimed. 'What *don't* you bloody know?'

'When you're telling the truth!' There was a sharp, shrill note in Alice's voice.

'*Nobody* knows that,' Grace said then with a giggle. 'Not even Daisy herself.'

'Fuck you!' Daisy screeched.

Martha heard someone whisper what sounded like 'touché' and a moment later the sound of flesh slapping flesh. She rushed forward as the screaming began, to find Alice and Daisy fighting furiously, while Grace, clad like the others in blue jeans and white T-shirt, straddled a rotting tree trunk, watching.

'Stop that!' yelled Martha. 'This instant!'

Neither of them took the least notice. They went on tussling and kicking and punching, moving ever nearer to the edge of the bank. Grace, however, waved her hand and said, 'Hello, Mrs Rathbone.'

Martha ignored her. She strode through the wet grass to where her daughter and Daisy were now rolling on the ground, locked in each other's arms, a hair's breadth from tumbling into the water. She snatched hold of the back of Alice's shirt and, with every ounce of her strength, tugged and pulled until she had freed her from Daisy's embrace. Suddenly released, Daisy spun like a wheel, right over the lip of the bank.

Horror-struck despite herself, Martha dropped to her knees. She crawled forward until she had Daisy in view, expecting to find her dashed on a rock or already snatched by the tide. Laughing uproariously, the girl was spread-eagled on the sand, her eyes alive with devilment.

12

Torrance was propped up in bed against a mountain of pillows, her flaxen hair glinting in the sunlight. When Dewi walked into the room she smiled at him, then, without warning, began to cry. 'Hell!' she croaked, scouring wet cheeks with her fist. 'Why am I bawling?'

'You're still in shock, dear.' The policewoman sitting with her handed her some tissues from the box on the locker. 'And you must be in pain.'

'Are you kidding? I hurt in places I didn't know I had.' She massaged her throat. 'It even hurts to speak.'

Dewi dragged a chair round to the other side of the bed. 'I've just looked in on Imogen,' he said. 'She seems to be holding her own.'

'How many pills did she take?' Torrance asked.

'Thirty or so.'

'It's my fault,' she said bleakly, plucking at the damp tissues on the bedspread. 'I shouldn't have let her have them. Up to a couple of weeks ago I was taking the pills away after she got them from Matron. She had to ask me when she wanted one.'

'Why were you doing that?'

'Because she's a suicide waiting to happen!' Angrily, she balled up the tissue. 'She *promised* she wouldn't overdose. She said she'd felt a bit more human lately, but I still counted them every night and every morning.' She stared at him. 'Damn it to hell! I should've *known* she'd crack after Sukie died.'

'None of this is your responsibility,' he insisted.

She touched his hand. 'You're wrong, David. Justine and her crowd did what they could, but Imogen always kept them at arm's length. She *had* to let me get close; I didn't give her a choice. She was a real uptight Brit long before the accident, you know.' Then she fell silent, lying motionless. Caught in the air currents, her hair wafted about with a life of its own. Eventually, she said, 'Vivienne told me Dr Scott and Matron got fired. Is that true?'

He nodded. 'And not before time.'

'Don't be cruel,' she chided. 'Matron's got nothing except the school and I guess she did her best.'

'No, she didn't. She stuck her head in the sand and let Scott do as she pleased.'

'You think?' She pondered the matter. 'Maybe you're right.' Letting her head rest on the pillows, she closed her eyes.

'I need to talk about the accident,' he said gently. 'Are you up to it, or d'you want a nap?'

'Hell,' she said mischievously, eyes still closed, 'I wish you'd speak proper English. I get one word out of three. Napping is what horses do.'

'It's also what tipsters do when they think they've picked a winner,' he added, sure she was teasing him.

'Fancy your knowing that.' She smiled sleepily, yawned and within seconds fell asleep.

Thinking it would be better to come back later, he was about to move when she lunged towards him as if galvanised, eyes wide open and face aghast. Her fingers hooked like talons round his arm.

'What's wrong?' he gasped.

Shuddering, she whispered, 'I'm so *scared*!' She stared at him fearfully, mouth working. 'Of the dreams I had. The nightmares!'

He laid his free hand on hers, feeling the strength in her fingers. 'A massive bang on the head like the one you got would give anyone nightmares,' he said comfortingly. 'They don't mean anything.'

'Don't they? I dreamt about Sukie.' She paused. 'And about Purdey. I dreamt she was impaled on a broken jump. There was blood spouting everywhere.' A spasm crossed her face. 'I was drenched in it. It was dripping from my fingertips.' Involuntarily, she yanked her hands free and held them up, turning them this way and that.

'See?' he said. 'No blood. And Purdey is absolutely fine. She gave Miss Attwill a hell of a ride this morning.'

'A *donkey* would give Miss Attwill a hell of a ride,' she remarked bitingly. 'She's so nervy she spooks the horses.'

'Was Sukie a nervy rider?'

Torrance clasped her hands. 'She was no real match for Purdey, but she had to try because her family expected big things from her. Purdey cost an awful lot, you see; about five times as much as Tonto.' She glanced up with darkened eyes. 'Maybe Sukie expected it of herself, too. She needed something to take pride in. There was nothing left after she and Imogen broke up.'

'Do you know why that happened?'

'No. I wondered if there was some feud between their parents. They live very near each other.' She looked at him, frowning. 'You know, don't you?' Once again, her fingers reached for his arm. 'Tell me!'

'I may as well,' he said, after a moment's thought. 'Everyone will know soon, in any case.' He related the myths that lay behind the tragedy, wincing as her fingers dug ever deeper into his flesh. 'But before she downed the pills,' he added, 'Imogen wrote us a letter, saying *she* was driving, not Sukie. She claims her parents took advantage of Sukie's amnesia about the crash.'

Torrance put her hands to her face and moaned, 'Oh, God!'

'Which puts a different complexion on things,' he went on, 'if, say, Sukie had suddenly recovered her memory.'

'Does it? How?' Then witheringly, she exclaimed, 'Hell! You surely don't think Imogen killed her? No chance!'

'Someone did. We're sure of that now.' He rubbed the marks her nails had left on his arm. 'I think she was enticed out of the building, but I don't know how.'

'She'd go like a shot if she thought Purdey was hurt, or in danger,' Torrance said. 'But how would she know? You can't see the paddock from the school.' She paused. 'You could *hear* a horse screaming, but then, everyone would have heard that and I certainly didn't.' Her voice dwindled away.

'Yes?' he prompted.

'I did hear something,' she said slowly, 'but not a horse. I couldn't sleep and I was looking out the window when a jet

293

plane came over so low it made the trees rustle.' Her dazed mind was so sluggish it hurt to remember. 'Then I heard another noise,' she went on, a faraway look in her eyes, 'like someone had kicked a stone, you know?' Her eyes focused. 'There was someone in the woods, I'm sure, but it was too dark to see them properly.'

'But not for them to see you.' He looked at her, imagining how she must have appeared to the watcher, her hair like a halo in the night, marking her out as the next to die.

13

Long after Martha went in search of her child, Janet had remained at the water's edge, absently picking out landmarks along the Anglesey coast but mostly killing time, with little enthusiasm for much beyond an early escape from this enervating place. Eventually she began reluctantly making her way across the lawn back to the school and, rounding the side of the building, circumnavigated the fire escape rather than take the shorter route beneath.

From the forecourt, she could hear the slam of car doors and the sharp crack of raised voices. She arrived there as Charlotte was being pushed into the rear seat of a squad car, a policeman's hand heavy on her blonde head. Nancy's nasty face was pressed to the window of another car. Both cars then roared away with a flourish of spurting gravel, watched in sullen silence by a crowd of girls. Some were Charlotte's worshipful subjects from the sixth form, some those who hung about Nancy like flies trapped in a spider's web, but there were many younger ones, whom Janet assumed were the hangers-on and apprentice courtiers. When they noticed her there was a shuffling of feet and swivelling of cold eyes, and she felt their menace as if she faced a pack of wolves. Then, to her enormous relief, Jack appeared.

Taking her arm, he pulled her out of earshot. 'Those two are going to the station to be interviewed.'

'Why?'

'Eh?' He frowned, then his face cleared. 'You're a bit behind, aren't you? Nancy's the school bully, Charlotte's her second-in-command and Sukie was one of their victims. Mr McKenna thinks it's just possible they bullied her to death.'

'I doubt it.'

'So do I,' Jack conceded. He watched the girls still crowded about the entrance, feeling their ugly mood. There was not a teacher in sight and he wondered if they were already gone, like rats deserting a stricken ship. 'Have another chat with the younger ones,' he told her. 'Nancy's conspicuous absence might loosen a few tongues.'

'I doubt that, too,' she commented.

'Watch your step,' he warned, opening the door of his own car.

Janet stiffened. 'I'm sorry, sir. I wasn't being impudent.'

Voice low, he said, 'I meant, watch your step with that lot. They could get mean.'

She waited until he had driven off, then purposefully strode towards the phalanx of bodies, nodding here, half-smiling there as she forged a way through. They moved aside to let her pass and immediately closed up behind her, pressing so close she could hear their breath and smell their bodies. To a girl, their faces were hostile, their demeanour intimidating, their deliberate silence terrifying, and the nearer she came to the door, the more slowly and unwillingly they moved out of her way. Any second she expected a stunning blow across her head or neck and, close to panic, imagined herself in a nightmare where the door was forever just beyond reach. Then, miraculously, she stumbled into the chilly gloom of the lobby and slumped against the wall gathering her breath, while her heart thudded in her ears. The girls at the back of the crowd stared in at her.

Suddenly one half of the double-front door crashed open and Alice, clothes filthy, face mutinous, lurched into the hallway, prodded from behind, like a recalcitrant heifer, by her mother. Martha was clearly furious. She glared at Janet. 'There are two more of them outside,' she announced. 'Grace and Daisy, and Daisy's in an even bigger mess than this stupid little madam,' she added, gesturing to her daughter. 'They've been fighting like bloody hooligans!'

'What about?' Janet asked.

'God knows!'

Janet turned to Alice. 'You'd better get changed,' she told her. Alice met her gaze and, with something like despair in her eyes, made for the stairs as a movement outside distracted Janet's attention. Daisy, face and arms covered in scratches, hair streaked with mud and sand, was by the door, looking in. Grace tramped up and down behind her, kicking gravel.

Temper rising, Janet marched to the door. 'Come in, now,' she insisted.

'Why?' Daisy demanded.

Janet dived for her. 'Because I say so!' she snapped, grabbing her arm before she could run off. She pulled her in, waited for Grace to follow and shut the door.

'They were down by the Strait,' Martha was saying, 'even though they know damned well it's out of bounds.' Her breath was harsh and fast. 'You'd think that would be the last place they'd want to go after that poor girl died there, wouldn't you?'

'Yes,' Janet agreed, watching Daisy's smirking countenance. 'Particularly as Daisy reckons Sukie's ghost is about.'

Grace blenched and swayed once, eyelids fluttering wildly.

'Oh, pack it in!' Daisy snapped at her. Tittering, she said to Janet, 'It was a *joke*!' *Everyone* knows it was. *She's* just pretending.'

'And *you're* just plain nasty,' Janet said coldly.

Daisy went rigid. She stared at Janet unblinkingly and challengingly, instantly defensive, instantly aggressive.

Martha was also staring at her. 'What shall I do with Alice?' she asked. 'Can I take her out of school?'

'Not until Mr McKenna gives permission,' Janet replied, her eyes still on Daisy. 'He's in the mobile incident room if you want to see him.'

Alice had left a trail of wet footprints on the stairs and as Daisy ran up she added to the mess. Janet followed her, wary of more mischief, Grace in her wake. When they reached the landing Alice was walking towards them from the dormitory, dirty clothes in a bundle under her arm, her face so pinched it was almost wizened.

Daisy, her expression unreadable, stopped and seemed to shrink against the wall.

Alice, drawing level, also halted. 'I'll never speak to you again!' she hissed. '*Never.*'

Throwing back her head, Daisy tried to sneer. 'Suits me!' she lisped. 'Just fine!' With that, she took off along the corridor.

'Your mother's waiting for you,' Janet said to Alice.

Without looking at her, Alice mumbled something unintelligible and slunk down the stairs.

Grace, creeping up beside Janet, said, 'Alice is quite uncouth.'

'From where I'm standing,' Janet replied impatiently, 'you could *all* do with learning some manners!'

Her face crumpling, Grace scuttled into the dormitory. She snatched an armful of clothes from her cupboard and rushed back to the door.

'Where are you going now?' Janet demanded.

'To the sick bay. Matron said I can go whenever I want.'

'Matron's not around any more,' Daisy commented, rummaging through the clothes in her own cupboard.

'For heaven's sake!' Janet snapped. 'She can still go if she wants to.'

'Did I say she couldn't?' Daisy turned, a pair of expensive-looking black trousers in her hands. She glanced at Grace's locker and called out, 'You've forgotten your precious jewels.'

As Grace dashed back in and grabbed something off the locker, Daisy said, 'You daren't lose those, dare you? They must have cost your holy father all of ten quid.'

Grace fled.

'Why are you so positively hateful to her?' Janet asked.

'Because, for one thing, she's a snide cow, and for another, she's a wimp.' Daisy kicked off her trainers, pulled the T-shirt over her head and stepped out of the dirty jeans, letting the garments lie in a heap on the floor. 'She was just the same at prep school.'

'I didn't realise you'd known her so long.'

'There's a lot *you* don't realise,' Daisy retorted. 'Like *my* mother is Grace's godmother, for instance. And like I'm trying to toughen her up for her own sake. She's got to survive at least another two years here.'

'Is that how you see it? As survival?'

'Isn't it?' Daisy padded back and forth from the cupboard to the bed, selecting and discarding various items of clothing.

Janet wondered if she were deliberately displaying her sumptuous body and the fine, hand-stitched lingerie. 'You're not getting ready for a night on the town,' she said. 'Hurry up.'

Pausing for a moment, Daisy stared. 'Did *you* go to boarding school? You behave as if you did. You're a real bitch.'

'As they say, it takes one to know one. Now, hurry up.'

14

Martha leaned against the ornamental wall in the forecourt, watching Alice kick a tiny pebble across the paving. 'I don't think I should bother Superintendent McKenna,' she told her. 'He's got more than enough on his hands already.'

'So?' Alice muttered, her eyes fixed on her feet.

Inwardly Martha seethed. 'So as it looks as if we're stuck with each other for the time being, we'll go for a walk.' She pushed herself away from the wall and moved off, stomping down the tarmac path towards the stables, clamping her lips on the angry words trying to force their way out, telling herself Alice was a complex person who needed to find her own answers, whose inner restlessness betrayed itself in the constantly shifting, volatile moods. But whether or not, she argued, she was fated to be both the rock against which Alice threw herself time and again and the haven she sought when the storms exhausted her, the battering Alice was now giving her was beyond all reason. She glanced round, to see Alice trudging behind with her head sunk into her chest, as if a horrible drama were being fought out inside her head, and the anger suddenly evaporated. The girl looked utterly pathetic.

Martha rounded on her. 'What's wrong? Why were you and Daisy trying to beat the living daylights out of each other? What's *really* going on?'

'Nothing!' Alice went on walking, with a foot-dragging slouch that might be the first sign of impending disability or simply the joyless gait of adolescence.

Scrutinising her, Martha let the distance grow. She had been Alice's age when arthritis first showed itself in a swollen, tender knee; diagnosed as such and not the cancer her parents feared, the relief had been enormous, but she had often thought since that if she must be assigned a disease, cancer might have been preferable. By now, she would be either dead or cured.

Alice stopped eventually and simply waited, staring ahead. When Martha caught up with her, she said, 'I'm hungry.'

Martha took two large bars of chocolate from her bag, handed over one and unwrapped the other for herself. She could eat relentlessly now without gaining an ounce, yet at thirteen, as her child's body began its metamorphosis into womanhood, she had ballooned almost overnight. When her brother died the weight fell away as if it had never been, burned to a vapour by searing grief. More and more, she saw Danny in Alice, in little comforting ways that offered fascinating glimpses of the gene's power to survive the death of one carrier and the interference of others.

As they neared the stables Alice's mood seemed to lift. Her head came up and her step quickened.

'Where are your new glasses?' asked Martha.

'Eh?' Alice turned. There was a smear of chocolate at the corner of her mouth.

'Your glasses,' Martha repeated. 'The ones I paid a fortune for so that you could have the frames you wanted.'

'In my pocket.'

'Then be careful you don't break them.'

'They *won't* break! They've got those special frames you can even tread on. That's why they cost so much.'

'Yes, well, you don't need to prove it,' Martha commented. She followed Alice into the stable yard.

Planting her elbows on the paddock gate, Alice nibbled the chocolate, holding it in both hands like a squirrel with a nut. When she had stuffed the last of it into her mouth she wiped her hands on the seat of her jeans and, her gaze fixed on the animals, said, 'Aren't they gorgeous?' She turned to her mother with a brilliant smile. 'Especially Tonto. He looks like he's jumped through the screen out of a Western movie.'

Martha regarded the huge, bold-eyed palomino. 'He's certainly striking. What's Torrance got in mind for him?'

'Dunno. It'll depend on whether she stays another year to try for Oxford.' She picked at a splinter on the top of the gate. 'I hope she does. She's offered to teach me to ride.'

'Not on Tonto!'

'Why not?' Alice turned sharply.

'You couldn't possibly handle him.'

'Stop treating me like a baby!' Alice flared.

Martha bit back a sharp retort. 'It's hard not to. I'm your mother and you'll be my baby even when you're my age – if I'm still around, that is.' A different emotion crossed Alice's face then. 'I expect Daisy's parents treat her like a baby at times, too.'

'I wouldn't know,' Alice said dismissively. 'I've never been to their house.'

'But you've met them when they visit the school.'

'They hardly ever come.'

'Don't they? That must be pretty miserable for her.' Martha frowned. 'Then how do you know so much about them? You gave me chapter and verse on what she'll eventually inherit from her mother.'

'Stop interrogating me!'

'I was simply making conversation.' With another enormous effort Martha kept her voice quite neutral.

'You shouldn't need to *make* conversation with your own child!' Alice glared ferociously. 'I'll bet Gran and Grandpa never had to make conversation with you or Uncle Danny. They already knew everything that mattered because they were always there!'

Martha glared back at her. 'They only knew because we used to tell them. So you'd better tell *me* what that disgusting brawl between you and Daisy was all about.'

15

After footling about with her clothes for another five minutes, Daisy had announced she was going for a shower. While she waited for her Janet leaned on the window ledge, blowing the smoke from her cigarette through the open window and praying she would not be caught. The gloss paint felt a little tacky under her bare arms. In the corners of the actual frames she could see pinkish stains beneath the white, where rust from the metal was already eating its way through and she thought it rather a neat metaphor for what had happened within the school, for all the gloss in the world could not conceal decay for long.

Daisy returned, clad in black from head to foot, looking much older and rather malign. Her sudden scowl exaggerated the impression. 'Why are *you* still here?'

'I want to talk to you.'

'You already have.'

'Well, you'll just have to put up with me talking to you again.'

Daisy walked over to her cupboard. The black clothes fitted her like a second skin and with every step her buttocks, sharply divided by the trouser seam, jiggled. Busying herself examining the scratches on her face in the mirror fixed inside the cupboard door, she said, 'And if I don't want to? Why don't you,' she went on, fingering a mark on the side of her neck, 'sod off? Then I won't have to grass you up for smoking in the dorm.'

'You'd have to prove it first.'

'I can smell it!'

'Can you?' Janet sniffed, ostentatiously. 'Aren't you a clever girl, then?'

Daisy turned round, regarding her rather admiringly. '*You* could give Dr Scott a run for her money.' Slamming the door, she threw herself on the bed. 'That's if she wasn't already history. Did you know Mr Nicholls sacked her and Matron because of me? The place was like a madhouse when he got here, so I told him why. I said Matron had gone off her rocker and done something to Therese, and Imogen had tried to top herself.' She licked her lips. 'Is *she* history, as well? She was obviously all prepared to die 'cos she was wearing her false leg for the occasion. When they put her in the ambulance, I could see what looked like two legs under the blankets.'

Janet shivered and, wishing she had not left her sweater in the car, shuffled away from the window and the chill creeping up and down her spine. Sitting down on the bed that faced Daisy's, she asked, 'How do you know Imogen tried to kill herself?'

Crossing her legs, leaning back on her arms, Daisy raised her eyebrows. 'Bush telegraph. *Everybody* knows.' Gazing at Janet with eyes that were almost opaque, she went on, 'Like everybody knows you've arrested Nancy and Charlotte.'

'They've been taken for questioning,' Janet told her. 'Not arrested.' She paused. Her head was beginning to ache, for the effort of making sense of the sounds coming from Daisy's lips was taking its toll. 'In case you want to update the bush telegraph, I can tell you they're being questioned about their penchant for violence. And Imogen isn't dead,' she told her. 'Torrance, as you probably know,' she finished with undisguised sarcasm, 'is very much alive and *almost* ready to start kicking.'

Her face expressionless, Daisy turned to look out of the window.

'Why were you fighting with Alice?' Janet asked, watching her. Daisy shrugged wordlessly.

'Was it something to do with Grace?'

Another shrug. 'Why should it be?'

'Well, what was all that about her "precious jewels"?'

'Christ! You're nosy! Her father bought her a pendant for her birthday last month. Grace swears it's a real diamond, but it can't be. He couldn't afford anything so big.' She swivelled her head to glare at Janet. 'Satisfied?'

Ignoring the display of temper, Janet took out her notebook and made a show of riffling through the closely written pages. She had no clear idea of what she wanted to know from Daisy, only that instinct was telling her there was something to find. 'I'd like you to tell me,' she began, 'how much contact there is between the juniors and the sixth form. Do you get on with them? Justine, for instance? She's your acting house captain, isn't she?'

With an ostentatious sigh, Daisy said, 'She's OK. She's quite sweet, really, and a super rider.'

'That's almost word for word what you said about Sukie.'

'So?'

'So is that a generalised or a personal opinion?'

'Je*sus*!' Daisy rolled her eyes. 'You're like a bloody dog with a bone!' Then, her voice a monotone, she commenced on a series of terse little descriptions that told nothing of consequence, concluding by stating that Ainsley was 'bizarre', Charlotte an 'airhead', Nancy 'OK if you don't let her piss you about', Françoise 'stinks like an old ashtray', Therese was a 'fat slob', Vivienne was 'out of her tree on drugs', the two Russian girls were 'bloody Commies' and Imogen was 'pathetic'.

As she droned away, Janet mentally ticked off names and when Daisy stopped speaking, she said, 'You didn't mention Torrance.'

Daisy looked at the floor.

'You must have *some* opinion. She's your house captain.' Slowly, Daisy raised her eyes, but they were empty, as if the girl behind them had suddenly decamped. 'Oh, give me a break!' Janet snapped. 'I'm asking you to answer a few simple questions, not explain the Theory of Relativity!'

Putting up her hands, Daisy flicked at the still-damp curls tumbling about her face. There was a fine sheen of perspiration on her brow.

'Does Torrance bully you?'

'No.'

'Do you like her?'

Suddenly reddening, Daisy squirmed. Realising she had probably lumbered on to the tender ground of adolescent love,

Janet involuntarily reached across the gap between them to pat Daisy's hand.

She recoiled violently. 'Don't *touch* me!' She sounded both horrified and terrified.

'I'm sorry!'

'That's what Torrance did.' Daisy's eyes were no longer empty. Janet was appalled by the misery there. 'She'd pat your hand, or stroke your hair. That's how she started it.'

'Started what?'

'I saw her in the stables.'

'Saw whom?'

'Torrance.' Her tension was almost palpable.

Carefully, Janet said, 'I'm a bit lost. What are you trying to tell me?'

Some unfathomable expression crossed Daisy's face. Letting each word hang ominously before she spoke the next, she said, 'I was coming up from the pool. I heard someone crying in the stables. I went in.' Once again, her voice droned. 'She was there with Sukie. She was raping her.'

'Did they see you?'

'No.'

'Are you *sure* that's what you saw?'

'Yes! Anyway, Sukie was so upset she came straight to tell me. She was going to report Torrance.'

'She told *you*?' Janet could not hide her astonishment.

Daisy stamped her foot on the floor. 'She *told* me! I was her friend; her *secret* friend. She called me "little sister".'

Janet frowned. 'Isn't it Torrance who calls the Tudor girls "little sister"?'

'It was Sukie's special name for *me*!' The words emerged with a horrible sibilance.

'No one's said anything to us about you and her.'

'I've told you!' Daisy snarled. 'It was a secret!'

'Why? Why did it have to be that way?'

The question threw Daisy into confusion. She gaped at Janet, face contorted.

'Why did your friendship with Sukie have to be kept secret?' persisted Janet.

Then, as the answer presented itself, Daisy relaxed. 'Because of Torrance, of course. She'd have gone absolutely *mad* with jealousy. She wanted Sukie all to herself.'

'Sukie told you *all* this, did she?'

'You don't believe me, do you?' Daisy demanded. 'You think I'm making it up. Well, I'm not, so there! Sukie was going to tell on Torrance, so Torrance killed her to shut her up. And I'm not the only one who knows.'

'No?'

'Alice does, too.' Again she licked her lips. 'Just you ask her.'

As Janet escorted Daisy across to the mobile incident room, the echo of her childish, lisping voice, luxuriating in the tale of sordid violence, whispered in her head. She pushed the girl into a chair, told Nona to make sure she stayed there and knocked on the door of the little office.

McKenna looked up. 'I was wondering where you'd got to,' he said. 'Dewi called. Torrance thinks she saw someone in the grounds on the night Sukie died. More pertinently, whoever it was must have seen *her*; hence the sabotaged saddle, no doubt. There's no way of knowing if any of the sixth form were out, but did anyone report absentees from the dormitories?'

'I'm not sure, sir,' she replied a little impatiently. 'And it might not matter, anyway. Daisy's come up with what sounds like a cast-iron motive. You need to speak to her.'

Reluctantly, clearly embarrassed by McKenna's presence, Daisy repeated her story and, because it was without embellishment, Janet found the second telling more persuasive than the first.

'You say Alice knows,' McKenna commented. 'But how?'

'I told her,' Daisy said.

'When?'

'Thursday night.'

'Why then? Why not before?'

'Because Torrance asked her to help with evening stables on Thursday. I wanted to warn Alice in case Torrance tried anything next time they were alone.'

'How did Alice react?'

'She went absolutely crazy.' She looked at Janet. '*That's* why we were fighting earlier.'

'Did she go crazy because she didn't believe you?' McKenna asked.

'No,' Daisy replied witheringly. 'Because she didn't *want* to believe me!'

'Do you think Sukie had told anyone apart from you?'

'No. There was no one for her to tell.'

'Why not?'

'She didn't have any friends after she stopped talking to Imogen.'

'She might not have had any *close* friends,' Janet intervened, 'but she was still popular with the sixth form.'

Daisy's eyes snapped. 'Who told you that. garbage? They *hated* her. They treated her like shit!'

'Did they?'

'When she wasn't being cut like she didn't exist, she got thumped and spat on, her clothes got nicked and her room was messed up nearly every day.' Daisy paused, her mouth working. 'They even threatened to slash Purdey.'

'Who did?'

Daisy glanced at him, then her eyes slid away.

'Nancy?' he suggested. 'Charlotte?'

Stiffly, she nodded.

'Anyone else?'

'I don't know.'

McKenna watched her, but she refused to meet his eyes. 'I think you do know, Daisy, but we'll leave it for the time being. Now, did you tell anyone, other than Alice, about what you say you saw in the stables?'

'No.'

'Could anyone have overheard?'

'I don't know.'

'Where were you?'

'In the bogs.'

'What time was it?'

'Nearly dawn.'

'Is it likely that Alice has confided in anyone?'

'I don't *know*!' Suddenly she gulped, put her hands over her face and began to sob noisily. Tears came trickling through her fingers and down the back of her hands.

He waited, regarding her thoughtfully. When the weeping abated to snivelling, he said, 'For the time being, we've got to keep you apart from the rest of the school. We'll put you in one of the empty staff flats, but you won't be alone,' he added hurriedly, as she dropped her hands to expose a face blotched with terror. 'There'll be someone with you constantly.'

Janet took Daisy to the dormitory to pack an overnight bag while McKenna went in search of the newly promoted deputy headmistress. He scoured the building from top to bottom, but found only a few junior teachers, randomly attached to various groups of girls. Miss Knight, he was told, had called the senior staff to a crisis meeting at her house. When he asked who held the keys to the vacant staff flats, no one appeared to know, so, using those Jack had taken from Nicholls, he breached Freya's erstwhile redoubt.

There was still faint whiff of her perfume about the room. As he rifled the key safe screwed to the wall, he half expected to feel her hand on his shoulder and, when he looked at the empty chair behind the magnificent desk, he could have sworn he saw her shade. Removing a pair of keys labelled VACANT STAFF FLAT 1, he realised that he wished she were there in person, so that he could thrust in her face the terrible harm she had done.

16

Halfway up the path from the stables Martha said exasperatedly, 'You *still* haven't given me a decent explanation. What's the matter? Has the cat got your tongue?' She grabbed Alice's shoulder. 'For the last time, why were you and Daisy fighting?'

Alice shrugged her off and, staring mutely and determinedly at the small patch of ground in front of her feet, plodded on towards the school.

Martha walked behind her on to the forecourt, sorely tempted at every step to help Alice along with a few kicks. Then she saw Daisy and Janet Evans, going in the direction of the staff accommodation block. A bulging leather backpack hung from Daisy's shoulder.

Expecting comment on this, if on nothing else, Martha glanced at her daughter, but Alice seemed not to have noticed them. She walked straight in through the double doors and all but cannoned into McKenna, who was standing in the dim lobby. Nona was at his side.

'I've been waiting for you,' he said. 'We need to talk.'

He led them into the visitors' room and something about his manner alerted Martha long before they were seated. When Nona closed the door and leaned against it, barring escape, she began to worry. 'What is it?' she demanded. 'What's happened?' When he remained silent, she asked, 'And where's Daisy gone? I saw Janet Evans taking her somewhere.'

'Daisy's been moved to one of the staff flats,' he replied.

'Please, don't prolong the agony.' Martha put her hand to her forehead. 'What's going on?'

'She's told him about Torrance.' Alice's hands were clenched into tight, white-knuckled fists.

Martha frowned at her. 'Told him what?'

'She said she saw Torrance raping Sukie.'

Martha's mouth fell open.

'She's lying,' Alice added.

'It's a devastating allegation,' McKenna said. 'She also claims that Sukie intended to report the rape.'

Alice met his eyes defiantly. 'And she *also* said Torrance killed Sukie to keep her quiet. She's lying about that as well.'

'How do you know?'

'I just do!'

'Why didn't you tell us about Daisy's allegations?' he asked. 'You've had plenty of opportunity.'

'Because I don't believe her.'

'What you believe is immaterial. You deliberately suppressed absolutely crucial information.'

'Only if it was true,' Alice retorted. 'And it isn't!'

Finding her voice, Martha said, 'You can't possibly know whether it is or not. You had no right to keep it to yourself.' She looked searchingly at her daughter and saw yet another stranger. 'Were you trying to protect Torrance?' she asked. When Alice nodded warily, Martha responded savagely, 'Well, you went a funny way about it! If you'd reported what Daisy told you, Torrance probably wouldn't have had an accident. Don't you realise that? Suppose she'd been killed? It's pure luck she wasn't.'

McKenna intervened. 'We can't be certain of a connection,' he said. He turned his attention to Alice. 'You like Torrance, don't you?' he asked softly.

'So?'

'Is that because she lets you help with the horses, or is there another reason?'

'Like what?'

Almost imperceptibly he shrugged. 'Perhaps she's made inappropriate overtures to you as well.'

Alice clamped her lips together, breathing noisily through her nose, her chest rising and falling sharply. Her skin was grey, and here and there dark bruises were beginning to show themselves.

'She's going to have an attack.' Martha struggled to her feet. 'Where's that blasted inhaler?'

Gazing fixedly at McKenna, Alice shook off her mother's ministrations. 'I don't need it,' she said, a gasp between each word.

'Then when you feel ready,' McKenna told her, 'perhaps you'll answer my question.'

'Oh, for God's Sake!' Martha snapped, standing protectively behind Alice's chair. 'Can't you see she's almost beside herself?'

'All the more reason to get to the truth,' he said shortly. 'If only for Alice's sake.'

'All Torrance has ever done,' Alice began, 'is be nice to me.' The breath whistled in her chest. 'Oh, and she occasionally ruffles my hair.' She challenged McKenna once more. 'I'll bet Daisy never told you what *she* did to Sukie, did she?'

'No. What was it?'

'She stuffed some broken twigs under the saddle.' With another pause for breath, she added, 'Sukie was thrown as soon as she put her weight on Purdey's back. Daisy laughed herself sick.'

'Why did she do it?'

'It was her idea of a joke.'

It was attempted murder, and only a psychopath would find amusement in that, Martha thought despairingly. 'She must have tampered with the girth,' she told McKenna. 'She *must* have done.'

'Not necessarily,' he replied.

Voicing the thoughts now besieging her own mind, she went on as if he had not spoken, 'And God knows why, but she probably killed Sukie.'

'Don't overreact,' he chided. 'I'm not defending Daisy's actions, but pranks like that aren't uncommon. A warped sense of humour doesn't make someone a killer.'

Alice groped in her jeans pocket for the inhaler. She snapped off the cap, rammed the end into her mouth, drew in a draught of medication, then glanced up at Martha. 'I wish you'd sit down,' she said curtly, before turning away. 'You're crowding me.'

Looking down on her daughter's small, dark head, Martha

was tempted to slap her, while at the same time wanting to weep. Her child was all but lost to her, befouled in the murk of Freya Scott's nether world. She leaned over to pick up her bag, a sob welling in her throat. Barely able to trust her voice, she said to McKenna, 'Let me know when you've finished.' Then, pushing blindly past Nona, she made her escape.

Once outside the visitors' room, Martha sank into the nearest chair. Her whole body ached cruelly, especially her legs, confined as they were in trousers that were still wet from when she had crawled through the grass after Daisy.

McKenna followed within moments. Standing over her, his mood indecipherable, he said, 'I can't continue to question Alice if you're not there.'

'Good.'

'Are you coming back in?'

'No, I'm not.' Painfully, she straightened her back and meeting his gaze, added, 'I'm banking on your compassion, Mr McKenna. You know as well as I do that she's not up to it.' Then she offered him a bleak, lopsided smile. 'You don't look too good yourself,' she remarked. 'About ready for the knacker's yard, I'd say.'

He perched on the edge of the chair next to hers, staring at his clasped hands. 'Not only am I beginning to feel as if we've been here for ever, but we seem to be going backwards rather than forwards.'

'But that's not as bad as feeling you've been dragged down to Freya Scott's destructive level, is it? Because you *have* been and the more you pursue Daisy's story the deeper you'll sink.'

'Come on, Mrs Rathbone,' he chided. 'You know I've got no choice.'

'But you've got a choice about the *way* you do it. And when.' Massaging her thighs, rocking gently in her seat, she went on, 'God forbid you might think I'm trying to tell you how to do your job, but I know these girls much better than you. Granted, I'm prejudiced, by being Alice's mother and by disliking Daisy so intensely, and I'm well aware that prejudice will always find ways of disguising and exploiting itself; nonetheless, I just don't believe Daisy's telling the truth.' Frowning, now rubbing her shins, she said, 'And that's not because I don't *want* to believe it, or because I'm trying to prevent Torrance from being destroyed.' She looked across at him. 'She will be, whatever happens. Not to put too fine a point on it, innocent or guilty, she's damned either way. You can't save her, but you could perhaps save someone else in the future.'

'I don't understand.'

That lopsided smile made another brief appearance. 'I'm not sure *I* do, either. My brain's getting somewhat ahead of itself.' She paused, marshalling her thoughts. 'If you take Daisy's story to its logical conclusion, Torrance could end up on trial for killing Sukie and with denial as her only defence she wouldn't fare too well. Now, if Daisy *is* lying, imagine how crazed with power she'd become if that happened.'

'And because feelings like that need constant stimulus to keep them alive,' McKenna added, 'she'd try it on again.'

'Yes.' Martha nodded. 'I'm sure she would. Not perhaps so much for the malicious satisfaction, but because she loves drama and the buzz it gives her. She seems to *need* it, to make her feel she matters and that's probably why she tells lies.' She turned in her seat to face him. 'She and Alice were knocking ten bells out of each other earlier, but Grace Blackwell actually provoked the fight by saying even Daisy herself doesn't know when she's telling the truth. Daisy swore at her, then I heard what sounded like a slap.'

'So why was Daisy fighting with *Alice* and not Grace?'

'Perhaps Alice was stopping her from battering Grace – I don't know, but I'd like time to find out. That's what I meant when I said you had a choice about how and when you deal with things.' Her next smile held a little optimism. 'And don't think Alice won't come clean. Once she really understands the implications of all this, not only for Torrance, but for Daisy and herself, she'll tell me the truth, at least about the brawl. People's behaviour, you see, is a circle of consistency. Alice only digs in her heels *so* far – in the end her intelligence gets the better of her mulishness.'

'Are you clutching at straws?' he asked gently. 'Barely ten minutes ago you were convinced Daisy killed Sukie and tried to kill Torrance.'

'Heat of the moment,' she replied wryly. 'And as I said,

prejudice will out.' Her face fell then. 'You warned me yesterday about usually finding the killer close to home, didn't you? *Please* give me time to talk to Alice,' she entreated, touching his arm with her gnarled, trembling fingers. 'I can't bear the thought that Torrance might have done something to her. I must find out!'

17

With Nona beside him, McKenna stayed on the forecourt until Martha's car vanished around the first bend in the drive. A moment before then Alice, in the passenger seat, turned to look, not at them, but at the school.

'Aren't you taking a bit of a risk, sir?' Nona asked doubtfully. 'Suppose they don't come back?'

'They will,' he told her, setting off for the mobile incident room. 'Stupid is one thing Martha Rathbone definitely is not.'

'Where's she staying?'

'Down the road, at the pub. She says the food's good and it's very homely.'

'She's an odd woman. Considering how rich she is, she's got absolutely no side to her at all. It's like her feet are literally screwed into the ground.'

'She simply has her priorities straight.'

Nona followed him up the steps. 'By the way, sir, I've packed up Imogen's things and done a list, and I took her room apart in case I missed something. I moved the bed, and looked behind the shelves and cupboard as well as the radiator.' Trotting after him into the little office, she added, 'I even stripped the bedding and shook out the pillowcases and duvet cover.' As he sat down, she leaned against the doorpost. 'I put her jewellery in the safe here. There's quite a bit of it, including a platinum and diamond tennis bracelet that must have cost a bomb, but I'm not sure if I found the particular necklace she was talking about in her letter. It would've helped to know what I was looking *for*,' she went on. 'I mean, is it an actual *necklace*? If it is, it could be a match for the bracelet. On the other hand it could be a pendant. She had a couple of those and both looked as if they could've cost what Sukie paid out.'

'If that's in fact what Sukie bought. It could have been a present for her mother.'

'Mr Tuttle was going to ask Sukie's father about it.'

'We'll leave him to do that, then,' McKenna replied. 'It's the least of our worries at the moment.'

'What if Imogen's parents bring it up?' Nona argued. 'They're due here any time, aren't they?'

'They don't know she's lost it,' he told her irritably. 'They haven't seen her letter yet.' Then he smiled an apology. 'I'm sorry, Nona, I'm very tired. You will be, too, if you don't get off home for a few hours' sleep. You've a long night ahead of you.'

She swallowed. 'What d'you mean, sir?'

'Didn't I tell you? You're babysitting Daisy. I want you back at eight to relieve Janet.'

McKenna was finishing his lunch when Jack telephoned from the police station.

'I thought you were going to see Avril O'Connor.'

'She wasn't in, so I came back here,' Jack said. 'I'll try again later.'

'Are you making any progress?' McKenna asked, lighting a cigarette.

'What do *you* think?' Jack replied. 'Nancy's standing on her rights, with the aid of her brief, and Charlotte's collapsed in a fit of hysterics, also aided and abetted by her brief.'

'Why?'

'Well, because Imogen took a swipe at her yesterday, Nancy reckons she's the victim of an assault. She wants to know what we intend to do about it and the solicitor's simply jumped on the bandwagon, as they do.'

'What's that got to do with the bullying they indulge in?'

'A great deal, apparently,' Jack said. 'They claim they're just protecting themselves from other bullies. Therefore we can't pick on them to the exclusion of these alleged other bullies. Needless to say,' he went on mordantly, 'Nancy and Charlotte reckon it'd be more than their lives are worth to give us names, so they've got us over a very big barrel.'

'You're being conned.'

'Probably, but I've no intention of risking an official complaint, which would be the next step if I don't back off.' Jack paused. 'That said, I'm not releasing them just yet; they can sweat a bit longer.'

'Daisy Podmore claims they threatened to slash Sukie's horse,' McKenna told him. 'She's also come up with a nasty tale about lesbian rape.' Quickly he relayed the gist of Daisy's interview. 'So, if she's telling the truth, Torrance has to be prime suspect in Sukie's murder.'

After a long silence, Jack said, 'I'm *extremely* dubious. The Torrance *I've* seen just doesn't fit the picture.'

'But in actual fact we know very little about her,' McKenna pointed out. 'Everyone has a secret face.'

'Maybe,' Jack conceded, 'but she nowhere near fits the profile either.'

'We just cobbled together some ideas, not a proper profile. And at its best, profiling is far from being an exact science.'

Jack sighed. 'It makes no odds, anyway. You've got to proceed on the assumption. When do you intend to question her?'

'She won't be fit for interview under caution before tomorrow at the earliest. And I haven't taken Daisy's formal statement yet – I can't until the protocols are sorted out. Her parents are abroad, so we'll have to get her a responsible adult as well as a solicitor.'

'Where are her parents?'

'Italy, according to Miss Knight. She's going to ring their hotel. It's very civil of her to find the time,' McKenna commented acidly. 'She spent most of the morning in a staff meeting and now I'm told she's burning up the telephone lines trying to get Nicholls to change his mind about sacking Scott.' After a moment he added, 'But not about Matron, apparently. She must be expendable.' He pulled on the cigarette, then coughed. 'Why don't you,' he went on when he had caught his breath, 'challenge Nancy and Charlotte about their threat to slash Purdey?'

'Is that wise?' asked Jack. 'As soon as they set foot back in the school, they'll be out looking for whoever grassed them up and taking reprisals when they find out.'

318

'I've got Daisy under guard in one of the staff flats.'

'Yes, but Nancy and her cohorts could have given most of the school a thrashing before they realise who snitched. It's too risky.'

'You're not thinking straight,' McKenna said rather testily. 'They already know *someone* ratted on them.'

'Needless to say, Imogen's suicide note was common knowledge before she was even carted off to the hospital,' Jack said. 'They assumed it was her. I didn't see any need to correct them. What I could do, though,' he added thoughtfully, 'is have another go at them about Tuesday night, because if I remember correctly, none of the sixth form has an alibi, not even to the extent of being able to alibi each other. Nor did any of them apart from Torrance – if she was telling Dewi the truth, that is – remember hearing anything out of the ordinary.'

'Suppose,' McKenna began, fidgeting with a pen, 'Sukie was lured out, by someone who knew about the threat to Purdey, on the pretext that it was about to be carried out?'

'Sounds good,' Jack agreed. 'So who knew, apart from Daisy?' Without waiting for a response, he went on, 'Who else has made allegations about Torrance? Who else has suggested Torrance had a motive for killing Sukie? Unless Alice is being very economical with the truth, *she* only knows what Daisy told her.' He paused. 'And as Daisy likes seeing people thrown off horses, she's an ideal candidate for the sabotaged saddle. Not only that, she fits the profile beautifully.'

'Martha Rathbone overheard Grace Blackwell accuse Daisy of not knowing herself when she's lying, just before *Alice* and Daisy started knocking hell out of each other. There's real tension between those girls, but whether it's relevant to us is another matter.' McKenna stopped speaking, then said forcefully, 'This investigation gets more labyrinthine by the minute. It's one person's word against another's from start to finish – not only that, we have to re-evaluate every word as soon as it's uttered and every nuance as soon as it suggests itself, and I doubt if we'll be any the wiser once Daisy and Torrance have been formally questioned.'

'Eifion might still be able to lift fingerprints off Sukie's shirt,' Jack reminded him. 'And there's the partial footprint on her

319

jeans. But I wouldn't advise,' he went on, 'waiting on the outcome. There's a horrible sense of danger in the school, but from where or whom, I've no idea. I just don't think the run of disasters is quite done with yet.'

'I hope you're wrong,' McKenna said. 'Still, Daisy's out of harm's way, or, depending on your point of view, temporarily neutralised. Alice is, too. As for the rest, we've taken every possible precaution.'

'Are you sure about that?' Jack asked quietly. 'Aside from the fact that we may be looking in entirely the wrong direction, I've been thinking about the pressure Nicholls was putting on for us to pack up and leave. It occurred to me he might have got rid of Scott and Matron because he knows they cooked up Sukie's murder between them and, following the well-trodden path, decided to let them disappear into "retirement", the way bent coppers slither off the hook.'

'Neither possibility had escaped me. That's why I've still got fifteen per cent of the force's manpower placed strategically around the place, why Matron's confined to her flat and why Freya Scott isn't allowed to set foot over any threshold except her own.' McKenna was about to disconnect the call when he remembered something. 'By the way, Eifion faxed a name and telephone number for you.'

'That's for you, as a matter of fact,' Jack replied. 'The old cottage by the pier is coming up for sale privately and that's the contact, if you're interested.'

McKenna made several more telephone calls, first to establish that Imogen's parents had arrived at the hospital, then to find out if Berkshire police wanted him to interview them about the allegations in her letter. He was asked to hold fire until Imogen was fit to give a preliminary statement.

Next, with great reluctance, he called John Melville, for a description of the jewellery Sukie had purchased the previous Christmas.

'Yes, I saw it,' John agreed. 'But I'm afraid I have only the vaguest recollection of what it looked like.' His voice was clipped, even brittle, and he sounded completely sober. 'I'm sure you'll understand, Superintendent, why that is. As it was the festive season, I was bound to be more drunk than usual, wasn't I?'

Ignoring the barb, McKenna asked, 'But it was a gift for Imogen?'

'I believe so.'

'And it was a necklace?'

'It was a gemstone drop on a chain and that's as much as I can tell you.'

McKenna smoked another cigarette while he mulled over the various factors, mostly imaginary, that were sure to thwart any plans to buy the cottage by the pier. In the end he reached a compromise with himself: unless there was sufficient garden space for his cats he would go no further and thus block disappointment before it was able to frustrate him. He called the number and made an appointment to see the cottage on Monday evening, then set about wondering how to repair the rift with the pathologist, immensely touched by the man's refusal to stop caring, even in the face of wilful and unreasonable hostility.

18

When Jack recommenced interviewing Nancy, he only succeeded in broaching the issue of the threat to slash Purdey before the solicitor intervened, demanding to know if the horse had in fact been harmed and wanting sight of the written statement of complaint, from the horse's owner or from any other interested party, that related to the alleged threat. 'And I mean "interested" in the legal sense of the word,' the solicitor added.

While Nancy's smirk grew, Jack was forced to admit defeat on both counts and, soon, compelled to release both girls. Charlotte left the police station with her hair in disarray, her clothes limp with perspiration and her face blotched with tears and streaked with mascara. Nancy, dry-eyed and cool, strutted out ahead of her, flame-red hair glowing and green eyes hard with triumph. She sat imperiously in the back of the police car that was to return them to school, making an obscene gesture as it drove from the yard.

Avril O'Connor was barely less hostile when she opened her front door to his summons. 'The neighbours said you'd been hammering on the door earlier,' she told him accusingly. 'And last night young Dewi Prys was here, looking for our Sean.'

'Right on both counts,' Jack replied with a tired smile.

'If you're wanting our Sean *again*,' Avril said meaningfully, leaning on the jamb as if to bar his entry, 'he isn't in. He's gone to Tesco to do my shopping, like he does every Saturday. He's a good son.'

'I'm sure he is,' agreed Jack.

322

Narrowing her eyes, Avril peered up at him. 'Have you spoken to Paula yet?'

'Not personally, but one of my colleagues has.'

'Well?' she demanded. 'Is our Sean still under suspicion?'

'No.' Jack smiled again. 'He never was, really.'

Avril sagged against the frame. 'You'd best come in, then,' she muttered, sniffing. Her eyes brimmed with tears.

Just like the other morning, he followed as she padded into the kitchen. Today she was baking. A tray of buns in paper cases was ready to go into the oven and a wooden spoon stood on end in a big Cornish-ware bowl where she was mixing fruit and dough for a bara brith. 'Sit down,' she invited, then turned her back to open the oven door. 'Cup of tea?' she asked, picking up the bun tray.

'If it's not too much bother.'

Without replying, she put the tray in the oven and filled the kettle before returning to the table. She picked up the spoon. 'If you've talked to Paula,' she said, stirring the fruit mix, 'why d'you want to see our Sean again?'

'I don't. I thought *you* might have things to tell me you wouldn't feel right saying in front of Sean.'

'Did you, now?' she commented. 'What sort of things would those be, then?'

Jack shrugged. 'Women's stuff, I suppose,' he said vaguely.

Avril smiled. 'That'll cover at least half the world's business, won't it?' She moved two lined loaf tins within reach and began spooning the mixture from bowl to tins.

Jack could smell the spices and tea in which the fruit had been steeped. 'Personal stuff, then,' he said, watching her level the loaves with the back of the spoon. Next, from a small white bowl filled with thick, clear liquid, she brushed on glaze. 'Women notice an awful lot,' he added encouragingly.

She opened the oven, checked the buns, then placed the loaves on the shelf beneath them. Once that was done, she rinsed her hands at the sink and turned her attention to making tea, saying nothing.

'If I were you,' he remarked, 'I wouldn't feel obliged by any sense of loyalty to the school. Dr Scott said she'd sacked you because your work wasn't up to scratch, but I've only got to look around your house to see she was giving me a cock-and-bull story. You've obviously got very high standards of cleanliness and so on.'

'Stop flannelling,' Avril said. 'I like housework. I always have. It's satisfying. A clean, tidy house and regular meals make life easier. You can't relax with dirt and clutter at every turn and your stomach rumbling with hunger, can you?' She lifted the teapot lid to stir the brew. 'I've always thought these women's libbers got it all wrong.'

'You mean they chucked out the baby along with the bathwater?'

'Something like that.' She nodded. 'They'd probably call me every name under the sun for looking after our Sean the way I do as well. But you see, it's all about give and take. I do what I'm good at, he does what he's good at, and when you work out who's actually done what, his share's often bigger than mine.'

'You'll miss him an awful lot when he gets married, won't you?'

Avril poured out the tea. Putting milk and sugar within Jack's reach, she said, 'He was barely a week old when I realised I'd be spending the next twenty years – perhaps more – rearing him just so he could one day up sticks and leave home. But that's what having children means, doesn't it?' She smiled. 'Anyway, when I'm not cooking man-size meals every day I might even lose a bit of weight. I certainly won't take so much trouble just for myself.'

'It's still sad,' Jack said.

She nodded. 'It's still sad, but at least I know I've done my very best for him, which is more than Dr Skinflint'll ever be able to say *she's* done for any of those girls at the Hermitage.' Picking up her tea, she gazed at him over the rim of the mug. 'Did she really call me a slattern?'

He was about to say not, but changed his mind. 'I suppose she did, in so many words.'

'She wants to be careful,' Avril commented. 'I might even ring up and remind her what slander means.'

'Did she ever give you a written warning about your work or anything like that?'

'Did she heck!' Avril said disparagingly. 'She didn't have

cause. I told you yesterday, she got rid of most of us to save money and it wasn't much of a surprise when she did, either. We'd seen the way the wind was blowing when she sacked the two assistant matrons. They were both qualified nurses, so they cost her. Instead, she took on two young chits just out of school with barely a brain between them.' After a moment she added, 'Matron told her at the time she was storing up trouble, but Dr Skinflint wouldn't have it. Told Matron to mind her own nose and get on with her work, or else *she'd* be needing another job, too.'

'Bit of a bully, is she?' Jack suggested.

Avril eyed him up and down. 'You mean to say you haven't found out yet? What have you been doing since Thursday, then?'

'We've heard there's some bullying among the girls,' he replied.

'Only "some"?' she commented tartly. 'Still, I suppose people have different ideas of what "some" means, don't they?'

'Did you come across much of it?'

'I'd hear about it more often than actually see it,' she told him, 'and it wouldn't be fair to say they were all at it. But then, you don't need many to make life hell for everybody. Maybe six or seven of them ruled the roost and that was it. When they left, the next lot moved up – there was always another group in waiting, so to speak.'

'What sort of things did they do?'

'What bullies usually do.' She rose, rather quickly, and went to the cooker and when she opened the oven door the smell made Jack's mouth water. She removed the tray of buns and put them on the counter, leaving the loaves of bara brith to bake a while longer, and standing with her back to him, began laying out the buns on a cooling rack. 'Plus taking advantage of what opportunities came their way because of being in a girls' school,' she added slowly. 'I dare say you've heard stories about what goes on in women's prisons, so you'll know women can be very vicious with each other in a sexual way.'

'Are you talking about lesbian rape?' he asked.

She ran a bowl of fresh dishwater and put the tray to soak before replying. 'I don't know about actual rapes,' she said, turning to face him, 'but there were whispers about a sort of ritual called "breaking in" when a girl started her periods.' Taking the few short steps back to her seat, she went on, 'I was on my way home one evening when I saw this girl creeping up the path with her skirt pulled between her legs. She made me think of a woman I'd seen in the hospital when our Sean was born – like she'd just given birth and could barely move because of all the stitches she'd had. She was on her way from the sports hall, so whatever was going on probably happened there. Anyway, the caretakers were forever complaining about soiled knickers blocking the drains.' Seeing Jack's expression, she remarked, 'You might well look sick but like I said, women can be very vicious.'

'Can you remember the girl's name?'

'They used to call her "Charlotte the harlot", on account of her mother's goings-on, so I heard. She must be in the sixth form if she's still there.'

'Did you ever talk to her about what you'd seen?'

'I tried,' Avril said. 'The very next day. One of the other cleaners found her bedding soaked with blood, so I used that as an excuse, but she just blanked me – too terrified to open her mouth, in my opinion.' With a grim smile she added, 'So I took it upon myself to tell Matron and I let Dr Skinflint know, but I don't expect for one moment that either of them did anything.' She took a few more sips of her tea. 'But don't set too much store by all this where young Sukie's death is concerned,' she cautioned. 'Bullying there may be, and stomach-churning stuff at that, but I'd be surprised – *really* surprised – to find there's any connection.'

'Would you? I'd have thought the connection's obvious.'

'Then you're not reading things right. Dr Skinflint controls the bullying like she controls everything else. She lets it go *so* far, but never far enough to cause *her* grief.'

'She's up to her eyeballs in grief at the moment,' Jack said. 'Maybe she isn't so clever after all.'

'Or maybe somebody else is *more* clever.'

'Like who?' he asked.

'Somebody desperate to hide something?' she suggested. 'Somebody desperate to *have* something, maybe. People can be made very single-minded by what they want.'

'Sukie didn't seem to own anything especially covetable,' he told her.

'Somebody could want something that you or I wouldn't look at twice,' Avril said. 'Like clothes, for instance. Our Sean said about that dog of yours sniffing out a girl in one of Sukie's old skirts.'

'We've been told that handing on outgrown clothes is common practice.'

'Outgrown *uniforms*, maybe, but those girls hang on to their other clothes like grim death. I've seen plenty of fisticuffs because one of them's "borrowed" something or other, usually when they were cleaning the seniors' rooms. There's an awful lot of pilfering.'

'There's nothing missing from Sukie's belongings. We've checked.'

'Well, if I were you,' she advised, 'I'd check again. *And* again, after that. Now,' she went on, getting up from the table, 'can I tempt you to another cup of tea and a bun with a dollop of cream under the top?'

'Butterfly cakes?' Jack asked, his eyes lighting up. 'I haven't had those since I was a child.'

19

When McKenna sent her away early, Nona was both angry and dismayed: angry because she would probably miss her favourite Saturday evening television and dismayed by the prospect of being alone with Daisy. By the time she had made a half-hearted trawl of the Bangor shops, in a fruitless search for the kind of stylish clothes Janet wore, she was positively dreading what the night might hold.

Gwynfor was watching football on television. 'You're home early,' he remarked, keeping his eyes glued to the screen. 'I wasn't expecting you before five.'

She threw her bag on the nearest chair. 'McKenna's making me do a split shift,' she said bad-temperedly. 'I've got to go back for eight.'

'Why?' Gwynfor jerked his head back and forth, following the progress of the ball.

'They've had to put one of the girls in seclusion in the staff flats and I'm babysitting.' She sat down beside him. 'Overnight.'

Absently he patted her knee. 'Tough.'

'Tough' was the right word, Nona said to herself, as for the umpteenth time she tried to find something that would keep Daisy occupied for more than two minutes. She felt completely exhausted, partly because she had been too keyed up to doze off at home, even for a couple of hours, but mostly with sheer tension.

Before she left, Janet told her that Daisy had spent the afternoon quietly reading magazines in the bedroom. She had chatted desultorily while they ate the evening meal that was sent over from the school, but retreated again to the bedroom when the washing-up was done. Once the door closed behind Janet, however, Daisy emerged. She spent almost an hour mercilessly harassing Nona like a spoiled toddler, before agreeing to watch the programme Nona was desperate not to miss. Sitting cross-legged on the floor, Daisy stared at the television for no more than ten minutes before announcing that the programme was 'shit'. She picked up the remote control and began punching buttons, her eyes skidding back and forth across the screen and, Nona was sure, taking in nothing. When she tired of channel hopping, Nona suggested doing the jigsaw they had found in one of the cupboards. Daisy co-operated long enough to sort the edge pieces, but suddenly scooped them back into the box.

Watching her, Nona felt a confusing mix of emotions. The incongruity between Daisy's behaviour and her appearance was unsettling, for although she looked like a young woman, albeit one rather bruised and battered, her limited attention span and constant need for novelty brought to mind the disturbed children Nona helped to process through youth court or met in the children's homes.

Shortly before ten she took respite in the kitchen. The school had provided a pint of milk, six teabags, a tiny jar of instant coffee, an old jam jar half filled with instant chocolate, four sandwiches wrapped in cling film and a packet of digestive biscuits. She unwrapped two tuna and mayonnaise sandwiches, made tea for herself and poured a glass of milk for Daisy. Then, supper over, she began persuading Daisy to get ready for bed.

Daisy ignored her. Restless and irritable, she roamed about the small flat, poking into dusty cupboards, pulling out empty drawers, going back and forth to the kitchen for biscuits, another glass of milk.

'Make that your last drink now,' Nona told her. 'I don't know when we'll get more milk and we need some for the morning.'

Daisy's tongue snaked around the milky moustache on her upper lip. 'Suppose they forget about us?' she lisped. 'We'll starve.'

'Don't be so silly!' Nona said snappishly and was instantly

afraid she had unconsciously aped that awful voice. *Had* she said 'Don't be tho thilly!'?

'We will!' insisted Daisy. 'We daren't go out in case the killer's lying in wait.' A frown creased her high forehead as she munched the last segment of biscuit. 'They could be outside right now, ready to kick down the door and batter our heads in.'

Chills ran up Nona's spine, lifting the hairs at the back of her neck. She opened her mouth, then closed it, trying to compose a reply that contained no sibilants. 'Time for bed,' was all she could muster, her voice wavering between false cheerfulness and optimistic determination.

To her immense relief, Daisy rose and carried her glass to the kitchen. 'I won't sleep,' she announced, but made her way reluctantly to the bedroom.

Nona followed her, to collect blankets and pillows for the couch, where she would spend the night. 'Don't run off all the hot water when you have your bath,' she said, as Daisy dragged her towel off the bed.

Daisy stood as if turned to stone. 'No *way* am I having a bath!' she breathed. '*No* way!'

'Why ever not?' Her arms full of bedding, Nona closed her eyes in near despair.

'Because the killer could break in and hold me down in the water until I drowned like Sukie!'

'Oh, for heaven's sake! Have a shower, then.'

'I had one this afternoon.'

'Have another!'

'I was going to!' Tossing her head, Daisy stalked to the bathroom.

For almost an hour she fidgeted between bathroom, bedroom and sitting room, while Nona, flicking through one of the magazines she had taken from the bedroom, tried to ignore her periodic and pointed reappearances. At last the bedroom door clicked shut, the bed thudded as Daisy threw herself down and the flat grew quiet.

That quietness soon became disturbing. All Nona could hear was the wind, fussing with the trees that grew almost close enough to scrape the windows, and her heart, which fast began pounding in her ears. Pulling herself together, she breathed deeply and steadily until her heartbeat subsided to a slow throb, then switched on the television, just loud enough to convince her she was not alone in this sinister little world.

The lumpy divan in the staff flat was even less comfortable than Daisy's cot in the dormitory. Lying atop the covers, she wriggled this way and that, staring at the fuzzy, yellowy oval the bedside lamp threw on the ceiling and, terrified Nona would sneak away at the first opportunity, listening so hard for sounds of life that her ears started to hum, only relaxing when voices began to chatter quietly from the television. Next, footsteps made for the bathroom, the lavatory flushed, the shower ran briefly, a toothbrush rasped against teeth and the light cord snicked. Soon afterwards the television was addressing a snoring audience and, once more, she felt frighteningly alone.

As she drifted to the brink of sleep, a lightning-strike of her own electricity cut her from head to toe, leaving her empty, nauseous and wide awake, and, as ever when that happened, she saw herself like the dead frog she had galvanised back to life in first-year biology. Touching electrodes to the frog's legs, she had watched with utter astonishment as the corpse bounded off the bench. Besotted with her Frankenstein power, she retrieved the cold, flaccid body and repeated the experiment again and again, laughing frenziedly each time the corpse jumped. When Alice intervened, standing between her and the teacher who, her voice hoarse with shrieking, was about to slap down her hysteria, Daisy was furious.

That was the first time Alice rescued her from her own excess, but now Alice, at the end of her tether, had finally abandoned her. Threshing about on the bed, Daisy wanted to beat herself to a pulp for opening her mouth.

Nona had dozed off, slumped on the couch with her hands folded across her chest, and she woke with her head hanging over the side and a vicious crick in her neck. Momentarily disorientated, she sat up slowly, massaging the pain, squinting at inane antics on the television screen. Then, remembering where she was and why, she switched off the set. Into the silence, noises intruded from the adjoining room. 'Oh, hell!' she muttered, struggling to her feet. 'What's she up to now?'

Daisy was hunched against the bedhead with her knees drawn up and her eyes awash with tears. Her bare feet looked cold.

'What's the matter?' Nona asked.

'I can't sleep.'

'D'you want some hot chocolate?'

Nodding, Daisy slid off the bed and trailed after her to the kitchen.

'You must find being cooped up here very strange,' Nona remarked, filling the kettle. 'I expect you're missing your friends in the dorm.'

'I don't miss Alice. I hate her!'

'That's only because you two had a fight,' Nona said. 'I used to feel the same when I'd had a bust-up with my best friend, but we'd be back to normal in no time at all.'

'I *do* hate her!' Daisy insisted. 'She gets on my nerves. She coughs all the time.' She imitated Alice's irritating, asthmatic cough. 'I feel like strangling her. And she nags, in that horrible voice of hers. It's like a rusty hinge.'

'She probably only nags because she worries about you. Friends are like that.' Nona unscrewed the lid of the chocolate jar and spooned powder into two cups. Daisy lolled against the counter, the bright overhead light exposing the tear tracks on her cheeks. 'Why were you crying?'

'I wasn't!'

'There's no need to bite my head off! You look a bit peaky, that's all.'

'I'm due soon.'

'Why didn't you say, then? Have you got stomach-ache?'

'No. I never get it.'

'Lucky you,' Nona remarked, pouring boiling water into the cups. 'I have dreadful cramps and I throw up.' She stirred the chocolate vigorously until froth billowed over the rims. 'When did you first get your periods?' she asked, making her way to the sitting room with a drink in each hand.

'Four years ago.'

'You were very young.' Nona put the cups on the floor, then sank on to the couch. 'I was thirteen.'

Daisy sat beside her. 'Alice hasn't started yet and she's nearly fifteen. There's probably something wrong with her.'

'I doubt it. People develop at different rates.' Gazing at her companion, she added: 'You're a big girl, anyway.'

'That's what Matron says. Bitch!' Daisy stared at her feet. 'When I'm due, my boobs get so swollen and sore they actually bleed if I do gym or games, and all *she* says is, "Big girls have to grin and bear it."'

'It strikes me,' Nona said slowly, 'that it's a good thing she's had to retire.'

'She'll probably come back as soon as your lot go. So will Dr Scott.' Daisy picked up her drink. 'That's what Miss Knight thinks, anyway. I heard her talking to Bebb after breakfast.' She paused. 'They live together, you know.'

'So I gather.'

Licking chocolate from her lips, Daisy said, 'Miss Knight seems fairly normal, but you can tell Bebb's a dyke from a mile off.'

'What's that got to do with anything?' Nona frowned. 'I expect they live together because they're sisters.'

Daisy shrugged. 'It's useful when you can tell just by looking.'

Tentatively, Nona said, 'From what I've seen of her, Torrance looks *very* normal. She's actually been told off for flirting with Sergeant Prys.'

Daisy, her face buried in the cup, said nothing.

'Still,' Nona went on, 'people can swing both ways, can't they?'

'I wouldn't know.' Daisy drained the cup, dropped it in the saucer with a clatter, then rose quickly. 'I'm going back to bed,' she said and almost ran from the room.

Daisy's breasts felt more swollen and tender by the moment; by Monday, when her regular-as-clockwork period would begin, she would not have been surprised if they had burst like over-ripe melons. Whichever way she lay, sat, crouched, or contorted her body, they hurt, and she realised she could barely remember a time when eight days out of every twenty-eight were not girded first by this burden of pain and then by the outpouring of blood, that made her stink like a barrel of rotting fish before stopping so abruptly it was as if someone had turned off a tap.

She tried to lie on her back, but the weight of her breasts was suffocating, so she rolled off the bed and picked up her bra from the pile of discarded clothes on the only chair in the room. Once the engorged excrescences attached to her chest were again harnessed in the pearly grey silk and lace, she buttoned up her pyjama jacket, then stood by the chair, wondering why she could still barely breath. When she realised the drawn curtains at the single window must be cutting off the air, she ripped them apart and, throwing open one half of the casement, leaned out, savouring the touch of the cool wind and a totally unfamiliar view.

The ground on this side of the building fell away quite sharply – yet another unsuspected aspect of the enormous enclosure about the school that could, Daisy had often thought, quite easily hide a whole herd of elephants. Here the trees parted, either naturally or by design, to allow a glimpse of dark water in the distance, the way to the Strait marked out by towering shrubs, ghostly and luminous where moonlight touched their blossoms.

What she saw, but more important, *why* she could see it, was one more of the myriad things that would always be beyond the capacity of her deformed speech to communicate. She took pen and diary out of the inner pocket of her backpack, dropped the pile of clothes on the floor and, angling her chair so that she could glance at will through the window, uncapped her pen.

At one time, she had used a conventional diary, but the compulsion to make an entry under each date seemed to drain her of any thought worth recording, so just before returning for the second year at the Hermitage she bought a stack of blank-paged books, bound in tooled leather of differing colours, and began a new one each autumn, at the start of the school year. The old books, some barely half-filled, some crammed from cover to cover with her small, rounded script – the records of the events and people who had made her what she was without handing her any clues to show how she might extricate herself – were in a brown paper parcel secreted under a loose floorboard in her bedroom at home. This year's book, bound in a bright topaz-blue, was already threatening to be full before term end. While she decided what to write, she leafed back and forth, reading whatever caught her eye, satisfied that every word was the truth.

15 October

The vicar from Bangor came this evening for the Harvest Thanksgiving service and he said the chapel looked more beautiful this year than last, which was nice, because I'd been allowed to help with the decorations. It was actually my idea to put candles round a vase of gold and yellow chrysanthemums on the altar. When we came out of chapel, the full moon was <u>enormous,</u> and so low in the sky I imagined, if I reached out, it would just fall into my hands. For some strange reason, even though it looked so cold, it made me feel better. Sunset was horrible and frightening, one of those times when the Strait seems to be running with blood.

19 October

The thousands of grey squirrels that live in the woods have finished stripping the nuts from the trees. The first frosts came last night, after nine days of relentless rain, and the leaves are already falling. Sexy Sean will start raking up the huge, sodden piles for his bonfires soon. He toils like a zombie in a horror film, endlessly filling barrows to overflowing with a long-handled shovel, wheeling the barrows away and coming back for more, while the smoke rises above the trees and darkens the sky, and the smell hangs in the air for days on end. <u>Everybody</u> watches Sean, noses pressed to the windows, drooling because he's so beautiful. Except Alice, of course, but I never did think she was quite like the rest of us. She's above that sort of thing.

29 October

I <u>hate</u> it when the clocks go back. Every year I tell myself not to be such a wimp, but I want to crawl into a hole and stay there until the spring. I wish I could hibernate, like the squirrels. It's already dusk when we come out of lessons and full night even before tea's over. The world shrinks. We have to stay indoors, but there's still only a few thin walls and artificial lights between us and the fearsome black wilderness outside. Sean's taken down the nets on the old tennis courts and put them in the pavilion. I always think the bare posts are like mournful reminders of summer. Last Friday, his boss drained the swimming pool. As soon as the water went, the dolphin at the bottom stopped laughing and leaping and shimmering, and turned into a motionless mosaic of tiles. Until the water comes gushing back next year, that's all it is.

30 November

Miss Knight made me go to the sports hall with a message for her bloody dyke of a sister. Matron <u>told</u> her I'm afraid of the dark, but Knight pushed me out of the door, calling me a silly baby. The indoor lights made bright rectangles on the forecourt and I could see the sports hall lights through the trees, but the path was just a pitch-black hole. I could hear the bare branches clacking together like dead bones. I ran as fast as I could. When I got there I was boiling hot, my heart was nearly exploding and the lights blinded me. The place <u>always</u> smells of stale sweat, even when it's empty. I went looking for Bebb. She wasn't in the changing rooms. I had to put on the lights and wait for the tubes to stop flickering and popping before I could go any further. She wasn't in the showers, either. They smell wet and steamy, and it's never quiet in there. Water drips from the faucets, plops on the tiles, and hisses and gurgles in the miles of pipes that run under the ceiling and come down into the shower stalls. It's very spooky and when Bebb suddenly appeared from the sluices I thought she was a ghost. What are you doing here, she wanted to know, very sharp. I gave her Knight's message and she didn't even say thank you properly. She left me to go back to school all alone through the dark.

26 March

Somebody – Sean? the caretakers? the fairies? – put all the clocks forward for summertime while we were asleep. I'd say Hurrah! except it just means seeing the rain for longer. It's been teeming down since the beginning of the month, so hard the tarpaulin over the swimming pool collapsed and Sean had to drain out all the water. I've never known a place where it rains so often. This must be why the Welsh people can sell water to England. Miss Attwill taught us about that.

3 April
Yesterday was Mother's Day and I didn't post her a card. I didn't forget, I just thought it's about time I stopped being a shitty little hypocrite. If she doesn't love me, why should I pretend to love her? I hope she's forgotten when I get home for Easter, but knowing her she won't have done. It'll be another sin of omission to harp on about endlessly and add to the zillions of others I've committed.

6 May
Since Thursday (nearly three days now) the weather's been utterly glorious. Matron, the old misery, says it's a freak, due to the new moon, and Sean's boss will soon regret refilling the swimming pool when the next lot of gales (in twelve days or so when the <u>full</u> moon makes the weather change <u>again</u>) tears the new leaves off the trees and fills the pool with sludge. I think she must be a lunatic, ha, ha! Imogen was first in the water. She must have been wearing her swimsuit under her clothes because she stripped off at the poolside, unstrapped her false leg and, after sort of hopping around one-legged for a moment, dived straight in. <u>She is so brave</u>. She can still swim like a fish and she actually looks like one now. Her stump isn't half as horrible as I'd expected, considering the fuss Charlotte made about it. But <u>she's</u> a dreadful ninny. I remember when she fell and cut her knee playing tennis, and she fainted when she saw the blood.'

27 May
We've done it again! Tudor House juniors have completely <u>trounced</u> the others, and provided the seniors don't let us down, we'll win the inter-house sports trophy for the <u>second year running</u>. The final matches get played out on Sports Day next month. Bebb, who despises me as a person as much as I despise her, still has to admit to my sporting talents. That's

why I've captained Tudor's junior lacrosse, cricket and tennis teams for the past two years, which has a lot to do with our success. Pat on back and three cheers for Daisy Podmore, even if she is stupid. Bebb sees through me, like I see through her and I'm not surprised her husband died on her. Matron doesn't, or can't, or won't. She treats me the same as always. I suppose the old me is in there somewhere, showing itself now and then, conning people into ignoring the other one, so Matron responds to the me she just remembers. Alice doesn't like the new me, but she sticks by me, no matter how often I tell her to bog off. Grace sticks in a different way, like a tick or something else you're desperate to get rid of. She leeched on to me in prep school. We've got to be best friends, she said, because our parents are. Bollocks to that. Who in their right mind would want to be friends with my parents, never mind hers? But I'd never tell her to her face. She might act like a drip, but it's just a front. She can get very nasty indeed.

28 May

I went in the pool myself today and God! the water was cold. It took my breath away, even though the sun was furnace-hot beating down on my head and dried me off in minutes afterwards. Some of the second formers were waiting to go in, including the one who missed a dead-easy return at deuce and nearly lost us a crucial tennis match on Wednesday, so I pushed her in while she'd still got her flip-flops and robe on. She shrieked like anything. On the way back to school, when I was passing the stables, I heard Torrance shouting and somebody crying. I sneaked up and hid behind the door. Sukie was being bollocked because she wouldn't tell Torrance how she'd come by the bruises on her arm, which Torrance had only now noticed because Sukie was wearing long sleeves until today. Torrance knew Sukie hadn't fallen off Purdey recently, or off anything else for that matter, so where had the bruises come from? I knew. I could have walked in, very nonchalant, and told Torrance. I could have also told her Sukie probably had lots more bruises under her clothes. She got them off Nancy, a week after the pool was filled up again. Sukie was by the pool-house door, watching Imogen swimming – or more likely, watching <u>out</u> for her, even though they hadn't spoken to each other for <u>ages</u>, when Nancy snaked her arm round Sukie's throat and dragged her inside. Sukie got the treatment, over and over, but she didn't say a single <u>word</u> until Nancy threatened to smash up Imogen's <u>good</u> leg.'

1 June

Sukie looks <u>awful</u>, like she can see the gates of hell waiting open for her wherever she goes. Your heart really does go out to her. She might have had another beating, but more likely she's scared to death Nancy will go after Purdey. Nancy's been talking about biblical revenge, but a leg for a leg instead of an eye for an eye. I don't believe it's Sukie's fault Imogen had her leg cut off. In the pool house, when Sukie told Nancy <u>she</u> was driving the car that crashed, her voice didn't sound right. It sounded like she was just repeating something, the way voices do if a teacher makes us say ten times I must not fart in the classroom. I don't know what to do. Nancy and Charlotte have kept completely schtum about what Sukie said – knowledge is power. I should've told Torrance last week, when she was ranting at Sukie, but I'm not speaking to her unless I'm absolutely forced because she's offered to teach Alice to ride, <u>and</u> on Tonto, but <u>she</u> <u>won't</u> <u>teach</u> <u>me</u>. The bitch! The only good to come out of all this is that Nancy's stopped molesting Imogen. She'd been under positive <u>siege</u> for months, but now Sukie's given the game away, whether it's true or not, Imogen's getting a bit of peace at last. Does she know why, I wonder?

There were only seven blank pages left in the diary. Forcing her pen to fashion the smallest possible configurations, Daisy wrote:

10 to 11 June, night

I've been put in an empty staff flat, all alone except for a policewoman called Nona. I don't like her very much and I don't think she's very taken with me. She might even be a bit scared of me. She tried to pump me about Torrance, trying to worm her way round to asking if I'd <u>really</u> seen what I said I had. Janet, the detective, is coming back in the morning, so I'll tell <u>her</u>. She <u>definitely</u> doesn't like me. She's a total bitch, but she seems to understand me and it's not because she's sort of one of us when Nona isn't. Janet knows I'm sad, and she didn't actually believe me about Torrance and Sukie. Alice didn't believe me, either. That's <u>really</u> why she said she'll never speak to me again, not because we had a fight. Alice meant what she said and that <u>hurts</u> <u>so</u> <u>much</u>. It's all my own fault. I've gone too far, told one lie too many. I don't know why I do these things. Being hurt and wanting to get back at Torrance and Alice about riding lessons isn't a good reason to cause so much dreadful trouble. The police will probably put me in prison, but I don't care. I never realised before today how awesomely powerful words can be, even if they're not the truth – <u>much</u> more powerful than Nancy's fists. I wonder if Sukie ever understood that. Did she <u>know</u> she was going to die? Did she feel it coming? Is <u>that</u> why she looked so awful? I must remember to ask Janet if Grace <u>has</u> told her about Tuesday night. She <u>said</u> she had, but I want to be sure.

Daisy was yawning as she put away pen and diary in the backpack. She padded to the bathroom for a drink of water, then slid into bed, still wearing her bra. Despite the pain in her breasts, she was soon fast asleep.

On the sitting-room couch Nona dozed fitfully, aware of Daisy's restlessness. The subtle light of a false dawn was touching the lowest reaches of the eastern sky before the girl at last fell quiet.

I

Janet awoke with a dull ache behind her eyes and the dead weight of foreboding in her heart. Sunday was the day she wished away before it had dawned, for it towered over each week like a threat and no sooner was one laid to uneasy rest than the next appeared, marking her passage like a row of stones that stretched ahead to the end of her life and infinity. The day rightly belonged to God, but her father, as God's representative on earth, had taken it to himself. He *determined* Sunday, she thought, climbing reluctantly out of bed, and when at last he went to meet his maker, what he had made of Sunday would forever circumscribe her own thoughts and deeds.

Her reflection in the bathroom mirror showed a face creased with sleep, but still firm and youthful. She put two painkillers on her tongue, took a sip of water and, as the pills slid down her gullet, wondered how long it had taken Imogen to swallow what she hoped was a lethal dose.

She brushed her teeth until the gums tingled, turned on the shower and stepped inside the cubicle, turning this way and that to let the water massage her head and neck. Shampooing her hair, soaping her flesh, covering herself from head to foot in delicately scented froth, she thought it sad that the younger girls at the Hermitage were not encouraged to take care of themselves. She had been tempted to comment several times, and to Matron especially, about the sour, unwashed smell that hung about them, the sweat stains on their clothes, the ugly little glimpses of underarm fuzz. Nor were all Freya's elite sixth form as groomed and glamorous as Charlotte.

The headache began to disappear, gurgling down the

plughole with the suds and night grime – if only the brooding threat of Sunday could go the same way, she wished. When she opened the shower door, steamy vapour coiled like ectoplasm towards the ceiling. She wrapped herself in a fluffy towel, then went to the bedroom to dress. Not knowing what the day would hold beyond guard duty with Daisy, she picked out canvas slacks, a silk shirt and a silk sweater. Once her hair was dry, she gave it a vigorous brushing, throwing up her head afterwards so abruptly that stars spun before her eyes. While the stars burned themselves out, she remembered the carousel of faces that had haunted her dreams, as one after another of the Hermitage girls flashed past to the eerie sound of a hurdy-gurdy played by some unseen hand. Each girl was herself yet subtly different, as if her true nature were only revealed by the night and, plagued by thoughts of mirror images and doppelgängers, Janet shivered as she made her way to the kitchen.

The front of her flat overlooked the lower end of Bangor High Street, the kitchen the back terrace of the Ship Inn, where flowering shrubs in giant pots tossed in the breeze. Waiting for the kettle to boil, she watched fallen petals swirling about with Saturday night's litter, vainly trying to organise her equally confused impressions of Daisy and her lurid tale.

2

Nona opened the door of the staff flat very gingerly. Seeing Janet on the threshold, she breathed a huge sigh of relief.

'Who else were you expecting?' Janet asked, puzzled by her pale face and fearful eyes.

'Oh, I'm being silly!' Nona led her to the kitchen, where the kettle was grumbling as it began to boil. 'It's this place. It really gets to you. I barely slept a wink.'

'Where's Daisy?'

'In bed still. I'm not sure what to do about breakfast. There's a couple of sandwiches left over from last night, but that's all.'

Janet glanced at her watch. 'It's after ten. Has no one been over from the school?'

'No,' Nona replied shortly. 'It's almost like Daisy was right. She said they'd forget about us and we'd starve.'

'Hardly.' As Nona dropped teabags in two mugs, Janet noticed her hands were trembling. 'What else did she say? You seem really rattled.'

'Believe me, "rattled" is an understatement! I feel positively neurotic.' Nona busied herself taking milk from the refrigerator, looking rather sheepish. 'But like I said,' she went on, 'it's this place. The trees sigh and moan all night long. It's unbelievably eerie. To tell the truth,' she added, picking up the kettle, 'I left the telly on so I wouldn't hear them.'

'Did Daisy sleep well?'

'It took her ages to get off. I made her some hot chocolate about eleven, but even that didn't settle her. Still, I'm not surprised. These girls must be scared out of their wits.'

'So, apart from winding you up,' Janet began, 'has she said anything of consequence?'

Nona slowly stirred the teabags round and round. 'I don't think so. Superintendent McKenna told me to note every word, but she didn't actually say anything worth writing down, except that she overheard Miss Knight saying Scott would be back when the fuss died down. Oh, and I tried to pump her a bit about Torrance, but she wouldn't take the bait.' She yawned, then rubbed her neck with her free hand. 'What she *did* say was awfully hard to understand because of that horrible lisp. She complained over and again about being bored, said everything on telly was "thit", then set my hair on end talking about the killer lurking on the other side of this very door, ready to pounce if either of us set foot outside. That's why she reckoned we'd starve, you see.'

'She's not a very nice young woman,' Janet remarked.

'She isn't a young woman,' Nona replied flatly. 'She just *looks* like one. Oh, and that reminds me,' she added, still stirring the tea, 'her period's due. She says her breasts are very sore.'

Janet waited until Nona left, then telephoned the school to ask for breakfast to be sent over. Daisy, looking rather drawn, was long about by the time the food arrived. She perched on a stool at the kitchen counter shovelling first cereal, then scrambled egg and toast into her mouth, chattering incessantly and inconsequentially between every mouthful.

Now and then Janet made the odd response, but most of her attention was fixed on the enigma of what dwelt behind that ever smiling face. Daisy had a strange aura, she decided, that was both cold and overheated. In one way she could almost see her, smiling broadly while she plunged a knife into someone's heart or battered their head to a pulp, yet she also recognised the dreadful, dispiriting fear that haunted every glance from the girl's strange eyes.

'Why are you looking at me like that?' Daisy demanded, breaking her train of thought.

'Like what?'

'Like you did yesterday.'

'As I don't have a mirror stuck in front of my nose day and

344

night, I can't answer for the way I might look at any given time. Sorry, but there it is.'

Daisy spluttered with laughter. 'Charlotte does – well, almost. She's always gawping at herself. She never makes any proper expressions either, so she won't get wrinkles and lines.'

'She must have heard about Diane de Poitiers.'

'Who was she?'

'The mistress of a French king, a long time ago.'

'Dunno about that,' Daisy replied, picking up her orange juice. 'Her mother told her, never frown, never laugh, never cry.' She wiped a bead of moisture from the rim of the glass.

'Well, from what I've heard, she was crying her eyes out yesterday at the police station.'

Daisy's eyes flicked over Janet and away. 'I'll bet Nancy didn't. She's hard as nails. You should have put one teeny-weeny spider in a cell, then locked her in with it and she'd have freaked out completely. She'd have gone absolutely *ape*!'

'I thought you didn't know them particularly well?'

'*Everybody* knows Nancy's scared of spiders,' Daisy said dismissively. Then her eyes took on that opaque appearance that made Janet shiver inwardly. 'Where are they, anyway?'

'Back here.'

'Are they going to court?'

'For what?'

'For whatever you arrested them for.'

'They weren't arrested. They were questioned.' Janet lit a cigarette. 'About Sukie.' Again, Daisy's eyes flicked over her. 'Nancy was also questioned about being the school bully. Her antics seem to be common knowledge, but unfortunately, unless someone makes a specific complaint, we can't do anything about her.'

'You couldn't anyway.'

'Bullying isn't one of your school games!' Janet snapped. 'And you don't win prizes for it. In the real world, bullies get prosecuted for assault. They even get sent to prison.'

'So? Why tell me?'

'Because you asked.'

'Did I?' Daisy slid off the stool and carried the used dishes to the sink. 'How long am I going to be here?'

'I don't know. Why?'

'It's boring. I want to go back to school.'

'You're here for your own protection, as you've already been told.'

Wide-eyed, Daisy said, 'I thought Torrance was still in hospital.'

'Oh, stop acting dumb! You know perfectly well we can't risk your gossiping about her.'

'Why didn't you say that, then? Anyway, I only talk to Alice, but she isn't here, so I couldn't.' She looked at the floor. 'And even if she *was* here, she wouldn't be speaking to *me*. You heard what she said yesterday.'

'You talk to Grace, too.'

Crossing the room in three small strides, Daisy said, 'But not *properly*. I told you, she's stupid.' Then, breathing in Janet's face, she added, 'To save us *both* getting bored out of our skulls, why don't you take me for a walk? Everyone will be in chapel, so you needn't worry about me talking to anyone. There won't be a soul in sight.'

3

As McKenna negotiated one of the crazy turns in the Hermitage drive, a security van suddenly materialised in front of him. Trailing in its wake, he peered right and left, but was no wiser about where it had come from when he reached the forecourt. He parked between two unfamiliar cars and watched the van bump along the track towards the arena.

Small groups of police officers, wearing an air of boredom, stood about in the lobby. McKenna learned that one of the cars belonged to the Roman Catholic priest who took Sunday morning Mass in the refectory, the other to the Protestant minister who, with the bulk of girls and staff and another group of officers, was in the chapel in the grounds. Until religious observances were completed, it seemed there was little for anyone to do.

He wandered back to the forecourt, to stand, hands in pockets, gazing at nothing, while the wind whispered through the trees, touching his face with cool fingers as it went on its way. The sky was a chilly blue, criss-crossed with vapour trails and torn cloud.

He had two hours to kill before the solicitor and social worker arrived to sit in with Daisy while she gave her statement and was interviewed about the sabotaged saddle. Long, empty hours, he thought, strolling across to the mobile incident room, a hiatus in the frenetic activity of the past three days. Torrance would be cautioned and questioned, provided her doctors allowed it, once Daisy's allegations were down in black and white. Alice was due back at two thirty. Imagining the various kinds of purgatory she would have made her mother suffer since yesterday, he went into the little office and sat down.

When he called Janet, she asked if she might take Daisy for a walk in the grounds and, seeing no harm in the suggestion, he agreed. Scribbling himself a reminder to obtain Daisy's consent for her things to be searched for knives, scalpels or suchlike, he next called Dewi, who was at the hospital, waiting to speak to Imogen if she regained consciousness.

'She's still completely out of it, sir,' Dewi told him. 'And she's still pretty sick. One of her kidneys is threatening to pack up.'

'How are her parents taking that?' McKenna asked.

'They don't know yet. They left in the early hours and they haven't come back.' Dewi paused. 'They were giving Vivienne a lot of grief because she wouldn't go away.'

'I hope you told them she saved Imogen's life?'

'Yes, I did. I don't think it made much of an impression. They're far more bothered about screwing money out of somebody for negligence. The school's first in line and us second. They've got their solicitor in tow, you see, and she decided it was "only fair" to tell me "which way the wind was blowing", so I told *her* that as the local weather's famous for being completely unpredictable, an almighty storm could suddenly blow up from an entirely unsuspected direction.'

'Berkshire won't question them without Imogen's formal statement.'

'Maybe not, sir, but it won't hurt to give the Olivers something to think about.'

'As long as that's all you say,' McKenna warned. 'By the way, keep an eye on Vivienne. Make sure she's fed and watered at least, and find out when she intends to come back here.'

'She doesn't, except to pack her bags,' Dewi replied. 'She's had the Hermitage, so she said, "up to the gills, and more".' After a moment, he added, 'I couldn't swear to it, but I'm sure she hasn't smoked anything apart from ordinary ciggies since she's been here and not many of those. Let's hope I'm right, eh?'

Two new pieces of paper had been put in front of McKenna while he spoke to Dewi, one a fax from the pathology department, the other a photocopied and faxed page from a jeweller's catalogue.

Eifion Roberts's efforts to identify the smudges left by the

348

killer's fingers on Sukie's T-shirt had proved fruitless, and as his attempts to extract evidence from the partial footprint on her jeans had been equally futile and disappointing, he intended to send both garments to a laboratory in the Midlands for a last-ditch round of tests.

McKenna glanced at the other paper before putting it aside for Nona, who would know if the jewel in the rather grainy photograph matched either of the pendants she had found in Imogen's room. The piece was not priced and McKenna wondered if it were one of those things people could not afford if they had to ask the cost. It looked expensive, but a pear-cut diamond weighing almost a carat was bound to be, he thought. The setting – a starfish-shaped platinum claw – was particularly unusual.

Jack was at the police station, supervising a thorough cross-check of every single item of information that had come their way since Thursday. He had nothing to report.

Shortly before eleven, McKenna took himself for a walk, setting off down the tarmac path towards the sprawling complex of swimming pool, sports hall and playing fields. As ever, the trees closed about him within yards and the air was heavy with earth smells. Where the trees cast their deepest shade, the path bloomed with moss, and as it began its downward slope he could see the distant roof line of the sports hall to the right. To the left, embraced on three sides by the woods, was the paddock. Some of the horses were moving about, searching for grass among the bald patches and tracts of mud. Purdey, her coat glistening, stood with her head over the fence, nose to nose with Tonto. Two figures suddenly came into view: Daisy, instantly recognisable, still garbed in black, and Janet, slender and pale-clad. Daisy ran towards the horses, reaching out to Tonto. He threw up his head, reared and, wheeling on his hind legs, took off at the gallop. Purdey followed suit, making the others stampede. Daisy seemed to be laughing.

He quickened his pace, but lost sight of them when the path veered to the right and they had gone when he neared the paddock. Now in the far corner of the field, the horses tensed as he approached and the skewbald mare advanced, ready to defend her herd. Head extended, neck dished, nostrils flaring, she stopped some ten feet from the gate and he was shocked to find himself afraid. Quietly but hurriedly, he walked away, listening intently for pounding hooves. Preoccupied, disconcerted, his sense of direction went the way of the four winds.

4

'You frightened those horses,' Janet said, rather accusingly, as she and Daisy meandered through the woods towards the swimming pool.

'I didn't! Tonto was just fooling around.'

'It didn't look like that to me.'

Daisy stopped. 'But do you know much about horses? Have you ever kept your own?'

'Have you?'

Favouring her with a scowl instead of replying, Daisy took off at a jog trot, her dark figure camouflaged by the dappled sunlight striking through the branches. Janet strode after her, imagining she was the cat stalking the mouse in this game they seemed to be playing and reminding herself that she could be caught unawares by a reversal of roles. Every so often, Daisy glanced over her shoulder, to make sure Janet was still with her.

Who was leading whom? Janet wondered. Then, her attention caught by a snatch of music on the wind, she paused, and hearing voices lifted in praise somewhere not too far away, felt again that stab of nostalgia. But for what? she asked herself, as the rustle of leaves overwhelmed the hymn. For games of tennis so hard fought they blistered the hands; for Sunday morning service and the scent of incense; for dew-kissed grass to roam on a summer morning; for twilit rendezvous in hidden places; for secret passions and shared secrets; for the agonising extremes of youthful emotion; and for the first experience of love that simultaneously opened the gates of Hell.

'What's wrong with you?' Daisy blocked her way.

Janet's heart thumped in her throat. 'Don't *do* that!'

'Why? Did I scare you?' Daisy's eyes gleamed. 'Did you think I was Sukie's ghost?'

5

The path McKenna next found himself following was gravelled, snaking through a plantation of massive ancient oaks. As the wind stirred their crowns, the trees groaned mournfully and low-hanging branches touched his face and body. Completely disorientated, he crunched onwards, hoping to find a clearing so that he could feel the wind and see the sun, but the further he walked the more lost he became. Like the crazy drive, the path led him towards each compass point in turn and when he stopped to peer skywards through a break in the great leaf canopy he saw only that the sun must be nearing its zenith. Then he heard a car door slam somewhere ahead. Almost at the run, he reached the top of a gentle slope, where below was what his bemused eye perceived as a fairy-tale cottage. He expected to see smoke curling from the chimney, peeping fawns, a wood-cutter, Snow White, the Seven Dwarfs, but all he saw was the witch. She was stowing suitcases into the boot of a sleek red car.

He pulled up short and, supporting himself against a tree, in full view should she glance in his direction, he watched her. She put away the last suitcase, hesitated briefly, then made for the open door of a square white house that was as stark as the memory of their Friday encounter, which continued to play in the theatre of his mind like a blatantly contrived bit of drama, where he was at once audience, actor and critic.

She emerged carrying a large carton, which she placed on the ground beside the car. Twice more she went back and forth, adding to the stack of paraphernalia with each trip, working methodically and systematically, and despite the ignominy of her exit, looking as cool and collected as ever. At one point her head jerked up, as if, like the horses in the paddock, she sensed his presence, but the moment passed. Shutting the car boot, she went into the house and closed the door decisively.

6

Arms loosely folded, Janet stood beside Daisy at the side of the swimming pool, gazing about admiringly. At one end the tiered diving platform hung against a backdrop of trees, its austere lines complementing nature's inconclusive arrangements. The pool house at the opposite end balanced the other structure, pulling the eye back and forth across the great expanse of water. The wind disturbed the water's surface, fragmenting reflections and making the drowned dolphin wriggle among the brilliant blue tiles. The scene reminded her of a David Hockney painting, where a quiet emptiness touched on a sense of something gone but something to come. The soft plashing noise as the water hit the sides of the pool and the whispering wind evoked the ghostly cries of girls at sport and, mesmerised by the shivering dolphin, she imagined Imogen upon its back, cleaving the water as if whole. The ghostly cries became the jeers of Nancy's cruel games when Imogen hauled herself back into the solid world and was forced to beg for mercy and her crutches.

Daisy nudged her. 'Had Sukie been chewed up by rats and crabs?'

Janet's flesh threatened to crawl off her bones. 'What a *horrible* thing to say!'

'Why? It happens, doesn't it?' Daisy touched her again. 'Well? *Had* she?'

Turning on her heel, Janet moved away from the water. Her legs were suddenly stiff. 'No,' she replied curtly. 'She had not.'

'That's good, isn't it? Otherwise, it would have been even *more* horrible for her parents when they identified her.' Trotting to keep abreast, Daisy asked, 'Have you seen lots of bodies? Did you see Sukie's body? What did she really look like?'

Janet stopped in the lee of the pool house. Refusing to meet Daisy's eager eyes, she said, 'Yes, I've seen lots of bodies. No, I didn't see Sukie. However,' she went on, teeth gritted, 'my colleagues tell me she simply looked very dead and very sad.'

'They must mean before she was cut up. We dissect corpses in biology, you know. They look *awful* when they're in bits.'

'What is it with you, eh?' Janet rounded on her. 'You're like some damned ghoul!'

Daisy stepped back as if she had been struck. Her face sagged, she mumbled something unintelligible, then took off in the direction of the playing fields. She moved fast and, once under the cloak of trees, became as one with the other shadows.

Janet went in pursuit, the play of light and shade constantly deceiving her, as if the woods were a magic place where people could lose their bodily selves. She caught up with her at last by a set of tennis courts that were, like the pool, relics of another era. Daisy had her fingers hooked into the high, dark-green netting surrounding the complex and was staring at the puddles still lying on the dusty clay and the angular shadows cast by the umpire's tall seats. Separated internally by the green netting, the four courts lay at the foot of a broad sweep of shallow steps leading to a wooden pavilion with an ornately canopied veranda, but courts and pavilion wore an air of abandonment and the veranda was heaped with drifts of dead leaves.

'I don't suppose anyone's played here for a long time,' Janet commented, when the heavy silence began to weigh on her.

'Well, you suppose wrong,' Daisy replied sharply. 'The sixth form use it for exhibition matches on Sports Day while the parents and teachers have tea in the pavilion.' Unhooking herself, she wandered towards the building, trailing her fingers along the netting. Twice she stopped to open the gates to the courts and the squealing bolts set Janet's teeth on edge.

'Did Sukie play in the matches?'

Daisy shook her head.

'I wish I knew why she went into the woods on Tuesday,' Janet said. 'Wild horses wouldn't drag *me* in there after dark.'

'Maybe she thought Nancy was going to hack off one of Purdey's legs.'

Janet felt sick.

'Nancy reckoned it would be a properly biblical revenge for Imogen's leg, you see,' Daisy went on, coming to a stop by the pavilion. The white-painted brick walls on which the building rested were stained with moss and damp, while trumpet-flowered bindweed crept upwards and outwards from a tangle of roots on the ground.

Shocked into immobility, Janet asked, 'How did Nancy know about the accident?'

'Sukie told her.' Daisy began beating a passage through the undergrowth.

Watching her batter the plants, Janet imagined how Sukie had been persuaded to open her mouth. 'And how did you find out?' she asked.

Instead of answering, Daisy disappeared round the corner and Janet was forced to follow. Her legs felt weak and she trod gingerly on the moss that carpeted the paving behind the building.

Daisy was standing at the foot of a steep, narrow flight of concrete steps leading to a slatted door green with mould. With a triangular space underneath, the steps leaned against the building like a small replica of the fire escapes at the main school. The handrail looked very flimsy. 'We can get in this way if you want,' she suggested. 'There might be some racquets and balls inside.'

'I don't want to play tennis.' Janet snapped. 'I want you to answer my question.'

'I overheard. OK?'

'And when did Nancy dream up that diabolical idea about Purdey?'

Daisy shrugged. 'Dunno.'

'Well, then, when did she intend to *do* it?'

Daisy sat on the bottom step. 'She was probably just tormenting.' Picking dirt from under her fingernails, she added, 'Like Therese *said* she'd wrecked Charlotte's clothes to upset Dr Scott.'

Absently, Janet brushed away a dandelion puff sticking to her sweater and watched it drift in Daisy's direction. 'But like Dr Scott,' she said, half to herself, 'Sukie couldn't know it was an empty threat.'

Pursing her lips, Daisy blew back the puff.

As the delicate little seeds touched Janet's face, she focused on Daisy. 'Who else has found out?' she asked.

'What about?'

'The accident.'

'Charlotte.' Daisy paused, then said, 'Imogen didn't need telling, did she?'

'Do you really expect me to believe you haven't spread it around? It was dynamite.'

Daisy's eyes flickered. 'Nancy doesn't know I was listening. She'd kill me if she found out.'

'Would she? Perhaps *she* killed Sukie.'

'No way!'

'What about Charlotte, then?'

'Oh, get real! She can't stand the sight of blood. She was sick all over the school the first time she saw Imogen legless.'

'So that leaves you, doesn't it?'

Daisy flexed her fingers. 'What does?'

'As the only other person who knew how to lure Sukie into the woods.'

Daisy escaped up the steps. Near the top, she stumbled when her foot slipped on a clump of lichen. Recovering her balance, she unhooked the hasp on the door, pushed it open and vanished.

Again forced to follow her, Janet wondered if she were not, like Sukie before her, being led straight into a death trap.

7

When Nona arrived home, she found a note from her husband stuck under the tomato-shaped magnet on the refrigerator door. 'Gone to Mam's,' it read. 'Back for lunch. Love, Gwynfor.'

A mug of coffee at her elbow, she leafed through the Sunday papers, before going for a long, leisurely soak, taking a colour supplement with her. The hot water and a generous dollop of foaming bath lotion were balm to her aching body, and as her eyes began to close of their own accord she dropped the magazine over the side of the tub.

She had no recollection of dreaming. Instantly awake, heart once again pounding thunderously in her ears, words hung in front of her eyes as if on a banner. Scrambling willy-nilly out of the tub, she grabbed a towel and ran to the bedroom, leaving a trail of sodden footprints on the carpet and bubbles floating everywhere.

As she punched out numbers on the telephone, her fingers felt as stiff as twigs. Janet's mobile rang and rang, but no one responded. She tried to call McKenna, but heard an echoing void. Frantically she called the operations room. 'Get hold of Superintendent McKenna!' she cried, when the duty operator answered. 'Tell him Janet's in terrible danger! Daisy Podmore killed that girl.' As the operator started to ask for details, Nona shouted her down: 'Just *tell* him! Now!' She cut the connection and again rang Janet's mobile, but there was still no response. Weeping, she slumped on the side of the bed, the telephone clutched in her wet hands. When she next called McKenna's mobile, a disembodied voice told her to leave a message.

'Last night,' she began, choking back the tears, 'Daisy kept saying the killer could be waiting outside the flat and she wouldn't have a bath, because, she said, the killer "could break in and hold me down in the water until I drowned like Sukie".' Sobbing uncontrollably, she went on, 'I've only just realised what she said. She could only know about that if she killed her.' Then, in a whisper: 'I'm sorry. I'm so dreadfully *sorry!*'

8

Bent over a large wicker hamper, Daisy was rummaging for something.

Janet remained by the door, well out of her reach. As her eyes adapted to the gloom, she saw more hampers stacked against a wall, stools upended on each other, rolled-up nets in a corner, and rows of folded deckchairs and trestle tables. There were three doors on the opposite wall, and she thought they must lead to the changing rooms and perhaps a kitchen. Dust motes drifted across the light that slanted through the closed louvres at the windows, and the place stank of mildew.

'Sod it!' Daisy dropped the lid. 'There are just plates and things in here.' She turned to Janet. 'Help me lift that top one,' she said, pointing to the stack. 'I know there are racquets somewhere.'

'I've already said I don't want to play tennis.'

'Why not?' Daisy demanded. 'What else are we going to do?'

Janet shrugged. 'Talk?'

Daisy sat down heavily on the lid and began to swing her legs, heels cutting swaths through the dust on the floorboards. 'What about?' She looked up. 'You're not allowed to talk about Torrance or Sukie unless I've got a solicitor with me.' Her eyes were accusing. 'You shouldn't have made me say what I did. You'd get into trouble if I snitched.' Then she offered her ghastly smile. 'But I won't, so you needn't worry.'

Playing for time, Janet glanced at her watch. 'I suppose we *could* have a game of tennis,' she said. 'Tell you what, you put up one of the nets and I'll look for the racquets.'

'I knew you'd see sense.' Daisy jumped to her feet, trotted

over to the corner and gathered up the nearest net.

As Daisy started towards the door, Janet walked around the wall. She put one of the stools on the floor, climbed on to it and, stretching for the lid of the topmost hamper, called over her shoulder, 'I'll give you a shout if I need help with anything.' She thought she heard Daisy grunt, but the sudden clatter as two golfing umbrellas rolled off the hamper and hit the floor obliterated any noise from outside.

9

Ready to accost her, McKenna waited for the headmistress to re-emerge from her house, but the door stayed firmly shut. Eventually he started back along the woodland path, facing the fact that she was likely to get away scot-free – a humourless pun – trudging on unawares when the gravel gave way to tarmac. A frantic horn blast from the driver of the security van jolted him back to his senses. Barely avoiding the van's front bumper, he staggered on to the verge just in time.

He concentrated on taking stock of his surroundings. Between the trees, the bright blue glimmer of the swimming pool was now visible. Briefly, Janet and Daisy were once again in sight, but they were soon absorbed by the woods. Fixing his eyes on the point where they disappeared, he set off at a fast walk, but had barely covered fifty yards before he was forced to drop his gaze. The glitter of sunlight on water, the swaying branches, the shifting shadows, played tricks with his vision, and more than once he was sure he glimpsed Janet retracing steps she had already taken.

10

Once Janet agreed to a game, Daisy stepped out of the pavilion's rear door feeling almost light-hearted. While they were knocking the ball back and forth – not too strenuously because her breasts hurt more than ever – she would unload her burden of guilt and shame and fear, without having to stand still, look into Janet's eyes and witness her scorn and disgust. Hugging the net loosely to her chest, she was about to descend the steps when there was a violent tug on her trouser hem. She glanced down into the face of her killer, and in the split second before she crashed earthwards realised how easily, and how bitterly, she had been duped.

The net unfurled, winding itself around her. There was a dull crack as she hit the bottom step, and when she came to rest, her head was lolling at an impossible angle.

The girl who had been lying in wait beneath the steps darted towards her. Snatching a handful of curls, she lifted Daisy's head. It flopped heavily and had it not been for the grinding of broken bone, Daisy might have been a rag doll stuffed with sawdust.

Exultant with success, the girl let go and, without a backward glance, melted away into the woods. She stopped once on her way back to school, to extract a strand of Daisy's hair that had stuck between her fingers.

The water in the pool plashed gently against the coping and the wind whispered through the leaves, and as McKenna entered the tunnel of trees beyond the pool house the sound of hymn singing hung in the air. The sudden bleep of his mobile was a strident intrusion in that harmonious world.

The trees interfered with the signal. With the handset angled skywards, he asked the operator to repeat the message. The shock anchored him to the ground as firmly as the shadow of each tree was held fast about its roots. When he began to run he had to look down to be sure his feet were not embedded in cannibal mud.

Stretching endlessly ahead, the tree tunnel was alive with shadows and menace and snatches of music; abruptly, it debouched into what seemed like a huge green cage. He clung to the netting, gasping for breath, seeing the puddles, the lofty umpire's perches, the leaf-strewn veranda of the pavilion. Then a movement to the side of the building caught his eye. He turned slowly and his blood ran like ice as a figure emerged from the snarl of undergrowth. Bindweed tangled with her hair and clung to her clothes, her face was streaked with dirt and for one breath-stealing moment he thought she was Sukie's ghost.

Janet staggered a few paces, then fell to her knees. 'Daisy's dead,' she moaned, holding her head. 'She lost her footing on the steps and it's all my fault.'

When Sukie's funeral was being arranged, John Melville exercised the one prerogative left to him and forbade McKenna from attending. Everything else was taken out of his hands by Hester's parents.

The service was held in the medieval chapel on their estate, where generations of ancestors had submitted to their rites of passage. Topped with a spray of white roses, Sukie's casket lay on the floor before the altar. Shoulder to shoulder, Hester's parents occupied the first pew. John was behind his father-in-law, his left hand curled round the time-worn carving on the arm rest, his right pulling wretchedly at his black silk tie.

Hester, sinking fast in a sea of grief whipped up to storm force by her own guilt, sat as far apart from her husband as decency permitted. When the shuffle of feet disturbed her and she turned to see Jack Tuttle take his place, she barely recognised him, although she had a faint recollection of his being kind to her at some dreadful time in the past.

As brief and furtive as the christening, Hester thought her daughter's funeral was almost squalid, as if the life that began in shame must end thus. All within the space of a few minutes, it seemed, the vicar spoke, prayed, spoke again, offered a final prayer, then beckoned the undertaker's men to heft the casket on their shoulders. When the small procession moved down the aisle, she fell into step two paces behind her parents. Her mother was grimly erect, iron-grey hair upswept under a huge black hat, stony features veiled in black. Her father marched to Chopin's funeral dirge, playing on the windy old organ. One or two petals, falling from the rose spray, were trampled under his marching feet.

The day was humid and overcast. As she emerged from the chapel, Hester noticed a group of estate workers standing very quietly beyond the wall, caps and hats doffed in respect. They stared reproachfully at her mother, who looked neither to right nor left as she pursued the jolting casket to the mouth of the open grave. The procession never wavered: the vicar, the casket, her parents, herself, her husband and that kindly policeman. She heard him trip on the loose flagstone that had rocked beneath her own feet.

At the graveside, a fine drizzle began to settle on their heads and shoulders. On the rose petals it glistened like tears. There were more words from the vicar, the smoke and scent of incense and a spattering of holy water before the casket was lowered. Hester was dry-eyed as her daughter sank into the earth, for she had already made the decision to join her.

She was planning her death with the same precision her grandfather was said to have applied to his military campaigns and, unlike Imogen Oliver, would not make a botch of it. Imogen had already lost one of her poisoned kidneys, and although anyone could survive with one leg and one kidney, Hester knew, in her heart of hearts, that this was only the beginning. Imogen would die by degrees, and Hester prayed it would be a long and harrowing process, for Imogen had killed Sukie as surely as if her own hands had thrust her into the greedy waters of the Strait.

On the day the coroner issued Sukie's burial certificate, the Olivers' solicitor sent a cheque for every penny they had swindled out of the Melvilles, together with six months' interest. Explaining that Imogen had suddenly and inexplicably recovered her memory, the solicitor trusted that the money would be accepted in full reparation for an error beyond anyone's control and closed with an expression of sympathy for Sukie's tragic death.

Daisy's funeral was a grand affair, in a huge Victorian church luminous with candles and stained glass, her coffin on a draped bier above a carpet of flowers that filled the nave with their scent. Grace's father, imposingly robed, took the service and Grace, childlike in her surplice, led the choir.

With Martha at her side, Alice sat ten or twelve rows from the front. Apart from Grace, Daisy's parents and the police, who were relegated to a pew at the back, she recognised no one among the hundreds of richly dressed people around her. She had looked in vain for their school friends, the teachers, Ainsley, the house captains, and even for Dr Scott, who had vanished from school two days after Daisy's accident. Matron, with nowhere to go, was still holed up in her flat when term ended.

Martha prayed that bringing Alice to the funeral would break the last shackle binding her to Daisy, even if she never forgot her. Nor, Martha knew, would she forget Torrance. The emotional experiences those two girls wrought upon her would be there for the rest of her life, ebbing and flowing in her memory, evoking responses according to the climate, much as the silver water forever rushing back and forth past the school must subject itself to the four winds and the temper of the heavens. Half listening to the Reverend Blackwell's exequies, Martha wondered for the thousandth time what lay behind Daisy's dreadful allegation about Torrance, unless it was simply the truth. Her only comfort came from the hope that Daisy had made a mistake, judging a different kind of encounter by the light of her own prejudices.

By craning her neck a little, Alice could view the coffin through the forest of necks before her. She had never seen a body inside a coffin and could not picture Daisy in that ornate box, although in her mind's eye she saw every horrible detail of Daisy smashed to ruins at the foot of the pavilion steps. Imagining how the people in front would look if their necks suddenly snapped, she groped rather blindly for Martha's hand.

Good Catholic that he was, McKenna felt deeply uncomfortable in an Anglican church, almost as if he were committing an act of betrayal. He had no idea what to do with himself, how to present his worship and respects, when to kneel, to stand or to pray, despite discreet instructions on the Order of Service set before each mourner.

The territory must be alien to Janet too, he thought, glancing surreptitiously at her bowed head. Her face was pale and she had lost weight in the past few weeks. The fine cloth of her black suit hung very loose.

During the investigation into Daisy's death she was suspended from duty. Two independent autopsies, exhaustive inspections of the site and finally, a coroner's inquest, determined cause of death as misadventure, to which poor maintenance of the school grounds had been a contributing factor. Janet was officially exonerated, but nonetheless, continued to blame herself, and confessed to McKenna that because Daisy had thoroughly unnerved her, she had encouraged her to leave the pavilion. That small, so human, lapse of professionalism, had held the most devastating consequences – if, he reflected, that were her only lapse. He glanced again at her bowed head, then at the hands clasped loosely in her lap, knowing he was not alone in being plagued by doubts. *Were* those pale, blue-veined hands stained with Daisy's blood, he wondered, yet again? Was that why she seemed almost paralysed with guilt? Or had she simply taken on her own shoulders the lion's share of their collective liability? Nona Lloyd had been on sick leave since the day after Daisy's death, so crushed by the weight of her own self-reproach that she now needed psychiatric help. Suddenly, he realised he had not had a chance to ask her whether the necklace in the jeweller's photograph matched any of those she found among Imogen's possessions. One more oversight, he told himself, and although it was probably of no importance, it might, on the other hand, be the key to solving the puzzle that had outwitted them all.

Janet felt suffocated by the press of black-clad bodies at every turn. She could see nothing of the service, bar the occasional glimpse of Grace's father bobbing up and down before the altar. She stared blankly into space, seeing instead Daisy in a heap on the ground, remembering how she first thought the girl had tripped over the tennis net and stunned herself, and how annoyed she was when she set about disentangling her. She would never forget the absolute horror of realising she was dead.

The coroner had been satisfied that the marks on the top step and on Daisy's shoes proved unequivocally that she had slipped on one of the clumps of lichen that grew like tumours on every surface. Daisy's own words to Nona were accepted as condemning evidence that she had killed Sukie, although no one could suggest a motive, beyond the tenuous theory that she had harboured a lunatic compulsion to avenge Imogen's leg.

Janet had seen Daisy's parents at the inquest, but doubted that she would today be able to pick them out from the crowd. She had no idea whether they accepted either theory or verdict, although there had been no murmurings to the contrary. What do I believe? she wondered. In her heart of hearts, she believed Daisy had been terribly wronged, and that both truth and retribution were being sacrificed to the easy answer.

For Jack, Daisy's funeral was surrounded by so much ceremony that, thankfully, there was little room left for feeling. He had found Sukie's funeral one of the saddest experiences of his life and he could still hear Hester's voice, telling him she did not care who had killed Sukie, or why, for it only mattered to her was that Sukie was dead.

After Daisy's death, convinced the resolution to hand was simultaneously too plausible and riddled with too many doubts, he and McKenna had argued furiously with their chief constable for permission to continue the investigation. Given limited authority until the final forensic tests on Sukie's clothes were completed, they had searched Daisy's effects, watched over by her parents, but found nothing to indicate whether she had or had not killed Sukie, or attempted to kill Torrance. As the Podmores' chauffeur was about to shut Daisy's trunk and a suite of leather suitcases in their car boot, Jack remembered her backpack was still in the staff flat, and because she had been under constant police scrutiny from the moment she opened her mouth with the steamy allegations about Torrance, he let her parents take it away without bothering to rummage through its contents.

In the light of Daisy's revelations to Janet about Imogen's accident, Nancy and Charlotte were again questioned. Remembering what Avril had told him, Jack approached Charlotte with cautious sympathy, wondering what soul-destroying assaults she had suffered from those whose mantle she would later inherit, but she had learned her lessons well and, in Avril's words, she 'blanked' him.

For some reason he knew he would never fathom, Nancy capitulated. She admitted to 'putting pressure' on Imogen and Sukie, presenting the police with a confused, and confusing, justification centred on the need for information, where she tried to explain the fear and threat arising from ignorance, concealment and uncertainty in a place such as the Hermitage. 'You've got to *know*,' she had told them. 'If only *some* people know about something that's so bloody important, you can't be sure they're not holding back something else that could affect *you*.' Her sentiments were very similar to those Justine expressed to McKenna, but spoken from a totally self-centred perspective, the voice of a personality deformed and brutalised by the years of bullying Nancy herself had endured. She flatly and consistently denied any involvement in Sukie's death, or indeed, any knowledge of it. Charlotte was dismissed as a possible candidate with a contemptuous comment. 'She wouldn't have the bottle,' Nancy said. 'And she can't stand the sight of blood.'

Jack went from the subjects, as he saw them, to the deposed monarch, but Freya Scott had already reorganised her defences. Far from expressing any contrition, she laid the blame 'fairly and squarely' at the feet of the police. 'Your response to Sukie's death was sluggish and shallow,' she said. 'Had Superintendent McKenna set his mind to the task in hand, instead of allowing himself to be – shall we say too easily, and most inappropriately, sidetracked? – Imogen would not have tried to kill herself, Daisy would not be dead, and I would not have been made the scapegoat.'

'And how was Superintendent McKenna "sidetracked"?'

'That,' she replied, with a dark hint, 'is something you must ask *him*.'

'On the contrary, Dr Scott, if you're aware of police misconduct or negligence, you're under an obligation to report it.'

He left the ball in her court but sure she would somehow, sometime, hit back, he had reported the conversation to McKenna, and suggested they organise their own defence.

'But first,' he had said, 'I need to know what she's getting at.'

McKenna, squirming with embarrassment, eventually told him. 'When I was in the lift with her, going up to Imogen's room after the incident with Nancy, she suddenly fell against me.'

'Why?'

'She sort of collapsed. In despair, it seemed.'

'What did you do?'

'I put my hands on her shoulders.'

'Then what?'

Offering a stiff little shrug, McKenna said, 'Nothing.'

'Nothing at all?'

'No.'

'She's implying a lot more.'

'Yes, I'm sure she is.'

'Well,' Jack remarked, 'if she *does* try to make capital out of it, you just say you reacted as any normal person would when somebody looks like they're about to keel over.'

'It's as easy as that, is it?'

'You hardly had time to get into her underwear,' Jack had said trenchantly. 'Even if you'd wanted to.'

Dewi's knees were aching. He had lost count of the times he had already knelt, stood, and knelt again, all to the subdued shuffle of hundreds of other feet and the rustle of as many garments.

He thought it wrong for them to be there. However indirectly, they were to blame for Daisy's death, for negligence, unwitting or not, always ended in disaster. Torrance was as good as dead, and that was their fault, too, because the truth about her had died with Daisy. Remembering the devastation Daisy's story wreaked upon the Torrance he had first encountered on the ride through the woods gave him the same, sick wrench in the pit of his stomach that he experienced when he saw her thrown from Purdey's back. McKenna had been utterly averse to questioning her about the allegations, but the fact that Alice had been party to them forced his hand, and although Alice doggedly maintained that Daisy had lied, Torrance was, as Martha had predicted, destroyed. As soon as she was allowed to leave the school, she had loaded Tonto and Purdey into a horsebox and driven away, all her vividness permanently tarnished by the dirt of uncertainty.

At Sukie's funeral, John Melville told Jack that she had paid them more for Purdey than the mare originally cost, and then, commenting on the sudden upturn in their monetary fortunes, said bitterly, 'And much good it will bring.'

Much good avarice brought anyone, Dewi reflected. The Olivers were facing several criminal charges, for despite the likely consequences for herself, Imogen had co-operated willingly in her parents' downfall, and provided the police with a damning account of their conspiracy. That was perhaps the only certainty in this morass of ambiguity, for when Sukie's clothes failed to yield up their secrets to the most intense scrutiny science could apply, the police lost their last opportunity to uncover the truth of her death.

He was sitting closer to the aisle than the others and could see a procession beginning to form at the altar. When he glanced round, he saw the doors being opened in readiness and the light breaking through had a silvery edge, an uneasy glitter. A black-garbed figure standing in the shadow of a column caught his eye and for a moment, he thought it was Freya Scott.

Every bone in Martha's body ached. When the final prayers were done and the Reverend Blackwell signalled for the choir to move from their stalls, she hooked her fingers over the pew in front to pull herself upright. Little flurries of activity rippled through the nave like a soft wind as the congregation readied itself.

Daisy's mother felt as if someone had torn open her chest, closed their fingers around her heart and were pulling it shred by bloody shred from its moorings. She had never imagined such a sensation possible, but she had never imagined her child's death. All the love she had never shown Daisy, all the emotion she never suspected might exist, had come out of hiding to destroy her, and inside the coffin from which she could not take her eyes was what remained of a whole human being she had simply never known. When she unpacked Daisy's baggage, she found the diary in the backpack, but read no further than the first few entries before grief threatened to annihilate her. Her husband said the diary, the clothes, the toys, the books – every relic of Daisy's existence – should be burned. She said she would kill him if he laid a finger on one single thing, then locked Daisy's room, hid the key, and squirreled away the diary for a time when she might have the strength to read on.

Grace, her godchild, was looking at her, yet again; doe-eyed, sorrowful, cloyingly sympathetic. Daisy's mother wanted to kill her, too, just for being alive.

Shielding her candle from the draught, waiting patiently for the rest of the choir to line up behind her, Grace swivelled her gaze from her godmother to peek past her father's skirts to the coffin, where her secret was totally safe, screwed down tight with Daisy and destined for the incinerator.

She could still barely believe how miraculously chance had played into her hands. Matron's dismissal was especially fortuitous, because in her absence, it fell to one of the assistant matrons to watch over the girls in the infirmary. The assistant, who worked nights as an office cleaner to augment her lousy wages, was, as always, tired: too tired to argue with Grace when she said she did not feel well enough to go to chapel on that fateful Sunday morning. She took the other girls and left Grace alone and unsupervised.

Grace had slipped out of school through the French doors in the visitors' room, crept along the front of the building and into the woods. Learning from the near fiasco that Torrance's hurriedly improvised accident turned out to be, she had made extensive contingency plans for Daisy, but none of them was necessary. Within minutes, she had seen Daisy and the police-woman meandering through the grounds.

As the pall bearers began to lift the coffin, Grace nodded gravely in response to her father's brief, proud smile, thinking yet again how Daisy had all but co-operated in her own death. She must have known *why* she had to die, Grace decided, for when she took flight off the pavilion steps, her face was a picture.

In most respects Daisy and Sukie could not have been more different, but they shared the fatal flaw of not knowing when to keep quiet. Despite Daisy's own multitudinous imperfections, she had been very quick to insist that Grace owned up to being out of the dorm on Tuesday night – 'you could've theen thomething the polithe'll want to know,' she had said, in that excruciating voice. Her snide remarks about Grace's 'prethiouth jewelth', made in front of the policewoman, put Grace through sheer hell. Sukie had done nothing more than urge her to confess, but on pain of exposure, and to return what she had stolen from Imogen. Under the surplice, against her flesh, Grace could feel the cold weight of the beautiful diamond pendant that soon, she would be free to flaunt to her heart's content.

The congregation rose as one when the Reverend Blackwell started down the altar steps. Alice saw the people in front swivel round to watch the coffin pass, and steeled herself for her turn, conscious that this was the beginning of another ending.

She recognised that her time at the Hermitage was done when Martha drove her down the crazy drive and out of the gates at the end of term. Those last few weeks had been terrible. There was no Open Day, no Sports Day, nothing but the school's lifeblood leaking away. She thought Vivienne Wade had somehow made the first, fatal cut when she played her 'get out of gaol' card the day after Daisy died. Other girls followed her, in dribs and drabs and then in a flood. When the police caravan disappeared, the horrible but so believable rumours about Daisy began, plunging Alice into a new despair. The night Sukie died, she had fallen asleep as soon as Torrance switched off the lights and would go to her grave wondering if it were true that Daisy left the dorm to murder Sukie.

When the coffin glided past, she shivered, but could still not imagine Daisy inside. Her abiding memories were of Daisy alive, yet the lisping voice and dark presence already haunted her dreams. One day, perhaps, she would be able to mourn, for all that was lost and all that must remain unknown.

Janet hoped fervently that once Daisy's funeral was over, she might start learning to live with her guilt, for it would certainly never leave her. Even more passionately, she hoped that Freya Scott was equally burdened. It was rumoured the woman had already wormed her way back into the army, and God help them, Janet thought, if she served the fighting forces as well as she had the school. When the tall iron gates closed on the last pupil, everyone knew they would never open again. Except for Matron, who was left to her own grim fate, the Hermitage was abandoned, but not because the reality of Freya Scott's little empire had been exposed. Once she had gone, the school lost all its lustre for the many parents who unswervingly believed in her and the dreams she purveyed. She had, many said, been ruined by the wayward girls she tried to guide through the stormy waters of adolescence. Sukie was already being touted as the architect of both her own and of Freya Scott's destruction; before long, Janet thought, she would also be blamed for Daisy's death.

Music soared heavenwards from the organ as the procession advanced. With the rustle of robes and the whisper of feet on stone, the Reverend Blackwell halted briefly before turning for the door. For a moment, Grace was in full view. Her chorister's garb lent charm, and with candlelight mellow on her face, she resembled a story-book child, dressed in a nightgown and bearing a candle to light the way to bed. As the procession moved off once more, she offered Janet a brief, knowing smile.

Past and present collided. With brutal clarity, Janet recalled those first few hours at the school, and retrieved the memory that had wilfully eluded her since the evening she collected Imogen's new stick and crutches from the hospital. She had been in the refectory, reviewing her notes before talking to the next batch of girls, when she chanced upon a snatch of conversation.

'You *mutht* have theen *thomething* on Tuethday night,' Daisy had lisped.

'I didn't!'

'Bollockth!' Daisy snapped, glaring at the girl Janet would come to know as Grace Blackwell. 'I timed you,' she added. 'You were out of the dorm for more than an hour.'

'I've *told* you!' Grace insisted. 'I was waiting for Matron outside her office.' Face puckering, she had begun to snivel. 'I wanted something for my headache. So, *there*!'